PROSPECTS UNKNOWN

PROSPECTS UNKNOWN

A MYSTERY WITH A DIFFERENCE

JAMIE DOPP

Canadian Cataloguing in Publication Data

Dopp, Jamie
    Prospects unknown

ISBN 1-896860-71-0

    I.Title.
Ps8557.O63P76   2000   C813'.54   C00-910488-7
PR9199.3.D5565P76   2000

© Jamie Dopp, 2000.
Author Photo: Linda Sheldon
Cover Art: A detail from a painting by Michael Lewis.

Published in 2000 by:
Ekstasis Editions Canada Ltd.   Ekstasis Editions
Box 8474, Main Postal Outlet   Box 571
Victoria, B.C. V8W 3S1   Banff, Alberta T0L 0C0

The Canada Council | Le Conseil des Arts
    for the Arts | du Canada
    since 1957 | depuis 1957

Prospects Unknown has been published with the assistance of a grant from the Canada Council and the Cultural Services Branch of British Columbia.

For Wendy Wasilewski
lover, mother, mystery woman

And for the real Phil Tucker.

Keep a diary or notes. Stop and record where you go, what you see, and what you do. Do not trust all these details to memory at the end of the day or end of the trip. You do not have to produce a literary masterpiece, just something that you can follow.

> E. L. Faulkner, *Introduction to Prospecting*

I

TO THE LETTER

Charles Gould, in his unshaken assurance, was absolutely convincing.

Joseph Conrad, *Nostromo*

CHAPTER ONE

What led to the bodies was my discovery of Camilla's left shoe. It appeared to me as a white dove, eye-high in the crook of a young maple tree, balanced there, it seemed, deliberately, perhaps as a sign. Some of the people of Silver imagined the shoe as a flagrant gesture by the assassins, a calling card reading *Fuck you!* or *Beware!* Others saw it as the result of an heroic struggle by the victims, a trace left against great odds to mark the location of the murders.

To me, in that first moment, the shoe evoked neither heroism nor danger. What came to my mind was two lovers, laughter, explosions of fallen leaves, cool damp skin meeting on hastily spread jackets and—sometime later—a good-hearted hiker raising a lost shoe. You could explain this by the fact that I was from out of town and knew nothing then about the strike at the mine, but also by the fact that I had arrived on the scene, driving my VW microbus nearly twelve hours from Vancouver, with a newly broken heart.

Of the drive I don't remember much; it went by more or less in a blur. I do remember darkness growing ahead of me, the Fraser going down on my left, the last flash of sun-glare on the windshield of an approaching car. Later on, as I climbed into my first real set of mountains, rain spattered the windshield like a handful of thrown seed. I stopped for gasoline, had a piss, got a large coffee to go. And drove on. All the time I was thinking of Jayne. I'd be angry and then sorry for myself and then a little smug about my dramatic departure. When I replayed our break-up in my mind (as I did over and over) it came out like a role-reversed version of *Frankie and Johnny*: "She done me wrong...."

About three o'clock in the morning, I banked around a long turn, and the landscape, even in the pitch dark, seemed different. I was in a valley, a cupped plateau between two mountain ranges. There was a sign, *Silver Next Right,* followed by a small commercial strip, mostly deserted and eerily lit by a row of halogen lights on tall hooked standards. A couple of fast food outlets, a cluster of motels and inns—The Rocky Mountain, The Ponderosa, The Red Grizzly, The Sportsman—and three competing service stations. One of the stations, the Igloo, had a restaurant still open; on its lot were a half-dozen eighteen-wheelers, lined up as neatly as freight cars in a railway yard, engines idling.

At the end of this strip there was another sign: *Danger. Stubborn Mule Pass 2 KM. Extreme Grades. Check Brakes.* It might as well have read: *Far Enough.*

I veered onto a side road. There was the shadowy bulk of fir trees, the popping corn sound of tires on gravel. I found out later that I drove three kilometers on this road, my eyes scanning the shoulders for a place to park, that eventually I turned off onto an even smaller lane, but I don't remember it. I only remember my lights hitting a gate where the lane finally ended, a clearing, a field dotted with sheep. I shut down, crawled back between the seats and wrapped myself in a blanket.

Sleep, of course, wouldn't come. Two or three times I dozed off only to bolt awake again. In my few moments of unconsciousness, I dreamed of storms, of whirlwinds, of falling. Near dawn I gave up, threw off the blanket and squirmed back into my shoes. I kicked open the van's side-door and discovered that the clearing was in fact a cemetery, the sheep, grave markers.

I eased myself down, blew a trombone of steamy breath into the air. Then, slowly, I walked.

For a while, I went from marker to marker until, on the far side, I followed a path into the woods, a short climb into a level area covered in scrubby growth. What I could see of the sky was flat grey, the colour of a dirty plastic milk container, with fog low enough to eat at the tops of the trees. With each step I felt my thighs, the ache of life in them, and heard the shifting tide of blood in my ears.

I slanted towards the shoe for no reason except that it seemed different, a scar of brightness in the early-morning late-autumn gloom. For a brief moment I thought of a bird, but soon saw the truth, imagined lovers' laughter, felt regret . . . and made to turn away. Then I noticed more white on the ground nearby.

It was one of those moments. So many clichés come to mind: the fork in the road, the window of opportunity. I was a man in the woods who sees something gleaming, something out of the ordinary, a prospect. Do I investigate? I thought at first the white patch might be snow, which seemed strange since I hadn't seen any other snow this low yet. Then I wondered if, against all odds, it was the other shoe. Then, inevitably, I thought of Jayne.

From this, everything followed.

I high-stepped off the path and pushed aside leafless underbrush, until the white became a rectangle showing through leaves and twigs. It was a man's shirt, Enrique's shirt, like a fallen flag of surrender.

Heading the investigation was RCMP Inspector Charles Gould. He arrived the day after my discovery of the bodies. With him was his right-hand man, Sergeant George Viola, four detective constables, a forensics team and a police photographer.

Some people wondered why the RCMP had to send in outside investigators when the town was already crawling with police. Frankly, it's hard to blame them. Since the first week of the strike a 58-member Emergency Response Team had been stationed in the town. That works out to about one cop for every fifty inhabitants. To get that ratio you'd have to have 30,000 officers in Metro Vancouver, enough to pack two Canucks games or ring Stanley Park shoulder-to-shoulder (helmets shining, batons at the ready). With so many officers it meant that one-half of all rental accommodation in Silver was occupied by the police. It meant that, by the sheer law of averages, any gathering of reasonable size (most evenings at the Legion Hall, the Selkirk Inn, or the Igloo Family Restaurant; curling night, hockey night, or film society night at the Rec Centre; Sunday service at any of the larger churches) was likely to have at least one officer at it. Which, of course, was precisely the kind of calculation the police hoped everyone would make.

Here's how the response team got there. On the first day of the strike, replacement workers sent in by the company tried and failed to cross the picket-lines. Shouts, pushing, two or three broken thermos bottles. A few hours later, Judge J. (Stump) Douglas of the B.C. Superior Court, Kootenays Division, granted an injunction limiting picketers to five at a gate. On the second day the replacement workers showed up again and were similarly beaten back. Name-calling, a few meetings of palms, cloudbursts of rotten fruit or balled up copies of the injunction. Only this time, footage of the confrontations found its way onto some television news broadcasts, along with excerpts from an interview with Lena Stahr, owner of the mine, denouncing the lack of law enforcement. On the third day, Nelson Smith, the provincial Attorney General, spent much of his time defending the government's handling of the strike. Smith was a self-professed champion of law and order; he was also, along with his Conservative colleagues, in the middle of an election campaign. At three o'clock that afternoon Smith had a meeting with the Premier. At four o'clock he called a news conference, and after a lengthy speech in which he made four references to his daughter's fear of downtown Vancouver, three references to his grandfather's coal-mining days in Nanaimo and twice let slip the phrase *state of apprehended insurrection*, announced that he had called in the Mounties.

Smith and his government were defeated in the election. A Socialist government replaced the Conservative one. Six months later, however, members of the response team were still escorting armoured school buses filled with replacement workers past the union pickets, ignoring cries of *fascists!* and *lackeys!*, getting physical when necessary.

There was, of course, no official explanation for assigning Gould to the case. It was understood that the RCMP was a professional police force, well-trained and independent, and that each of its investigators was equally capable of handling an investigation. Unofficially, Gould's superintendent emphasized the volatile situation in the town.

"When the victims disappeared," the superintendent explained, "—this was on Friday last—each side in the strike accused the other of murder. Now that the bodies have been found . . . ."

"Both sides had a motive?" asked Gould.

"It's not clear whose side the victims were on."

"Not replacement workers?"

"They went through the picket lines on the buses with the others, but it's not clear what they did inside. They didn't work underground or in the office. They seemed to be working directly for Lena Stahr, the owner of the mine. But some think they were using this as a ruse, that they were actually trying to organize the replacement workers or were spying on the mine for the union. They were, after all, union people originally. That's how they got to Canada, refugees from"—the superintendent checked his notes—"from Costaguana."

"I know the place."

"South America." The superintendent offered a vague explanatory wave of the hand.

"Well then," said Gould, "I'll expect more tension than usual in the town."

"Not only that."

The superintendent, whose name was O'Brien, raised two fingers to the bridge of his nose. O'Brien was a thick, burly man with an elephantine neck, a nose that looked like it had once been broken, and a deeply lined, coarse, almost brutal face. In spite of his formidable appearance he had a certain charm of manner. He had a trick of resettling his spectacles on his nose which was disarming, in some indefinable way cultured, as if he spent his free hours reading Joyce or listening to Mahler or playing chess. He pushed back his spectacles now. "Also, there is the politics of the thing."

"Of course."

"More than that. Yes, the strike has been a hot potato recently, arguments for and against the new Labour Code and so on. But think of it, Gould: political killings in rural British Columbia! Where do you think that could lead?"

"Maybe the killings weren't political."

"All signs so far . . . ."

"I don't like to prejudge things."

"I know, I know. That's a reason I want you to handle the investigation. Still, I've got a gut feeling, and with the possible politics of it—well, that's all the more reason for you to be the one on the case." Gould, as I discovered later, had a reputation for an almost unnatural stability, for a dispassionate steadiness of mind, for being, in short, a professional's professional. Mainly he dealt with homicide, but he was sometimes used on other cases when extreme tact was necessary. A spare, tall man, with a flaming moustache cropped short in the military fashion (a style I've never liked), he had clear blue eyes, auburn hair, and a thin, fresh, red face. Combined with a very straight-backed way of walking, his appearance created an impression of ramrod correctness, an impression which, in the line of duty at least, he was careful not to contradict.

The walk, in fact, was the result of years of equestrian training, Gould's main passion from boyhood until early adulthood. As a youth he had particularly loved dressage, the precision of it, the careful disciplining of horse and rider. While other boys his age were off playing baseball or hanging out at the arcade, young Charles spent hours at his riding club working on the basic moves: the shoulder-in, the half-pass, the volte (a circle exactly six steps in diameter). Dressage taught him to develop the lightest of touches, to use a gentle tug at the reins to channel the horse's energy without triggering its resistance. His greatest joy was the collected canter, in which horse and rider start at a trot and then slow by half halts, the horse's steps shortening, its knees rising higher, until horse and rider achieve a graceful light march with the horse's back hooves landing exactly in the hoof prints of the fore.

Gould, in later life, was aware of how his walk and manner affected people. He knew that some junior officers considered him to be a rule-obsessed prig or, worse, a snob. But he made no effort to change. In fact he found the impression rather useful; it contributed to his reputation as a professional, as someone who could not be influenced by outside considerations or distracted by any means from the task at hand. One of his greatest assets as an investigator was the aura of authority and firmness which he projected, an aura often successful at commanding co-operation from a witness. His ability to present himself as beyond influence was assisted by his true dislike of politics. He claimed to have few set political opinions, none that had to be masked or elided during an interview, and he had never had a party allegiance. In spite of his lack of interest in politics, or perhaps because of it, he was considered to be politically astute when necessary (a contributing factor in his assignment to the Soledad case). Interestingly, both traits—his dislike of politics and his intuitive understanding of it—could be traced to his family background: his mother was the daughter of Jimmy McPherson, a beloved advisor of W.A.C. Bennett during the first Social Credit government in British Columbia, and his father was Senator Robert Gould, longtime political gadfly, man of principles, and one-time Premier of New Brunswick.

How Gould and I became friends is a part of this story too, though the account of our friendship comes mostly later. Suffice it to say that we were not an obvious match. Except for the fact that we are both left-handed, we had almost nothing in common. I have never been a fan of our Boys and Girls in Blue—or Scarlet. To be honest, I even have a criminal conviction (nothing serious, cultivation of marijuana . . . and no, I never told him). Even putting aside the fact that Gould was a cop, you have to consider the class difference. Though I came to like him very much during our time together, and though I miss him now that he is gone, Gould never did shrug off the weight of his upbringing, that heavy coin of mansions, servants, security guards—the privilege and the stiff upper lip that went with it. None of us can escape the past, of course (a truism we both had to confront in Silver), but let's face it: if I had met Charles Gould at any other time in my life, I would have written him off as an Upper Class Twit.

Jayne would say that my attraction to Gould was proof of my masochistic need to sell out, proof of my groveling worship of authority, of the boot that holds me down. Proof that, for all my radical posturing, I am a Daddy Knows Best at heart.

It's hard to contradict her. So much of what followed upon my discovery of the shoe has left me confused, disoriented, with only a fraction more understanding than when I packed up the microbus and fled Vancouver. It's ironic that the shoe, which was the starting point for the Soledad investigation and remained in many ways the centre-piece, the one clue that Gould kept coming back to, was for me the beginning of a long detour, an evasion of the original purpose of my trip. I left Vancouver hoping to make sense of things, of myself, of what I wanted. Above all I needed to sift the debris of my relationship with Jayne. Until almost the end of my time in Silver, I claimed that Jayne was another story, a different story, not this one. I told myself that she had nothing to do with the Soledads, nothing to do with my interest in Charles Gould. Then, by the most common and yet strangest of turns, my long detour led me back to what I had to face. Amazing how many different ways you can be wrong at the same time.

Political astuteness is not something that could be said for Inspector Breeze, the officer who took my statement. Only hours later, before the investigation had even properly begun, Breeze held a press conference to not-very-subtly implicate the union in the murders. I saw the video-clip while drinking coffee in the Igloo Family Restaurant. Gould had to listen to Breeze's voice every hour on CBC radio as he drove from Galiano Island to Cramdown, then again the next morning, as he made his final preparations, then journey, to Silver. In answer to the inevitable "Any clues as to the identity of the killers?" Breeze said, "Not yet. I should say, however, that for some weeks now we have been investigating extremist elements in the Brotherhood of Mineworkers Union. Of course I can't say anything more at this time."

That night, as Gould slept in his apartment in Cramdown, and as I camped obliviously in the Igloo parking lot, all hell broke loose (again) in Silver. First, fist-fights broke out at the Selkirk Inn (a supposedly neutral drinking site). The fights roiled out into the street and when the police arrived they became targets themselves. Someone rammed a police car with a pickup truck. The police called for back-up and the attackers fled. Some of the combatants ended up at the Legion Hall (anti-union) and spread inflammatory stories about what had happened. Not long after, a mob had gathered in front of the union office on Henry Street.

At nine-thirty the next morning, Gould, driving in the first of four cars into town, passed the burnt out remains of the union office. The office front looked like a jagged-toothed mouth that had vomited up a pile of paper, chairs, drywall and brick. Yellow crime scene tape closed off the sidewalk. Most of the broken glass had been swept up, but somehow one large shard had been left in the middle of the road: it lay there gleaming, like a giant accent. Gould noticed that steam still rose from the building's blackened husk. The steam mingled with a cold mist that was already in the air to give the town an eerie, almost tropical appearance. For the space of a heartbeat, Gould felt like he was falling. The mist reminded him of his time in Costaguana, years ago . . . . Then, catching himself in a net of irony, he observed to himself that since the day was now November 2nd the bodies of Enrique and Camilla Soledad had appeared on the Day of the Dead.

He began, as usual, with the crime scene. It turned out that Inspector Breeze had secured a very large area, including the entire cemetery and part of the access road, a move of which Gould approved. A roadblock was in place not far from where, barely thirty hours before, I had pulled over my microbus to camp.

Gould and Viola first made an estimate of the situation. They paced off the distance between the cemetery gate, beyond which a motorized vehicle would have had trouble proceeding, and the footpath into the woods. From the path itself they contemplated the shoe, still in the tree, and the police tarp over the bodies. The first officers on the scene had been careful to limit their movements to one narrow track, from the opposite side, so as to avoid damaging any foot impressions that might remain in the damp ground. "We'll need some orientation shots from here," Gould said to Special Constable Fulton, the photographer, "then we'll start close ups." Then to Viola: "I'd like a couple of men to help remove the tarp. Is the coroner here yet?"

Gould's examination yielded two sketches and a number of pages of notes. He took the notes in his usual precise hand, left-handed. Though he carefully avoided premature interpretations of the data, there were a few features that immediately stood out. It was likely, for instance, that the victims had been killed at this spot. There were no signs of bodies being dragged, even after the layer of leaves on the ground had been carefully lifted to reveal the soil underneath, and the victims were found face down, as if they had fallen forward from their knees, with visible traces of blood in the immediate vicinity. Camilla Soledad wore one shoe; how the other got into the tree was a mystery (there were some foot impressions between the bodies and the tree, but the quality was too poor to be of much use). Within six metres of the bodies there were a number of human-made objects: a cigarette butt, a crushed American beer can (Banner Premium Ale), twenty-six cents in Canadian money (one quarter, one penny), and a strip of plaid flannel fabric not matching any article of clothing on the victims. Most intriguingly, near the heads of the victims, and less than a metre apart, were two lead coloured stones that were obviously out of place with the surroundings. A later mineral analysis proved them to be what they appeared: palm sized nuggets of silver ore.

While Gould carried out his examination, Constable Fulton took photographs and the forensics team combed the area for less visible clues. A search of the victims' clothing yielded only a wallet, apparently untouched, in the right back pocket of Enrique's trousers. At the appropriate moment, in consultation with Dr. Dean, the regional coroner, Gould ordered the bodies to be transported into Silver for autopsies.

The causes of death seemed clear enough. Hands bound, a single bullet to the back of the head: death, execution style. From the condition of the bodies, Dean guessed that death had occurred three to five days previously. A closer estimate would have to wait for the autopsies.

Gould, as always, was shocked not by the violence but by the logic evident at the scene, the well-tied knots at the wrists, the two bodies laid out in parallel lines, each bullet hole a neatly touched period. And the apparently deliberate signs: the nuggets, the shoe. What horrified him most were crimes not of passion but of reason.

CHAPTER TWO

Gould, on the job, was a model of systematic inquiry. When I became privy to them, I was astounded by the detailed accuracy of his notes, the careful lists of items observed, the interview accounts that were virtual transcriptions. He also had the neatest left-handed writing I have ever seen (my own is readable but fluctuates between neatness and scrawl depending on my mood). My own notes about the Soledad murders, penned into the black sketch book that I'd bought for another purpose, were, as usual, a mishmash. I started out determined to offer an objective account of the investigation beginning with my own discovery of the shoe. I spoke to people in the Igloo, or rather they spoke to me, and I dutifully recorded their words. But as time went on I found myself getting bored with this—it seemed to be going nowhere—and my entries began to change. Eventually I ended up with the same contradictory mess of documentation, literary pretension and personal confession that has gotten me into trouble before.

Gould warned me not to make too much of his method. "I'm sure you know how it is," he said, "what with your experiences as a researcher. Just because you are thorough and try to stick to the facts, people—some people—think of you as a narrow-minded fanatic. Obsessed with order, with making everything fit into some neat little pattern and so on. The fact is, and it is one of the first lessons of being an investigator, not every crime can be solved. Your job is to try to solve it, yes; but if a crime remains unsolved it doesn't mean your investigation is a failure. A successful, professional investigation only collects all available information pertinent to the case. The rest is . . .

well, a bonus, a pleasant but extra payoff."

He told me this only hours before the Soledad case came screeching to a halt, only hours before his self-assurance collapsed and—in a contradictory attempt to both avoid and reveal the secret that tormented him—he began pouring his heart out to me. During the long caffeine-driven night that followed, it became clear that Gould was absolutely desperate to prove his theory about events in Silver. How then was I to take his claim that solving the crime is "a bonus?" Of course, I didn't believe it at all. I didn't believe he actually believed it himself. Even then, so late in the game, I had trouble accepting that Gould could be quite as contradictory as myself.

Gould's team set up shop at The Red Grizzly, a no star establishment bumped up against the Trans-Canada Highway. They took over a series of adjoining rooms on the second floor. The largest, from which two queen sized beds had been removed, became the murder room. Advance work by two constables yanked from the E.R.T. meant that this room was already operational. It contained tables arranged in a horseshoe, with space at one end reserved for the indexers, who would cross-reference every piece of information acquired during the investigation. Two telephone lines and an answering machine had been specially installed, and a photocopier commandeered. The other rooms were for Gould and his team. Gould's was directly across from the murder room and looked out towards the highway. He insisted on a few changes. He had a proper desk brought in along with a small, secure filing cabinet for documents. On the desk he set the portable typewriter he always traveled with. He asked that the heavy curtains over the window be removed, or at least adjusted so that they could be pushed aside, and that the window be fixed so that it would open. And he insisted on something to cover the mirror over the bed.

There was a certain amount of gallows humour amongst the officers about the accommodations. On his way in Gould had asked a cabby about the place, and the cabby had simply pointed to the wooden pub-sign over the entrance, which showed a red grizzly on its hind legs as if ready to box. Someone had tried to bag the grizzly with a shotgun. Where the grizzly's hip should have been, there was dense cluster of holes—like a distant galaxy of imploded stars. The lobby was done up in a style that blended hunting lodge motifs and icons from English heraldry. Framed reproductions of coats of arms, old hunting rifles, fake armour, and stuffed animal heads decorated the dark paneled walls. A deep red carpet ran throughout—perfect for hiding dirt or blood—and there was a peculiar fishy smell, part vomit, part disinfectant, that seemed to be everywhere. Hence Gould's insistence that his window be made to open.

Just after noon on that first day, while the forensics team carried on at the crime scene, Gould and Viola drove back to the RCMP station to meet with Inspector Breeze.

The public area of the station had been converted into an operations room for the strike. On the bulletin board was a 72 hour duty roster for the response team, photographs of five union men who had been banned from the picket area, and various notices to remind officers of recent developments. Nearby on the wall were two maps: one of the town and environs, with the Cyclops Silver Mine blocked out in red magic marker; the other of the mine property itself, showing entrances and exits, access roads, buildings, and a complex pattern of current and derelict shafts. Portable dispatch equipment was set up in one corner behind the counter, where a hatless uniformed officer now bent low over a microphone.

Breeze was in his office. The duty officer showed them the way. When the door opened, Breeze rose from his desk, smiled, and said, "*Bueñas dias,*" a greeting that, under the circumstances, Gould found in very poor taste. The other inspector was a square-jawed man, with salt-and-pepper hair, heavy eyebrows, and brown eyes. He was dressed in a charcoal grey business suit. After introductions he leaned out the door and said, "Scobie! You wanna tell Wright we're ready for him?" Then, "Can I get you a coffee? You had lunch yet?"

"We grabbed a bite on the way over. And—no thanks."

"Then let's sit."

The room had a look of impermanence about it, like a portable office at a construction site. At right angles to the desk, against one wall, was a table with an apparently out-of-use computer on it; the computer screen was turned partly away, with the key-board, accordion cord dangling from one end, balanced on top. The rest of the table was taken up with papers and files. Above the table were the same two maps Gould had seen outside. On the other side of the room, still in front of the desk, were a couple of chairs and a half-sofa, above which hung a metal-framed generic landscape. More papers had silted into a pile on one end of the sofa. The desk itself was very cluttered: an open laptop computer, papers, file folders, a couple of computer disks, a desk-lamp, an in-and-out tray, a cup of pens and pencils, and—somewhat incongruously—a vase with some wilted flowers in it. Except for the flowers there was nothing on the walls or desk of a personal character.

Breeze gathered the papers off the sofa, dropped them on the floor, and signaled for Gould and Viola to sit. They had just settled in when an uniformed sergeant came into the office. Breeze did the introductions, then continued, "Wright was in command here before we had to come in with the E.R.T. He's got a good knowledge of the town."

"Glad to have you on board," said Gould.

Sergeant Wright looked to be in his late thirties. He was a big blond man, taller than Gould and with a broad chest and bullish arms and neck, the kind of cop who projects a quiet kind of power, the kind that comforts you when it is on your side and terrifies you if it is not. He had hulking brown eyes and a wide jaw, which, combined with his way of carefully mouthing words, created the impression of some large grazing animal, a steer or an ox—an impression belied by the obvious intelligence of the words themselves.

For a moment, Gould had an odd feeling about Wright, as if he'd seen the sergeant before. He searched his memory but couldn't think of when or where they might have met.

Wright sat. Breeze pulled up a chair of his own.

"So—what've you got for us?" Gould asked.

"You know the basics already," replied Breeze. "Two murder victims, Enrique and Camilla Soledad, a husband and wife. Disappeared six days ago, on the 27th. They left their house at 7:30 in the morning, dropped their children off at James Cook Elementary at 7:35. Were supposed to go from there to the replacement workers' camp to board a bus into the mine, but didn't show."

"And the bodies?"

"Found four days later, on the 1st, by a Phil Tucker. Says he was passing through on his way no where in particular. He'd just broken up with his girlfriend."

"Hell of a way to have your mind taken off a broken heart! Have we checked his story?"

"Confirmed his address. Apparently he was a graduate student at Pacific Western University, but recently quit. We got the girlfriend's number from him, but there doesn't seem any particular reason to contact her."

"I should probably take a look at him before we let him go."

"I figured. He's camping at the Igloo station on the Trans-Canada."

Gould lifted a page on the preliminary report, which he had taken out of his briefcase, and let it drop again. "So our time frame is from 7:30 on the morning of the 27th until eight on the morning of the 1st. From the conditions of the bodies, death probably occurred nearer the beginning of the frame than the end. Any word yet about the Soledad car?"

"Nothing."

"And the last people to see them were"—Gould consulted the report—"a couple of people who saw their car at the elementary school, their children, and Mr. Wallace Lies."

"That's right."

"How old are the children?"

"Felipe is ten, Gabriela seven."

Gould sighed. "Where are they now?"

"With Reverend Bentley and his wife. Bentley sponsored the Soledads to come to Canada, through the Unity Alliance Church, and they lived with him for their first few months here."

"Who's Lies?"

"Next-door neighbour. Also mayor of the town. He saw the family get into the car as he came out to go to work. 7:30 exactly. He's sure about it."

"He also reported the disappearances. How was that?"

"Seems that the Soledads were supposed to report directly to Lena Stahr, owner of the mine. When they didn't she telephoned Lies, who is an acquaintance, and Lies, who'd seen them leave in the morning, thought it odd. So he called. We first discretely talked to the children at school, then initiated a search."

"When was this?"

"Lies called at 8:25. Said he'd just talked to Stahr."

"Okay. Now tell me about this other possible sighting."

"David Thatcher. Caretaker at City Hall. Says he may have seen the Soledad car shortly before eight. He was cleaning up some glass out front when he thought he saw it go by. Made an impression on him because it was going the wrong way, north on Queen Street instead of south, away from the mine instead of towards it."

"And in the car?"

"He wasn't sure. He knew the Soledads a little—knew they were working at the mine—and he was fairly certain about the car. Also that there was a man and a woman in it. Beyond that, however, he couldn't say. Latinos all look alike to him."

"And this was at five to eight, ten to eight at the earliest?"

"Yes."

Gould set aside the file he was holding and pushed himself to his feet. "Show me the locations of the Soledad home, the school, the mine, city hall, and the crime scene."

Breeze followed Gould to the table with the unused computer on it. He leaned across with a pencil and marked the map on the wall.

"And where is the replacement workers' camp?"

"Down this side road here."

"So normally this is the route the Soledads would take in the morning. And this is where Thatcher may have seen the car."

"Right."

"Definitely not on the route to the mine. Though it is on the route you'd take from this area to get to where the bodies were found. Assume for a moment that Thatcher's story is true. If the Soledads left the school, here, at 7:35 and drove to City Hall, how long would that take?"

"Two, three minutes. No more."

"But Thatcher says he may have seen them fifteen to twenty minutes later."

Gould tapped his moustache. "Can I have this map?"

"Certainly."

Gould and Breeze made their way back to their seats. Gould consulted the preliminary report again. "Anything else from the time of the disappearance?"

Breeze thought a moment and shook his head.

"Okay. Let's move on then—"

"Alexander MacKenzie." It was Sergeant Wright who spoke.

"Excuse me?"

"Alexander—"

"Ha, ha, ha. That's right, Wright." Breeze lounged back in his chair. He had a pleased look on his face.

"Who is Alexander MacKenzie?"

"An old prospector. Lives in a cabin on the side road that leads to the replacement camp. He came in to see us yesterday. Claimed to have seen a large, black, Mercedes sedan on the side road about the time the Soledads disappeared."

"That's interesting."

"I wouldn't put much stock in it," said Breeze.

"Why?"

"Besides the fact that MacKenzie only came forward yesterday, a week after the fact, which suggests he is fishing for attention, he is an extremely unreliable witness. Alcoholic. Close friend of Al Goodwin (though that's neither here nor there). He has a reputation around town for spreading fantastic stories to get attention."

"What kind of stories?"

"Prospecting stories. You know, the mining equivalent of fish stories, the big one that got away."

"And any other reports of this car before or after?"

"None. But"—and here Breeze wagged his finger for emphasis—"I have a prediction for you, Gould. Before this case is over, you're going to have people left and right reporting glimpses of this car. Even retrospectively. They're going to say, oh I never thought it was important before. It'll be like, I don't know, Elvis or Big Foot. You know what I mean? People claiming to have seen it, like they needed to see it, or needed the attention that came with seeing it."

"What do you make of MacKenzie, sergeant?"

Wright shifted, it seemed a little uneasily, in his chair. After a moment he said, slowly, "I've always liked Alex MacKenzie. He's always been straight with me."

"So you believe his story. You don't think he just made it up after he heard the bodies had been found in order to get attention?"

"I honestly don't know. Like I said, he's always been straight with me."

"Do you have his number?"

Wright shook his head. "He doesn't have a phone. The easiest way to catch him is to drop by the Miner's Museum. He's there every weekday afternoon. It's a good place to get some background information on the town too if you're interested."

"Okay," Gould said. "Let's move on to motive. Who had something against the Soledads?"

There was a pause. Breeze grimaced slightly and crossed his arms. "I should say something before we begin," he said.

Gould waited.

"I suppose you heard the clip of me on the news the other night? I feel rather badly about that. I'm usually more circumspect. Still, I want you to know that we have been investigating the union, and, there is no doubt, there are some real hotheads in that organization."

"So you think the union heads our list of suspects?"

"They had the strongest motive. There are also the incriminating circumstances."

"The two meetings between Enrique Soledad and Al Goodwin?"

"They top the list. We don't know about the October 11th meeting, but our surveillance team saw Soledad leave on the 26th. Just after he went out the door, Goodwin rushed out after him. He shouted *You'll rot in hell before I do, you stupid Spic!* and Soledad yelled something back, apparently an epithet, but it was in Spanish and our men couldn't understand it. But there is also the night someone vandalized the Soledad home."

Gould checked the report. "This was on the 9th?"

"They spray-painted slogans, *Eat Shit Scabs* and *Go Home Spic*, stuff like that, and threw human excrement against the door."

"Maybe Soledad went to the union office on the 11th to confront Goodwin about it?"

"Possible."

"What about Goodwin himself? What do you know about him?"

"Fanatical S.O.B. That's all I know."

"His father was a miner in Cape Breton," explained Wright. "Killed in an accident in the 70s. Goodwin was one of the first employees on board when the Cyclops mine opened in 1980. Before that he worked in Northern Ontario."

"Does he have family here?"

"No one. From what I know, he's a bit of a loner."

Gould asked his next question to no one in particular.

"What about the rumours that the Soledads might have been working undercover for the union?"

Breeze jumped in. "Personally, I believe those rumours were started by some people in the union itself. Part of a disinformation campaign, a way to deflect attention."

Gould raised a fist to his mouth and pressed his finger into his moustache—tapped, once, twice, feeling the bristles. "Okay," he said. "What about other people who knew the Soledads? Sounds like Reverend Bentley would be an important person to talk to."

"Definitely."

"What did he have to say after the disappearance?"

"Not much. He was quite reticent, in fact. You know, things didn't work out very well between the Soledads and Bentley's congregation. Personality conflicts. A lot of hard feelings. I don't know all the details—you'll have to get them from Bentley himself. Anyway, when we talked to him, I think Bentley was embarrassed by the way things turned out."

"And Wallace Lies—he obviously knew them too."

"As well as anyone except Bentley."

"What's Lies like?"

"A wheeler dealer. Zips around everywhere in that airplane of his. An ambitious, manipulative bugger, to tell you the truth. He's always got a dozen business schemes on the go."

"Would any of these schemes involve the principles in the strike?"

"I wouldn't be surprised. Hell, knowing Lies, he's probably trying to make money off both sides."

"What about the Soledads?"

"He had dealings with them—definitely. Sold them their house. That was in August. They moved in over the Labour Day Weekend, just before they started working at the mine. According to Lies, they used $40,000 cash as a down payment. At the same time they deposited $10,000 more into their account at the bank. Of course, the house caused quite a lot of bitterness in the town, particularly amongst those sympathetic to the union. Foreigners taking Canadian jobs, that sort of thing. Six weeks after they moved in, like I told you, the place was vandalized."

"Any explanations about the money?"

"No. Lies says he had nothing to do with it."

"What else did Lies have to say?"

"Not much, really. He talked mostly about himself."

"Does he stand to gain financially in any way from their deaths?"

"Not that I know of. He is executor of their estate, and he volunteered a copy of their will immediately after the discovery of the bodies. It leaves everything to the children."

Gould observed Breeze for a moment. Though he tended to be aloof with the lower ranks, he usually felt a fairly strong affinity with his fellow senior officers. But not with Breeze. There was something about the other inspector that rubbed him the wrong way. Partly it was that initial greeting, so in bad taste. Partly it was Breeze's obvious bias against the union, which suggested something unprofessional in his approach. But there was something else as well. Something more subtle. Oddly enough, he decided it had to do with Breeze's clothes. Breeze's suit was a cut above what most senior officers usually wore, and it was topped by an expensive-looking tie and gold-coloured tie pin. There was something of the aging leading-man about Breeze, the careful haircut, short but with a hint of curl, the dimpled jaw, and a general paunchiness that suggested muscles on their way to flab—a whiff of decadence and self-indulgence.

"Okay," said Gould, after a minute. "What about other friends or acquaintances?"

"None that I can think of."

"What about Lena Stahr? They seemed to be working directly for her, didn't they?"

Breeze frowned again. "True," he said, with a stare of concentration. "I didn't interview her myself, but if I remember, after the disappearances she said she knew of no one—outside of the union—who might have anything against them. Otherwise, she didn't know them personally. She's a pretty reclusive individual."

"Can you see any motive for Stahr herself to be involved?"

Breeze shook his head. "If we discount the story of the Soledads working undercover, I don't think so. I wouldn't absolutely rule it out though."

"Why not?"

Breeze laughed. "You know as well as I do, Gould, that at this

stage you can't rule out any possibility."
Gould put away his copy of the preliminary report in his briefcase. "That should do for now," he said. "A bit later, I'll want to get a clearer picture of the Soledads as people."

"I can help you with that," said Sergeant Wright.

"Good."

The four men rose to their feet. Wright and Viola led the way to the door. Before Gould could follow them, Breeze caught his eye and said, "Before you go, Inspector, I'd like a word with you alone."

The sergeants filed out and Breeze closed the door behind them. Then he walked to the desk and stood for a moment with his back to Gould. He reached out and cupped the flowers with his fingers. "I hate to have to speak to you this way," he said, as much to the browning petals in his hand as to Gould, "but I have to tell you something. About Sergeant Wright."

"Yes?"

Breeze turned. "You'd have probably gotten this from someone else, so you might as well get it from me. Let me be frank with you, Gould. Wright and I have had our problems. His nose is out of joint because, well, because my strike operation has had to take over the policing in this town. This was his office, you know. He had a pretty cozy posting here. Six officers and him. Small town, nice and quiet. His own little fiefdom."

"I'm not interested in personal grievances."

"Of course not. But I wanted to tell you because word has it that Wright's anger has affected his judgement. I don't have any concrete examples for you, but that's what I've had reported to me by more than one of my men. I just thought I should warn you so that you know what you're getting."

"I'll take it under advisement."

CHAPTER THREE

Viola and Gould had worked together for over six years. They were a good match, more for their differences, which complemented one another, than for what they had in common (which was little enough). Viola was two years from retirement and projected the plodding, indifferent manner of someone going through the motions. Like many officers, he had been gradually worn down by the intractability of the problems he had been asked to face. In his early years as a beat cop he had been extraordinarily idealistic and dedicated, a real champion of the people, but now he was like a revolutionary whose great battle had been fought long ago and lost. Sometimes he was nostalgic for the heroic men he had fought side by side with, sometimes he shed tears for the hard lives of those, like his Sicilian immigrant parents, who had had to claw a living from the hide of a corrupt world, but more often than not—like so many disillusioned revolutionaries—he tended towards scorn for the populace he had once sought to liberate.

Viola was content to hover in the background, silent as a monk, in a bad suit, with his tonsure-like stubble of white hair and broad, lined, peasant face. When Gould gave an order, he drifted into motion. Gould always put him in charge of the murder room, where his plodding manner was an asset, leaving the inspector to roam where the key inquiries would take him. Towards other officers Viola tended to a mix of comradery and fatherliness—he loved to down a few pints and dole out half-cynical words to the wise—but towards Gould he kept an instinctive distance. Now and then he would drop a comment about his two married daughters and the astonishingly beautiful grandchildren they had borne him, but he never expected—and never received—any confidences in turn.

After the meeting with Inspector Breeze, Gould sent Viola and Wright back to The Red Grizzly. He asked them to make sure the lists of individuals to contact were complete. Once the preliminaries were dealt with, the investigative team would need to interview all the replacement and striking workers at the mine, the Statewide Security agents hired by Lena Stahr, and the neighbours and acquaintances of the Soledads.

Then he drove to the Silver and District Hospital. He asked at the main desk for Dr. Dean. The nurse said, "Around the corner that way. There's a constable on guard outside the door."

According to Dean, the autopsies suggested that the manner and location of the killings were as they appeared. "It's quite evident," she said, "that the victims died in the positions in which they were found. The way the blood has settled in the bodies is quite conclusive. And death itself was definitely caused by the bullet wounds."

"Murder weapon?"

"A .38 handgun with hollow point ammunition."

"Other signs of violence?"

"Numerous. The male received a head blow, from behind, not long before death—not enough to kill him, but certainly enough to put him out for a while. My guess is he was clubbed with something resembling a policeman's billy club. Both bodies also have bruising on their faces and torsos, consistent with a beating, and bruises also on their arms, which suggests they were dragged or maybe carried to the spot they were killed."

"Tortured?"

"Not specifically. Though, as I said, they were both seriously beaten before death."

"Time of death?"

"I fix it quite close to the time of the disappearances. The state of the bodies suggests some time on the 27th, certainly no later than the 28th, and the stomach contents, though pretty decayed, contained raspberry seeds, probably a sign that they were killed not long after breakfast."

"Toast and jam."

"Exactly."

They were standing not far from the slab on which the body of Enrique Soledad lay. Further off, on another slab, lay the body of Camilla. Both bodies were naked, uncovered. Labels had been tied to their left ankles and around their wrists; the heads, both shaved bare, were in wooden blocks, with the napes of the necks resting in the curvatures. Enrique's face was dark and distorted from the blood that had settled in it, the eyes were clamped shut, the mouth slightly agape, the killing wound just visible at the base of the skull. Sutures showed where the skull had been reassembled after removing the brain. What expression was left to the face was so contradictory, containing equal fragments of awe, surprise, anger, sadness, and bliss, that it was impossible to interpret. An almost black incision, now sutured up again, ran from under the chin to the pubic region, by which organs had been removed for study. The incision had a slight curve in it to avoid the umbilicus.

Gould had seen many corpses in his time and had witnessed many autopsies. There was not much that could shock him. In fact, in some ways, he had always felt his position to be privileged. Of all the people who might see the body of a murder victim, the witnesses, the family, the coroner, the mortician, the priest, he was the one most directly charged to act on the victim's behalf. Justice, he knew, could never undo what had been done; but until the killer was brought to justice, until some meaning was brought to the crime, the emptiness and horror flowing from the murderer's act—and the victim's absence—could never, in any significant way, be staunched.

On this day, however, he was unusually moved. Perhaps it was because Dean had not yet completed reassembling the bodies. For although the abdominal incisions had been sutured up, and although the skulls had been reassembled, neither Enrique's nor Camilla's hands had yet been reattached. Under certain circumstances, it was necessary to amputate both hands at the wrist in order to examine them properly, to do scrapings under the fingernails, to examine all the intricate creases and joints for anything—food or dirt or blood or skin tissue—that might throw light on the victim's fate. But something today about a husband and wife, almost side by side, so close and yet eternally separate, and without hands.... Gould turned away.

In an attempt at diversion, Gould now indicated a clipboard hanging above the worktable, which contained some of the forms the coroner would have to fill out. At the appointed spot on the top form was the doctor's name.

"Excuse me asking something personal," he said, "but your first name, Misao, is it Japanese?"

"Yes."

"But?"

"It's true. I'm not Japanese. I was named after the woman who delivered me. A very remarkable person, to be a woman and Japanese and a doctor in Canada at that time."

"Was it hard growing up?"

"Not in the way you think. The hardest part was that it made me think I had to become a doctor. That I was fated somehow, or required, to live up to the name." Dean now laughed somewhat ruefully. "And of course I did become a doctor after all"—gesturing around the lab—"but with a difference."

Gould slipped back into professional mode. "Is there anything else at this time?"

"One thing. I'm not sure how to say this, Inspector, I know you know your job, but something about execution style killings really sends a shiver up my spine. Accidents and suicides are tragic, gut-wrenching, particularly if children are involved, but you can at least partially blame God and circumstance; with crimes of passion, you can blame it on booze or drugs or the insanity of love. But with these killings"—she gestured to the two slabs—"these are the products of evil. Not chance. Not despair. Not madness. Just evil, pure and simple.

"What I wanted to say was that with killings like this, if they were done by a real professional, there won't be mistakes. Which means the physical evidence is not likely to get you very far. In fact, from what I've seen, the physical evidence in this case seems planted, almost taunting, as if the killer has deliberately created a puzzle for you that cannot be solved. At least not from the evidence given. Over the years, I've learned that to solve a crime like this one you have to find out the meaning of the crime in a larger sense, if you know what I mean, to go beyond the narrow logic of the crime scene, to explore the larger issues involved, the history, the struggles between groups or factions, and then to work backwards. Otherwise . . . ."

While Dean talked Gould nodded once or twice, but his eyes wandered, to the bodies on the slabs, to an instrument trolley gleaming with surgical tools, and finally to the workbench, its microscope, Bunsen burner, and various beakers and containers. He took in the orderly arrangement of clear plastic bags, each one carefully labelled, including four bags each containing a severed human hand. When the coroner's voice had trailed off, Gould said, "Thanks for the advice, Doc. Send everything to Cramdown a.s.a.p., all right?"

"Of course."

"I look forward to your full report."

Gould made for the door. Then, with his fist on the handle, he stopped and, over his shoulder, said, "Oh—and everybody makes mistakes."

He returned to The Red Grizzly. On his way in he stopped at the desk to ask if the changes were completed to his room.

"I don't know about that," the woman there said. "You talk to Arnie?"

"The owner?"

"Whatever."

"I talked to a Mr. Keller."

"That's him. Then I guess it should be done."

"Another thing. I'm going to be here for a week or so. Is there a good place along the highway to eat?"

"Our bar opens at noon. But they only serve munchies."

"I was thinking of somewhere . . . else."

"Well, I guess the most popular place is the Igloo just down the road. Kind of touristy but also a truck-stop. Open twenty-four hours."

"Thank you—"

"—Margot. You're welcome, Inspector."

Indeed the improvements, except for something to cover the mirror, had been completed to the room. The curtains were now pulled aside and the window opened a couple of inches, enough to create a distinct coolness in the room. The smell—that cocktail of upchuck and Mr. Clean—was still noticeable, but whether it was because of the open window or because he was getting used to it, Gould found it less pronounced.

It was time to map out the wider investigation.

He began by recording most of his conversations with Inspector Breeze and Dr. Dean. In this he was aided by a family trait, for like his father and brother, Gould had a remarkable memory. The gift of memory had taken different forms in the Gould men: in Senator Gould, it translated into a vast mental reservoir of government policies and legal minutiae; in Gould's brother, into an astonishing facility with music. In Charles himself, the gift allowed the recall of entire conversations verbatim.

This ability had not always worked to his advantage. He had first discovered it when, as a child, he was able to parrot word for word his father's dinner-time lectures. At first he did it simply to gain his father's attention (at the time, Robert Gould was not only Premier of New Brunswick, but had an older son on the verge of a dazzling musical career and a glamorous young wife on the verge of spectacularly and scandalously divorcing him). Unfortunately for young Charles, his father misinterpreted his gesture for an interest—indeed, a true calling—in politics (the usual subject of the lectures), and Charles spent much of the rest of his youth dodging the political mantle his father became intent on bequeathing to him.

The talent also did little for his social life. Like many gifted children, he was considered freakish by his peers. As an adolescent and young adult, when his riding schedule permitted, he carried on a fairly active social life, and his ability to recount entire classroom lectures or conversations from a party of the night before brought him a certain amount of notoriety. But, back then, outside the confines of dressage, he had a poor sense of discipline. Sometimes, once he had captured an audience, he would drone on for twenty minutes reproducing every trivial detail of a previous conversation, oblivious to the growing boredom, then irritation, of his listeners. He also thought it amusing to publicly replay other people's drunken ramblings, a habit that left a number of acquaintances beet-faced and led to a consensus amongst his peers that the joy of conversation was seriously threatened by the presence of a human tape recorder.

The ability, however, was a godsend in investigation. One of the more difficult decisions for an investigator is when to bring out his or her notebook. When interviewing a witness or interrogating a suspect, important statements, like a confession, need to be recorded verbatim.

But if the matter under investigation is sensitive, as it always is with a homicide, the obvious use of a notebook or tape recorder can inhibit candor.

After making his transcripts, Gould highlighted the details for further pursuit. Then he made some notes to himself about how to approach the interviews ahead.

At this point, the investigation would likely centre on Al Goodwin and Lena Stahr. Goodwin was an obvious suspect, but Gould intended to give equal attention to Stahr, particularly until the role of the Soledads (scabs or spies?) had been clarified. Before he interviewed either of those two, however, he needed to increase his store of wider information. Better information was necessary for him to ask the right questions when the time came and to recognize the right responses. In any case, a more indirect approach can sometimes have a useful effect: the uncertainty, the anxious wait with an investigator in the vicinity, can unnerve the lies out of someone when the rap on the door finally comes. In extreme cases, it can even goad a perpetrator into doing something stupid—like trying to skip town—that is halfway to a confession.

So he began by calling the Church of Christ Redeemer. Reverend Bentley answered. They agreed to meet the next morning at ten.

Then he tried the office of Wallace Lies. A secretary answered. After he had identified himself and the nature of his business, the secretary put him on hold, and for a minute and a half he was treated to a Muzac version of *Maxwell's Silver Hammer*, replete with chimes when the hammer allegedly came down upon her head. When the secretary cut back in, she informed him that the Mayor was out of town and would not be available until Monday.

This second call caused Gould to pause. Had he just been put off? He could of course subpena Lies to testify, but he didn't like to work that way, particularly early in an investigation. Witnesses were a little like horses. They needed to know who was in charge, but only to a point: too heavy a hand on the reins triggered resistance. He decided to let Lies run free for the moment.

He went into the bathroom, ran some water into his hands and splashed his face. His toiletries—shaving soap, brush, razor, nail-clippers, deodorant, comb, toothbrush, toothpaste, and shampoo—were neatly lined up on the shelf provided. He dried his face, beginning as always with his eyes, then dabbing his moustache with a corner of the towel. Close to the mirror like this, he could see the parts of his face inherited from his father, the thin mouth, the eye-lid that drooped a little, like an inverted tent, the line that seemed to contradict all the others, following the contour of his cheek bone to connect the corner of his eye with the corner of his mouth. He was not one to spend much time in self-reflection; he had always considered it effete. In this he was like his father, who governed his own life by rationality and will; his father, at the age of 82, still beginning each day with fifty push-ups and fifty sit-ups. It wasn't that he denied the value of the inner life. No. Just that he thought of it in the same way as he would a range of wild horses—all those feelings and memories and fears—something that could carry him forward but only with the proper discipline (light-handed but firm). Still, sometimes lately he was irritated by doubts. Sometimes he wondered if now, at the age of 41, the careful choices he had made for his life had started to unravel. Take, for instance, the distinctions he had drawn between himself and his father. For a long time he had been very clear about their relationship. He respected his father, his single-minded determination, his adherence to principles, but he saw himself as operating differently, less rigidly, with a greater appreciation of the complexity of life. His father, for one thing, had no sense of irony. And he was so partisan, so deadly earnest about politics—the complete opposite of his younger son. And yet, these days, the Senator's expression or voice seemed more and more to inhabit Charles Gould's own. As if by the very fact of aging, as his body came to resemble the body of the father he remembered from his boyhood, a genetic memory, a cellular recording started to play. The sound of that recording sometimes threatened to drown out his own words and thoughts.

    He was also having dreams. Nightmares. With an intensity that had happened only once before in his life. On some nights, just five minutes into sleep, he would bolt awake with a sensation of falling, then slide back into elaborate, shimmering narratives. He would be at a reception, say, one of the receptions that punctuated his childhood, and an adult in formal clothes would bend down to shake his hand and ask him his name . . . and he would not be able to remember it. Or he would be reviewing a police report, one that detailed some gruesome crime, and it would become urgent to solve the mystery of it. He would see by the cover page that he had worked on the case himself, and would remember, abruptly, that he had already worked out the solution. But when he flipped to the last page he would discover that it was in a foreign language, a language that he might once have understood but whose meaning was now lost forever.

Thinking about police reports brought Gould back to the present. The mirror, his ruddy, long face in it. Now, in the harsh light of the bathroom, he shook off the memory of his dreams. His doubts receded before the steely assurance of his own gaze. He found his face, the fixed mask of it, reassuring. All things considered, he decided, narrowing his eyes a little at himself, it was truly the face of a professional.

The towel was still in his hand. He folded it in half length wise and carefully scrolled it back onto the towel rack.

It was nearly six o'clock. Night had fallen. Gould's window was now dominated by the orange glare of a halogen streetlight. A steady beat came from the highway, punctuated here and there by the bass rumble of a transport truck.

Gould gathered up his papers, put on his suit-jacket (a somewhat worn, blue blazer, with a specially tailored bulge on his gun side), and, trench coat and briefcase in hand, left the room. Across the hall, the sergeants had pretty well finished with their lists. The map from Breeze's office was now tacked to one wall. Another wall was mostly covered by a white board on which Viola had posted the known facts of the case, including a brief description of the Soledads—names, ages, occupations (with a question mark)—and photographs of the crime scene, which Special Constable Fulton had recently delivered. One constable sat at the horseshoe table flipping through papers. Another was entering information into a laptop computer. Wright was just putting on his coat as Gould stepped in the door.

"Off?" asked Gould.

"I can't do any more today," said Wright. "I have to get back home. A family matter. I'll be back bright and early tomorrow."

"We've pretty well finished up anyway," said Viola.

"I'd rather like to pick your brain about the Soledads," said Gould.

"Definitely. In fact, it's important that we talk. I have some things to confess. Things that go beyond just my knowledge of the Soledads."

"I'm already aware of your conflict with Inspector Breeze."

"Beyond that—though Inspector Breeze is definitely off my Christmas card list." Wright smiled ruefully for a moment and then grew very serious. He lowered his voice and turned his body slightly to shield his words from the constables, who continued to work on behind him. "The fact is, Inspector, I think I may a played a part—a minor and unwitting but rather shameful part—in the murders."

"Then we must definitely talk."

"Yes. But I really must get home at the moment. I'm expecting a very important phone call and I have to be there for it."

"Later on tonight?"

"I'll be free again by eight. Why don't you come by a bit after?"

"Fine."

"Do you know the way?"

"Give me directions and I'll get there."

"Interested in something to eat?" Gould asked Viola, when Wright had left.

"Had it. Once things are wrapped up here a couple of the boys and I are going for a pint."

"Then let's quickly review our approach for tomorrow."

"Sure thing. Oh, first. There was a message for you from the Super."

Gould set his trench coat and briefcase on the table and followed Viola to the answering machine. Viola pushed a button.

"Thought you'd want to know, Gould, something interesting has come up," said the voice of Superintendent O'Brien. "I got it from Vancouver city police but it was also on the mid-day news if you were listening. Two men, Terrance Sherwood and Edward Berry, were arrested yesterday in Vancouver trying to sell off bars of silver bullion. Eight bars in all. This is the thing: turns out they're members of the B.M.U. local in Silver. A couple of your striking miners. I don't know what it means exactly, but you should send someone down there to check it out. The investigating officer is Detective Surridge."

Gould raised a curled finger to his moustache. After a moment, he said, "Do you think Sergeant Wright could run the murder room?"

"No doubt."

"Well, depending on what comes out of my talk with him tonight, he may get his chance. Fancy a drive to the big city, George?"

"I've always enjoyed a change of scene."

Not long after, Gould gathered up his things. His stomach was gnawing at him—a combination of the hour and the long, adrenaline driven day. Before he left the room, he gathered up a file of clippings Breeze had passed on about the strike. Something to make his time eating more useful.

He made his way downstairs. Margot was still at the check-in desk, smoking a cigarette and writing, it seemed, in an accounts ledger. She was a short, thick-boned woman, in her early to mid thirties, with a faintly Churchillian face. Gould imagined her equally capable of staring down Nazis, neo-Nazis, or guys in pickup trucks with too much Banner Premium Ale in their bloodstreams.

Gould had an idea.

"Excuse me, Margot," he said, "could you make a phone call for me?"

"Sure thing. Where to?"

"The Igloo."

"Hold on a sec." Margot took a drag from her cigarette, stood up from where she had been working, leaving the cigarette to smolder in a tin-foil ashtray, and, expelling smoke from the corner of her mouth, ran her finger down a list of numbers taped to the desk. She starting punching buttons.

"Ask if someone named Phil Tucker is there."

She nodded, listened for the pickup, and asked the question. A few seconds later, she gave Gould a mildly flirtatious smile and handed him the receiver. "They say they'll get him for you."

Chapter Four

One of the things I was curious about, once I got to know him, was how Gould ended up in police work. When I had learned something about his family, his silvered upbringing, it made me even more curious. Why would someone whose family was jowl-to-jowl with the Canadian political elite, who only had to show up breathing to land a cushy job in Ottawa, do something so proletarian and thankless?

When I brought the question up, Gould gave me his in-the-line-of-duty look. His unwavering blue-eyed if-I-was-American-I'd-be-a-fighter-pilot look. And said, "A man must work to some end."

"Yeah, yeah," I said. "Now tell me the real story."

Eventually, he told me two of his earliest memories.

The first had to do with his brother. Seems that one day when they were living in Fredericton, back when their father was still Premier, he and his brother had contrived to escape the family home. A squad of RCMP officers was supposed to be guarding the family, and the boys were never to leave the house without a bodyguard. They hated the bodyguards. The bodyguards were men with beefy arms and huge feet who lumbered after them like slightly irritated pet elephants, intimidating their friends and stamping out their fun—men who chattered nonsensically or condescendingly at them or who were stony cold. The boys made a game of trying to escape. Charles remembered numerous occasions in which he and his brother made a break for it. They would fly like bandits until there was heaving and puffing behind them, the pachydermal *thunk thunk* of police heels that proved the hopelessness of their case.

On this occasion, however, the two boys timed their escape perfectly. Their nanny had just left the room; their latest bodyguard was downstairs in the guardroom. His brother led the way down a rope ladder from the second story window, and the two of them raced across the back lawn of the family estate and disappeared like rabbits through a hole under the fence.

They didn't go far. Far was not the point. Instead they went to the most public space around, The Green, that thin, heavily used ribbon of park between the Saint John river and the Legislature. On one side, brown-blue water; on the other, glass, granite, gargoyles; in between, trees, benches, people, prams, dogs, kites . . . and them. They bought ice cream from a vender with a bicycle cart. They swaggered. They glared into the eyes of strangers, defying anyone to recognize who they were. They threw rocks in the general direction of the university rowing team.

When the staff realized what had happened, a great panic set in. Radios squawked. Police cars flailed off in various directions. Foot-patrols *thunked* about the neighbourhood.

Fifteen minutes later, the escapees had been spotted.

"My mother had a lot of trouble dealing with security," Gould explained; "it was one of the many things she hadn't bargained for when she married my father. Anyway, one of the few ways she had of asserting herself around the staff—servants and security alike—was by insisting that nobody but she, my father, and our nanny could discipline us. She told me she had these nightmares of us having a wild day only to be yelled at or bullied by a dozen strange adults. So when the security men found us by the river they stationed themselves quietly and waited for her.

"She tried to be discrete. She understood our impulse to escape all too well. Everything would have been fine except that my brother chose then to throw one of his tantrums. He was like that. He fought and clawed and screamed at the top of his lungs, he denounced my mother, called her a witch, until two officers in full uniform ran from their car to help. Which of course only made things worse. Now instead of having a nice quiet walk back with my mother, with a security patrol discretely trailing behind, we were dragged across The

Green in front of dozens of gaping people and packed into the back of a police car. My mother also seemed to be dragged along. She ended up on the seat beside us with her face in her hands, weeping.

"Funny thing was, that night, when we were up in our room (we were sent to bed early), a whole parade of people came in to see my brother. My father came to give him a lecture. My mother came to scold him and ended up weeping, again, into his blankets. Our nanny, Miss Grant, came in to see if he was all right. 'What an eventful day you've had,' she cooed. All the time these people were coming in I was in the next bed, lying there awake and quiet. I had been perfectly willing to go back when my mother came for us. I hadn't created a fuss. I understood that what we had done was wrong. And yet, for all my virtue, nobody paid any attention to me."

The other memory had to do with Corporal Cleary. It seems that one result of The Great Escape was that Annie Gould, the boys' mother, finally had it out with Inspector Blank, the officer in charge of security. She was angry about her own treatment but particularly angry at the bodyguards assigned to the boys. "They wouldn't try to run away so much if you didn't always assign such creeps to them," she said.

"And what do you mean by a creep?" the Inspector asked.

"A creep is a big lumbering ox who's always got his hand on his gun. He thinks guarding my sons is degrading, a job for a baby-sitter, not a big tough policeman. He's a bully and pushes the boys around psychologically all the time."

And so a compromise was struck, at least when it came to the boys' protection (a few weeks later, Annie looked after herself with a Great Escape of her own). The result, for Charles and his brother, was Corporal Cleary—Corporal Tom as they called him. Cleary was a pleasant, kindly man in his late thirties, a family man who had an intuitive sense of when to be visible to the children and when not. He never blundered in when the boys were with their friends or fighting amongst themselves. Sometimes, when the three of them were alone, he joined in their games. And he told them stories, of his first assignment up in northern Ontario, of growing up on a farm on the Prairies.

Gould's memory of Cleary was an emotional composite, an accumulation of the all the warmth and security he felt when the corporal was around. Cleary stuck with the boys through the crisis that followed their mother's departure until their father's humiliating defeat in the election of 1961. Charles, amongst other things, marveled at the corporal's stories, a number of which had to do with horses. He remembered lying in bed retelling the stories word for word to himself. He also remembered admiring Cleary's uniform. All the RCMP officers wore their red tunics and baggy pants with the yellow stripe down the side when protecting the Goulds (Robert Gould insisted on formality). But only with Cleary did Charles look up close: the corporal stripes, the brass buttons, the whistle on a white lanyard, the polished black boots. Only with Cleary did he connect a real officer around him with that red-tunicked upright hero of postcards, movie matinees, and cereal boxes.

He also admired Corporal Cleary's gun (much to his brother's disgust). The gun was always there in its hideaway black leather holster. Sometimes, in a clandestine moment, they would huddle under a tree out back, and Cleary would release the silver buckle and lift the holster's flap. He would pull the gun out by the handle and then, ever so carefully, lay it across Charles's hands. Charles would run his fingers under the barrel, close a palm around the wooden grip, and marvel at the weight of it.

According to Corporal Cleary, the pistol was for shooting snakes.

"Very touching," I said, the night Gould told me this. "But aren't you contradicting yourself? In one case, you learn that the goody-two-shoes of this world get ignored, that to get attention you have to act up like your brother. In the other case, you learn to admire a benevolent goody-two-shoes like Corporal Cleary."

"Seems entirely consistent to me," said Gould.

"How so?"

"Maybe I never wanted attention."

Sometime later, however, he admitted that he hadn't told the whole story. "If you really want to know why I got into policing," he said, "you have to understand more about the riding."

Remember that Gould had a very erect walk. An upright, uptight walk. A tight-assed walk, you might think (I did the first time I saw him). I can imagine him all those years on some horse or other, the Upper Class Twit doing the Upper Class Thing, and his private coach stopping him to tap his lower back with a riding whip: "Upright, Gould, upright—don't slouch!"

When he was sixteen or seventeen he got very serious about making the Canadian national team. He prevailed upon his father to give him the money to buy the best horse he could find, not a mean feat in itself, considering Robert Gould's notorious miserliness and his skepticism about this project in particular. Still, arguments were made, the money was produced, a horse purchased, and with the aid of a coach and trainer Charles began the long, slow process of raising himself and the horse—whom he christened Pierre—to international standards.

He approached competition with an almost fanatical intensity. He was meticulous in his preparations, the careful schedule of training before an event, the willed sleep of the night before, the competition day riding in. His father liked to point out an irony: that the rider worked so hard to achieve precision only to await the imprecise interpretations of the judges. But Charles liked that aspect, the humanness of it, as opposed to the cut-and-dried time-clock and fault system of show jumping, and he believed that, in the end, excellence would always win out.

The year he tried out for the national team, the trials were held in Ottawa, on a muggy June weekend with thunder drifting in like applause from over the horizon. Lansdowne Park was an advantage. Charles had competed there a number of times; it felt almost like home turf. On the day of the dressage test, Pierre was edgy but lost his tension quickly during the riding in. They assumed position. In a moment, the signal, and Pierre stepped smartly forward.

During the ride Charles was only vaguely aware of the crowd, its summer colours and polite silence, the ribbons decorating the judges' tables. He was more aware of touches and smells, the humidity on his face, horse-hair on the backs of his fingers, the aromas of turf, saddle polish, Pierre. It seemed to him that Pierre took the bit calmly and confidently, that they moved smoothly through their paces, made fluent transitions, and, most importantly, that they maintained from beginning to end a near perfect balance.

Afterwards, Charles's coach, who was a taskmaster and not prone to easy praise, nodded . . . satisfactory. In the finish area they assumed position again. A wait, breath gradually slowing, Charles bending now and again to stroke Pierre's neck. One minute. Two. Then, on the scoreboard, a flicker of lights. Charles's coach, one of Canada's most eminent equestrians, had always emphasized the gentlemanly elements of riding, how riders gave proof of their self-control by submitting to the judges' verdict without argument or protest. But this day the scores were so low that it sent a murmur through the crowd. Charles blushed. Then he yanked on the reins and, with Pierre half-rearing in protest, kicked clods out of the arena.

That evening he was inconsolable. He was convinced, partly on his own and partly from goading by his father, that the judges had been politically motivated, that the performance had been interpreted not on its own merits but because of who he was.

The failure began an angry, unsettled period in his life. A period of travel and self-searching. He quit the University of Ottawa, where he had been an undergraduate, sold Pierre and used the money (against the furious protests of his father) to buy the first of many plane tickets. Two years later he had toured Europe and Africa, had spent time in Mexico, Argentina and Costaguana, and had fallen in love. He was twenty-two years old. Six months after returning to Canada he joined the RCMP, vowing to be the most principled and a-political officer ever.

"All right," I said, "now we're getting somewhere."

The Igloo is not at all shaped like an igloo. From the highway its complex—three-bay garage on one side, restaurant on the other—is just another generic roadside stop whose main asset is the weariness of the traveler. You might say that the building looks a little like two flattened ice-cubes bonded together, all those straight lines and windows, with a glass-fronted atrium in between, but that would be stretching it. The only thing that distinguishes this stop from any other is the sign: a stylized black-and-white igloo on a metal standard. If you're from Alberta or B.C., you know the sign I mean.

Igloo Oil is not exactly one of my favourite companies. If you do a little research you'll find that it was one of the first all-Canadian successes from the Alberta oil fields. A local company that made it big. Eventually it grew into a fully-integrated oil and gas producer, controlling everything from initial exploration to that guy with the Igloo cap on his head cleaning your windshield, but then, following the next logical step in Canadian business, apparently, it sold itself to a multinational conglomerate which promptly rationalized local operations. The rationalization put two thousand people out of work.

The other problem, of course, is the company logo, which is not a sterling example of Political Correctness. I mean, we've stolen enough from the native peoples already, do we have to steal their images too? In fact, there were some protests about the logo a couple of years ago. Jayne, not surprisingly, was right in the thick of them. There was a march in downtown Vancouver, a rally, some picketing. Some ingenious protesters slightly distorted the Igloo symbol to make it look like a skull. They created a palisade of skulls on poles, blocked off the entrance to a tower in the business district, beat drums, sang, clapped and chanted down the corporate imperialists. Unfortunately, because of the change in ownership, the head office was by then in Denver. When rumours of the protest finally reached that far, the board of directors shrugged them off, claiming they had two much *goodwill* riding on the logo to change it now.

None of this stopped me from loving the Igloo the moment I walked in the door. What can I say? As improbable as it may seem, the restaurant lived up to those corny TV ads: "Come in under the igloo, a sign of shelter from the storm."

The franchise owner, Wallace Lies, met me just inside. There was something about his face that was hard to pin down, something that made it hard to remember afterwards. He had features like everybody else—eyes, nose, mouth, hair—but when I tried to recall them to myself they seemed somehow undefined, like a slightly blurred photograph.

In any case, I can't complain about the way he greeted me. He guessed right away who I was (the microbus was a giveaway) and pumped my hand up and down and said I could camp in the parking lot as long as I wanted. Given what had just happened to me. Given that the police had requested me to stick around for a day or two.

Not long after, I staked out the corner booth that became my habitual haunt. From this booth I could see out both long banks of windows, one facing down the valley towards town, the other facing a sheer wall of dark rock, the West Columbia Range, the tops of which are usually lost in cloud. At that time of year, early November, with tourist season over and ski season not yet begun, the main customers were drivers of the rigs parked nearby, travelling salespeople and various mobile workers (road crews, B.C. Tel technicians). A selection of locals was usually there too, including a sampling of striking miners and replacement workers, a fact that demanded a special diplomatic tact from the waitresses.

It wasn't just Mr. Lies's greeting that made me warm to the place. The place itself also seemed so—how can I put it?—so real. I know that's vague—what is *real life* anyway?—but I can't think of any other way to put it. Take that first morning, after I settled into my booth and gave my order to Marlene (name stitched onto her uniform). Around me men in nylon bomber jackets with the names of their football teams on them, or in heavy faded checked shirts, contemplated their fried eggs and hash browns or hot turkey sandwiches before forking them into their mouths. Two tables away, a Hydro crew nodded hard hats of yellow plastic over mugs of coffee. The music, which was just fractionally louder than the talk, was country-and-western, the old-fashioned variety, Johnny Cash, Merle Haggard, Hank Snow. While I sat there, a tractor-trailer rumbled to a halt on the lot and blocked my view of the mountains.

Something about that corrugated broadside, about turning back to take in the room again, about the short-order cook coming out from behind the counter to personally deliver my order: the total effect made me feel *I have arrived.*

The other thing was, I was a celebrity. Talk about attention. Once word got around that I was the one who had discovered the Soledad bodies, a succession of people, reporters, staff and customers, locals and out-of-towners, slipped into the seat across from me to ask what it was like. As I told and retold the story, people gave me looks of sympathy and understanding. Now and then, at the end of my tale, someone would pat me on the arm or look into my eyes and say "well, take care."

Some of the truckers called me *kid*.

When Inspector Gould pushed in through the door, every person in the Igloo knew who he was. Partly because I had passed on word that he was coming. Partly because his description had raced through town earlier in the day. Partly because his appearance—the short hair, the moustache, the posture, and especially that jacket-and-tie—was a dead giveaway.

When you think about it, is there anything more transparent than a cop in plain clothes? When was the last time you were fooled by those beefy guys in one-button grey and blue jackets trailing some dignitary? Seems to me that if you really want to disguise a cop you should dress him up in a parody of a police uniform. You know, the equivalent of army surplus: an old police shirt, mismatching trousers, a Metropolitan Police baseball cap. Make the guy look like the equivalent of a sixties anti-war protestor in army fatigues, someone flaunting his contempt for the uniform (an eco-button or peace symbol on the cap would be a nice touch). Or better yet, make the guy look like he wished he actually was a cop. Someone who never misses those *real life* cop shows (there are those two words again). Sort of like the guys who wear gold-braided officers' caps with the names of American aircraft carriers on them, guys who dream of being fighter-pilots but who will never even learn to fly.

Normally, when someone comes in the door of the Igloo, nobody pays much attention. If it isn't too busy maybe a waitress or the short-order cook looks up, but none of the customers; they're too busy chowing down or arguing about the merits of Burnaby Joe versus Eric Lindros. This time, however, things were different. I won't say conversation stopped or anything as cliché as that. But there was a definite change amongst the clientele, a ripple-effect that started at tables nearest to the door and spread out until it took in the entire room. Attention shifted—split (mouth still making the case for Lindros, eyes sizing up the cop at the door).

Gould, for his part, didn't seem to notice. He just stood there and calmly surveyed the room. Blue jacket, grey pants, white shirt, dark blue tie with red somethings on it (turned out to be miniature schooners). His auburn hair was faintly back lit by the light from the glass door behind him. His briefcase was against one thigh.

There are a dozen signs you can use to signal recognition. To say *over here.* To say *I am the one.* All those hand and arm gestures, the placard in the airport crowd, the wave, the shout. But the most powerful signs are often the subtlest (don't ask me why). In this case, someone watching Gould or I individually would have had a hard time noticing when the message passed. Just a momentary stasis in the eyes. Then a slow stride, that remarkably upright equestrian stride, the Royal Family pickle-up-the-ass walk ... down the line of the lunch counter, past vinyl upholstered metal stools bolted into the floor, past juice and pop machines and mirror-backed shelves of pastries ... right turn at the high counter sectioning off the grill, the two on-duty waitresses retreating from their hangout by the warming light ... past the studiously unconcerned rig drivers at the prime location *Truckers Only* table.

He introduced himself. He showed me his badge. He took a copy of my statement out of his brief-case.

"Are you a writer?" he asked.

"Not that kind of writer," I said.

Marlene brought him a menu.

What was it that attracted me to him? Me, Phil Tucker, convicted cultivator of marijuana, a man who wears his left-wing convictions like red dye on his hands? Was my attraction really the ultimate sell-out, as Jayne would say, proof that I was just waiting for the right moment (the *right* moment!) to become one with the powers-that-be?

I could make excuses. How tired I was of the melodrama with Jayne. My nightmares of storms and falling. How shaken I was to find two dead human beings at my feet.

What it came down to, in our first meeting, was that aura of resolution. That implacable calm, the walk, the manner. In retrospect I can see I let my imagination get the better of me. Who could ever live up to what I yearned for? Even so, I bet the so-called decision makers of our day make half their judgements on equally impulsive and human grounds, the way you size up a restaurant or a glint in the bush in a second, decide in less time than it takes to tie a shoe whether you will stop or carry on. And Charles Gould, remember, had presence. As he sat on the other side of the booth from me and snapped the catches on his briefcase, he seemed so tangible, so there, as if he was the only real person in the room and everybody else was faintly fictional. He asked me a series of questions. I don't even remember any more what they were. I was aware of his eyeing me for inconsistencies, probing for signs of bad character, and I just submitted myself to it. I remember thinking, "Wow, this guy really knows what he's doing," and "I'd hate, no I'd love to see him interrogate a suspect!"

Then, as suddenly as it began, the interview was over. He put his papers away, closed his briefcase and turned his attention to his Dashaway of the Day. Split pea soup and an egg salad sandwich.

In the silence that fell between us as he worked on his food, I picked up my journal again. I had laid it on the seat beside me when he sat down. *Are you a writer?* "A funny thing," I began, flattening the journal open in front of me. "In the three days that I have been here I have spoken to maybe thirty or forty people. Some locals, some passing through. Everybody, it seems, wants to talk to me about the murders."

I let that sink in. Gould betrayed no interest.

"Of course, it's because I found the bodies. People want to know what it was like and so on. But they also think, for some reason, that because I found the bodies I can fill them in on the investigation."

Gould looked up from his soup.

"I can't, of course. But the funniest thing is, you'd be amazed at all the things they've told me in return. After I tell them my experience, it's like they need to unburden themselves. Know what I mean? In two days I've learned more about the situation here in Silver than I could ever have thought possible."

He had stopped eating now. Soup spoon in his left hand. "People have talked to you about the murders?"

"The strike, the murders, everything. I've talked to striking miners, replacement workers, local joes and janes. Everybody has a theory and, well, I've written them all down in here."

He seemed to consider my journal for a moment. Then turned back to his soup. "If you have anything pertinent to the case...."

"That's the thing. I mean, how do you tell? Maybe something is pertinent and may it's not. It's the kind of thing you need to discuss and work out."

"What is pertinent is whatever helps me to identify the killer or killers of those people. Is that clear enough?"

His tone set me back a moment. Frankly, I was a bit surprised. I had expected him to be a lot more interested in the information I had collected. Had expected, well, some praise or encouragement. *That was very resourceful of you, Tucker. Keep your ear to the ground and let me know if you find out anything else.* Instead he seemed annoyed.

I tried another tack.

"I'd be happy to photocopy everything I've got so you can look it over for yourself."

"Suit yourself."

"What I was going to suggest—" But I hesitated. Gould was staring at me with a knowing, a warning expression. "I thought I could be of some—"

He set down his mostly-eaten sandwich. Lifted the napkin from his lap and dabbed his mouth. Examined me with his cold blue eyes. And sighed. "Why is it always the intellectuals?"

"What?"

"The intellectuals. The people I always have trouble with, the ones that always want to get involved—to meddle in an investigation. So often they are intellectuals. It's as if all those years when they are slogging away at their intellectual duties, teaching, writing academic papers, all that time what they really want to do is write mystery novels. And then, by accident, they end up with a minor role in a real criminal investigation. And suddenly they start taking notes in journals."

I flushed. Then went on the attack.

"First of all, Inspector, I'm not an intellectual. I never was much of one and now I've given it up entirely. And second of all, second of all—" But I couldn't think of anything else to say.

Gould listened to my outburst with a slightly bemused expression. He squeezed a crumb up off the table with his finger and put it in his mouth. "So, what exactly was your field anyway?"

The way he said it—with a kind of casual coyness—made me suspect a trap, as if he had seen into me in some way, as if he had discovered something to his advantage. It was a feeling I was to have a number of times during our acquaintance and, later, friendship. Even when I knew him fairly well, I rarely figured out the line of his thinking until it was too late.

I resorted to generalities. "To tell you the truth, the proposal I gave in for my dissertation was not accepted. It had certain flaws. And I was looking around for another project when, well, when I decided to quit."

He nodded as if I had just confirmed something for him.

"I don't see how—" But I did see what he was getting at now. "I told you," I said, flushing, floundering, "I've quit. It doesn't matter to me any more. I'm no longer interested."

He waited for me to finish. Then, quite deliberately, he ate the last bites of his sandwich and drank the last spoonfuls of his soup. He signaled Marlene for the bill.

And turned on me.

"Don't tell me that I didn't warn you," he said. "If you want to photocopy your journal for me, fine, I will look at it. Otherwise, your presence here is no longer required. I can't order you to go home, but I strongly suggest that you do. I don't want to talk to you again or see you again. If I catch you meddling in my investigation in any way I will have you arrested for obstructing justice. Is that clear?"

CHAPTER FIVE

Gould returned to his room. He was, no doubt, irritated at me. I don't blame him. Let's face it, I was angling to get taken on as an assistant on the case, to play Watson beside his Holmes, Adso beside his William of Baskerville. Pretty stupid, I admit. I've seen enough cop shows and read more than enough mystery novels to know what cops think of meddling civilians. Chalk it up to Gould's dazzling presence . . . or, more likely, to my desperate state, to how far I had fallen: down on my knees and lunging with both hands towards his ramrod gleam.

In the interest of honesty, I should also admit that Gould was not far off in his insinuation about my motives. Though I wouldn't admit it to myself at the beginning, there is no doubt my interest in the Soledad murders was partly triggered by the parallels I saw between them and my rejected PhD dissertation. My proposal had been interdisciplinary, which is another way of saying that it was a mishmash, a hybrid, one of those things that no department really wanted. It focussed on the Nanaimo coal strike of 1916 and the political climate that had led to violence being used against the workers (including the killing of one union leader by a Mountie in the hills above Comox). I had discovered a statement by James Dunsmuir, the Premier of the province and one-time owner of the mines, at the Royal Commission into Labour Relations in 1903, that he would take any measures necessary to resist unionization. My idea was to write a commentary, part political and part historical, with certain fictional dramatizations for special effect, pinning the violence of the strike on the anti-union sentiments of the Dunsmuirs and then drawing parallels to the political climate of today.

My supervisor, a historian, looked at it and sighed. "Some of this is okay," he said, "but most of it seems vague to me. I don't see the logic behind some of your connections. Remember that the Nanaimo coal strike was a long time ago and took place within a particular context, the First World War and the war-driven labour policies of the time. And the fictionalized episodes, I have definite problems with those. Seems to me you have enough trouble keeping the facts straight without giving yourself license to make things up. Like, what do you really know about what Dunsmuir said to his cronies over drinks? Do you even know that Dunsmuir drank? And besides, it's a serious stretch to pin the violence of 1916 on the Dunsmuirs. After all, by that point, they'd been out of the coal business for a generation."

Jayne, predictably, thought my proposal was a copout. "There's potential in your idea about the fictional bits," she said, "but it looks like you're going to force them into some tight fitting little pattern—a pattern that proves the Dunsmuirs were guilty, surprise, surprise. It's like a fucking who-done-it: the Dunsmuirs in the board room with a pen and paper. Bo-ring. Real life isn't so tidy, you know. And, anyway, your whole project looks like just more male history to me. All those guys fighting over guy things, written about in guy language. There's a couple of bells and whistles to get attention, but ultimately it's just following the academy's rules. Next thing you know, they'll be offering you a job."

The irony behind Gould's irritation with me, of course, is that my presence in Silver remained a temptation to him. When things went bad for him, he sought me out. He came to my booth at the Igloo. Talked to me. Poured out his heart. Along the way, he violated the most fundamental rule of being an investigator: to protect the confidentiality of a case.

Neither of us knew, the first time we met, how quickly the game could change.

There was still time before his meeting with Wright, so Gould took out the file of clippings from Inspector Breeze. These came from a selection of out-of-town dailies and the weekly Silver *Claim* (owned, as it turned out, by Wallace Lies). From them, Gould learned that the

B.M.U. had only organized the Cyclops workers the year before, and that Lena Stahr, as a matter of principle, had refused to negotiate. In one quote she expressed a feeling of betrayal: "I have run a non-union mine all these years and the workers have been very well treated. They even say so themselves. So why unionize? Why now? It's just a few hot-heads who want to do it to prove that they can." The news stories also gave graphic evidence of the violence of the strike. There were inflammatory statements by Al Goodwin ("Killing a scab is like killing somebody robbing your home") and Lena Stahr ("I don't care if I have to kick ass from here to Texas—the mine stays open!"). There were stories about picket line incidents, break-ins and vandalism. In one incident, the American security personnel brought in by Stahr turned their attack dogs loose on the union pickets. In another, a tractor-trailer attempting to enter the mine was attacked with baseball bats and bricks. A brick shattered the windshield and the driver, a man named Luke Carson, suffered a "life-threatening head injury." According to the article, Carson was taken from the scene unconscious and remained in "critical" condition in hospital.

There was no mention of the Soledads until their disappearance. The articles that followed all related the Soledad story to the strike. They added nothing to what Gould already knew.

After reading through the news file, Gould went back through the original Missing Person reports on the Soledads. In the rush to get started on the case, he had only looked at these quickly before. Now he read them carefully, beginning with the statements from fellow workers at the mine, then moving on to the statements of neighbours, the children, Goodwin and Stahr, and anybody else who had anything to do with the Soledads. These interviews would have to be updated, now that the disappearance had turned into a murder, but they still contained some useful bits of information. Gould wrote down a number of items for further inquiry.

By then it was eight o'clock.

Sergeant Wright lived in one of the older, wooden houses near the town's core, on a street with few fences and many front porches. The porches were of the kind that seem to catch the overflow from daily life; they were tangled with old arm-chairs, bicycles, forgotten hanging plants, stacks of newspaper waiting to be recycled, and bowls of water and cat food. All the porches, that is, except the porch at the Wright house. There everything was swept clean. All the lights in the house were on and the windows were brilliant rectangles, the curtains pushed out of sight or gone entirely. Gould took the front stairs at a regular pace, his large feet in their black leather shoes scuffing out a polite signal of his approach. The front door—restored oak with a tell-tale milky grain, bright brass mail-slot and door-handle—was ajar; a spill of light crossed the porch at Gould's feet. Gould planted his heels where a welcome mat might once have been. He leaned in to knock with the back of his knuckles. Then pulled up short.

Through the doorway, there, a section of wood floor. And someone, face down. He could see the tire-tread soles of the running-shoes, toes touching, heels angled out to form a V. A bit of athletic sock, pale flesh, and two blue-jeaned legs to the thigh.

A man. Not moving.

He hesitated to the count of two.

The only thing to do was knock.

At the sound, the man rolled onto his back and sat up, hands appearing on the floor by his hips. Then a head, slightly cocked, eyes focused upwards. "That you, Inspector? Come on in."

When Gould had pushed the door wide, he could see what he would have guessed from the outside: the house was empty. Wright sat on a bare livingroom floor, in a room with blank walls, no curtains, no furniture. To Gould's left, towards the centre of the house, was a red brick fireplace with a stained oak mantle. The fireplace had been swept out, the glass doors left open; the mantle was an unbroken dark line, like the bar between two halves of a fraction.

Wright, on the way to his feet, said, "This place was seriously wrecked when we moved into it, cracked plaster, pissed on carpets, things like that. We ripped out the worst of it, put in new plumbing, wiring, did just about the whole place over again. Including this floor." He gestured with his hand. "Want some tea? I've got a kettle in the kitchen."

Wright was now in civilian clothes, a bulky orange wool sweater, hand-knit, it seemed, from the rough loop of the stitches, as well as the blue jeans. As he lead the way to the kitchen, Gould had that odd feeling about him again. Surely he had seen him before somewhere. Then it came to him: Wright was the spitting image of Corporal Cleary.

The kitchen, like the livingroom, was a hollow shell. Besides a few odds and ends, including the kettle, the only things in it were a few cardboard boxes and a real estate sign lying flat in a corner, the tip of its wooden stake still beaded with dirt. On the way in Wright nodded in the sign's direction. "That was my important call. It came maybe two minutes after I got back. Confirming the deal on the house. Soon as I heard I went outside and yanked it up."

While the kettle heated, Wright explained. "I've already sent my family ahead to Vancouver. We didn't want the kids to change schools in the middle of a term. One of the hardest things I've ever done. You got any family?"

"A brother. I almost got married once, years ago."

"You run or did she?"

"Neither. She was killed."

Wright opened his mouth to say something, but Gould waved him off. "Nothing sinister. A car crash. Victim of reckless youth."

"I didn't mean to probe."

"No problem. I rarely think about it anymore."

"Well. I won't bore you with my own family life. Just say that it's important to me. But I should tell you something else, up-front, before we begin: I've decided to resign from the force. I was going to do it at the end of last month, but now—for personal reasons—I want to stay on until this case is wrapped up. It's the accumulation of a lot of things: Breeze, the way the strike has been handled around here, my own stupidity. Anyway, I thought I should tell you. Nobody around here knows yet."

"What'll you do in Vancouver?"

"What do ex-cops do? Become a P.I. and write detective novels about my experiences...." Wright lined up two mugs on the counter and dropped a tea bag into each. "No—I don't know. Might do some security work, but I might try to get into something entirely different. We've got some money saved and Karen already has a teaching job. It's going to take me a while to get my bearings back."

Wright started to pour the water, then stopped. "Oh, sorry, you take milk?"

"Black is fine."

After a minute, Gould plucked his tea bag out by the string and tossed it, after Wright's, into a garbage bag tied onto a drawer handle.

"Maybe we should start with what you know about the Soledads."

"Sure," said Wright.

He led the way back to the livingroom. There he stretched out on the floor with his back against the wall. When Gould had done the same, he sighed. "The Soledads . . . ."

"Did you know them well?"

"Average. Maybe a little better than average. I've always—I mean, I used to make a point to meet new people in the community. So I talked to Enrique and Camilla a few times and we had their family over for a barbecue in late-July or early-August. It was pleasant enough. The kids had some fun though they couldn't understand each other very well. The adults talked, just social talk mostly. You probably know that few people got close to the Soledads, kids or parents."

"Except for Wallace Lies and the Bentleys?"

"I guess. Actually, there was something about the Bentleys I wanted to bring up earlier." Wright paused for a moment, then continued slowly, "I think it's a bit strange that Felipe and Gabriela are staying with them."

"Why?"

"The Bentleys and the Soledads did not, as they say, depart on speaking terms."

"I gathered that from this afternoon. Personality problems and so on."

"There was more to it than that. Just a week or so after our barbecue, sometime in early August, the Bentleys filed papers against the Soledads with Social Services. They withdrew the papers again almost immediately but, you know, small town, word gets around. Rumour was they were trying to have the Soledads declared unfit parents."

"On what grounds?"

"I'm not sure. Neglect, possibly. To be honest with you, though, my gut feeling is that the grounds are beside the point. From what I've heard, the real reason the Bentleys filed is because they wanted the children for themselves."

"Declare the parents unfit and then adopt them?"

"Something like that."

"Is that possible?"

"I don't know. Must have been terrifying for the Soledads, though. I mean, they wouldn't have understood the system at all. Anything must have seemed possible to them."

"Why did the Bentleys withdraw the papers?"

"That I don't know. Maybe they just realized it was a hair-brained strategy."

Gould pressed a finger into his moustache. He wondered if Wright had just had the same thought: Maybe they realized there was a better way to get the kids.

"Now that I think of it," said Wright, "the Soledads did have a reputation for leaving their kids alone a lot. Maybe this was justified, maybe not. There was one incident at the beginning of the summer, I'm guessing early June, when they left the kids with the Bentleys and went to Vancouver. Ten days, maybe, they were gone. They'd only been in town a couple of months by that point, and the kids were going through tough times adjusting, so you can imagine how tongues wagged."

"Some kind of holiday?"

"I really don't know. The one to ask about it would be Wallace Lies. Apparently he flew to Vancouver to pick them up."

"One thing puzzles me," said Gould. "I was going through the interviews with the other employees earlier on and their impressions of the Soledads are contradictory—to say the least."

"They were enigmatic people. I don't imagine any of the other employees got to know them very well."

"But the comments. Some thought the Soledads were too forward, that they talked too much and were pushy social climbers. Others thought they were extremely reticent, that they never talked, never socialized, and seemed totally uninterested in the life of the town. The only thing the interviews had in common was that nobody liked them."

"I liked them, but I was one of the few."

"But why? That's what I want to know. Surely it wasn't just red neck prejudice."

"I wouldn't discount prejudice entirely. We've got our share of red necks around here. But, really, I think the Soledads, whatever they did, they just seemed to challenge people. They both had a way of looking, I don't know, sort of ironical or knowing, that made it look like they were thinking something not-too-flattering about you. But that might just have been the way they looked. Do you know about Enrique's summer classes at the highschool?"

"No."

"He was hired to do some language tutoring and a few social studies classes on South America. The principal, the trustees, I guess everyone expected him to give the usual watered down survey of the region. You know, the Conquistadors, the Mayans, a bit about local customs and key exports. Instead, he brought politics into it, and not just local politics, but about how Canada and the U.S. are complicit in the worst of the problems down there. This, of course, did not go over very well with some of the parents."

"Did the Soledads ever show sympathies for one side or the other in the strike?"

"As I understand it, at first they took no sides. They were too fresh off the plane. But eventually they came out in support of the strikers, or at least Enrique did. He sounded off about it in his summer course (which was a major no-no: the trustees had imposed a complete ban on all talk about the strike in the classroom). By mid-summer, though, about the time of our barbecue, things were changing. I can't remember how it came up exactly, god I was sick of the whole thing by then, but somehow the strike came up during our barbecue. It was the only really serious moment in the whole afternoon. Anyway, it was quite startling. Camilla spoke. She'd hardly said anything all afternoon, but suddenly she launched into this speech about how greedy and stupid Canadians were. She put it that way: *you Canadians* . . . . She said she couldn't believe the two sides in the strike. How oppressive and exploitive the company and their hired goons were and then how stupid the strikers were. 'In my country,' she said, 'people risk their lives just to steal a living from the rich criminals who control everything, but here, workers earning sixty thousand Canadian dollars go on strike for more. It is madness. How can you expect your country to survive with such madness?'"

"And Enrique's reaction?"

"He didn't say anything then. But I understand he was saying similar things around town just before he and Camilla started working at the mine." The two men sat at right angles to one another, sipping their tea, their feet not far from touching on the hardwood floor. Gould had folded his trench coat into a neat square and laid it out, with his briefcase, to the side. Leaning forward as he was, with his blue blazer unbuttoned and his forearms on his knees, his gun was visible in its holster below his right armpit. Wright had one blue jeaned leg out flat along the floor, and from time to time he seemed to inspect the lace on his running shoe, turning his ankle this way and that.

"And now," said Gould, "we come to the heart of the matter."

Wright continued to turn his ankle.

"I'm beginning to think that everybody in this town had a motive to kill the Soledads."

"Wait'll you hear my story . . . ."

Wright downed the last of his tea, then pulled himself to his feet. He stretched, while Gould, still on the floor, observed. Wright took a few long strides over to the fireplace and put his empty cup on the mantle. "Karen and I had really expected to settle here," he said. "I made some sacrifices to get the posting, put in some years in pretty tough situations. Even here the job had its ups and downs. But I really felt like a member of the community. Like there was a community, and I was an important part of keeping it that way. Maybe, if anything good comes of these killings, maybe it'll just shock people into realizing they were being stupid and greedy, like Camilla said. For me, though, it'll be too late."

Wright seemed to sweep away some lint from the mantle. In the meantime, Gould himself rose to his feet. After a minute, Wright turned and said, "Okay. Here's the story. Let me start by saying that I blame Inspector Breeze for a lot of what has happened in Silver. You know about our differences. But, objectively, let me just say that Inspector Breeze's manner of policing is extremely divisive. You know, it's so often a paradox with strikes. Before the police are called in to keep the peace the level of violence on the picket lines tends to be fairly minor. It's only after we arrive, only after we start using our muscle that the picketers go wild. Forcing scabs through the lines . . . . Even with the best of intentions, even if you try to be as diplomatic as possible, your presence inflames the situation. And Inspector Breeze . . . well, like I said, he has been absolutely not diplomatic about it."

"Not everybody in police work manages to be as diplomatic as they should. I'll admit it's not professional . . . ."

Wright took a deep breath. "Maybe I've blamed Breeze too much. I don't know. It's a question I've asked myself. The thing is, Inspector, it goes beyond a lack of professionalism. What you have to know about Inspector Breeze is this: from very early on in this assignment, he has been in bed with the company."

Gould, in a rare show of emotion, raised his eyebrows.

"That's a very serious charge," he said.

"I mean it at its most literal and damning."

"Can you prove it?"

"Now we do come to the heart of the matter."

Wright put both hands into the pockets of his jeans and took a step, two, away from Gould. Then he turned.

"On October 19th, a little more than a week before he and his wife disappeared, Enrique Soledad came to me for help. He said that he had been cheated, that was his word, *cheated*, by Lena Stahr at the Cyclops mine. He seemed angry and desperate. Frankly, I didn't go into details with him. I don't know Stahr very well, but I know she is extremely tough when it comes to her own interests, and the way she has reacted to this strike . . . well, cheating the Soledads seemed quite in keeping. Anyway, what Soledad wanted was my help in getting some leverage on Stahr to make her, as he put it, *treat him fairly*.

"Now. Rumours of a relationship between Breeze and Stahr had been circulating since shortly after the response team came to town. The two of them, though, had managed to be very discreet, so the rumours stayed just that, rumours. Enrique came to me and said, look, we both know of these rumours, is there any way you can help me to prove them? If I had proof, he said, I'd be able to force Stahr to treat me fairly. He appealed to my sense of decency. My sympathy for the little guy. My reputation for being an honest broker. But really he knew—how could he not?—that I had my own score to settle with Inspector Breeze. Obviously, Breeze was the one who would be most hurt by proof of the relationship coming out. So, the long of the short of it is, I did it. I got the proof. A parting shot. A last, malicious, stupid act."

"What kind of proof?"

"I pulled some strings—I have friends on the E.R.T.—and my

friends pulled some strings of their own, and some person or persons on Lena Stahr's security team made a video using the security cameras on her estate. Apparently, on the next Saturday, the 22nd, this person or persons trained a camera through a partially opened curtain and recorded the results."

"Which were?"

"Damning—I assume. The cassette was dropped off at my door with a note that read *Mission accomplished* or some such thing, but, frankly, Inspector, I never actually looked at it. As soon as I saw that cassette I felt ashamed. Like I had been drawn into this conflict at the lowest possible level. I mean, character assassination . . . ." Wright shook his head.

"But you did pass it on to Enrique Soledad?"

"On Monday the 24th. And the next day, two days before he disappeared, he went to see Breeze, presumably to threaten him with it. He probably demanded that Breeze use his influence to make Stahr treat him fairly. If he didn't, curtains for his career and embarrassment for Lena Stahr too."

Gould raised his hand to his moustache. "I wonder what happened to that cassette?"

"I can tell you that after the disappearances, Breeze himself supervised a search of the Soledad house."

"And?"

"He didn't find it. I can't be absolutely sure, but the men I talked to—men I can trust—say he did not."

"That would only have been a first stage search."

"There would have been no way for him to justify going any further, not without drawing suspicions on himself."

Gould added his cup to the mantle. It sat there side by side with Wright's own. He turned and walked slowly to the uncurtained window that dominated the long wall of the room. Outside, ghost light fell on the railing, the empty porch. Beyond that the night was dense and still.

"Sounds to me like you're looking for some kind of redemption here, Sergeant," said the inspector.

"I suppose that's true."

"Well—I've decided to give you a chance at it. What you did for Enrique Soledad was highly unethical. It was a serious failure of judgement and may have, in fact, contributed to the murders. Under the circumstances, however, I can understand why you might have done it, and I respect your coming clean like this."

"Thank you."

"So. It seems to me the next step is to search the Soledad house again, this time doing a proper job. But I haven't got the people to spare for it. And the issue is sensitive."

"I would really like to do it. I'd do it alone if necessary."

"No. I'll assign somebody to assist you. You pick out the man. But you're going to have to work during your off hours. Starting tomorrow I'm going to need you to run the murder room for me. I've got to send Viola to Vancouver."

"I can handle that."

"I'm sure you can."

"It might take a few days to go through the whole house."

"Frankly," Gould said, with a stare off into the future, "I'm not looking forward to dealing with that tape, assuming that you do find it."

Chapter Six

The interview with Wright put Gould in a pensive mood. The kind of mood that, if he were another detective, might lead him back to his room to toy with a pocket chess set. If he were Albert Einstein he might get out his violin and play some Mozart. But he was no Einstein and no Marlowe, he was just Charles Gould, a man without a musical bone in his body and not inclined to games of any kind, and so he did what he often did in times like this: he drove. A part of him would have preferred to saddle up a horse and ride along a trail or around a practice ring, but under the circumstances, he thought, with a pat on the steering wheel, this old horse from the car pool would have to do.

He came out to Henry Street. It was wide, lined with shops, mostly dark now, and lit by old-fashioned electric lights on wooden poles. A few cars were angle-parked on either side of the street, like the last of an old duffer's teeth just hanging on. Two or three people passed on the far sidewalk. East on Henry, at the end of the shops, was the RCMP station, and after that the bridge over Whatcom Creek into a neighbourhood carved out of the foothills below Mount Flag. To the west lay the Legion Hall, the remains of the union office, and the T-intersection where Henry ended at Queen. Gould turned that way. As he did, he imagined that on a clear day Henry Street would be stoppered at either end by mountains. The Legion Hall was a blaze of light. From the cars fly-gathered around the building, it was obviously in for a busy night.

Two blocks on there was a yellow fire department pumper in front of the burnt-out union office. The pumper was showing its four-way flashers but not its overhead beacon. Gould slowed down. Sure enough, there was a white finger of smoke rising from the ruins of the building, a steady, seemingly controlled stream of white, like the smoke from a signal fire, a white finger with its tip buried deep in the black night above the arc of the street lights. A volunteer fire-fighter stood on the sidewalk with his back to Gould. He was dressed in full gear and had his legs planted firmly apart. As Gould continued past it became clear that the man was holding a fire-hose, the nozzle pointed into the ruins. Gould saw no other firefighters in the area. Nothing was coming out of the hose.

At the intersection with Queen he stopped. The light was green but no one was behind him. Straight ahead was an open space, a mini-park, two or three benches and what looked like a war memorial. Beyond that was an emptiness that marked the Columbia River, and beyond that, invisible but somehow making their presence felt, the West Columbia mountains. From where he idled, Gould could just make out a corner of the Silver Municipal Hall. This made him think briefly of Wallace Lies, how the early part of the investigation had looped back, more than once, to him. North on Queen was the interchange with the Trans-Canada and the relative comfort of his room at The Red Grizzly.

What he wanted, he now realized, was to see the house where Camilla and Enrique Soledad had lived. That was the other way, south, in the direction of the turnoff to the mine. He put on his left turn signal and waited for the traffic light to turn green again. Then made a left turn from the right hand lane.

The house was in a neighbourhood called Putty Hill. At first Gould thought the name might refer to the kind of soil there or to the shoddy quality of the houses, which would have been ironic, since Putty Hill was the most expensive neighbourhood in town. Some of the locals did in fact use the name as a joke. The area had originally been settled by managers from Henry Nathan's Three Shaft Mine, the original silver operation begun in 1897, and, following tradition, a number of the Cyclops managers now lived there. For some locals the putty in Putty Hill referred to what these managers were in the hands of Lena Stahr. . . . The original name, however, was a reference to the source of the wealth behind the comfortable houses. For the first silver strike in the area, the chance find by William Tingley in 1884 that serendipitously led to the prospering of the town, was of ore so pure that it was called buttermilk silver—ore so soft that it could be dug out of the rock with a putty knife. Tingley actually made his discovery another five kilometers southeast, closer to where the Cyclops mine now operated, but local legend had come to associate his find with the hill now dotted with the executive homes that it had made possible.

Gould had no trouble finding the neighbourhood. He passed the Selkirk Inn (also in for a busy night) and took the first street left. Within a couple of blocks this street started to rise and wind. He made one false turn and had to consult his map. Then he was on Confederation Crescent. The Soledad house was Number 6, right next door to the home of Wallace Lies.

What immediately struck him was an odd symmetry between the two houses. The Lies home and the Soledad home had obviously been built from identical plans, but reversed, so that the houses were mirror images of one another. Both were big solid cool-looking places, with burgundy brick walls, terra cotta tile roofs, and white trim—an unusually spanish or southern style for this area. Ornate iron grills guarded the lower windows. Both houses had evergreen bushes in their front gardens and long gentle slopes of lawn down to the street. The lawns flowed around trees in neatly cutout circles like dark green tides around rocks. The trees, for the most part, were ruthlessly trimmed up, which allowed the houses to be clearly visible from the street, another oddity in a neighbourhood where most of the landscaping emphasized privacy. There were no sidewalks.

The symmetrical arrangement meant that the car ports and driveways of the houses were side by side, separated only by a narrow line of hedge. This set up a stark contrast. For the Soledad driveway was an empty unlit expanse, while the Lies driveway contained three vehicles: a white Mercedes sports coup, a dark sedan rather like Gould's own, and a silver Cadillac with a custom license plate, ONE EYE. Beside the Lies driveway, a lamp with the number 8 on its glass shone atop a squat brick pillar. The identical lamp next door was unlit, the number only a darker heart on dark glass. The Soledad house had not a single light burning, which made it seem half-swallowed by encroaching forest. The Lies house, on the other hand, was a fortress of brightness: the entire bottom floor and three of four windows on the second were ablaze. Shadows streamed outward from the Lies house, giving long tails to the trees and faintly crossing the lawn next door.

Gould killed his engine and lights and meditated for a few moments on the scene. Then he turned the key again and drifted down to the end of the street, where there was another cul de sac.

As he came out of the loop another vehicle approached the Lies house. A red land rover with yellow fog lights and a heavy grill, a kind of cow catcher, on the front. It pulled up near the spot where Gould had just parked himself. As Gould rolled past, the driver's door swung open and he caught a glimpse of a dark haired man he did not recognize.

Back at The Red Grizzly, he recorded his conversation with Sergeant Wright, then closed up his notebook and rested with his forearms on the desk. The air was cool. He could feel a draft from the window. Outside there was the rhythmical sound of traffic on the highway, a sound like waves on a beach cut through now and then by the pitch-change of an engine gearing up or down or the explosive hiss of air breaks. He got up, palmed the window tightly closed and arranged the curtains.

He went into the bathroom, washed his hands and face, and brushed his teeth. His bathrobe was hanging on the back of the door. He took the robe down, flicked off the light and came into the other room again. He folded the robe over the back of a chair and then took his clothes off, item by item, double-parking his shoes beside the bed, arranging his jacket, tie, shirt and pants on a single hanger, and balling up his socks and underwear and dropping them into the plastic bag he used for dirty laundry. For a moment he stood there naked, a long lean man faintly freckled from nose to toe, and felt the coolness of the room raising goose-bumps on his pale flesh. He leaned over to turn off the light . . . and something moved on the ceiling.

The mirror, or rather mirrors—for the larger mirror was made up of sixteen smaller mirrors arranged in a square. It was still not covered. He made a mental note to ride Arnie about it in the morning, and then, forming a contradictory thought, pulled his hand back from the light. For some reason he wanted to see himself. He eased himself onto the bed and stretched out on his back, legs slightly apart, arms at his sides, head on a pillow. When he looked up he saw his complete body reflected back to him in the sectioned mirror. Like Galileo's famous drawing. At first glance the reflection seemed perfectly true, but as he gazed more intently he could see minute distortions where the smaller mirrors fit together, a slight bevel here, a warp there, so that it seemed that his body was broken up into eight or ten not-quite-fitting pieces.

The cool air in the room washed over him, his arms, his torso, his genitals. And he remembered that his habit of sleeping naked had begun during his summer in Costaguana. All those years—all that life—ago. The nights were tropical, then, and the effect of humid air on his naked body was deeply sensuous.

To his surprise his penis had begun to stiffen. He lifted his left hand up off the bed and slid it like a starfish down his stomach and between his legs. He made a fist around his penis and drew up his legs. All the while his double did the same in the faintly distorting mirror. He half-closed his eyes.

And then something, the thought of Costaguana probably, triggered his memory-tape of the conversation with Sergeant Wright. Their words began to replay in his head. "That you, Inspector?" he heard. "Come on in . . . . This place was very run down when we moved into it . . . . You want some tea? . . . . You got any family?"

His hand dropped back to his side.

"You run or did she?" he heard.

When he finally came around to talking about Elizabeth, deep into that long night of confessions triggered by the apparent breakdown of the case, Gould began with an apology. "It's so cliché," he said. "It's the kind of thing every second pulp detective has in his background."

"But it is the reason you got into police work?"

"Not on its own. Everything else had a part to play too."

"Yeah, yeah. I don't mean to suggest you're one-dimensional. Still . . . ."

"Still. You're right. She was the most immediate reason."

"So tell me about her."

Well.

In May 1975, Charles Gould found himself in Buenas Aires. He was twenty-one years old, almost twenty-two, a veteran of two years on the road. For most of that spring he had traveled with an American couple, Dawn Neill and Bob Schuler, whom he had met in the Yucatan. The couple wanted to drive to Tierra del Fuego and back but they were a little nervous. There were rumours of bandits in Belize and worse in Guatemala. As a result, they struck a deal with Charles, whom they met one morning at the Mayan ruins of Palenque. In return for accompanying them on the road and taking his turn at the wheel, Charles could have a free ride to the farthest point of South America and back.

Whether it was because of the extra body or the blind luck of audacious youth, they had a relatively uneventful and very pleasant drive south. They all had to fight off diarrhea at one time or another; there were a few bleak moments trying to figure out where the hell on the map they were; and the tensions between Argentina and Chile made the approach to Tierra del Fuego a bit uneasy. But there was also spectacular scenery and those magic moments when they roared like a light airplane into a some village (the muffler having taken a number of hits by this point) and the residents opened the shutters of their whitewashed homes with wonder and welcome on their faces.

By the time they turned back north again, however, Charles was bored. Bored with all the driving. Bored with Bob and Dawn (nice enough people in their way, but so American). When they reached Buenas Aires again, he thought briefly of flying back to Canada, but then decided against it: though he wasn't sure what he was looking for, he was sure he hadn't found it yet.

As it turned out, leaving Dawn and Bob was made easy for him. In Buenas Aires they met two strapping young hitch-hikers from New York state, one of whom claimed to be an auto mechanic. Bob and Dawn were immediately for adding them to the party (they'd all fit in the microbus somehow). According to the hitch-hikers, the place to be that summer was going to be Costaguana, especially a beach town called Puerta des Mujeres. Dawn and Bob were all for stopping there on the way north (they had bypassed Costaguana on the way south to go straight from Columbia to Peru). At this point Charles said, "Look. Why don't the four of you go on without me? I've got money. I'll fly ahead to Costaguana. I'd love to just lounge on the beach for a while. We could all meet there in a couple of weeks."

So, it was agreed. Charles bought a ticket from Buenas Aires to Sulaco (via Bogotá) and the four Americans started out in the microbus.

"I never saw them again," Gould explained. "I made it to Puerta des Mujeres but for some reason the Americans never showed up. For a couple of years after that, I thought about trying to track down their address in Pennsylvania, but what with everything else happening in my life, I never got around to it."

The flight into Sulaco from Bogotá reminded him of flights he had taken to Vancouver. A white desert of glaciers below and the jet gradually descending, no end of the mountains in sight until the peaks flew by so close they seemed about to gouge the fuselage . . . then, suddenly, as if he'd stepped over a cliff, empty air and gentle green-brown hills far below. For some reason the jet had to fly past the city and make a great slow turn over the ocean before landing, something to do with landing patterns or the prevailing winds (although the place was famous for its lack of wind). As a result, from his window, Charles had a panoramic view of the Placid Gulf, the Gulfo Placido, shining green-blue in the sun, and its two bordering peninsulas, Punta Mala to the north and Azuera to the south. He also glimpsed the three small islands, the Isabels, that half closed off the mouth of the gulf.

He looked particularly closely at Azuera, not only because Puerta des Mujeres lay on the other side of it, but because the guide book he carried had described it as a place rich in local legend. The book described it as "a wild chaos of sharp rocks and stony levels cut about by vertical ravines" and said that it was haunted by the spirits of two American adventurers, wandering sailors, who had set out to discover "a vast treasure of silver" said to be hidden there. Charles could just imagine them, these gringos, their stolen donkey, revolvers at their belts and machetes in hand. On the second night after their departure from Sulaco, "an upright spiral of smoke" was seen from the razor-backed head of the peninsula. People watched the strange portent with "envy, incredulity, and awe." But the adventurers ultimately gave no other sign. The legend was that the Americans found the silver but died in the process and that "their souls cannot tear themselves away from their bodies mounting guard over the discovered treasure."

In Sulaco he bought a bus-ticket and rode with a collection of poor men in straw hats, women in headscarves, children, chickens, and frayed wicker baskets, in a bus with no glass in the windows, over the low thorny spine that connected Azuera to the mainland, and down the coast to Puerta des Mujeres.

The Americans were right about one thing. It was a hopping place that summer. Charles checked into a hostel already two-thirds filled with young people. The hostel was in a cinder-block building with a red-tiled roof near the beach. The tiny rooms contained three-high bunk-beds with wooden bottoms and straw mattresses. Square holes in the walls served for ventilation. Through the holes you could catch glimpses of blue sky, palm trees, yellow-green grass, sand. The sand was everywhere, white and granular, like a dusting of salt on the floor of the hostel, in the folds of clothes, under the mattresses. And always, in the background or on the edge of awareness, was the sound of the sea: crash of waves and the long slow hiss of receding water.

Within two weeks the hostel was full, there were people camping in the dunes, and the town market was crowded with long-haired tourists from Australia, Europe, Canada, and especially the United States. During the days there was swimming, surfing, sunning and frisbees on the beach. At night, guitars and beach fires, warmed over Taoism, Kahlil Gibran, rum, beer and pot. Occasionally a couple disappeared hand-in-hand into the inland darkness. For the singles, the in-thing was to party all night and then sit on the beach and wait for sunrise. Wait for dawn, the sun, the light. Nobody cared—or maybe nobody noticed—that the beach actually faced west....

There was something apocalyptic about Puerta des Mujeres that summer. Partly it had to do with the concentration of young people, the contradictory feelings of youth, how the eye of the cosmos is on you and yet nothing you do is of any worth, how you are both immortal and about to die tomorrow. Mostly it had to do with the war, the American war in Vietnam which had just finally, dramatically ended. Wave upon wave of Americans broke upon the town, each with its own tangible sense of flight. A number of the kids talked about their need to escape, about the moral collapse of their country.

Charles made friends with a number of young vets, men his own age with experiences that filled him with awe and momentary desire (to have done that and survived!) but mostly with relief that he was Canadian. The vets were bitter about the climate back home, how half the people hated them because they embodied the failure of their country and the other half hated because they were baby killers. One vet, a young man named Mike Best, had been discharged in '72 and had enrolled in medical school. For two years he seemed to pick up where he had left off before he volunteered for the service. Then one day in the fall of '74, in the middle of a lab class on internal organs with a cadaver on a slab half-dissected before him, he quietly snapped. He put down his instruments, peeled off his gloves and gown, left the building, packed his car, and headed south. Two months later he was in Puerta des Mujeres—and had been there ever since. "I guess I'd just seen enough bodies," he explained.

Another vet, a guy named Jarman (first or last name Charles was not sure) said, "All I want out of life now is to have a farm in New Hampshire, a place totally away from everything. Only thing is bucks. So, what I'm gonna do is get a load of cocaine and take it in a boat from Sulaco all the way up the coast to Canada."

"Canada?" asked Charles.

"Sure. If you want to smuggle stuff into the States you go through Canada. Everybody knows that. Through Vancouver. Easiest port in the world to smuggle stuff into. After Vancouver you've got like 5,000 miles of undefended border to pick from. Once I've sold the stuff, that's it, I'll never do anything like that again. I'll just buy my farm and then fuck'um, just fuck the whole damn fucking country."

"What can I say about her?" said Gould. "She arrived in early July with a couple of high-school chums. They had all just graduated. They were travelling for the summer. I overheard their conversation with one of the hostel managers and stepped in to tell them about some vacancies down the beach. They asked for directions and I said *Why don't I walk you there.*

"I remember that walk, the road, the bleached white asphalt below my sandals, the sun on my back. I showed off my knowledge about the place (I had been there four weeks!). Actually, at that point, I was more attracted to one of her friends, a blond girl named Shiela, than to her. We found the other place. I said *So long* and then stopped and said *Oh there's a beach party tonight down near our place, you should all come.* They said they would.

"Only she came. She sought me out from the crowd as the only person she knew. She said that Shiela and her other friend had spent too long on the beach that afternoon and were sick from sunburn. I was a little disappointed at first (I was looking forward to meeting Shiela again) but then we got to talking.

"You know, I don't have a single photograph of her. I never got one. I remember her auburn hair, small freckled nose, her slightly in-turned teeth, her blue, blue eyes. She was eighteen. Fairly tall, small breasted, white skinned, thin. Her name was Elizabeth but her friends called her Archie, in part because of her family name, Archibald, but also because of the comic book character—red hair and freckles. Maybe the reason I wasn't attracted to her at first was that she looked like she could have been my sister.

"Anyway, that night, over rum and Cokes, we talked. And danced. Talked and danced and talked and danced. And, as the night went on, there were, I don't know, signs. Coincidences. Like we were fated somehow. Like, for instance, we started off with the usual *Oh you're not American either?* and *What part of Canada are you from?* Then: *Hey, I was born in New Brunswick, too. What part? Fredericton? Me too!* It turned out that our families had lived only a few blocks apart. Thousands of miles from home to meet someone who grew up around the corner.

"She pried my family name out of me. Dangerous emotional territory. Then she said, *That's amazing. I think my earliest memory is of you, at least of your father and brother and you.*

"Turns out she was four years old at the time. My father was campaigning for re-election, his desperate campaign in 1961, the election he lost so decisively. Archie had been downtown with her mother when her mother stopped and grabbed her shoulders. *Look,* she said, pointing to a man in a suit, *there's the Premier!* The man was shaking hands on the opposite sidewalk. Nearby him were two big beefy men also in suits and two boys, us, my brother and I. In his desperation, my father was using us to try to pull in votes, trying to get marks for being a single parent now taking care of his sons.

"The reason the moment stuck in her head all those years was us.

The boys. She wondered what it would be like to be a child of the Premier. At this point I interrupted her and said, *It's not all it's cut out to be, you know.* And she said, *Oh no, not that. I imagined from the start that it would have been horrible.*

"Not only that. It also turned out that we had the same birthday, four years apart. Just co-incidence, I suppose, but after enough rum and the accumulation of words it seemed pretty mystical.

"The long of the short of it is, we had a wonderful summer. We walked beaches, ate at outdoor canopied restaurants, talked about everything, and, after a few days of getting to know one another, made almost daily love. I had been a virgin. She was not. Her girl-friends hung around for about two weeks and then moved on with a different group.

"What can I say? I was in love. I felt I had finally found what I was travelling for. At the end of the summer we flew back to Canada together. She was starting at U.N.B. that fall. So she went back to Fredericton and I went to Ottawa. The plan was for me to go back to the U. of O. and for her to do a year at U.N.B. and then transfer. I figured that the goodwill I would get from my father for going back to school would be enough for lots of money to travel back and forth.

"Two weeks later, I had attended a week's classes at Ottawa, had written her six letters, had talked to her on the phone as many times, and had a return plane ticket in my pocket for the end of the month. And she was dead.

"How she died is about the most common story in the book. It turned out that she had broken up with a high school boyfriend not long before she met me. His name was George Roberts. A rich boy from the same neighbourhood. When she got back to Fredericton that fall he was waiting for her. He followed her around, to her classes, on the street, until she finally confronted him. She told him about me. And he said, okay, he would leave her alone forever if she would just go out to dinner with him one more time. A night to talk properly and say goodbye. She agreed.

"They had dinner at a local restaurant. Afterwards he insisted on taking her for a drive in his car, his father's car. He took her into the country and was showing off how fast the car would go when he missed a corner . . . and he was bruised up and broke his leg . . . and she was killed.

"It turned out that he had boozed it up all through dinner. He had twice the legal amount of alcohol in his system. And according to the police report he was driving twenty miles-an-hour over the speed limit when he crashed. He was charged with impaired driving, dangerous driving causing death. But when it came to court, all the charges were reduced, practically dismissed, on a technicality. The papers wrote about some expert evidence, but really, anybody who knew anything knew it was because he was a rich kid, a Roberts, and rich kids don't go to jail for crashing their Daddy's car no matter who gets hurt or how fast they were going or how much booze they had in their system."

It was deep night at the Igloo. Almost three o'clock in the morning. Not far down the highway two squad cars were stopped with their blue and red flashers on. Every once in a while the RCMP did that, set up a spot check on the highway near the Igloo between two and three A.M. At two the bars emptied, and shortly after there was a rush to the only twenty-four hour restaurant in town. Groups of loud-voiced revelers—all men—stamped in to drink coffee. Judith, the night cook, sneered that they did this so they'd be sober enough when they got home to beat their wives.

Gould and I were in my corner booth. We had already been there for five hours. We had each finished seven or eight cups of coffee. Gould was entirely absorbed by his strange, confessional mood, the mood he had arrived in after making what he thought was the biggest blunder of his career, a mood in which his words were lucid and his manner, for the most part, calm, and yet in which the very fact of his speaking so intimately to me hinted at extreme emotional pain.

We slouched towards each other from opposite sides of the table. I was still astounded to see his body so curled, so unerect. I was still dazzled by the changes in him, his flaunting of certain professional standards, his insistence on making me his confidant, his co-equal, his friend. I said, "So you decided that no more rich kids were ever going to beat the system again. Not if you could help it."

"Something like that," he said.

Chapter Seven

The next morning, Gould assembled the investigative team in the murder room. There were fifteen officers in all, including a half dozen seconded from the E.R.T. The small room was humid, musty, electric, like a crowded lecture hall. A few officers sat on chairs around the horseshoe table, most leaned with their backs against the wall, balancing their notebooks on a raised thigh.

Gould began by giving an overview of the known facts. Viola, for added emphasis, pointed out various things on the white board or the map taken from Breeze's office. Then Gould handed out assignments. To Constables Miller and Grove-White, he gave the task of interviewing the Soledad neighbours. Constables Blank and Burgar he assigned to question rank-and-file union members, Allison and Dagg to question replacement workers (with special attention to those on the bus the Soledads were supposed to have taken). Corporal Elderkin he assigned to investigate the financial structure of the company. And so on. At the end, he announced that Sergeant Wright would be in charge of the murder room. "Hand in your reports to him."

After the meeting had broken up, Gould and Viola sat down for a few minutes to discuss the sergeant's aims in Vancouver. Neither of them knew quite what to make of the case of Sherwood and Berry. It was probably just a side-show, but there was no way of knowing for sure. At a minimum, Gould hoped that Viola could leverage the two miners into telling what they knew about Al Goodwin.

Viola, as he buttoned up his coat, said, "I'm looking forward to this. Going back to Vancouver always reminds me of my days in uniform."

Gould grinned. His ironical knowing grin. "Still hankering after the old heroes, George?"

"Your day will come, Inspector," Viola laughed. "Besides, I'm too old and fat and cynical to bother with heroes anymore."

Gould had been up for over two hours before this. While it was still dark out, he had taken an early breakfast in the Igloo (where he cast an icy glance at my empty booth) then walked back to The Red Grizzly and climbed into his car. He drove south on Queen Street, through the quiet grey town and out again, into the country side with the Columbia River like a moon-shadow of the road on his right, down what was now Highway 38, past the turnoff to the mine, which was marked by two signs, *Cyclops Silver 3 KM* and *Caution: Large Trucks Turning*, and on until he reached the next intersection. Then he turned.

This road—Regional Road 4—was winding and rough and crowded in on either side by scrub bush. There was still only a faint sheen of daylight in the sky, enough to veil the stars but not enough to light the way. A good time and place for an abduction, Gould thought. Whoever had waylaid the Soledads had only to wait a few hundred metres off the highway, here, in the half-light, around some tight corner.

The replacement workers' compound was in a clearing about three kilometres in. It was one of those ambiguous fortress-like places that looked like it kept people in as much as kept them out. A high, chain-link fence topped by three strands of barbed wire. A front gate with a guard house. Just inside the gate there was a trailer that seemed to be an administrative centre; it had spot-lights at its corners that were still glowing white. Parked nearby were two yellow buses with wire mesh over the windows and some black Statewide Security vehicles, a command car with roof lights, two vans, a jeep. These had the Statewide logo—a green map of the United States in the pupil of a red and white eye—on their front doors. Farther on there was an empty helicopter pad, a paved rectangle with a white bull's-eye on it surrounded by a low fence. A wind sock hung limply from a pole. Beyond the administrative area, Gould could see rows of trailer homes, the occasional light standard, a few cars, and a jumble of rocks and tree stumps.

He identified himself at the guard-house and explained his purpose, then took up position outside the gate.

Soon workers started appearing from the doors of the trailer homes. They came quietly, in ones and twos, down the beaten track road that ran the length of the compound. Jackets, jeans, lunch-pails, the occasional flair of a cigarette lighter. From the nearest trailers came men with black jackets and shoulder patches identifying them as Statewide Security agents. The agents entered the administrative building and came out again with side-arms, shotguns and other equipment. Two agents were assigned to drive the buses; eight or ten others climbed into the two black vans. In the end, a convoy of four vehicles set out, with a van in front and behind and the two buses in between.

Gould drove on ahead. He made his way back to the highway, then north to the turnoff to the mine. The road to the mine was much like Regional Road 4, though wider and better serviced. About four kilometres in, the bush opened up into a wide clearing.

The scene in this clearing reminded Gould of one of those staged political campaign events moments before the candidate appears. All the props and supporting cast were in place. Off to one side were three RCMP cruisers, a CBC television news van, and a smattering of other vehicles. Off to the other side was a small camp, a tent, a picnic table, an oil drum with a smoldering fire in it. Some union men were gathered around the fire. Others—five men exactly—waited with picket signs near the gate to the mine property. Not far from the union men stood six RCMP officers. Not far from the officers was the television crew. The gate itself was tall and chain-linked, with a guardhouse to one side; behind it were two Statewide agents, shoulder to shoulder, arms crossed. Other agents were conspicuously present, some lounging further back on the access road with video cameras and weapons, others patrolling the nearby fence with guard dogs.

Not far inside the gate, Gould noticed, was the hulking rig once driven by Luke Carson. The rig had obviously been towed inside after the attack described in the newspaper. It rested at an oddly tilted angle, one set of its wheels in the ditch and the cab jack-knifed out of alignment with the trailer. With its smashed windshield and twisted posture, the rig looked like one of those vehicles featured in news footage after some natural disaster, a transport off the side of a highway ruined by flood or earthquake or tornado.

As if to cue the action, a helicopter now whumped into position overhead. A moment later, the convoy of vehicles from the replacement workers' camp rolled into view.

What happened next reinforced Gould's perception of the staged quality of the scene. First, the union picketers formed a line across the road. They held up their signs for the convoy vehicles and the cameras to see. They shouted slogans, the words of which were drowned out—perhaps intentionally—by the sound of the helicopter. The convoy came to a halt. After a count of ten, the RCMP officers moved in and escorted the picketers off the road. The gate swung open, the convoy passed through, and the gate closed again. Then everybody seemed to return to the wings. The helicopter whumped away, the picketers rejoined their comrades around the oil drum fire, the CBC crew returned to its van, the officers to their cars, and the Statewide agents drifted away from the entrance. The first rays of sun struck out from between two mountain peaks, and Gould marveled at the beauty of the scene, the clearing, the trees, those pale yellow bands of light and the looming towers of rock and ice from which they seemed to descend.

Then he drove back to town.

A few minutes before ten, with the sun shining a little ways above the eastern peaks, Gould made his way to the Church of Christ Redeemer. It was at the high end of Henry Street, at the crest of the first big foothill, so that the glacier of Mount Flag seemed almost directly overhead and the Silver business district was spread out below. A clear, almost mild morning, with a high blue sky and a gentle southerly breeze.

The parking lot was at the rear of the church and gave directly onto a newer annex that apparently housed the church offices. Gould locked his car and walked slowly back around to the front.

The main building was old and wooden, white-washed, with a blunt steeple above its front entrance. Some of the paint had flaked from around the chapel windows, which, Gould noted, had only large geometrical patterns in their stained glass, no human figures or other intricacies of design. He climbed the wooden front steps and tried the double doors. Unlocked. In a moment he found himself in an antechamber: a guest-book on a plain wooden podium, a bulletin board with notices, some stacked hymnals and Bibles. A walk-in cloak room opened off to one side.

He paused to take in the smell of the place. It seemed to him that churches all smelled like this, something about polish, the presence of stone and wood, residues from human beings. Old flesh, perfume.

Just inside the chapel proper, against a back wall, there was a long wooden display case with a glass top. It was about the size of a human being. Gould expected it to contain church photographs or books (this was not the kind of church to display corpses or saintly remains). In fact, as it turned out, the case contained a hand: a six-foot long, carved wooden hand. The hand was laid flat on a bed of blue velvet and was in the position of pointing; mounted differently, it could have made a giant, three-dimensional road sign. Attached to the side of the case was the following explanation:

Carved in 1901 by William Markham, this hand pointed heavenward from our church steeple, reminding Silver of the One and Only Way, until February 15, 1965, when it was toppled by a freak storm. Though various plans were initiated for reattaching the hand, ultimately it was decided (for safety and other reasons) to bring it into the church, where now it testifies to our church heritage and continues to remind us to seek the greater glory of God.

"A typical Canadian compromise, wouldn't you say?"

Gould turned. At the front of the chapel stood a big, able bodied man in a dark suit. The man was posed with his hands clasped before him. To his right was the pulpit. On the wall behind was a functional-looking, square-timbered cross.

The man descended two steps and came down the aisle between the pews. Creaks and groans came up from the wooden floor. When the man had stopped again, a handshake away, Gould asked, "How so?"

The man's hands were still before him, folded together like a heart. He looked Gould over with eyes that were the same blue as Gould's own—a blue suggesting tropical seas—except that they seemed to glow from the bottom of two deep hollows, as if the sea in them were observed through a reversed telescope.

"Back in 1965, the congregation was deeply divided. Apparently, some wanted the fallen hand returned to its place, but others felt it was too ostentatious, that its time was past, that it should be burned or otherwise done away with. So, as a compromise, the deacons put it in this case. Out of public view, but still dictating its message to those inside."

"A clever compromise, though I wouldn't necessarily call it Canadian. A lot of the people I've known seem to thrive on proclaiming their beliefs in public."

"Yes, but do you believe them when they do? In my experience, the louder the proclamation, the more likely it is to be a lie. Public shows of virtue so often turn out to be disguises for shameful acts. Surely"—and now the man smiled—"you must have discovered that in your line of work?"

Gould instinctively reached for his I.D.

The other man waved him off. "No need, Inspector. Silver is a small town. I already know who you are."

"And you?"

"Philip Bentley. No need to call me Reverend. We don't stand much on title around here."

Reverend Bentley stretched out his arm, directing Gould to walk with him. He led on with a monk's slow gait. They passed out of the chapel and started up the stairs to the annex.

"But you did not answer my question," Bentley said.

"About virtue as a mask?"

"And your line of work."

Gould planted his foot on a polished wooden step. "Well, it's true that, as an investigator, you discover things are seldom entirely as they seem. That's why it's important not to jump to hasty conclusions. At the same time, you learn about disguises. And you're right, great shows of virtue can be a disguise. But you also learn that few people are capable of maintaining a disguise under the right kind of scrutiny."

They had reached the top. Bentley stopped and smiled, rather ruefully, it seemed. "That sounds a little threatening."

Gould showed his palms, a gesture that—with a silent appreciation of the irony—he recognized as vaguely Christ-like. "Only if you're wearing a disguise."

Bentley laughed. "My office is this way."

The reverend's office, like the chapel, was sparsely decorated, with square-backed, modestly upholstered furniture and little ornamentation. A book case built into one wall was almost empty; the shelves contained just a few copies of the same Bibles and hymnals found in the ante-chamber, three or four framed photographs, and—the only distinctive item—a Mayan doll in ceremonial dress. In one corner was an open closet containing some black gowns. On the minister's desk there was a green blotter, a black telephone with answering machine and little else.

When they entered, Bentley went to the window for a moment. "A glorious day," he sighed, "don't you think?"

"Nice enough," said Gould.

"Since you came to town—just yesterday, wasn't it?—the weather has vastly improved. We've had such a rainy stormy fall. But today it's almost like spring in November."

Gould waited patiently for Bentley to turn around. When he did, they both assumed their chairs.

"I want to thank you in advance for your co-operation," said Gould. "I'm sure that recent events have not been easy for you or your congregation."

"Quite." Bentley clasped his hands on the desk blotter.

"I'd like to know anything and everything you can tell me about the Soledads."

"I hardly know where to start."

"Why don't you start with how you came to sponsor them."

"Through the church, of course—the Christian Unity Church, I should say—which has a program in which member congregations can help secure passage for refugees to Canada. Once in Canada, the refugees are billeted by the sponsoring community and assisted with the claim process. Usually, with the right advance preparation, everything goes quite smoothly."

"And the Soledads?"

"Our local church board chose them from a list supplied by the central office in Vancouver. Then there were arrangements, negotiations. It all had to be done carefully, of course, what with the danger to the Soledads. As it turned out, the government seemed quite happy to be rid of them."

"So there were no problems getting them out?"

"None that I know of. The more difficult arrangements were of course managed by the agencies in Costaguana."

"Did the Soledads ever give you to understand that they were still afraid of the government of Costaguana? The reason I ask, of course, is that I want to deal with the possibility that the Soledads' former enemies may have tracked them down here."

"They never mentioned anything to me. And it doesn't seem logical, anyway. If the government of Costaguana wanted to kill them, why let them escape to Canada first? Seems like it would be a lot easier to kill them back in Costaguana."

"Indeed. Well, let's turn now to when the Soledads arrived in town."

"Before we do, I'd like to say something."

Bentley raised a finger, as if to hold the inspector in place. Gould waited. The reverend lowered both elbows onto the blotter and made a steeple with his hands.

"There are some things I need to tell you, Inspector, before we go any further. I want to be honest with you from the beginning. Let me speak to you without disguise." Gould narrowed his eyes.

"About the Soledads, Inspector. The truth is that they were a cause of grief long before the awful events of last week. For various reasons. Some of the fault is ours—mine. Perhaps we should have gotten to know them better before agreeing to bring them to Silver."

"In what way a cause of grief?"

For a minute Bentley seemed to pray, eyes fixed on Gould. "At first," he said, "there weren't really problems. I wouldn't call them problems. Disappointments, maybe. You have to understand that my congregation, though powerfully united in its Christianity, is not without its differences when it comes to other things. I had hoped that the gesture of helping fellow human beings in need would transcend—erase—our differences. That, in fact, it would strengthen the bond between us."

"But it did not?"

"It could have. I am sure it could have. Except that the Soledads had a way of bringing out differences."

"How so?"

"I can't recall anything specific. They must have made some comments or gestures, otherwise people wouldn't have reacted. Still, mainly, it just seemed that their presence, the very fact that they were in our lives and at our services Sunday after Sunday—somehow it just provoked people."

"That's very vague."

Bentley looked down at his hands. He seemed to notice a mark on the blotter and set a finger to work rubbing it out. "Put it this way," he continued. "Do you know very much about the Republic of Costaguana?"

"Some."

"One of the odd things about it, something that I learned from the Soledads, is that silver mining is a key industry. Enrique of course worked originally in the major mine there, the San Tomé. But that's not the point. The point is: the politics. Some of it having to do with the mines. But mostly the F.L.C., the Front for the Liberation of Costaguana. This is the group that the Soledads were apparently connected with."

Bentley made one or two more passes with his finger, then seemed satisfied that the spot on the blotter had been erased. He refolded his hands. "The point is," he said, "and I have to take some blame for this, for not foreseeing the problem—the point is, the F.L.C. is a Marxist organization."

"I see."

"I don't think you do. You think it's that simple"—one finger raised—"but it's not. Yes, the Soledads' Marxism created some tension in our congregation. The conservative members were understandably uneasy about it and even the more progressive members were put in a difficult spot. But politics—politics is just of this world. The bigger problem with the Soledads' Marxism was that, well, frankly, it meant they did not believe in God."

Gould held his expression.

"It was so naïve of me," said Bentley, after a moment. "I just assumed that since they were recommended to us by the church they would be, in some fashion, church people."

"Did the Soledads do anything specific to attack your religion?"

"No, no. Again—nothing specific. But their manner when they were in the church or when they were asked about their faith was so evasive. They weren't required to believe as the rest of the congregation believed. We're much more enlightened than that. But there seemed—no, there was something critical, judgmental, even mocking about their attitude."

Gould, who had remained very still until this point, now raised one hand and, by connecting thumb and middle finger, made a circle. He tapped the circle in the air once, like a musical conductor. "Let me get this straight," he said. "You say that there was nothing specific, just an attitude, an evasiveness. And yet the Soledads triggered so much animosity. Could it be that the problem was cultural?"

"I'm not sure what you mean."

"A matter of interpretation. I'm starting to believe that although they were here for six months, no one in Silver really figured out how to read the Soledads. Or at least different people seemed to read them in very different ways. Take their fellow workers at the mine. Some saw them as very warm, some as very aloof. Some thought they were very talkative, preachy almost, but some thought they barely said a word. What I wonder is, maybe this is simply because the Soledads were foreign. Maybe you just misunderstood their signals."

"No. We understood their signals all right."

Gould popped the bubble made by his thumb and finger and lowered his palm back onto the chair arm. "In a way it's immaterial," he said. "It doesn't matter all that much why people felt animosity towards them. What is important is if you know of anyone, in your congregation or outside of it, who might have felt enough animosity to do what was done."

Bentley met the Inspector eye to eye. Tropical sea to tropical sea. Then, very deliberately, he stood. He moved slowly from behind the desk, one of his hands trailing behind for a second over the green blotter, as if reading a Braille inscription, and came over to the bookcase. There he took down the Mayan doll for a moment and turned it over in his hands. He said, "You haven't asked about Felipe and Gabriela."

"I intend to interview them eventually, after they've had more time to begin dealing with their grief."

The reverend put back the doll. He returned to his desk, sat, and spread his hands before him. For a moment, he seemed to consider the position of his thumbs. Then he said, "I disagree with you that the reasons are not important. I know absolutely nothing that might point you to a killer of the Soledads, but this animosity, I do not want it misunderstood. I want it clear: there were reasons. The Soledads were a disappointment. Some reasons for this are vague. One reason is not. And don't tell me about cultural differences. I know very well about cultural differences."

Bentley's hands had tightened into fists. He noticed this now and gradually, as if by an act of will, flattened them back onto the blotter. "This is hard for me," he said, with the briefest flicker of a smile. "Look, Inspector. I told you I would adopt no disguises. Well, you were bound to find out soon, if you have not already: the Soledads were formally expelled by our church three weeks ago."

Gould did not react. Bentley waved a hand to show that this was not the main point.

"The decision was a while in coming. It was decided upon by the deacons at their monthly meeting. I made the announcement during my sermon of that week."

Bentley stopped. A long controlled breath.

"Was it something to do with the children?"

"Very perceptive, Inspector. Yes. It had to do with the children."

Bentley rebuilt the church with his hands. He seemed to look into his fingertips for the right words, then, all at once, fell back into language.

"When the Soledads first arrived in our town, they billeted with my wife and I, as you know. Needless to say, in the first months, Enrique and Camilla were very busy, trying to learn the language, beginning to build a new life, dealing with immigration issues. Enrique volunteered to teach a course at the high school; Camilla took computer lessons here in the church offices. During this time, Mrs. Bentley and I cooked and cleaned for them and very largely cared for the children. Which was fine. We accepted it with joy as our duty. But—and this is the point—the children, Felipe and Gabriela, were very badly behaved. They were rebellious and rude. They seemed to have no respect at all for their elders. They ignored house rules, they got into fights with other children. They seemed angry and wild all the time. And when we introduced the matter to their parents, we were told to mind our own business."

"Maybe the Soledads had their own way of raising children."

"I'm sure the Soledads did have their own methods. But, regardless of culture, there are certain absolutes. The Soledads were much too permissive to give the children a good moral grounding. But the real problem, the real source of the childrens' terrible behaviour was . . . . This is hard for me to say, Inspector. Especially considering all that has happened. But the real problem was inappropriate touching."

"Touching?"

"Molestation. Sexual abuse. Whatever you want to call it."

The only change in Gould was the appearance of concentration lines in his forehead. Now he lifted one of his long, spidery hands and tapped with a finger at his moustache. "How, may I ask, did you discover this abuse?"

"Mrs. Bentley first suspected it. She was concerned about the amount of touching between parents and children. Hugs and kisses and pats on the bottom. She didn't think it was natural. And then she discovered that the four of them were sleeping in the same bed together. Naked. I had the children come to me for counselling—ostensibly of a religious nature. I asked them about the touching and their answers were unequivocal. They admitted that their parents touched them in totally inappropriate places. If you want, I have my notes from the counseling sessions."

"And this is why the Soledads were expelled?"

"It was the last straw. Though of course I did not mention the abuse in my announcement. To protect Gabriela and Felipe."

Both men fell silent. Eventually, out of the silence, Gould said, "Tell me. If you had such hard and fast evidence of abuse, why did you withdraw your complaint against the Soledads with Social Services?"

Bentley seemed surprised for a moment by the question. Then he shrugged. "Why? A very complicated question, Inspector."

"I've got time."

"The easiest way to explain it is as a balance of interests. On balance, we decided that it was worse for the children for us to proceed at that time. The family is our most important institution, and it seemed that the Soledads should get a chance to work out their problems as a family. To be honest, I had hopes of counseling the parents about their behaviour or getting them to accept counseling from someone else. A naive hope, as it turned out. Once the Soledads moved into their new home, they refused to have anything to do with me."

"Just a couple more questions before I go," said Gould.

"Very well."

Gould assumed a casual tone. "Is Wallace Lies a member of your congregation?"

"Yes he is," said Bentley. "He is in fact on the church board, though I don't see that it makes any difference."

"Probably not. I'm just filling in details. How well do you know him?"

"Fairly well, I suppose."

"I'm curious," said Gould, "did you see Mr. Lies last night?"

"I went to his house. How did you know?"

"I saw you. Getting out of your vehicle. A red land rover, wasn't it?"

"Sometimes my ministering takes me to rather remote areas. Especially in the winter."

"And, last night, did you see Mr. Lies?"

Bentley brought his hands together again and rebuilt the church and steeple. It occurred to Gould now that the posture was rather like a family lawyer about to do some fancy arguing. Finally, the minister said, "I actually went over last night to see Mrs. Lies. I counsel her privately sometimes. She is a troubled woman. But that, Inspector, is a very private matter and not something I can talk about. Even in the interests of no disguises."

"I see. Well then, I guess that does it for today. Thank you for your co-operation."

Chapter Eight

Gould drove back down Henry Street. He crossed Whatcom Creek into the business district. Ahead of him, the road seemed to run straight into the West Columbia mountains. The air was clear. No finger of smoke scratched the sky.

He pulled in at the RCMP station. The duty officer showed him into the office of Inspector Breeze.

"Gould!" said Breeze. "Glad you dropped by. Have a seat."

It looked as if Breeze had been cleaning. The unused computer was gone from the side table; the half-sofa had been cleared of papers; the desk looked almost orderly. The vase of cut flowers had been taken away. When Gould looked in from the doorway, the other inspector stood with a load of files in his hands. He gestured Gould towards the half-sofa and carried the files to a metal filing cabinet. He chose a drawer and, with the files under one arm, seemed to consider a moment. Then he shrugged, dropped the files in as a bundle and closed the drawer with his hip.

Breeze patted his hands and gave Gould a broad smile. "A fine day, wouldn't you say?"

"It's mild."

"That too. But tell you what: I feel great. Just great. Call me an optimist, Gould, but I have a feeling that things are going to be okay around here. So, what can I do for you?"

Breeze grabbed the steel-framed chair from in front of his desk and spun it around. He sat upon it and stretched out his legs. He was wearing a navy blue suit with a red rose in the lapel. As he settled into the chair, his body threw a moist cloud of cologne.

"Mainly I'm just keeping in touch. How were things on the picket line last night?"

"Fine. More than fine in fact. Since the torching of the union office the other night, the picket line has been remarkably calm. Like everybody got something out of their systems."

"No other incidents? Break-ins? Violence?"

"Nothing."

"I see." Gould sat with his briefcase on the floor near his feet. He had one elbow on an arm-rest of the sofa. A finger of his other hand now gently tapped the bristles of his moustache. "How well do you know Wallace Lies?"

"Not well. Why?"

"His name has come up once or twice."

"Have you talked to him yet?"

"I phoned his office yesterday. He is unavailable."

"That's strange."

"Why?"

"Usually he's accessible. Too accessible, some people would say."

"Into this and that and everything?"

"Right. Do you want me to arrange a subpoena?"

"Not yet. I'm going to give it a couple of days. Do you know anything about Mrs. Lies?"

"Again, not much. The fact is, I've only seen her two or three times, and then very briefly, since I arrived."

A pause.

"There is one more thing," said Gould. "An unrelated matter."

"Fire away."

"What kind of car do you drive?"

Breeze shrugged. "A car-pool car, rather like the one you showed up in. A big Avro sedan. What's it to you?"

"Do you ever have steering problems?"

"You mean the car pulling left or right?"

"Something like that. A problem staying exactly in your portion of the road."

"Sounds to me like you have an alignment problem, Gould."

"You may be right."

"Hey, if you want I can recommend you to a local mechanic."

"Thanks. Not just now."

"Anything else?"

"That's all."

"Right." Breeze slapped his thighs and rose to his feet. He made a sweeping motion with his arm and released a laugh. "Hey, you can tell things have improved around here when I have time for this."

"Almost looks like you're settling in."

Breeze laughed again. "Could be worse things, Gould. Well, if anything comes up I'll let you know."

After lunch, he decided to interview Alex MacKenzie. The telephone book gave an address on Queen Street for the museum. He drove looking for a sign but couldn't find one, then turned around and concentrated on building numbers: no luck. So he parked his car a few blocks south of Queen and Henry and walked back north.

Queen was more of a mixed street than Henry, a street of houses rather than commercial buildings. Some houses had been converted into stores or offices—a law firm, a boutique, an optometrist—but many remained as residences. There were few people around. The ones Gould passed immediately recognized him as a police officer and either avoided his eyes or blew him exaggerated hellos. He walked slowly, keeping his eye out for a sign. Up ahead, the twin flags of the municipal hall slow-danced in the gentle breeze.

When he reached the War Memorial, he did a slow scan but still found nothing to point him the way. The memorial itself could have been in any number of small towns scattered across the country: a red granite monolith, with the names of those killed in the Boer War and World War I, below which had been inserted a newer column, not quite a perfect match, attesting to the surprise of the town elders in having to account for World War II and Korea.

Eventually a man came along and Gould stepped across his path. "Excuse me," he said, "could you please point me the way to the Miner's Museum?"

"It's right over there." The man pointed to a nondescript wooden building that Gould had taken for a private home.

"Thank you."

Even up close, there was nothing to indicate the existence of the museum. Only when Gould cupped his hand over the window in the top of the door and saw a light, a rack of pamphlets, and a man sitting behind a card table with papers and a strong-box on it, was he sure enough to try the handle. The door pushed in on a hydraulic arm and closed again slowly behind him.

The attendant looked to be over sixty, with a curtain of white hair around the dome of his head, dark leathery skin and deep lines on his face, as if, sometime in the past, his face had suddenly shrunk. When Gould stepped inside, he put down the book he was reading and looked up with rheumy grey eyes.

Taped to the card table was a sign: "Adults $2.00, Children and Seniors $1.00, Historical Pamphlets $2.50."

"Alexander MacKenzie?" Gould asked.

"Who wants to know?"

"Inspector Charles Gould. I'm in charge of the Soledad murder investigation. I'd like to ask you a few questions about the statement you gave on Wednesday."

MacKenzie looked out from under bushy white eyebrows. He cleared his throat.

"What do you know about the town of Silver?" he asked.

"Not much," said Gould. "Not yet, anyway."

"Know what a Widow Maker is?"

"No."

"Early pneumatic drill. So many miners died using them that that's what they called them."

"Interesting. Now, there are a couple of things about your statement I'd like to clarify. For instance—"

"Forget it, Inspector," said MacKenzie. "I'm working."

He picked up his book.

Gould stood stock still. He looked down from his side of the table for a full minute, expressionless, observing the attendant. Then he reached inside his suit jacket.

Two loonies dropped on the table. They spun like golden tops and then fell flat.

MacKenzie set aside his book. He lifted the lid on the strong box, slowly, took out a roll of tickets and carefully ripped one off. He held it out for Gould. Then he did something peculiar: he grinned, a gap-toothed, full-faced grin, a grin so dramatic that the man's eyes disappeared in whirlpools of wrinkles. Gould felt as if he were being mocked and welcomed at the same time. Then MacKenzie relaxed his face, wagged his finger and said, in a hoarse voice, "That way."

The indicated doorway led to what must once have been the house's living room. The walls had been painted a flat grey, and on them were mounted various black and white photographs. There was no obvious starting point, so Gould made a slow circle. Some of the photographs were of Silver, first as a small settlement in the 19th century, then as a turn-of-the-century boom town. Other photographs were of miners. One showed three men on a ledge working a wall of rock, backs turned to the camera, while a fourth man, facing the camera, tilted a wheelbarrow upward to reveal some recovered ore. Another showed two men with shotguns guarding a trolley of silver bars.

What was strange, if not disconcerting, was that the photographs were accompanied by only the most cursory of explanations. The picture of the men on the ledge, for instance, was simply captioned *Scraping surface*. The other picture was *Duty guard*.

As Gould proceeded from room to room, past displays of mining equipment, ore samples and many more photographs, the labels remained equally terse. Sometimes, as in the case of *Duty guard*, the caption was almost cryptic, as if it had been scribbled in a rapid shorthand (a number were actually hand-written) or roughly translated from a foreign language. By the end of his tour, Gould felt that he had learned little about mining in the region.

One thing he did confirm, by implication, was that Lena Stahr had been integral to the revival of mining in the area. He deduced this from the sheer number of pictures of her in the modern section of the museum. Here the photographs were in colour—a ribbon cutting, a site inspection, a portrait of workers and bosses, a banquet dinner—all with the same woman in them. Though the captions were uncommunicative and did not name the woman directly, there was a banner in the banquet photograph that read: *Congrats Lena On A Job Well Done!*

There was something a little disconcerting about a woman being the centre of attention in so many documents of what was, otherwise, an entirely male field. Gould was unsettled further by just how beautiful Lena Stahr was. In the earlier photographs she looked like she could not have been thirty years old: a dark-haired, dark-eyed young woman, tall and slender, with full red lips and a slightly in-turned smile. Mostly she was dressed in nondescript, functional working clothes, blue-jeans and overalls, but this almost seemed to magnify her feminine presence. There was something distinctly sexual in the way the men, her employees, gazed at her; their look was both predatory and servile. She, in turn, was usually looking at the camera, at ease, with an aura of knowing, as if she acknowledged the attention and thought in entirely natural.

In the later photographs, the sexual charge was, if anything, magnified. In these Stahr more often wore business suits: matching skirts and jackets with white blouses and one or two discrete but very expensive looking pieces of jewelry. In the banquet photograph, which seemed very recent, her hair was shorter, styled, with just a flicker of contrasting white. She wore a long black evening gown. She stood at the speaker's podium, smiling, her head slightly back, as if enjoying a great joke. The male heads to her left and right were turned and all looking up at her, all still serious, the men concentrating on her like off-stage actors waiting for a cue.

Though the confirmation about Stahr was interesting, the overall effect of the museum was to confirm Gould's prejudices about history. A lot of glittery worthless stuff that had nothing to do with his case.

When he returned to the entrance area, MacKenzie looked up from behind the table. "Interesting, eh?"

"Interesting."

"If you got any questions, any questions at all, I'm the man to ask."

Gould stood for a moment, sizing up the attendant. The old man was leaned back in his chair with his arms crossed. Gap-toothed grin, sunken face, shag of white hair. The man breathed heavily, with a faint gurgling sound on the exhalation. Gould detected a faint sour odor of cigarettes and something like burnt leaves.

"Tell me," he said, with an air of choosing a topic at random, "what happened to the captions?"

"The captions?"

"Yes. The little narratives that usually go with historical displays. The little white cards with explanations on them."

"You didn't like the captions?"

"They weren't very informative."

"Maybe that lets people make up their own minds."

"You have to give people more information. Otherwise—"

The attendant seemed about to blurt something out, but was seized with the need to cough. He successfully stifled it, his cheeks puffing, his back arching, and took in a long slow breath. Then he spoke in a raspy voice. "So," he said, "what's confusing for you? What's missing?"

"Take the last couple of rooms, the most recent displays. There is a woman present in a number of photographs."

"Lena Stahr."

"She seems to be a central figure, and yet there's nothing to explain about her. Her name isn't even listed—I only deduced it from evidence internal to one of the photographs. So what's her story? How'd she get to be that person in the middle of so many photographs?"

"You really want to know?"

"I use it mainly as an example. But, yes, it would be useful to me to know more about Lena Stahr. Within reason, of course."

The attendant laughed, and the exertion of laughing seemed too much for him: he doubled over in a paroxysm of coughing. When he had recovered himself he spoke again in a raspy, phlegm choked voice. "If you want the explanation within reason, you can find it in them pamphlets over there."

Gould glanced briefly at the rack.

"Actually, there's only two different ones," the attendant continued, "one about the early history of the town, Henry Nathan and the Three Shaft Mine and all that, and one about the last fifteen years or so. The newer one'll tell you all about Lena Stahr—within reason."

"That's not a very persuasive selling job."

"Frankly, I think the pamphlets are bullshit, but they sound like the sort of thing you want."

Gould's face was a mask. "Why don't you tell me about her?"

There was a challenging tone in Gould's voice that gave the attendant pause. His face grew serious. He took two or three laboured breaths, wiped his mouth with the back of his hand, then, all at once, grinned again. "Why not?" he laughed. "That's my job, ain't it?" He closed his eyes for a moment, as if concentrating, and then began to speak.

"Read that pamphlet and it'll tell you something like this: *Lena Stahr was born in blah blah blah in Denver, Colorado, the oldest of three daughters. Her father was an airline mechanic; her mother, Gloria, a homemaker. As a teenager, Lena put money away for college by working part-time in the office of Silver Eagle Mines, a company of well-known American tycoon Anthony (Tony) Jenkins, where she developed an interest in mining and precious metals. In 1974, she graduated from the University of Colorado with a B.Sc. in inorganic chemistry and took a job with the Tristero Corporation, a giant resource company based, in part, in Nevada.*

"*For the year or so, she was a junior member of a team doing feasibility studies of various properties. This team came to Silver, British Columbia in late 1974 to study Henry Nathan's lake, the lake where the tailings from the original Three Shaft Mine had been dumped. New extraction technology raised the possibility of salvaging the silver in the tailings. Lena—now Lena Stahr, having married businessman Munro Stahr—recommended in favour of developing the property. Her advice was not taken. This began a time of frustration, when her contributions to the team were consistently ignored or trivialized.*

"Turns out that Tristero had her pegged as a future company spokeswoman; even then, companies with public image problems saw the value of having an attractive woman speaking for them. They were letting her tag along with the feasibility team to give her a gloss of credibility and then they were going to shift her to public relations. When she figured out what was going on, she demanded to see the president. He admitted everything. She told him she wanted to do real work. He gave her an ultimatum, so she quit.

"She went back to university, this time to do a Master's in metallurgical engineering. She decided on Pacific Western University in Vancouver. For her thesis, she designed the processes necessary to extract the silver from Henry Nathan's lake. In 1977, having completed her thesis and divorced Munro Stahr, she returned to the offices of Silver Eagle Mines and made a pitch to Tony Jenkins for money to acquire and devel-

op the Nathan Lake property. Jenkins said yes, and his support was a turning point.

"It goes on from there," MacKenzie wheezed, "about how Lena learned to be a good manager, to lighten up with the boys, joke with them, tease them along, get them to communicate. But the really important part comes after the lake project is almost over. You want to hear it?"

Gould nodded.

"Well, she has made a sizable profit over two years, but now the silver in the old tailings at the bottom of the lake is almost all extracted. So what happens? As the pamphlet tells it, Lena Stahr had an inspiration. Yes, she read up on her history, about how the Three Shaft Mine and all the others seemed to dry up at the 300 hundred foot level, and she did her own careful examination of the terrain and thought, 'There's more silver here, but it's deeper down. I can tell by the lay of the land.' So in 1980, she started spending her profits on drilling teams who took core samples from deeper and deeper below ground. Six hundred feet, the crews drilled. One thousand feet. Thirteen hundred. Then, at fifteen hundred feet, twice as deep as anyone else had thought worth trying, and with her money almost gone, Stahr discovered the rich, large deposits that have brought long-term prosperity to the region. The rest, as they say, is . . . more bullshit."

There was a pause. Gould stood with one hand in a pocket and his briefcase on the floor by his feet. MacKenzie breathed heavily.

"Sounds like the usual background material," said Gould. "Not a lot of use to me, but—"

"Come here." MacKenzie heaved himself slowly to his feet. "Let me show you something."

The attendant took Gould to the room in which the modern display began, and stopped in front of a photograph of Lena Stahr cutting a ribbon. The caption read (unhelpfully): *Ribbon cutting.*

"This is a photograph of the official opening of the Cyclops silver mine," explained the attendant. "This, of course, is Lena Stahr. This fellow here, just in the background, is Al Goodwin. Good friend of mine. You talked to him yet? Well—don't believe all the propaganda about him. Now look here. The person right closest to Stahr. You recognize this guy?"

Gould looked. The hair was darker and better kept, the body less bent, but clearly it was the attendant himself.

"I'm not going to tell you about my personal relationship with Lena," the attendant said. "That's my history, and I ain't sharing it. But I'll tell you something. What really happened back in one nine eight oh when the silver was almost gone from Henry Nathan's lake. What really happened was this. I had been picking over the foothills around here for years. I had laid a few claims. Would've worked them too, if I'd had the dough. Anyway, I was the one who figured out about the deep veins of ore. I went to Lena with some maps I made. I explained to her about the lay of the land and what I knew about some of the old shafts (I'd done some scavenging). I said, *If you drill here and here, I'm sure you'll find something.* Well, one thing led to another, as they say, and we had a good time for a year or so. At the end of it, she owned my claims, her mine was almost in production, and I was out the door. Zip."

"Lena Stahr stole your ideas?"

"All legal, of course. All legal. She's a smart one that way."

Now MacKenzie led the way back. He walked slowly, as if he had to concentrate on the placing of each foot. When they got back to his table and chair he said, "Listen, that's enough about that. Enough history. I'm dying for a smoke and I gotta close up and go somewhere to do it. So—what did you want to know about my statement?"

Gould took a few seconds to clear his mind. Then he said, "I went to the replacement workers' camp this morning. I wanted to watch a shift change. On the way I took a look at your cabin."

"Yeah, so?"

"Your cabin is more than fifty yards off the road."

"So?"

"And at 7:30 in the morning, there isn't much light."

"What are you saying? That it would have been hard for me to recognize the car?"

"How much did you have to drink the night before?"

"Listen, Inspector. I recognized the hood ornament. You know, that thing that looks like a peace sign sticking up on the hood there."

"You recognized a hood ornament, through a window from sixty yards, in the half-light, after just waking up from a hard night's drinking?"

"I hadn't gone to bed yet."

Gould shook his head. "Well, thanks for the background about Lena Stahr," he said. "For the history lesson. But I'm afraid you're living too much in the past."

"Says who?"

"Mercedes don't have stick-up hood ornaments anymore, Mr. MacKenzie. The company stopped making them that way years ago."

Gould, as the interview with MacKenzie suggests, was suspicious of history. In this, oddly enough, he had something in common with Jayne, though for very different reasons. Gould, I think, hated the untidiness of history, all those irrelevant details, all those implications dragging your attention away from whodunit. Jayne, however, hated history not because it was untidy but because it was tidy. As soon as you start retelling past events, she would argue, you end up drawing connections that do no justice to the real complexity of life. You end up slanting your account to support your own biases. And since most historical accounts have been written by men (she would go on) they just perpetuate a biased male view of the world. For these reasons, she was reluctant to speak about her own past. When she did reveal things, she stuck to very specific stories—fragments, vignettes, discrete moments without connection to before or after—and usually refused to generalize about them. Early on in our relationship, this frustrated me: I wanted to know everything about her. "Tell me something," I'd plead, "anything. . . ." But she'd just smile and kiss me hard on the lips. "Anything I could tell you would be a lie."

Personally, I think both Jayne and Gould didn't want to face how their own pasts shaped their present. How they were not entirely free to live in the present or to make what they wanted of themselves. Not that "what's bred in the bone" is all-determining, as some literary types like to claim . . . no, we have more freedom than that. But the past has a way of blocking out the larger grid on which we move, of imposing limits to our choices, limits invisible but real nevertheless, like the borders of a country or the workings of an unconscious prejudice. The more you try to deny the existence of this grid, the more you try to live in some utopian free space of the present, the more likely you are to find your nose flattened against it in the form of an unexpected letter.

PROSPECTS UNKNOWN

Then again, I have no reason to be smug. One of the truths the events in Silver rubbed my nose against was that I have the opposite problem from Charles Gould and Jayne Whynot: I'm not very good at dealing with the present.

Gould returned to The Red Grizzly. He wrote out his interview with Reverend Bentley, his second interview with Inspector Breeze. He listed everything he'd learned at the museum. For a while, he reveled in the discipline of writing, the steady flow of ink from the pen in his left hand, the letters so remarkably legible . . . .

Then the telephone rang. It was Wallace Lies.

"Hello, Inspector," said a boosterish voice. "Sorry I missed you yesterday. My business was easier to complete than I expected; in fact, it has turned out to be an unexpected success, a terrific success! So I'm available. Why don't you come by my office later on. Say around five? We can have that chat."

Gould's stomach was bothering him again. Too much activity and not enough food. He decided to grab a bite before the interview with Lies.

He had just opened the door when he was met by Sergeant Wright.

"This just came for you."

In the sergeant's hand was a blue and red courier envelope. It was addressed to *Inspector Charles Gould. The Red Grizzly. 2349 Trans-Canada Highway. Silver, B. C.* The return address was *The Senate, Government of Canada, Ottawa.*

Ten minutes later, Gould was back at the desk in his room.

He was slouched slightly forward in his chair—an uncharacteristic posture. One elbow, supporting his telephone hand, was on the desk. His other hand was splayed out on the open letter.

Into the telephone he said, "Superintendent? Charles Gould here. I need to speak with you. In person . . . . No—in person. Will you be in your office the next couple of hours? . . . . I'm heading back immediately. I will be there by six."

II

BLANK PAGES

Faults often go in families; they tend to follow the same general direction or directions in a given area.

E. L. Faulkner, *Introduction to Prospecting*

Chapter Nine

Gould did not tell me about his father until the Soledad investigation had apparently broken down, after his failed attempt to employ the Third Degree, that-oh-so-literary device, as a short-cut to solving the case. Even then, he hummed and hawed, evaded, avoided, and did much dramatic posturing before finally getting to the point. He also vacillated between personal confession and trying to re-establish himself as the consummate detective, so one moment he would be telling me intimate details about his family life and the next he would be trying to solve the mystery again. After a while, I came to realize that all the detours were necessary, even if they bugged the hell out of me, even if they were designed to avoid the one thing about his father that Gould most needed to tell. It was as if he had to look away from his father, somehow, to look all around him but not directly at him, in order to finally see him clearly.

One detour had to do with his brother. When he brought his brother up, he spoke with pride and a hint of yearning. "Sometimes," he said, "I wish I was more like him, the way he's always known his own mind, the way he's stood up for himself. Though he's had his own problems too, of course."

"Are the two of you close?"

"Now. When we were kids, I worshipped him some of the time—he was my big brother after all—but hated him, feared him, was embarrassed by him a lot of the time. As teenagers, we drifted apart. The fact is, we were just so different. Even as kids, we were totally different."

They were, at least, both left-handed, though for young Charles this was nothing to celebrate. The last thing he wanted, on top of the burden of his family's notoriety, was another sign of his difference from the other kids, and it was clear to him, even in grade one, that the normal thing was to be right-handed: scissors, rulers, the direction of printing, watch stems, pencil sharpeners, language itself—all drove home the message that to be left-handed was to be a freak, gauche, if not downright sinister. For a while, he practised making letters right-handed. He fantasized about breaking his left hand in an accident, having heard that people, when forced in this way, always learned to write with the other hand. No luck. Not even Miss Power's coaxing (by this point teachers had at least stopped whacking left hands with a ruler) was enough to get him over the dumbfounded awkwardness that overtook him when he worked with his right hand. Eventually, he resigned himself to writing as his body seemed to demand, though with one important difference. By discipline and drudgery and doggedness, he managed to avoid the southpaw's typical tortured scrawl and was soon instead collecting—along with his first equestrian prizes—awards for penmanship. If his writing had to be left-handed by the pen, it would be right-handed on the page.

His brother, typically, was a different story. For him, being left-handed was just another excuse to assert his distinctiveness. While Charles never complained about being branded incompetent for failing to scissor a straight line or for dropping the ink bottle placed in his right palm, his brother screamed bloody murder. He took every instance of bias, personal or institutional, conscious or unconscious, as an affront. When Mrs. Donnelly explained that to make an "o" you drew a circle "counter-clockwise" he leapt to his feet and demanded, "What if you're left-handed? Wouldn't you go the other way?" He was positively gleeful in contradicting Constable Zietlow, who came in to teach bicycle safety and explained that to make hand-signals you motioned with your left and steered "with your stronger hand." And, predictably, he developed his own writing into an aggressive scrawl and charged discrimination against any teacher who claimed to be unable to read it.

For a long time, Charles was embarrassed by his brother's outrageous behaviour, the constant battles about left-handedness and other, more important, things, but, as an adult, he wondered if a cruder rebellion wasn't sometimes necessary. Faced by a world of oppression and disorder, maybe all that was left was the melodramatic assertion of self. He also realized, in retrospect, that there was a certain amount of envy in his attitude to his brother, a resentment for being lost in the glare of one who burned so brightly, a resentment of his brother's courage in defying authority—especially, in defying their father.

Twenty years after his parents' divorce, when Charles had reconciled with his mother, she, after serving him herbal tea in her hippie kitchen on Galiano Island, had smiled and waxed affectionate about her two sons of the left hand. "You were so different about it, you two," she said, the crow lines radiating from her eyes. "With you, Charlie, you were so eaten up. You saw it as a handicap, the mark of Cain, and you set out with your damn-the-barricades stubbornness (inherited from both your father and I) to overcome it. Almost succeeded, too. But Glen. With Glen, if he wasn't such a brilliant player with the left hand—oh so rare that ability on the lower end of the keyboard—if it wasn't for that, we would have thought that he was forcing himself. I can just imagine it. If Glen wasn't left-handed originally, he would have recreated himself that way, just to be ornery, to irritate the good bourgeoisie, just to make the absolutely biggest stink that he could."

I drank my coffee. My hand shook a bit as I lifted the cup, no doubt from all the caffeine I had taken in (the Igloo did not serve anything as big-city-pretentious as decaf).

"Your brother is a piano player named Glenn Gould?" I asked in disbelief.

"Not 'Glenn' but 'Glen'. Not two 'n's but one. 'Glen' was my grandfather's name and also the name of my mother's favourite uncle. How were my parents supposed to know he'd be interested in music? It doesn't run in the family."

"Wasn't that hard on his career?"

"Not at first. At first it just seemed like a joke. It would be the first thing people would ask him about at a recital: 'Are you related?' Ha, ha. Until he was about fifteen, he thought it was pretty funny too. In fact, he loved Glenn Gould, the other one. He had all his records and sometimes even imitated his methods and style, as impossible as that sounds. The problems started only when Glen started trying to develop a style of his own."

"People started making comparisons?"

"And, of course, when this happened, he could never win. If he took a less ambitious approach to a piece, they would say he was not living up to his name. If he took a more experimental or eccentric approach they'd say he was just imitating the other Glenn. After a while, anything the other Gould had recorded he simply could not perform. Eventually it really began to bug him. Imagine. Having to live with the notoriety of my family and with such a coincidence of name."

"Did he ever consider changing it?"

"He did, in fact. But ultimately he felt like that would be giving in. For a while, he gave up on classical music entirely. Then one day he discovered that all his years of practising with the radio on—he emulated the other Glenn Gould in that—had allowed him, somehow, to absorb popular music. Without even trying, he just knew all these songs. The family memory, of course. And at the same time he discovered that my father hated this music, that it would embarrass him no end to have his son, one-time classical music prodigy, playing Top 40 covers in a lounge-act rock 'n roll band. The band, by the way, was called Six Years Old. Which was appropriate in more ways than one. And to show his anger about what had happened to him, he began introducing parodies of classical tunes into his solos. Brutal parodies. You know, a little *Moonlight Sonata* in the middle of his solo in *Born to be Wild*. This went on for a while, until a funny thing happened."

"What?"

Gould sipped his coffee and took a slow bite of the pie he had just ordered. It was late night at the Igloo. We had been talking since just after ten. Three hours. The place was empty of customers now except for the two of us. Still an hour or so before the bar rush. As we sat there, our faces glazed with the recycled air of the place and our mouths fusty from all the coffee, it occurred to me that Gould, in the midst of his mania, his anguished need to confess, was actually, in a perverse sort of way, enjoying himself. Enjoying this recital of his own—and his brother's—story. That literary pause, the sip, the nibble of pie; like those moments when Philip Marlowe stops to give a few extra tidbits about a room when you know there is a body behind the desk. Wanting to savour it. The power of the telling. Making it last. Charles Gould wiped his lips.

"Thing was," he said, "my brother, when he wanted to make a name for himself, when he wanted to be an absolute original, discovered that he couldn't be. But when he wanted to just fade into the woodwork, when he wanted to be anonymous, he couldn't do that either. Word started getting out about his quirky solos. It meant the band had a sound. Next thing you know Six Years Old had a bit of a name, a following. And record company agents began to attend their shows."

"Never heard of them," I said.

"Nothing came of it. As soon as Glen realized what was happening he quit. Skipped out."

"Back to anonymity."

"Sort of. But he knew he had to make a living somehow and that my father was not going to give him any money. So he kicked around a bit, moved to Toronto, did some accompanying for a not-very-good dance company, even tried working at other things—retail—but that was a non-starter."

"I can't imagine your brother serving a customer."

"He was determined not to serve anybody. Well, the long of the short of it is, he came up with a more subtle strategy. A strategy that allowed him to play the classical music that he truly loved (because he discovered that he did love it when he was forcing himself through all those cover tunes) but in a way that he wouldn't be taken seriously, that he wouldn't be subjected, over and over again, to those impossible comparisons. That's how he became Glen Gould (The Other One)."

The image that stayed with Charles was from a few years back, when the brothers had begun to know one another again and to like one another for perhaps the first time. Glen had invited his police officer brother to a private party in the 52nd floor lounge of a bank tower in Toronto. Much of the Bay Street elite were there, the Mayor, a city councillor or two, ministers from the provincial cabinet. Charles wasn't sure why Glen invited him. At first he thought it was to show him that he had gone back to his original calling, that he was starting over again, as if the problems of his past did not exist or no longer mattered. Later, he realized differently.

So there was Glen, in black tie and polished black shoes, hunched over the white and black keys in the pose Charles remembered from their adolescence, a pose that had tempted him too when he grew tall and lean. But Charles had straightened his posture with dressage, and now only Glen arched his back that way, his hands, so pale and beautiful and longer even than Charles's own, seeming to take their life from the safe cocoon of his body. He played Chopin's *Polonaise in A Flat Major*, a stately piece with complicated rolls for the left hand. Charles sat at his front table, eyes half closed as the music swept over him. It filled him with bittersweet emotions to listen to his brother play this way, to hear him truly exercising his extraordinary gift. By turns he felt admiration and anger and regret.

Near the end there was a dramatic flourish, followed by a moment of expectation. Glen raised his hands over his head, held them for the count of three, and brought them down again. There was a jarring noise, followed by what seemed like the repeated sound of breaking glass. It was the same piece but now played at triple forte and double time. A series of bad notes—probably intentional—sheered across the melody. Glen threw back his head, shook his hair behind him. His eyes were clamped shut, his lips kissing empty air. More crashes, more white flashing hands—and, like a slammed door, it was over.

For a moment, Glen Gould (The Other One) hung limply over the keys, the maestro spent by his virtuoso performance. Then, with an impish grin, he leaned into his microphone and released a long, low, guttural belch.

Charles sat frozen, the blood high in his face.

Nobody in the lounge stirred. Not the mayor. Not the cabinet ministers. There were five seconds of complete silence. Then, from somewhere in the back, came a single spoken "bravo" and a pair of hands slowly clapping. An instant later everyone in the lounge, as if commanded by some force beyond their control, had exploded into laughter and applause.

There was a green-bottle fly in the Igloo the night Gould made his confessions. I watched it drop off the edge of our table and weave an unsteady line towards the kitchen. I couldn't help wondering what a fly was doing alive, in the mountains, in the middle of November.

When Gould had first appeared, shuffling with an aura of tragedy from the door of the restaurant to my booth, there had been a bearded man at the *Truckers Only* table. Gould, uncharacteristically, nodded to the man as he went by. The man, who had been writing in a notebook of some kind, looked up and bit the end of his pencil.

Gould collapsed into the seat across from me.

"It's over," he said.

"You solved the case?"

Hours later, after the bar rush had ended but before the first light would show in the sky, Gould told me about his mother. I had just pressed him again about the consequences of his disastrous confrontation with Lies, Goodwin and Stahr. I was very worried about his state of mind. It seemed more and more likely that he was going to give up on the investigation. "Surely, if you are patient, you can rebuild your case," I said.

"The other thing about my brother," he replied, "is that he kept in touch with my mother."

He hadn't said a word about his brother since shortly after midnight. He had, in fact, just finished telling me about Archie and Costaguana. But that was how his talk went that night, how it moved immediately and seamlessly from one story to the next. He kept giving answers to questions I had asked hours or days before, as if the questions, which he had scoffed at or dismissed the first time, had just been asked—or asked again. And he went from one event of his life to another without introduction, without context, without establishing a sequence. As if all the events were as accessible, as immediately present, to me as to him.

"He kept in touch," he continued, "despite or maybe because of my father's prohibitions, and in spite of or because of my mother's fatalistic inertia. My mother, you know, assumed that her leaving meant she would be cut off from her children. Remember, the separation happened in 1960. Attitudes to women leaving their husbands to live with someone else were not so liberal as they are today. Attitudes to a woman leaving to live with another woman . . . ."

"It would have been very brave. To come out publicly in 1960."

Gould nodded. "My father, of course, was furious. He didn't actually believe her at first. He thought she was doing it to sabotage his political career—which, of course, was partly true. But she had other, more personal reasons for going public in that way. She didn't want her relationship with Daphne to be sniffed out by the press (as it would have been, eventually). And I think she felt she'd lived too many lies too long. She wanted to be herself, her true self, and be up front about it."

"What a shock it must have been."

"Glen, for some reason, seemed to understand right off. That's why he kept in touch, why he insisted on it from the beginning. But me, I didn't understand. Frankly, I hated her for it. I hated her for a long time. Oddly enough, I hated her as much for what she did to my father's political career as anything else. Strange—considering how I loath politics. But my father was depressed for years after the election in '61. I mean, his party was totally wiped out, they lost every single seat! Now, of course, I can see that there was poetic justice in that."

"How so?"

"To tell you that I'd have to go back to the beginning."

I sipped my coffee, suppressing the caffeine tremor in my hand. I crossed my arms, leaned back in my seat, and grinned.

"I've got all night," I said.

It was like this.

In 1951, Gould's father was a 39-year-old junior minister in the New Brunswick government of John Babbitt McNair. He had been promoted into Cabinet just after the war as a rising young star (he was first elected in 1940 at the age of 28) but once there had made few positive impressions. His colleagues considered him to be elitist, pedantic, and unnecessarily abrasive, a turgid, uninspiring speaker who in spite of—or because of—his obvious intellect tended to bog down in arcane explanations of detail.

All that changed when he and Annie fell in love.

It happened at her father's funeral.

Annie's father, Jimmy McPherson, had been a respected advisor of W.A.C. Bennett, the Premier of British Columbia, and an old friend of Robert Gould's father, Reggie. After Reggie's death (he was a rich man who had lived for the good life and died largely of it, in 1933, at the age of 62), Robert visited the McPhersons in Vancouver, where Jimmy and his young wife had just had their third child. Every few years thereafter, as he criss-crossed the country for one reason or another, Robert visited the McPhersons, and when he was elected to the New Brunswick Legislature he occasionally called Jimmy long-distance for advice.

At the funeral, Robert was surprised at how the three children—all girls—had grown. The last time he had seen them, four years before, they had been only children. Now the youngest, Margaret, whom he had first seen only weeks after she was born, was 17, and the oldest, Jenny was 21. But it was the middle daughter, Annie, who truly caught his eye. She was 19 years old and a beauty.

Who can explain such attractions? In her autobiography, Gould's mother pointed out the obvious explanation: that she had latched onto Robert as a substitute father. Like so much else in *Contra-Diction*, however, it is impossible to be sure of the amount of irony in the statement. Robert, for his own part, was following in the footsteps of his own father, who had given his early adult years over to business and career, and then, in early middle age, had realized that he had no heirs. In truth, Robert was still a passably handsome man, with a lean athletic body (all those push-ups and sit-ups and ski trips to the Laurentians); he was well-traveled, rich, and, in small doses at least, an impressive conversationalist.

The marriage a half year later was a minor sensation. The Fredericton *Daily News* proclaimed: "LONG TIME BACHELOR MINISTER MARRIES GLAMOUR GIRL!" Gould's image suddenly and dramatically changed. As a result, when McNair announced his retirement in later 1951, Robert Gould became a contender for the leader's job. At the leadership convention of 1952, Annie Gould was the difference (all the historians agree on this); somehow, by her very presence, she contradicted all the negative elements in Robert's persona that had previously held him back. Not only was Annie beautiful, but she was soft-spoken and deferential, with a warm sparkle in her eye that made her a natural campaigner. In this, at least, she was her father's daughter. Those who had doubts about Robert were swayed by a simple calculation: how could a man be abrasive, turgid, and uninspiring when he had managed to inspire her?

After the convention Robert called a snap election. It was the same story, a love-in for Annie Gould that incidentally swept her husband to power.

There were two secrets of the 1952 campaign that only came out later. One was that Annie Gould was three months pregnant when the writ was dropped. All through the campaign, she had to excuse herself from some function or other to throw up. As she put it in *Contra-Diction*, she spent half the campaign on her knees in strange washrooms and the other half trying not to wretch as strange men pawed her hand. The media attributed her paleness to her dedication to the work of her husband; the paleness also had a way of accentuating her beauty, the white skin against her dark hair giving her an ethereal glow.

This first secret became evident soon after the election, when the pregnancy began to show. Before the year was out, a son, Glen, was born, only adding to the honeymoon with the voters.

The second secret came out only much later, when, in 1975 (the same year her second son, Charles, found himself in Costaguana), Annie published *Contra-Diction*. The book detailed the growing self-awareness that had led to her coming out as a lesbian and included intimate details of her first encounters with Daphne. It was Daphne, a writer herself, who encouraged her to write her life story.

In *Contra-Diction*, Annie claimed that when she agreed to marry Robert it had been on condition that he retire to private life. She had grown up in a political household and did not want her own children to do the same. Robert, she wrote, had agreed, but after McNair's resignation, when the movers and shakers in the party had come to him to run for leader, he had back-tracked. "He had such well thought out arguments for why he should make the attempt to be Premier," she wrote. "He spoke of destiny, of what a man must do. He spoke of what a better world he could make for our children. 'If you forbid it,' he said, 'I will not run.' But how could I forbid it? I was twenty years old, never good at arguments, not even understanding certain fundamental things about myself. I was totally in love with the man (or so I thought). After I told him I would not forbid him he kissed me on the forehead and said, 'Maybe this is our chance to get the political bug out of my system. Maybe I will lose and the whole matter will be settled.' But I told him, 'If you run, you will win.'"

"I've heard that story before," I said.

"According to my mother, it happens all the time."

"No. I mean that actual story. And I know a fair amount about your mother's book, I think, though I've never read it. It was one of Jayne's favourites. She used to quote it all the time. I recognized the title. I think she originally read it in a Women's Studies course she took as an undergrad. But I don't remember it being by Annie Gould. Annie Something, but not Annie Gould."

"Torrent."

"That's it."

"My mother changed her name, after she left and moved in with Daphne. She didn't want to change it back to McPherson, because, as she said, that was just another patronym. So she changed it to make it meaningful for herself."

This comment made me grow thoughtful. I remembered Jayne for a while, the discussions we used to have at her kitchen table, the smell of tea, how she would attack almost anything I said, out of principle (*problematizing* it, was her term), how she'd change tacks in the middle of a claim, contradict herself, and if I tried to point out the fallacy would denounce me as a demagogue. The sound of her black leather jacket as she reached across the table for my arm. The incense smell of her bedroom. The sensation, like fingertips gently descending, as our skin joined and unjoined in making love.

I thought of her room. The books in a bookcase of stolen planking and cinder blocks. Her clothes over a chair. Her futon with the oddly floral duvet on it. I thought of the end table by her bed, the ashtray made out of a cracked Peter Rabbit china cup. The partially opened drawer. The unopened letters to a woman I could never know.

"It's a fairly common thing, these days," Gould continued, "at least amongst women. Particularly women who've been abused. Take a new name as a way of taking charge of their own identity."

"If only it was that easy," I said.

"The funny thing is, I grew up believing that my parents' break-up was simply a result of the sexual thing, but in fact, now that I know my mother better, I realize that that second secret, the broken promise, was probably more important."

"Well, he didn't exactly break the promise. More like he weaseled out of it."

"The first election. But, apparently, my father also promised, after the first victory, that he would only serve one term. Then he went ahead and sought re-election, without consulting my mother. They were estranged by that point, according to my mother, so the whole issue was left unspoken. He just pretended that he had forgotten the original promise or that he hadn't made it, and she was off trying to understand who she was and how she had ended up in a silver cage."

"Your father, the man of principle."

"You remember his campaign against the latest round of constitutional proposals? Two, three years ago. He looked like a Roman senator on the news, toga around him, orating to a packed assembly. The man of reason . . . ."

Now it was Gould's turn to grow thoughtful. He looked into his coffee cup and frowned, as if disappointed, somehow, that it contained only coffee (though this was the umpteenth time he had checked). He lifted the cup, threw back his head, then set the cup back down again. He raised one long finger.

"I grew up with that," he said, looking at the finger. "The principle of non-contradiction: If A is the answer, then not-A cannot be the answer too. All my life I've had to live with a father who says things like this . . . ."

Gould raised himself up and adopted an oratorical pose—the one finger raised, other hand on his heart (rather like the Tin Man in *The Wizard of Oz*).

"What is wanted here," he intoned, "as in any province or country, is law, good faith, order, security. Anyone can declaim about these things, but a businessman like myself pins his faith to material interests. Why? Because only let the material interests once get a firm footing, and they are bound to impose the conditions on which alone they can continue to exist. Conditions of law, good faith, order, and security. That's how your money-making is justified in the face of lawlessness and disorder. It is justified because the security which money-making demands must be shared with the people. A better justice comes as a result."

"Is that a quote?" I asked.

Gould tapped the side of his head with his finger. "Family legacy."

"No wonder your father haunts you."

"Who says I'm haunted by him?"

"It's rather obvious."

"Yes, well, I admit, I've spent a lot of my life rationalizing away things about my father. Even when I came to know my mother again, and to love her and respect her, I still didn't believe a lot of what she'd said or written about him. Come to think of it, I was still rationalizing about my father when that letter arrived last Friday."

"And now?"

"You tell me . . . ."

Chapter Ten

As he climbed the steps to the Regional Headquarters at Cramdown, Gould thought briefly of his brother. How he wished he was more like him. Glen, in this situation, would have been working himself up, would have been preparing for a stellar confrontation with O'Brien, a supernova of ego colliding with ego: ID wristed onto the desk, lip snarled, exit taken with a prima donna's swirl of cloak. *Take this job and shove it* as libretto to Wagner.

But this was not Glen Gould (The Other One) pushing through the circular door of the Regional HQ. This was not Glen Gould returning the desk sergeant's nod of recognition, not Glen Gould at the elevators. No, this was only Charles Gould: a man who believed that a measured response was always the best response. A man who still believed, in spite of—or because of—all the violence he had been witness to, in the value of civility. A man who always held himself ready for the judges' marks.

O'Brien's office was on the top floor, the fifth, one floor above Gould's own. This floor was always quieter than the others, but at the moment it seemed entirely deserted. It was, after all, past six o'clock on a Friday night and though police work goes on twenty-four hours a day, the administration of police work is mostly nine-to-five. He passed no one along the long carpeted hallway down which he now walked. Two or three closed doors, then the frosted glass of the outer part of O'Brien's office. Through the clear glass portion of the door he could see O'Brien's secretary still at his desk. His name, he remembered, was Martin.

"The superintendent is waiting for you," Martin said. "You can leave your coat there."

He led Gould to a wide wooden door with a brass knob. Without knocking, Martin reached for the knob, turned it, and let the door ride gently inward. Gould hesitated a moment before the opening. He watched as Martin went over to the coat-rack and—passing by Gould's recently hung trench coat—lifted down his own heavy jacket.

When he stepped inside he saw that O'Brien was watching a television screen set into the wall beside his desk. The office was long-shaped and softly lit. The richness of the dark-green carpet gave him the impression of treading on velvet. O'Brien sat in front of wall-length, drawn curtains, also green; on the wooden desk before him was a green-shaded lamp, a computer, and a neat stack of papers and files. Even when Gould was fully in the room O'Brien did not turn his head. O'Brien's heavy face, lifted slightly so that it accentuated the line of his nose, looked both formidable and intelligent. He held a remote control in his hand and seemed totally absorbed in what was happening on the screen.

The Senate
Government of Canada

Dear Charles:

It is a matter of some pride to me that we have kept our respect for each other all these years. Though we have had our differences, and sometimes quite violent differences, I feel we have achieved the kind of mutual accommodation that could be a model between peoples, not to mention a model for the often vexed relations between fathers and sons. I realize that I have rarely spoken to you of love. I will not, therefore, engage in the hypocrisy of a grandiloquent expression of love now. Let me just say that I care for you, Charles, as father to son, and as one man to another. In short, your opinion matters to me.

So it is with a deep trepidation that I write to you now about a matter that I fear will lower your opinion of me, that may indeed, if you do not grant the adequacy of my explanations, permanently undermine the respect that I feel is the bedrock of our relationship. I will not be coy with you: it has to do with the murder of Enrique and Camilla Soledad. Word has come to me, it doesn't matter how, that you have been assigned to the case; the same sources helped me track you to the place where I now send you this letter. The point is this. When you have probed deeply enough into the case, you may very well discover that I, your father, Senator Robert Reginald William Gould, am complicit in the murders.

Let me explain. As you investigate the financial structure of the Cyclops Silver Mine—as you inevitably will, I know, exemplary investigator that you are—you will discover that Cyclops Silver is in fact 65% owned by an American mining concern called Amalgamated Silver and Bauxite of Houston, Texas. A.S.&B. is in turn controlled, through a series of holding companies, by our own Canadian Candough Corporation, of which I am member of the Board. When you have traced things back this far—as I know you will—you will discover that the Directors of Candough, worried about the profitability of Cyclops Silver, recently issued direct operating orders to it. In short, there are documents insisting that Lena Stahr take any steps necessary to safeguard the profitability of the mine.

This may sound harmless enough, but the context of the order—the history behind it—suggests otherwise. The general context, of course, is the strike and the frankly union-busting tactics Stahr has adopted in response to it (with the acquiescence, if not outright approval of the Board). The more specific context is a letter by Stahr detailing her difficulties in maintaining profits at the mine. In this letter she singled out Enrique and Camilla Soledad as workers who posed special security and financial problems for her. She said—without giving reasons—that she could not fire them. In response to this letter, the Board sent its terse imperative. The actual words we used were: "And in regard to your difficulty with E. and C. Soledad, you must take any steps necessary to maintain profit levels."

I think we expected Stahr to fire the Soledads. We simply ignored or discounted her assertion that she could not do so. But if you know anything about Lena Stahr, how much she loves that mine and how much pressure she has been under since the strike (partly as a result of actions by the Candough Board)—you know it was a recipe for disaster.

Let me emphasize that I have no proof that Stahr was actually involved in the murder. In a way, it is immaterial. The point is that the political damage to the board members—that they should have given such an order in such a context—will occur in any case once the connections are made (and I know they will, with you on the case, whether or not the actual documents are produced or not). I will not patronize you by listing the other prominent individuals at present on the Candough Board.

Also let me say that at the time of the order I had certain qualms but, ultimately, it seemed to me to be the right decision from a business point of view. It seemed to me that as a member of the Board it was my first responsibility to take good business decisions. At the moment, however, I deeply regret that we did not think things more carefully through. I feel responsible. This is the main reason why I am breaking Board confidentiality to reveal this matter to you. I will, of course, be forced to resign as a result.

I realize this puts you in a terrible position, Charles. It would have been infinitely worse for both of us, however, had you uncovered these connections on your own. I will not presume to tell you what I think your response should be. You will of course take the steps necessary to guard your own integrity.

Nothing would please me more than for you to clear what may soon become a stain upon our family name. Unfortunately, as I said, proving that someone else actually committed the murders is not likely to save us from a good deal of embarrassment. I hope only that this embarrassment will not extend into the relationship that you and I have for so many years managed to maintain.

Your affectionate father, R.R.W. Gould.

Gould took three or four steps. From his improved angle he could see that O'Brien was watching the news, a demonstration of some sort on Parliament Hill, shots of a crowd, placards, the talking head of a reporter. Something about cutbacks, a coalition—the sound was too low to make out clearly. For perhaps ten more seconds O'Brien watched. Then, suddenly, he zapped the television dead and laid the remote on a corner of the desk.

"It's important to stay up with the times."

Gould made no reply. He stood half the room away, at attention, his briefcase against one thigh. He held this pose until it became clear that the superintendent was waiting for him to speak. Then, for some reason, he could not leap into what he had come for. So—rather awkwardly—he said, "I hate television. Never watch it."

The superintendent smiled. "You are a throw-back, Gould, in more ways than one. And why do you hate it?"

"Besides the poor programming, I find that a television dominates any room it is in."

"But if you don't want to watch you can just turn it off. You just pick up your remote and . . . we all have that privilege."

"I still find it tyrannical."

"Come, come, Gould. It's not like the thing is two-way you know."

Gould stifled his response. Not yet. Glen, no doubt, would have said it out loud.

There was another pause, and this time Gould was determined not to fill it. Eventually, O'Brien rose from his chair and strode deliberately to within arm's reach. Close enough to touch Gould. Or strike him. The intimacy of it was magnified by the soundless carpet.

"Shall I say it, or will you?" O'Brien said.

"I will," said Gould. "I have come here to withdraw from the Soledad investigation and to register my extreme—"

The superintendent waved him off. "I thought that's what it was." He took Gould by the elbow and directed him to a sofa and chair. "Sit down, Charles, sit down. Before you say anything else we better have a drink."

He sat Gould on the sofa and turned to a liquor cabinet that soon unhid itself from the wood paneling. Inside was a decanter, from which he poured two glasses.

"It is called wine," said O'Brien with a faint smile. "You will have read about it in books, no doubt."

He passed Gould a very full glass and settled himself in the overstuffed chair.

"Now, drink. Then, before you tell me why you are withdrawing from the case, I want to say something."

They both drank.

"I've been watching you Charles," O'Brien said. "I've been watching your work over the last few years. And, generally, I like what I see. Just the other day, I was reviewing a case file of yours—the Vander Hoff file—at the request of the Attorney General's office, and I was admiring the work you had done on it. Treading so carefully through that political mine field. You reported the facts and made your recommendations with real clarity and balance. So clear and balanced there was a kind of elegance to it."

"Hardly elegant."

"I mean it as a compliment. Your writing, in fact, if I may say so, reminded me a little of your father's. The cogency of it, without, of course, the political bombast."

The mention of his father made Gould narrow his eyes.

"You know my father?" he asked.

"Everybody knows your father," O'Brien laughed. "Though I am one of the few, probably, to have read his political writings."

The superintendent poured more wine. While he did so, Gould drew his briefcase up onto his lap.

"The point is, Charles, that I think you could go very far in this profession. You could be a real credit to your family. To your family name. Except that . . . well, you still have one or two things to learn."

"What things?"

"All in good time. First, drink up. This is a quality merlot. And then, I suppose we shall have to deal with whatever it is you have for me there in your briefcase."

Gould had another swallow. O'Brien, his large body relaxed in the overstuffed chair, did the same. Then Gould set his glass back down, popped the catches on his briefcase, and took out the letter he had received two hours before.

O'Brien, with a faintly ironical shrug, accepted the letter from Gould's outstretched hand.

He adjusted his glasses. And read.

Gould sipped his wine. He now felt a small contradictory flush of euphoria, a symptom of that early stage with alcohol when you've had just enough to want some more. He did, two sips, three.

O'Brien lowered the pages. "That's it?"
"There has to be more?"
"Is there?"

Gould came forward on the sofa. Euphoria gone. A moment of adrenaline-induced clarity. "I think there is more. I think there is a whole lot more."

O'Brien shrugged. He reached for his wine, the letter crumpling on his lap.

Gould cleared his brief-case away and sat ramrod straight. He flattened his hands on his thighs—his interrogation posture. "You knew about this, didn't you?"

"That your father sent you a letter?"

"That he was potentially implicated in the investigation."

O'Brien ran a finger around the rim of his glass. "I did." Then he chuckled. "Really, Charles. What did you think? That I deliberately put you in an impossible situation? Could I be that Machiavellian?"

"I don't know. I really don't know."

The two men stared at each other, the seconds ticking off silently and disappearing into the forest depths of the room. Gould's blue eyes gleamed with moisture—a sign of the emotions dammed up within him. O'Brien's face was a paradox. It was deeply lined, scored, as if it contained a visible trace of every expression it had ever made, and yet the accumulative effect was one of expressionlessness, inscrutability.

"You know what I feel like?" Gould said suddenly. "I feel like running off somewhere, doing something reckless, crazy. I feel like fighting a war or hacking a thousand mile trail through the jungle."

"Lose yourself in action, Charles?" O'Brien spoke gently, but with a father's slightly mocking, critical edge. "Well, action does have this much going for it: *it is the enemy of thought and the friend of flattering illusion.* A novelist—a great writer—said that."

O'Brien laughed again. He raised his glass in a mock toast. "Drink up. Drink your wine. It's not as terrible as all that. Here, let me show you something."

Reluctantly, as O'Brien hovered over him, Gould reached for his glass again, lifted it, and tipped it against his lips. The wine had a musky taste, an old taste, a complex taste that was all the more seductive for its complexity. O'Brien topped up the glass again. Then he signaled for Gould to stay put, stepped between the serving table and the overstuffed chair, and padded softly across the carpet to his desk. From behind, his grey business suit seemed slightly rumpled, creased, like his face—with a similarly ambiguous effect.

O'Brien reached across his desk for a stack of files. He turned the stack around so that the labels were right side up, sifted three or four files, and shuffled some other papers that Gould could not see. A moment later he was back in his chair.

"If push came to shove," he said, patting the manila folder now across his knees, "I would deny that this file actually exists. And I'm not going to let you read what's inside of it. But, see, look—it has your name on it. This, Charles, is your personnel file. Not your official file. Your other one. Note how thick it is."

"But that's outrageous. All officers have a right to review their—"

"Don't be naive Charles. And don't worry. You misunderstand me entirely if you think there is anything sinister about this. In point of fact, there isn't much in this file that is damaging to you. A lot of it, in fact, is family history. I have a great regard for historical information, even if, from what I understand, you do not." O'Brien slapped the folder onto the serving table between them. He tapped it with his fingers. "All this means, Charles, is that I know you better than you think."

Gould stared at the folder almost brushing his knee. Out of reach. He could see the unreadable smile of the pages within, more than an inch of white paper. For a moment he had a vision of himself as Glen, on his feet, in a rage, about to . . . he wasn't sure what. Then, something in O'Brien's voice, a sapping combination of reassurance and threat, made the vision fade. He held his place.

"This is how I know you are not really interested in running off. In losing yourself in action. For one thing, you've done that before, when you were twenty-two, when you joined the Force in the first place. Not a terrible motive, of course, and not all that unusual actually, though it is a little like becoming a priest in order to deal with a crisis of faith. But here's the other thing. This file tells me that in spite of—or because of—your original motives, you have proven yourself to be an exemplary officer. A potentially great officer. You are talented and committed. You live and breath police work. Somehow, I just don't think you could imagine yourself doing anything else.

"But let me tell you something else. This file tells me that some of the way you are, your emphasis on absolute neutrality and impartiality, this manner, though commendable in many ways, is also an extreme reaction. A reaction to what you were running away from at twenty-two when you joined the Force. I guess I should say who you were running away from, because you were, of course, running away from your father. That's all in here. You wanted to distinguish yourself from him, to show that you were different. You wanted to be a-political. A worthwhile ideal, Charles, but you can take it too far. I mean, when you come right down to it, is what we do here really that much different from what your father does?"

"It's totally different."

"Why?"

"Because my father is a partisan. He takes sides."

"And we are just neutral upholders of due authority?"

"At our best."

"You are a throw-back, Charles. You really are. It is one of your most admirable qualities, but really, at a certain point . . . ." O'Brien chuckled into his glass for a moment. Then he took a sip and grew serious again. "Well, of course, you are right to a certain extent. We do try to be neutral in our enforcement of the law. We try to be balanced. That's why I admired—still do admire—your handling of the Vander Hoff affair. But you know and I know that laws don't just happen. Laws come about because politicians put them there. And there are good laws and not-so-good laws, just as there are good politicians and not-so-good politicians."

"It's not our job to decide what laws are good or not."

"Of course not. Not in that simplistic sense. But think of the implications of what I've just said. Let's face it, there are times when we on the Force have ideas for how the law should be—or not be. And in cases like that, there are politicians we can work with, politicians who are proven friends, and politicians who are not. We are not just disinterested bystanders, you know. We also have our vision of what is best for the country. And in our own way, either by working to have the law changed or by working with the discretion we always have in enforcement, we work towards that vision. Sometimes, in very rare cases, it is necessary to exercise this discretion to its fullest degree, to bend the law, if you will, in order to protect a larger vision of the law. It happens. You can choose to see that or not."

"And if I don't?"
"To choose not to see it is a choice too."
"Not to choose is to choose?"
"Well, yes. If you put it that way."
"Do you know what that sounds like?"
"What?"
"Double-think. Not to choose is to choose. Bend the law to protect the law. It's like *War is Peace* and *Freedom is Slavery*."
"That's a harsh judgement, Charles. I'm just trying to fill you in on some of the political reality that shapes our work. The living, modern—I might even say postmodern—reality we work with every day. We are impartial and partial at the same time. We are neutral and political at the same time. Those are the facts. And you are caught up in them whether you choose to acknowledge it or not."

There was a long silence. Time passed. For some reason, Gould remembered a sophomoric argument he had once overheard about time. How if a second were infinitely divisible, then, theoretically, a second was infinitely long. Say a bullet was fired at a target and the bullet needed one second to travel the distance between the target and the gun. To reach the target the bullet would have to pass the 1/2 second mark, the 3/4 second mark, the 4/5 second mark and so on. Problem was, there could be an infinite number of such marks, and if the bullet had to pass them all, wouldn't that take an infinity? At the time, Charles had thought, "Why don't you fire a gun at your head and find out?" But now, in the office of Superintendent O'Brien, what he thought of was the heads of Camilla and Enrique Soledad. Those black openings that each closed a life. And the hands, elsewhere.

O'Brien cleared his throat. "The long of the short of it, Charles, is that you are to remain on the case."
"But why?"
"The philosophical answer, I suppose, is that I think it is important for you, at this point in your career, to be caught up. To choose to be caught up instead of choosing not to choose. But the real answer is more directly political. In point of fact, my reasoning hasn't changed since I first assigned you to the case. I still value your judgement. I still think you are the man for the job. I still expect you to operate with the professionalism, the tact, the political savvy, with which you always have. But with one small difference."

"I can't believe you expect me to cover up—"

"Not cover-up, Charles. Not at all. I want you to investigate the murders in your usual thorough manner. The point is only this. Regardless of the outcome of the investigation, we need someone in charge who will ensure that the Candough Board's actions come to light only if absolutely necessary. And that someone, by every indication, is you."

"Because if they come to light I will implicate my own father."

"Well, think of the positive side: because you are such a professional. So a-political that you would not allow any political damage to individuals unless absolutely warranted by the facts. But, yes, let's be honest, it's also because of your father. Your father, you might say, is an added security."

"But what about my conflict of interest?"

"Charles, Charles, you haven't been listening. Look, I'll make a deal with you. If the investigation takes a decisive turn towards the Candough Board, you can bring the details back to me and I will take you off the case. We can say at that point that we just found out about your father's potential involvement. No one will ever know except you, me, and your father, of course."

"And what if, here and now, what if I choose not to take the case?"

"Well. At this point you have two options. You can either carry on with the case or resign from the Force. Surely, under the circumstances, you must see that there is no other option."

He did know.

He was, after all, Charles Gould.

More time passed. Gould felt like he was sinking into the green carpet at his feet. He reached up and pressed his moustache, hard, until he tasted blood inside his lip. Then he lowered his hand again.

"Just tell me this," he said, softly, almost in a whisper. "My father's letter—it was prompted, wasn't it? Someone at Candough has already leaked a copy of the Board's directive to Lena Stahr. Maybe Stahr's letter too. To the press. Or to us. Or both. Isn't that so?"

"What makes you think that?"

"My father would never have volunteered that kind of information on his own. Especially not to me. He would never have violated board confidentiality."

O'Brien sipped his wine. "Let's just say that your father, besides having been a long-time friend of the Force, has always been a very astute politician."

"But those documents could be evidence."

"There are complexities to this case that you are better off not knowing about, Charles. At the moment they would be needless distractions. If, later on, you need to know about them, trust me, I will fill you in."

"And if the press happens upon these complexities while I am still on the case?"

"Unlikely. Steps—steps that you needn't bother yourself about—have been taken."

"But the ownership of the mine is on public record."

"True. But the ownership structure is convoluted enough to make it unlikely any reporter will trace it all the way through. Reporters don't like that kind of hard research. Besides, if you are worried about your father, remember that he is going to resign. By the time anyone knows anything, he will already be on the high ground. Now . . . ." O'Brien set his glass aside. All at once he looked like a busy official not pleased at having been disturbed. "You have an investigation to get back to, Charles. An investigation to run, in your usual exemplary fashion."

Before he took his leave, Gould made a show of throwing back another full glass of wine. He had trouble closing the catches on his briefcase. When he pushed himself to his feet, he swayed unsteadily, theatrically, and O'Brien rose to help. Their bodies met. The superintendent staggered back two steps, three, and just barely avoided bruising himself on the arm of the overstuffed chair. Gould doubled over for a second and then, abruptly, straightened again. With exaggerated dignity he marched for the door. O'Brien caught up with him just as his hand found the brass knob and suggested that he let him call a cab, but Gould, ramrod straight and ready for the judges, declared that he intended to walk.

Only afterwards, when he had closed the door again and had started back to his desk, did O'Brien notice the empty place on the table where the personnel file had been.

III

WITHOUT A COMPASS

There are some people who boast that they have never carried a compass and they can find their way around . . . as well as anyone. It is no surprise to anyone knowledgeable . . . that search and rescue efforts are commonly needed to find these people.

> E. L. Faulkner, *Introduction to Prospecting*

Chapter Eleven

Why did Gould remain on the case? I've never quite figured it out myself. I mean, what could be more damning, more a violation of the professional code by which Gould seemed to live, than to carry on as if he didn't know—or didn't care—that his father might be implicated in the murders? And yet, on the surface, that is precisely what happened. Most likely, Gould was ensnared by mixed motives, the usual cat's cradle of yearnings and fears and feelings of obligation . . . exactly the kind of tangle I know too well myself. Part of him probably hoped that he could exonerate his father somehow, even as another part of him craved to expose his father's guilt. Part of him believed he should submit to O'Brien's authority, while another part of him was bent on revenge. One moment he thought he glimpsed a way out, a glimmering solution for his own life that was, improbably, connected to the mystery of the Soledads. The next moment he bitterly rejected any possibility of a solution. For a while he imagined himself acting like Glen, going on a rampage, belching in the face of authority, but then something else—the proverbial voice inside—reminded him that he was not Glen but Charles Gould. And then another voice, a voice that seemed at once most alien to him and closest to his heart, pointed out that the nature of "Charles Gould" was very much an open question.

The only direct comment he made to me about it came out of the blue, two days after his long night of confessions, when he said, "A failure of the imagination."

"What?"

"That's why I stayed on the case. I just couldn't imagine an alternative."

It was a funny comment, said that way, at that moment, as if the question had just been asked. It reminded me of the strange transitions in his speech during the night he told me so much. In fact, we hadn't talked about anything significant since that night, not about the Soledad case or his father or Archie or why he got involved in police work. All I knew about what happened after the confrontation with O'Brien was that Gould had gone for a long walk, leaving the HQ and the business district of Cramdown behind. Eventually, he found himself on a path overlooking the Thompson River. There were leaves drifting down, almost invisible, around him; now and then one would brush his cheek like a black butterfly. A stray dog hooked up with him for a while and sniffed and trotted and bumped against his briefcase, and for the second time in recent memory he wished he had a horse. He found a rock, mossy and cold but relatively dry, and sat down to stare out at the river, the water oozing along like a slowly moving channel of oil flecked here and there with light from nearby houses.

By the time he arrived back at his apartment, it was after nine o'clock. His thighs ached. He was queasy from lack of food but also, after so much exertion, past hunger. He turned on a light and dropped his trench coat, uncharacteristically, on a chair. Then went into the kitchen. There he turned on another light and placed his briefcase on the table. He set the briefcase down carefully, as if he were setting down a tray of tea things. He turned the combination lock. Shot the catches.

Inside was the file he had taken from O'Brien.

For a while he just stood there, staring at the file, the pale flesh colour of the folder, the white at three edges attesting to the bulk within. Then he turned away.

He set up the coffee maker for the morning, spooning the fresh grounds, that aromatic soil, slowly into the filter. He walked a not-really-dirty dish towel to the laundry basket. He went into the bathroom, turned on a third light, and splashed water on his face. He did not look in the mirror.

Finally, back in the kitchen, he sat down, lifted the file out with two hands and elbowed the briefcase away. At first he placed the file in an upright position so that he could read the green-edged tab—*Gould, Charles Robert*—then, all at once, he spun it ninety degrees and opened it like a book.

The top page was blank.

The others were also blank. All of them.

For a long time, he just stared at that mound of bleached nothingness, that empty text that had masqueraded as his life, his face, like the blankness itself, absolutely unreadable.

Then he went to bed.

"You mean O'Brien was right?" I asked.

"Pardon?"

"Didn't O'Brien say that you could never imagine yourself other than a cop?"

"He did."

"So he was right, eh?"

Gould hated to admit that O'Brien was right about anything. He stood with his back to his car trying to think of a way out of it, or maybe playing the silence game he was so fond of, though now with the new posture that had grown on him since his confessions. It's hard to describe exactly what this posture was. To someone who didn't know him well, he probably looked the same, still erect, chin up, eyes with their usual level assessing gaze, but in fact his bearing had softened, there was something less ramrod about it, as if his body had deteriorated somehow or become more human from within.

Finally, he pressed a finger against his moustache, his favourite gesture (or a parody of his favourite gesture), and said, "It just took me a couple of extra weeks."

"To imagine yourself—"

"—differently. Yes."

"How so?"

"I've decided to quit the Force."

"Quit the Force? But what will you—"

"I don't know what I'll do. Ultimately. I want my life to be a blank page—like that bogus file—for a while. In the short term, though, I'm going to take a holiday."

"Go riding?"

He shook his head. "Travel. To Costaguana."

I was, of course, dumbfounded. Afterwards I realized it was perfectly logical, so many elements in his life pointed to it, but at the time, like the file with the blank pages, it contained too many possibilities for me to properly grasp.

But I'm getting ahead of myself.

So.

Gould, for whatever reasons, stayed on the case.

The morning after his confrontation with O'Brien was overcast but calm. An indistinct day, no wind or rain or snow. The maple trees outside Gould's apartment were mostly bare, the last leaves clinging to the branches with a brittle, fragile look. One good blow, or one solid snowfall, would clear them off.

He had a large breakfast, two boiled eggs and three pieces of toast, as well as juice and the coffee he had set up the night before. He listened to part of the morning show on CBC radio. He finished dressing, a bit confused at first when his trench coat was not in the hall closet, and then, because he had left his car in the HQ parking lot the night before, set out walking to work.

The walk was very pleasant. Only a few Saturday vehicles passed him along Columbia Street. Leaves were drifted against curbs, into the wheel hubs of parked cars, in flowerbeds, across lawns. His breath steamed as he strode along.

The HQ was a grey cube of concrete and glass a couple of blocks from the downtown. It stood with its back to the river, not far from the metal span of the Yellowhead Bridge. Out front there was a sculpture that showed four bronze workers leaning together to raise an obelisk of granite, rather like the famous staged photograph of the American marines raising the flag on Iwo Jima.

He climbed the stairs and pushed in the circular door.

The thing to do, he had decided, was to go back to the beginning, back to the scene of the crime, or at least what was left of that scene in the crime lab. Which meant spending time with Sergeant Bacon.

Detective Sergeant Roger Bacon was in charge of the forensic lab. He greeted Gould in his windowless basement office, a short, roundish man, somewhere between forty and fifty, with thick brown hair except for a gleaming bald spot on the crown of his head. He had the suggestion of jowls, pinkish eyes, and a milky complexion, perhaps from spending too much time under artificial light. Gould had always liked him, his monkish discipline and attention to detail, his boyish enthusiasm for all the latest technical gizmos meant to aid in investigation. Like many police officers, Bacon shared a certain fatalism about the times in which he lived. No doubt things were going to rot, to pot, youth crime was up, crack was available on every second street corner, the poison of gangs was creeping from the big cities into the whole body of the country. Instead of following the usual line of argument, however, and maintaining that the solution was more prisons and cops, and cops with bigger guns, Bacon argued that the corruption was best fought through knowledge: study the principles of human psychology, study the fundamentals of matter, know some biology, economics, sociology, and—his pet peeve—invest in new scientific technologies, laser-scopes and infrared sensors and computers.

When it came to technology, Gould and Bacon had had many friendly arguments. The first time they worked together, Bacon was incredulous that Gould did not use a miniature tape recorder on the job. Gould, in turn, said that he was for anything that improved the close reading of the scene, but that in his opinion too much technology was a threat to the human element. For Gould, the key to any investigation was the watchful human observer with a pencil and notebook.

"One thing I have to say from the start," said Sergeant Bacon, this Saturday morning, "it seems like some of these items were planted."

"The nuggets?"

"Case in point. They were indeed composed mainly of silver ore, as you suspected. Here, let me show you the results of our mineral analyses."

Bacon punched some keys on his computer and swiveled the monitor so that Gould could see. A graph appeared on the screen, along with some writing below. "Trace elements," explained Bacon. Then he pushed a key and the screen cleared and a new graph appeared. "This one shows silver content."

"Commercial grade?" Gould asked.

"The nuggets were very similar. Each assayed out to about eighty-five ounces a tonne. How profitable would depend on the costs of production."

"Okay. What else?"

Bacon settled back in his chair, one of those swivel jobs with the high-tech back supports. Gould leaned towards him with his hands spread wide on the desk top. Besides the computer terminal and keyboard, the desk contained various files and papers and photographs associated with the Soledad case. The actual physical evidence was now boxed up and locked away in a storage vault.

"The shoe in the tree," said Bacon. "We found numerous microscopic elements in it, nylon fibers, blood traces that matched those of the victim."

"A blister?"

"On her heel. Absolutely nothing unusual. But in a tree?"

"It's a haunting image, I know. I've thought about it a number of times myself. Now and then I have this absurd notion that if I could figure out how it got there, the rest of the case would just fall into place."

"Maybe the killer was trying to tease you with it. Taunt you."

"Some people in the town think that the victims themselves put it there. A last heroic act to mark the scene of their own murder."

"Unlikely."

"Or it could have been put up by chance. Maybe Camilla Soledad lost her shoe as she was being dragged along and someone, later, found it."

"Found the shoe but not the bodies?"

"It's possible."

Bacon sighed. "You know, this case has a diabolic aura about it. Even just working with the physical evidence, there is something so flagrant, so premeditated. As if we are meant to read everything symbolically. Even an old scientist like myself...."

Gould now pushed himself back off the desk. He stood straight and smoothed his jacket with his left hand. Meanwhile Bacon surveyed the papers before him, lowering his head so that he had a frog's throat, and then reached out with a pudgy finger and tapped a photograph clear of a pile.

"Take the twenty-six cents found on the ground near the bodies. A quarter, a penny. You can't see them in this but the red circles show you where they were. Now, there were no usable traces on these coins;

from their position, it looks like they just fell out of the male victim's shirt pocket. But, look—"

Bacon pulled out another photograph. A close-up of the coins. "What are the chances?" he said.

"I remember collecting Centennial coins when they first came out."

"You and every other kid in the country. So what are the chances of someone today, thirty years later, having two of them at the same time?"

"Pretty slight."

"Or the beer can," Bacon continued, pulling another photograph. "It's hard to see how this fits into the *modus operandi*. A professional killer is not likely to have stopped to have a beer. There were also print-fragments on the can, not enough to identify anyone, but enough to suggest that whoever drank the beer was not concerned about leaving prints. So, you might be tempted to think of the can as unconnected, just an item left accidently at the scene, something dropped there before the crimes were committed."

"Except?"

"Except the beer was Banner Premium Ale."

"American. That's not unusual these days."

"No. But have you seen the TV commercials?"

"I don't watch television."

"The old resistance to technology . . . . Well, you should sometimes, Inspector, you know, just for what you would learn there. Sometimes it pays to keep up."

"So I've been told. What about the commercials?"

"Probably it's too much of a co-incidence. So flagrant it's practically literary. But in the commercials the nickname for the beer is The Silver Streak."

Gould lowered his eyebrows.

"It's like, with the coins, the killer might just as well have draped a Canadian flag over the bodies. And with the beer can, well, it's yet another allusion to silver."

"Like the nuggets."

"Like the rope with silver threads in it."

"A reference back to the town or to the Cyclops Mine or to another mine."

"A reference to a hidden treasure? See what I mean?"

"Yes and no. To me the nuggets, at least, seem like a signature, the killer's way of saying 'I did this.' Maybe, if we can find out whose signature they represent then we will know why the Soledads were killed."

"Well, Inspector, I'm glad it's your job to sort it all out, not mine. Too many coincidences for me."

Bacon and Gould talked this way for much of the morning, sifting through the mass of information generated by the forensics lab on the evidence from the crime scene. Gould, as usual, took careful notes, but only one item jumped out at him as an immediately promising lead. This was the cigarette butt found near the bodies. By using a series of elaborate techniques, including chemical samples of the paper and identification of certain additives in the tobacco (Sergeant Bacon had tried to explain the method in detail but Gould asked him to get to the point), the lab had identified the brand name.

"You won't find these in Canada," said the Sergeant. "Not in the U.S. either. They're only available south of the American border."

"Yes?"

"*Producto Equis*," Bacon said triumphantly. "That would translate as—"

"Brand X."

"Right. Manufactured in Guanajuato, Mexico. Available throughout Central and South America, as I said, but not available here."

The rope, on the other hand, turned out to be a disappointment. When asked about it, Sergeant Bacon turned up his palms in an empty-handed gesture. "I faxed pictures and descriptions to more than a dozen military experts, as you requested, but no luck. They all agreed it could have come from a military uniform, but nobody could tell which one. Probably nothing Canadian. I also asked Chris Keep, our best police historian, and he doubted if it was braid from a police uniform. The problem is that there are thousands of different uniforms in the world. In fact, as more than one person pointed out, the smaller the military the more likely it is to have elaborate uniforms for its soldiers."

So the morning went. At the end of the discussion, Sergeant Bacon sat back in his chair. "You know," he said, "over the years I've developed a pretty good sense of how long an investigation will take. A gut reaction to the forensic evidence. But with this case, I honestly don't know. On the one hand, it seems so solvable, as if everything is there, laid out, planted for us to find. On the other hand, the very deliberateness of it fills me with doubt. Maybe all the evidence was planted to mislead us.

"Take 'silver' again. So much seems to point back to something about 'silver' as the key. But the sheer number of things that point back to it, it's like a word that has so many meanings attached to it that it becomes unintelligible.

"And another thing. I have this strange feeling, like I've seen this m. o. before. Not just the execution style, which is common enough, but the surrounding clues. I ran the details through our computer and cross-checked every data bank we have access to, but nothing. I don't know. With the technology today, if someone had killed this way before in North America or even Europe I should have gotten a match. Or maybe I'm just reacting to the case itself. Like I said, I'm glad you're the one who has to figure it out."

Gould spent the afternoon in his office. During that time, he made two phone calls. The first was to Sergeant Viola in Vancouver.

"I interrogated Sherwood and Berry this morning," the sergeant reported. "They wouldn't say boo about Goodwin. Nothing good, nothing bad, no history. They weren't much more helpful about themselves. What they claim is that they found the silver bars in one of the deserted mine shafts near, but not on, the Cyclops property. There are dozens of those, apparently. They say they might be able to find the place again but maybe not: it was very far off in the bush and they came across it at night."

"What were they doing in the bush, at night, near the Cyclops property?"

"I put the question to them, of course. They said they had a right to be there, it was public land, and they weren't going to say anything more."

"What about the bars themselves?"

"Eight bars, about twenty-five kilos each. The distinguishing symbols on the bars had been obliterated, which is what spooked the dealer they were trying to sell them to."

"Two hundred kilos. That works out to about thirty thousand dollars."

"And something else. Sherwood and Berry are being represented by a hotshot lawyer retained by the Brotherhood of Mineworkers Union. He says his clients are going to make a claim for the silver as found treasure. He's also made a stink about us holding them over the weekend. If we don't get more on the silver soon, we'll have to let them go. The Crown says we haven't got a case until the origins of the silver are more clear."

"Did you contact the Cyclops mine?"

"Surridge did. And . . . well, it's very strange. Surridge talked to Lena Stahr, twice, and Stahr claims, absolutely, that the mine is not missing any silver. They keep a very strict record of the bars they produce, she says, and everything is perfectly in order."

"You don't think their story could be true?"

"Unlikely. If they really did find the silver, if it really is found treasure, why did they try to sell it on the sly? And why did they, or someone else, obliterate the bar markings?"

"I agree. Well—looks like we'll have to let them go on Monday, but we better keep an eye on them."

"You want a surveillance team?"

"Yes. And, in fact, I have a idea for how the surveillance team should operate. Rather unusual, but it might put some pressure on Sherwood and Berry to talk. If we can get approval. And find a few extra dollars."

Then he spoke at length with Sergeant Wright. Wright summarized the findings of the various interviews conducted on Friday. Gould showed particular interest in the results of Constables Allison and Dagg.

"They managed to contact all the workers on the bus the Soledads were to have taken," reported Wright. "Nobody saw anything unusual."

"Nothing about a black Mercedes?"

"Nothing."

"I've been thinking. Did anyone mention a black van on the road that morning? A Statewide Security van, say."

"Not that I know of. A van like that would not have been unusual, would it?"

"No. But I'd like to know. Get Dagg and Allison to check, will you?"

Wright also summarized the findings of Corporal Elderkin, which confirmed what Gould had already learned about the ownership of the Cyclops mine. Elderkin's sources confirmed that the Candough group as a whole was rumoured to be in financial trouble. According to one broker, there was a story going around that at least some of the group's divisions might seek bankruptcy protection. "There'll be a huge shakedown if that happens," the broker said.

Finally and reluctantly, Gould asked about Wright's search of the Soledad house. "Miller and I spent a couple of hours there last night," Wright reported. "We decided to start up top and work our way down. So far—nothing."

"Well, carry on Sergeant. I'll be heading back first thing in the morning."

At the end of the afternoon, Gould turned in his chair to look out his fourth floor window. Down below the Thompson River flowed on, grey like the grey day. A few cars passed on the Yellowhead Bridge.

Then he packed up his briefcase.

When he left the HQ that day, Gould appeared to be his usual ramrod self. A brisk, efficient officer, a professional's professional. During the time he had worked in his office, he had stopped, once or twice, to consider that O'Brien might be only one floor above. He had wondered what O'Brien was thinking, what his plan really was. But he didn't dwell on it. In general, he had successfully relegated the question of O'Brien, just as he had relegated the blank file and the possible implication of his father, to the back of his mind. Now that he was back, now that he had decided to continue with the case, he resolved, as always, to stick to the pertinent facts.

He came down the steps of the HQ. He strode past the sculpture of the heroic workers. The obelisk, resting in the hands of the workers, was frozen at an angle in space. There was no way to tell if it was about to rise or fall.

He headed for the parking lot and did not look back.

JAMIE DOPP

CHAPTER TWELVE

Gould arrived back in Silver just before ten on Sunday morning. The unseasonal warmth of Friday had given way to a second day of something more ambiguous, a day grey but not dark, cool but not cold, one of those days when the sky is a featureless slate and you can't locate the sun. He had it in his mind to begin again at The Red Grizzly, but, at the last second, turned off at the *Silver Next Right* sign and headed into town. He steered down Queen Street with the river on his right, past houses, a couple of commercial buildings, until he reached the municipal hall. At the traffic signal he waited, the War Memorial on its postage stamp of green now on his right, and then—when the signal changed—turned left.

The wide pavement of Henry Street was almost white with age. On either side were storefronts, every fourth or fifth one vacant. Far ahead, the road seemed to disappear into the base of Flag Mountain. Obviously some snow had fallen near the peak overnight, because the mountain's distinctive crevice was now filled in. The crevice formed a long narrow shaft that, connected to a roughly rectangular glacier on top, seemed to make the shape of a flag. The shaft was at an angle so that it seemed like the flag was bending in a strong wind or, conversely, like it had just been thrown down—a great white standard draped over the blue-grey rock.

Faintly, in the distance, he heard the pealing of church bells.

He had no particular plan. During the drive from Cramdown he had mulled over various scenarios but, for some reason, he could not quite decide how to proceed. When he had turned into town, it was with a vague hope that something along the main routes of Silver would suggest his next move to him.

The burned out union office, which he drove by now, seemed like an artifact from ancient history—a weathered ruin, meaning obscured, a charred face masked with plywood. He drove past the Legion Hall, past the turn-off to Sergeant Wright's house (or former house). Then, by the RCMP station, he slowed down. This was the place, after all, to which he had reported four days before with Viola and the forensics team. It was another obvious place to start again. And yet, now that he considered it, it seemed unlikely that Breeze would be in, and, anyway, what would he talk to Breeze about? The fact was that the other inspector was likely to be more of a distraction than a help in the next while. New beginning or not, he and Breeze had a history that promised its own questions and difficulties.

Then the church bells, which were now louder, gave him an idea. He accelerated past the station and continued straight on Henry Street, over the Whatcom Creek bridge and up the hill. He found himself in a small line of cars. The cars were turning in, one by one, at the bells' source. Now he could see the blunt wooden steeple with gill-like openings from which the sound emanated.

He found an empty slot in the back parking lot and turned off his engine. Other cars filled in the gaps around him. Some women clacked by in Sunday heels.

After a while, the bells stopped. Gould waited, observing, as a few last stragglers made their way inside. Then he stepped out of his car and locked the door.

He came in through the main entrance, feeling a gust of damp human-heat as he did. The ante-chamber was empty except for one man, an usher, who stood stiffly in the archway to the church proper. Gould kept his trench coat on. He took a copy of the program of worship from the usher and indicated that he would slip into an empty spot in the last pew.

The service began with two hymns. The music triggered a memory in Gould of his early days in Fredericton. Back then, his father had taken the family to Church on Sundays—a political necessity, though his father was not, by any other indication, a religious man. For Charles as a six or seven-year-old, those Sunday morning outings were even more stressful than usual. He had a great fear of arriving at the Anglican cathedral with the fly of his pants undone, or doing something during the service, like singing out of cue or farting, that would bring shame on his father. When the family walked down the centre aisle, with a body-guard or two trailing discretely behind, all eyes were upon them. They had to wear their public faces, cheerful and dignified, and it always seemed to Charles that his clothes were too tight, that the moment he was anything but vertical his seams would split apart and he would be exposed—ridiculed. Nothing ever did rip, but always, when he settled into his place, he would feel the vice of his clothes, a squeezing of his testicles that seemed to take his breath away.

After the hymns, the congregation rustled back into their seats, setting off a muddled cloud of fragrances. Then Reverend Bentley took the pulpit.

Bentley was an impressive sight this morning. He wore a black gown over his suit, so that only the shirt and tie were visible. His curly, dark hair was combed severely back. His cheekbones stuck out whitely on either side of his long face, giving him an ascetic, almost gaunt appearance. He stepped up to the pulpit with an impression of slow strength. Before speaking, he fixed his deep-set blue eyes on the congregation. The eyes seemed tired, with a hungry distant look.

"The text for the sermon today is from Luke, chapter 8 verse 17: *For nothing is hid that shall not be made manifest, nor anything secret that shall not be known and come to light.* These words from the Holy Gospel have a special significance for us given the tragic discovery of earlier this week. I speak, of course, of the discovery of the bodies of Camilla and Enrique Soledad, two people who worshipped with us for some months earlier this year. The Soledad children, Felipe and Gabriela, must be foremost in our prayers right now. So too should be the police officers charged with discovering the perpetrators of the crime. Let us hope that the passage from Luke is prophetic of the success of the police officers' task.

"But I want to concentrate on the deeper meaning of the passage today. I want to talk about what it means for each of us, each day, that Our Lord sees, not only what we do, but into our very thoughts, our very hearts...."

And Bentley went on to give a four-square Christian sermon about sin and prayer and the need for a daily examination of conscience.

Gould was struck by the almost tragic tone Bentley assumed as he spoke. It was as if Bentley were speaking to himself, reminding himself of certain fundamental truths he had forgotten. Because Gould had never heard him preach before, he couldn't be sure if the self-critical air was usual or adopted for the occasion. In any case, it gave the words the minister spoke an added emotional charge.

Part way through the sermon, Gould became distracted. He had been listening and observing at the same time, his usual habit, his ears registering the words while his eyes slowly swept across the backs of the parishioners in front of him, when, all at once, he realized that he was sitting not ten feet from Wallace Lies. Lies was three rows up, directly on the other side of the aisle. Gould recognized his profile from photographs in the file of clippings Breeze had given him.

From that point on, Gould kept his eyes primarily on Lies. The sermon ended, there was a prayer, a collection, and a final hymn. Still Gould watched Lies, not because he thought he would learn much by this, but only to revel in the man's presence, his corporeality, after four days in which he had seemed to hover tantalizing and unreal in the margins of the investigation.

Lies's presence also made clear Gould's next step.

After the final hymn, the parishioners remained standing while Bentley gave the benediction, then, after he had left the pulpit, they began to file out. Gould stepped from his pew and prepared to intercept Wallace Lies.

Just then, he was intercepted himself.

It was a woman in a green dress. She appeared, apparently, from out of nowhere, and planted herself in his way. She held her black leather purse in both hands.

"How nice to see you, Inspector," she said. "I was wondering when I would get the honour."

The woman's smile was welcoming—more than welcoming. It was one of those smiles that had a practiced quality about it but that made you believe in it anyway, an actor's off-screen smile, the smile of someone forced by custom to offer a greeting but who was nevertheless genuinely glad to meet you. A smile that had faced the world, that had been around, that knew where to encounter any number of marvels, but that, for reasons it suggested were obvious, had chosen to concentrate on you.

Maybe it was the smile. Maybe it was the woman's sudden appearance, against all his expectations. Maybe it was the mood Gould had been in since Friday night, carrying on with his usual apparent confidence and yet also, somehow, lost. Whatever the reasons, Gould did not recognize who this woman was. Her physical features were familiar: the styled dark hair with the flicker of white, the dark eyes, kind and aloof at the same time, the classic thin nose and red mouth. The only thing different was that she seemed shorter than in the photographs, an effect no doubt of the fact that in the photographs she was always the centre of attention, always elevated metaphorically if not literally.

Stahr seemed to read his uncertainty. "But you do know who I am, Inspector?"

"I—"

"Well!" the woman said, with a disbelieving laugh. Then she smiled again, apparently without a trace of irony. "This is not getting off to a very good start, is it?"

"Ms. Stahr, I do know your name. Of course. I'm sorry, you took me by surprise for a moment."

Wallace Lies, Gould noted, had headed towards the staircase into the church annex. Another few steps and he would be out of sight.

Stahr's dark eyes took him in. "When I saw you at service this morning," she said, "it occurred to me that there were many things for us to talk about. Obviously your investigation of the murders has led you in other directions. But, if I may propose it, I think an interview with me would be helpful to you. And it would allow me to clear the air for myself."

Gould suddenly became conscious of who he was, or rather, of the role that he was playing. "Perhaps," he said, feeling instinctively for his brief-case (which was locked in his car), "perhaps I should have started with you in the first place."

"There would have been a certain logic to it."

"Yes. What do you suggest?"

"Do you have plans this afternoon?"

"I'm afraid I do." Gould glanced towards the staircase up which Wallace Lies had now disappeared.

"Unfortunate. How about tomorrow morning?"

Gould considered. This was not the way he liked to set up interviews. He liked to be very much more in charge, to suggest the time and place himself. But, as Stahr had pointed out, there was a certain logic to it. "All right."

"Why don't you come out to the house. Say around 9:30. We can talk a while and if you're interested I can give you a little tour of the mine. If you don't mind a helicopter ride, that is."

"Fine. That would be useful. However"—Gould assumed his most professional manner—"one thing. Since I have you here, I'd like to confirm something with you."

"Yes?"

"Vancouver city police tell me that you have not had any silver stolen from your mine lately."

"That's correct."

"You know the story of Sherwood and Berry?"

"I do."

"But don't you think that is odd? So much in their story hints at a theft, and where else could they find silver bars in this area? You are the only producing mine."

"I can tell you quite unequivocally, Inspector, that no silver produced in my mine has been stolen. As I am sure you are aware, I have taken great pains with security recently."

"Then I suppose it is—"

"—a mystery, Inspector. But isn't that the whole reason for your job? Until tomorrow, then."

Gould went after Wallace Lies. He was determined that he would speak to him—today. He was irritated that Lies had slipped away from him in the church and was even suspicious of Lena Stahr for stopping him like that.

In retrospect, I suspect that his determination to track Lies down hinted at the pressures building up inside of him. There was no compelling investigative purpose to be served by interviewing Lies just then. The mayor's name had come up in proximity to that of the Soledads on a couple of occasions, and Lies's earlier stalling and then invitation to talk seemed vaguely suspicious, but Gould had no real reason to assume Lies was a suspect. Maybe going after Lies was a way of proving to himself that he was back in charge again, that he made the decisions about when and where a witness would answer questions, that nothing had really changed. The irony, of course, was that he had stumbled onto the idea of interviewing Lies because of his earlier indecision. This made his decision like so much else he did over the next few days: on the surface, it seemed perfectly consistent with his earlier reputation, with his role as the professional's professional, but examined more closely, it seemed not-quite-right somehow.

He drove to the Lies house. Parked across the street. And waited.

It gave him a rather haunted feeling to see the Lies house, with its Soledad mirror image, in the daytime. Something about the light, the grey day, blurred the contrast between the two houses that had seemed so evident a few nights before. The Soledad house still showed signs of vacancy, of decay, the grass shaggy at the front, unraked leaves drifted in around the trees. But there was something dingy about the Lies home in this light as well, something that made Gould expect to see a tear in a curtain or a crack in a window. . . .

Ten minutes passed. Then he got out of the car, walked up to the door, and rang the bell.

Margaret Lies answered. She was a slim woman in black slacks and a white blouse. She had bobbed salt-and-pepper hair, dark sad eyes, and an urchin mouth that suggested alcohol and cigarettes. The bony fingers of one hand held a cigarette now. When she raised it to her mouth, Gould imagined the click of wood on wood.

"Yes?"

"My name is Inspector Charles Gould. I'm in charge of the Soledad investigation. I would like to speak to Wallace Lies, if I may."

"Wallace is not home."

"I see. And may I ask, are you Mrs. Lies?"

There was a laugh, perhaps bitter. "Yes, I'm Mrs. Lies."

"I'm sorry to interrupt you at home like this, Mrs. Lies. Just that your husband and I have been a bit a cross purposes the last few days. We had agreed to meet on Friday but I was called away. So when I saw him at church this morning . . . ."

"Would you like to know where he is?"

"I would appreciate it."

"He went to see his lover, Inspector. Surely you have been in town long enough now—how long have you been here, four days?—surely you know about his lover, this lover, by now."

"I'm afraid—"

"—Lena Stahr, Inspector. He has gone to see Lena Stahr. She summoned him this morning. I listened in on the other phone."

The revelation caused Gould a moment of vertigo.

"Perhaps," he said, "we should talk about this in more detail."

Margaret Lies opened the door wide.

"You've probably wondered about the name," Margaret Lies said.

"Excuse me?"

"Lies. Not exactly a name that immediately inspires trust, is it?"

Gould was sitting on a couch in the living room, his briefcase a faithful dog by his foot. The house, from what he could see, was designer-decorated, but in a way that too obviously drew attention to the fact. Though his own tastes ran to the minimalist, Gould understood that the most impressive rooms always had a certain accidental quality to them, a minute dissonance, something to cast doubt about whether the design was intentional. This living room, however, was too studied, the colour scheme (blue, beige, white) too perfectly adhered to, the decorations—ornate vases, matching shaded lamps, original oil-paintings in wooden frames topped with brass lamps—seemed to have invisible labels on them: *Art Object*. The effect was of an expensive but characterless hotel suite.

"He thought about changing it, back when we were just starting out. This was in the Sixties, in Vancouver. You probably don't know, but Wallace started out in insurance. At first the name seemed a terrible burden. Imagine being a salesman and having to introduce yourself as 'Lies'! But one day he had an idea. Instead of trying to apologize for his name, to downplay it, he decided to play it up, and next thing it was a great joke, a great ice-breaker, a wonderful way to introduce himself: 'My name is Wallace Lies and I've come to tell you the truth about Life Insurance, ha, ha.' People remembered his name after that, which is a big asset when you are in sales."

"Was he a good salesman?"

"One of the best."

"Why did he leave?"

"A long story."

Margaret Lies, legs crossed in a chair at right angles to Gould, stubbed out her cigarette into the ashtray she had balanced on her knees. Then she reached for the package and lighter beside her. Her hand trembled as she raised a new cigarette to her lips. Just before flicking the lighter into flame she paused, removed the cigarette from her mouth again, and said, "He wasn't always such a bastard, you know." Then lit up and drew deep.

"Wallace didn't entirely like sales," she said, after a while. "The money was nice, but he saw himself as something bigger, something more managerial. Almost from day one he took courses to move up in the company. He saw himself as a V.P. someday, with a nice office, making big decisions, signing his name to important memoranda. The company strung him along. For years they promised him he would move up, all he had to do was work hard, do what he was doing, pay his dues. Eventually it was obvious they were lying. Then they changed their tune, told him he was too good of a salesman, that they couldn't afford to lose him. Personally I think it was because it was an American company and the managers were all Americans and they weren't going to let some hick from the North into the inner circle."

"So he quit?"

"He stewed for a long time first. Got bitter and more bitter. All this time we were saving money. I was working too, as a legal secretary. We didn't—couldn't—have kids. We had always had it in our minds to make a big investment someday, something to go along with his promotion in the company. But without the promotion we both felt kind of lost. Like what the hell, what's it all for.

"Well, one day my brother called. He was living in this interior town called Silver. He said it was a happening place, that the mines were about to open again, that if someone was smart enough to get in on the ground floor, make some investments, there was real money to be made. Frankly, I never liked my brother much, God rest his soul—he crashed his plane into a mountain. And I sure didn't like the idea of leaving Vancouver. But Wallace latched onto the idea, better to be a big fish in a little pond he said, and I thought maybe it would help bring us back together."

A while later, Margaret Lies said, "What the hell, I'm going to pour myself a drink. Can I get you anything?"

Then, "Here's to the friendly town of Silver. The town of many prospects!"

"And your husband?" asked Gould.

"I haven't decided," she said. "Maybe he should fry in hell. Maybe I still love him."

"I didn't mean—"

"I know that's not what you meant, Inspector. I know you just want to get me back onto the topic of Wallace and Lena. That's what you came in for, right? Not to listen to me. Do you want to take out your notebook for this? If you do, it's all right with me."

"I'll remember."

She raised her tumbler to her lips. Ice cubes jangled. She took another drag off another cigarette and then said, in a suddenly huskier voice, "What the hell, maybe he should fry, the bastard."

This is what she told him:

For years, almost from the day they arrived in Silver, Wallace Lies had tried to insinuate himself into the company of Lena Stahr. He claimed it was for business purposes. "She and I," he said, "we're the two biggest players in this town. She owns the mine, I'm going to own everything else. Imagine what we could do if we worked together."

Stahr never seemed interested. She was a solitary woman, a one enterprise woman, a woman who had made it in a man's world, and she saw instantly that Lies was interested in more than business.

Then, for some reason, that past summer, after more than ten years of resistance, she suddenly gave in.

"There had to be money involved," said Margaret Lies. "Some important business transaction. Stahr would not have changed her mind about Wallace without some powerful reason."

"Maybe she felt pressured by the strike."

"No doubt."

"Any idea what the business might have been?"

"At first I couldn't think of anything. Nothing had changed in our lives. No new situation, no opportunities had come up that I could think of. But then . . . well, I think it had to do with the Soledads."

"How so?"

"Again, I'm not sure. Wallace hasn't exactly confided in me the last while. But the Soledads were the only thing different in our lives. From shortly after their arrival, Enrique Soledad seemed to take a liking to Wallace. Maybe he just wanted to use him, I don't know. Certainly when the two of them were together—which seemed more and more often as the summer went on—Enrique was full of questions, about Canada, about Silver and the people in it."

"Wouldn't the mayor of a town be the logical person to ask those kind of questions to?"

"It went beyond that. Especially at the end of the summer I noticed that they were having long intense discussions about something. I caught them at it a couple of times, and after that they'd go into Wallace's study to talk. It seemed like they were planning something. I don't know what, but somehow, in some way, it also involved Lena Stahr."

"Can you tell me about your husband's behaviour, his attitude to the Soledads and to Stahr about the time of the murders?"

Margaret Lies hesitated. She tilted her head back for a moment and stared at the ceiling. When she looked at Gould again, she wore an expression somewhere between a grimace and a smile. "This makes him a suspect, doesn't it?" she said.

"Does that bother you?"

"No—I don't know. A part of me wishes I'd seen him with his finger on the trigger. But, the fact is, I didn't. I've only got suspicions."

"At the time of the murder?"

"Things did seem a bit tense between him and Enrique the last while. But it almost seemed to draw them closer together, like they were in something together that was not working out. Once I heard him arguing on the telephone with Lena. I tried to pick up the other line but they heard me do it and after that they were a lot more careful."

"Except this morning."

"That was different."

"In what way?"

PROSPECTS UNKNOWN

"I think, this morning, I was intended to overhear."

"Something has changed, then?" It was less a question than a statement of fact.

"Yes."

Margaret Lies, whose marionette hands had been so occupied with tumbler and cigarette, now grew still.

"It wasn't an arrangement, exactly," she said, after a minute, "we never actually talked about it, but over the years, with his various indiscretions, Wallace and I had learned to maintain a certain fiction. He always pretended that he had to meet someone for business reasons. I always pretended, if not to believe him, at least not to actively disbelieve him. And as long as we maintained our little fiction, though I wasn't particularly happy, I could cope. Now, for the first time, with Lena, the fiction has fallen."

"He told you about her?"

"They had a meeting at my house! Here! In this room! They made a very big deal about it. They couldn't explain it, they said. After all these years they knew it looked strange, they said. But suddenly, this past summer...."

"Did they hint at all about the business dealings that might have brought them together?"

"No. The opposite. They made jokes about how, after years of trying to lure her with business opportunities, Wallace had managed to have her fall for him simply and totally for himself. It didn't make sense, they said, but that was the truth."

"Did you believe them?"

"Is my husband's name Wallace Lies?"

Gould considered. "When did this meeting take place?"

"Last Thursday night."

"This may seem like an odd question. But was there anybody else there?"

Mrs. Lies looked puzzled for a moment. "But, of course," she said. "Inspector Breeze was there too. He sat through the whole performance. Didn't he tell you?"

"No."

"Reverend Bentley too. He took me upstairs after a while to give me some counseling. He said men are weak, that he knew Wallace still loved me in a deeper, spiritual sense, that if I only showed patience he was sure this affair with Lena Stahr would soon run its course."

"And Breeze?"

"I thought he was there as a stand-in for Reverend Bentley. You know, the steadying presence, the neutral friend who helps everybody keep things in perspective. Which makes sense, except that he didn't say anything the whole time. No pearls of wisdom. No calming words. He just sat there. Staring."

"Staring at what?"

"At whom. Unless—"

All at once, Margaret Lies broke into a laugh. The effect on her drawn face was quite startling: it looked like her cheekbones were about to push through the skin. Then she wiped her eyes with the back of a hand (*click, click*) and crushed her cigarette out with a vengeance.

"Don't you get it?" she asked Gould, still chuckling, still catching her breath. "Don't you understand? A woman like Lena Stahr. She wouldn't be satisfied with just one man, would she?"

"Sorry I'm late," said Gould, when he returned to The Red Grizzly. "I had an unexpected interview with Margaret Lies.'

"Anything interesting?" asked Sergeant Wright.

"A lot, though I'm not sure how any of it fits together yet. Any luck last night?"

"Nothing."

Sergeant Wright mouthed his words even more slowly than usual. He seemed tired. Obviously, he had been putting in long hours in his night-time search of the Soledad house. His face had the look of someone who has just come in from the cold: slightly rheumy eyes, flushed cheeks, deeply etched lines.

"How far have you searched?"

"The main floor is done. The basement is next."

"Anything from Allison and Dagg?"

"They're making the rounds right now. We should hear back from them in an hour or so."

"Let me know what they find. I'm going to my room for a while. I'm interviewing Lena Stahr in the morning and I want to prepare."

"One thing before you go. We got a message from Al Goodwin this morning. Basically, that he wants to talk to you as soon as possible. 'To clear the air,' he says. Apparently, the union has opened a temporary office in some rooms at the Selkirk Inn. He says call him any time."

Gould narrowed his eyes. For a moment, he seemed to read something on—or behind—Wright's face. Then he gave a minute nod. "I'll be in my room if you need me."

Chapter Thirteen

That evening, Gould reappeared at the Igloo. He came straight to my booth and asked if he could sit down. Needless to say, I was stunned. I yammered like an idiot for three or four seconds before I could say, "Sure." Then I tried to sweep a place clean for him.

Up until then, I had been drinking coffee (four or five refills over three hours), reading, and occasionally listening in on the people around me. I was also, I admit, feeling rather glum. To tell you the truth, the novelty of being in Silver had begun to wear off for me. The first day or two had been incredibly thrilling—the realness of the Igloo, all those people telling their stories, all those notes in my journal. But as the week went on and it became clear I would get no closer to the investigation, my curiosity about Silver and the Soledads began to wane, fewer people came to gossip and I found myself running out of things to write about in my journal. When I could think of nothing else about the investigation to write about, I found myself thinking—and writing—about Jayne. And when I fell onto the subject of Jayne, I fell into the same old confusions.

Just before Gould reappeared, one trucker and then another had sat down at the *Truckers Only* table. I could just hear their voices above the background murmur of country music and idling diesel engines.

"Been looking for you on the road," the first trucker said. "There was a ten spot waiting for you in Kelowna."

"Too bad you didn't pick it up. You'd be ten bucks richer."

The second driver had a poppy pinned to his Dekra-Ferrari cap. Like many of the drivers, he wore a sweat shirt with a hood and another sweat shirt over top. He had a Santa Claus gut and a dark goatee. Under the cap his head was shaved.

"Where you headed?" the second driver asked.

"Calgary and Regina and straight back. You?"

"The Island."

The first driver wore a leather cowboy-like hat with what looked like silver dollars around the brim. He had a scraggly beard and sunken cheeks and lit another cigarette from the end of his last.

"What's Rogers Pass like?" the second driver asked.

"Snow at the top. Fog here and there but nothing too bad." The first driver gave his thermos to Betty, the waitress, to have it filled. Then he went on, "Last time I went to the Island I missed the fucking ferry. So I tell the guy, you know what the problem is? It's all those motorhomes and trailers—all those tourist sons of bitches. They got nothing to do but take up space, and I got a living to make. I pay five times the taxes those guys pay and I still can't get on the fucking ferry. How far you going tonight?"

"All the way. Got to be in Nanaimo first thing if I don't want to dead head it back."

"Me, I go by my body, know what I'm saying? My body says go, I go. My body says lie down, I lie down. I don't care what any cop says."

I listened to this with my journal open. I was telling myself that this was great material, that I should write it down. Just then I looked up.

Gould covered the last few feet with his usual unhurried but unhesitating stride, eyes slightly narrowed, lips a near perfect straight line, almost invisible below the cropped moustache. When he stopped the grey flannel of his trousers just brushed the faux-marble edge of the table.

"May I?"

I closed my journal. I plowed some junk aside with my arm. The junk made quite a pile: half-a-dozen books from the armful I had brought with me from home, a greasy, half-emptied glass of water, an empty cup and saucer on a coffee-ringed paper place mat (Myths of Canada). In the end, the junk made an interestingly jumbled pile under the window ledge, a potential still-life subject for somebody, lots of odd angles and surfaces topped by the no smoking sign behind. The sign itself—the universal version, a circled cigarette with a red line through it—had seemed new when I first saw it, five days before. Now its plastic surface was scratched and had mustard and relish stains on it, and someone, when I wasn't there to see, had tried squiggle out the prohibiting line with a green felt marker.

Gould was dressed in his trench coat and flagrantly I-am-a-plainclothes-cop blue blazer. There was something Big Bird-like about him, the hockey player not the costume character: the high neck, the angular chin and nose, the red-topped height. I remembered the hockey player, Larry Robinson, from watching the Montreal Canadiens as a kid. Robinson was famous for devastating body checks that looked entirely unspectacular, just a meeting of shoulder against chest, a muffled umph, and the opposing player flat on his back with the wind knocked out of him.

Gould, when Betty approached, said, "Coffee. And do you have apple pie tonight?"

"Heated?"

"But no ice-cream. Thank you."

I kept my eye on him. My cheeks felt hot. I had a searing memory of our meeting just three days before. *I will charge you with obstructing justice* . . . . After he ordered his pie, Gould seemed to forget me entirely for a while. He just made himself comfortable (if that schoolmaster posture could ever be comfortable) and focussed his eyes elsewhere, waiting.

After Betty came and went again, Gould took a bite of pie. He raised his cup to his lips. He seemed to savour the coffee, holding it in his mouth before slowly swallowing, and then, all at once, gestured with his fork.

"Is that it?"

He was pointing to my journal.

"Is that the famous book?"

"Not exactly famous."

"Still interested in passing on what you've learned?"

"I—"

"Why don't you read to me? Read me some of those accounts that might be pertinent to the Soledad investigation."

I tried to decode his expression, but, as you'd expect, I had no luck. There was irony in the way he spoke, a hint that I was being mocked in some way, but I couldn't be sure to what extent or for what reason. It was quite possible that the request was a ruse, a delaying tactic, a way of drawing out my discomfort (I still expected him to blow up at me at any time). On the other hand, I couldn't think of anything else to do.

So I raised the journal to my chest in two hands. Opened it below my chin, like a prayer book. "Where should I start?"

Gould raised a corner of his mouth, a half-grin.

"At the beginning, of course."

I read to him. I read him the various accounts I had collected relating to the murders. There was something soothing about the exercise, the way it cleared my mind, the way Gould's attention made me feel that I was back at the centre of something. I grew a little in love with my own words.

Unfortunately, it became obvious, after three or four minutes, that Gould was not really interested. He admitted to me later that my journal had only been an excuse for sitting down across from me. In fact, when he pushed in the door of the Igloo that night, he had no clear plan. He hadn't even really planned to join me. His encounter with O'Brien, you might say, had destroyed his inner compass. Or rather, his meeting with O'Brien had transported him to one of the Earth's poles, where compass needles spin around and around in a free-space where all the electromagnetic lines cancel themselves out. All directions possible, nothing fixed. Then he saw me and, on a whim, did his pickle-assed walk to my table.

When it was clear that he was only half listening, I tried to pare my reading down to essentials, who said what, who they thought might have done it, why. A couple of times Gould caught me up over this. "You're editing," he said.

"I didn't think it was pertinent."

"I'll be the judge of pertinent."

He took no notes, which made me wonder (I didn't know about his memory yet). His eyes seemed to focus on something behind me, something right behind my head. I knew there was nothing there—I was sitting in the corner, against a wall—but still I had to fight an urge to look around. I tried little embellishments, dramatizations, to get his attention, and when this didn't work, or worked only enough to get him to tell me to stick to the facts, I considered an outright lie. I was curious if I could get it past him: "blah blah blah and Lies confessed to hiring the killers blah." I didn't risk it though. He was only listening with half a mind but even half of Gould's mind intimidated the hell out of me.

When I was done he stared past me again for a few seconds. He wrapped his coffee cup in two long pink hands and raised it to his lips.

"So," I prompted, "what do you think?"

He set his cup down, dabbed a finger at his moustache. Gave me that ironical half-smile. "Hearsay, speculations, a lot of posturing by people who'd like to imagine they were at the center of events."

I sagged a little. "I guess it doesn't add much to the case."

"Not much."

"You've probably heard it all before."

"But not so elegantly expressed."

We looked at each other. I looked at him. He looked at me. I wondered what he saw when he looked at me. Maybe—I don't know this for sure—he wondered what I saw when I looked back.

"Actually," he said, after a moment, "you've shown a couple of good instincts here. This booth, for instance, the way you've made it your own. That's a good instinct. It's always better to have some kind of controlled space to interview witnesses, sometimes a formal interrogation room, but often, when you have to, another space that you set up for the purpose. Like this. It's a basic rule of thumb that interviewing witnesses on their own turf makes it harder to get the truth. The witnesses tend to control things rather than the investigator."

"I didn't actually plan it that way."

Gould seemed to consider his next question a moment. "You want to get at the truth?"

"I—"

"Well, the key is to show your authority." He raised an index finger for emphasis. "Above all, stay firm—that's what I tell new recruits. If you show weakness or hesitate in any way, you invite evasion. If a witness is resistant, emphasize your authority by little gestures. Make him sit in a different chair or take off his hat or butt out his cigarette. Little things so that he understands who's in charge."

He raised his voice a notch. He pointed his finger at my chest. "Now, let me see your journal."

I pushed the book across the table to him.

And he pushed it straight back at me. With his one finger. Laughing. "See what I mean?"

I was annoyed. "I think my situation here, at this booth, drinking coffee with people who come and go, is a bit different than you going out to interrogate witnesses."

"Is it?"

And we both fell silent for a while.

What was going on? My senses were working overtime, trying to read Gould's expression, to interpret his words, his body language. The mere fact of his presence seemed like an invitation: stick around, let me show you a few things. I had a hard time believing it, of course, given how he had warned me off before. I decided to angle for a little confirmation.

"So," I said, after we'd wetted our lips with coffee and assumed our usual postures, "I've, um, I've decided to stay on a while."

He glared at me. His fighter-pilot blue eyes. For a moment, I thought I had fallen into a trap, as if everything he had done and said so far was meant only to lure me into betraying my intentions. But then, his face completely deadpan, he said, "So have I."

He played the professional's professional for me. He did not reveal anything specific about the Soledad investigation (though I gently prodded him once or twice). Mostly he lectured on method. He told me his views on the importance of the crime scene, on the need for absolute impartiality; he made two or three connections between investigative technique and horseback riding, the full significance of which I didn't yet understand. At one point, I thought he was going to tell me who I was by reading the pile of junk I'd swept aside. In the books he could have found evidence of my enthusiasms (*Nostromo* was there, *The Telling of Lies* was there, *An Introduction to Prospecting* was there, *The Long Goodbye* was there), but, ultimately, he seemed to want to keep his monologue abstract. When I look back now, it seems like he didn't actually say much that first night, that what he really did was strike a number of convincing poses: the investigator with his eyes narrowed in concentration, the investigator tapping his moustache in thought, the investigator with his arms crossed, the butt of his gun visible in the opening of his suit jacket, the ultimate arbitrator.

By all rights, I should have scoffed. So much in my background and education has taught me to be skeptical. Instead, I have to confess, I lapped it up.

Then he did something that caught me off guard.

He asked about Jayne.

"Huh?"

"Your girlfriend—or, rather, ex-girlfriend. Have you heard from her?"

I couldn't tell if this was a ploy by him to keep me off balance and hence, in the way he'd just described, to control the interview, or if it was just polite talk, guy talk, or if he just threw the question out for the hell of it (ask the broken-hearted lover about his ex, see what kind of reaction you get). Most likely he had no particular motivation, though it's easy for me to read into it now, these months later, given what ultimately happened.

"I guess you wouldn't know," I said.

"Know what?"

I savoured the moment a bit. I wished I had a piece of pie to bite into. I settled for a long satisfying sip of my now cold coffee.

"Well," I said, finally, "I telephoned a friend in Vancouver on Friday afternoon and had him pick up my mail. Turns out there was a note from Jayne. When he called me back I asked him to open it and read it to me over the phone. Here, I transcribed what he told me."

I turned some pages. Found the place in my journal, one of those I'd skipped over when I read to him, and flipped back and forth a couple of times, just to keep him waiting. "Turns out she's skipped the country," I said.

I cleared my throat.

"'Philip,'" I read, "'You will never know all the reasons, so don't go mad trying to figure them out. Don't wait for me. Don't bother trying to find me or follow me. If you really want to know—and I know you do—I've quit grad school (for real, not as some romantic gesture) and I'm off to South America. Got a ticket to Costaguana. After that, who knows? I don't believe in beginnings or endings. Here's to the present. Jayne.'"

So we began, Gould and I, though Jayne may have been right about one thing: maybe there was no beginning, maybe Gould and I had been entangled all along. Why did he seek me out? Even now, I can only guess. Maybe he really had no plan, maybe joining me was really a spontaneous act—though that's hard to believe of a man whose whole life was a testament to method. At the time, of course, I was convinced he had some hidden master strategy. Even as he sought me out on consecutive nights after that, even as he seemed to warm to me in various subtle ways—even then, part of me was convinced he was using me to a higher purpose, that there was some brilliant Sherlock Holmesian scheme behind it all. I kept waiting for him to unveil some dazzling solution to the murders in which I'd played an unwitting part.

Part of me, I admit, suspected the inner turmoil that drove him. When he started dropping hints about the investigation—a clear breach of his professional code—all kinds of warning signs went up. But, basically, I ignored them. I clung to the Gould who had dazzled me the day he told me off, the man with presence, the ramrod gleam, the steely-eyed professional. I quite deliberately suppressed the evidence most damaging to this image: the fact that he was talking to me.

For our own reasons, Gould and I each needed to play out a certain fiction, that I was the narrator and he Dupin, that I was Captain Hastings and he Hercule Poirot, that I was his mirror and he my flesh and blood. Something like that. Only when the investigation came crashing to a halt, when Gould shot apart his own authority by his clumsy attempt to use the Third Degree and in the process destroyed the comforting illusion I had cultivated about him, only then did the absurdity of our situation become clear. There we were, imagining ourselves into the ever popular roles of detective and side-kick, trying to avoid certain hard realities in our lives by pretending to identities that are some of the most hackneyed in all of fiction. It's amazing that we didn't start using expressions like "quite so" and "astounding" and "elementary." Even when we realized the phoniness of the roles we were playing, we did our best to avoid the significance of this: we hummed and hawed, told stories on other topics, talked and postured and talked some more, all to avoid the real reasons we were sitting across from each other. Only after we'd exhausted our evasions, after we'd followed every gleaming tangent and struck every dramatic pose, did we stumble, in good novelistic fashion, on a few truths about ourselves and the histories that had shaped us.

But the need for evasion runs deep. How deep can be measured by the fact that even today, months after the events in Silver and weeks after Gould, in his only letter to me from Costaguana, spelled out the definitive solution to the Soledad murders—even today, I am not comforted by the so-called truth that has emerged. A part of me misses Charles Gould too much. A part of me wishes we were still at my booth in the Igloo, still humming and hawing, still striking our silly-assed poses, still finding other impertinent and gleaming tangents to distract us.

PROSPECTS UNKNOWN

CHAPTER FOURTEEN

The one thing I didn't bargain for, when the crunch came, was Gould's interest in Jayne. Not just his romantic interest, if that's what his trip to Costaguana was really about, but his interest in forcing me to talk about her. I guess I should have read the signs—that apparently casual reference in our first meeting after his reappearance, his transparent ploy, a few nights later, to get his hands on my photograph of her. When he came right out and challenged me to talk, I thought it was a last ditch evasion, an attempt to avoid telling what he had to tell himself. I said Jayne was not pertinent, that she was another story, that she had nothing to do with the Soledads or his father. I said that giving time to her would be disruptive, self-indulgent. "Yeah, yeah," he said, "now tell me the real story."

By this point, it was early morning at the Igloo. Gould had just talked all through the darkness in that unpredictable way of his, moving from the investigation to his personal history and back again. He had just finished telling me about the letter from his father and the meeting with O'Brien. As a final, dramatic flourish, he brought out the file of blank paper and slapped it onto the table between us. Just then, something fell into place for me. "So that's it," I said. "That's what's really important for you about this case. Your father...."

He stuck his nose down into the steam rising from his cup and frowned in the way he had been doing all night. Then he looked up at me. Irony in his eye. "What's really important is what Jayne would make of that file."

Outside an engine revved. It was an eighteen-wheeler with chrome exhaust pipes rising vertical on either side of the cab. The pipes were perforated with holes near the top, like the muzzle of a machine gun. When the engine revved, black diesel exhaust jetted skyward.

The stars were gone. The world had a steely look.

"I don't think Jayne has anything to do with this," I said.

"That's what you keep saying."

"That's because it's true."

"Come now. Take a look at yourself. What's really behind your being here? It's not just curiosity."

"Well, in that sense, of course Jayne is important. Jayne is the reason I ended up here. But I am not haunted by her—not like you are haunted by your father. For me, this case, my time here in Silver—it's about moving on."

"Bull shit."

It was shocking to hear such words come out of Charles Gould's mouth. The man, until then, had absolutely oozed propriety, civility, upstandingness.

"This is not about moving on for you," he continued. "This is about evasion. All you've done the last ten days is avoid what you left Vancouver to deal with. You pretend you are here without an ulterior motive, without a plan, but every word you have said to me, every note you have taken in that book of yours—it's all about Jayne in disguise. You pretend she is not on your mind but she haunts everything you say. Why else would you try to change the topic when I bring her up? She haunts you so much that you can't even talk about her. What was she really like? Why did you break up?"

I was tired. So tired. I had just listened to him confess for nine or ten hours with very little pause. I had tried in various ways to get his reassurance that he would not, in fact, abandon the investigation. I had put back way too much coffee.

So I decided to humour him. I figured it was the only way I could get him back on track.

Lena Stahr lived on the old Nathan estate, two and a half acres of walled grounds on the far side of Putty Hill. To enter, Gould had to pass through an iron gate under the watchful eye of a uniformed guard. As he passed the window of the guardhouse, he noted a quartet of television monitors and, in a secured rack on the wall, a pair of shotguns. For about fifty meters he drove through trees, until the lane opened onto a wide sweep of emerald grass. On the grass was a helicopter, resting in a circle of orange pylons. The house itself was three stories of grey brick and white latticed windows. To one side there was a white, three-car garage, and on the other side, further back and partially visible past a corner of the house, was a large greenhouse with a domed roof. Beyond everything was the uneven, glacial line of the mountains.

He left his car, as instructed, under the portico extending from the main entrance, climbed the three steps and rang the bell. Stahr opened the door herself.

She was dressed in a knee-length, silver fox coat, under which she wore a black dress. Her hair was pulled back sharply and secured somewhere under the high collar of the coat. She fixed her eyes on him and, with a slightly ironical effect, smiled.

Gould had prepared himself for her eyes, to look at them but not into them. Those sophisticated, agate eyes. Now, thinking to take charge of the situation at once, he said her name and made to shake hands, but in the same instant that he extended his right hand she extended the left, and there was a moment of awkwardness. He hesitated, decided against turning his wrist over to shake backhand. Instead he withdrew his right hand, transferred his briefcase, and offered the other. Stahr clasped it as if to shake left-handed was the most natural thing in the world.

"Let me show you around," she said, doing up her coat. "After that, we can talk."

She took him up in the helicopter. The pilot made a slow circle around the Cyclops property before landing. Gould remembered the outline of the place from the map in the RCMP station, but it was much more impressive to see the real thing. The mine was pushed up hard against the mountains and was surrounded by forest. Here and there were openings in the trees, some natural outcroppings, some old mine shafts. As they approached the landing pad, Stahr said: "See that tall structure that looks like a grain silo? That's the main headframe. A hundred and twelve feet high. The main shaft goes down there. The structure itself contains the hoists that move workers up and down and bring up the ore. From there the ore goes along that long rising chute to the mill, the large square building over there. The other buildings are for equipment storage and repair, emergency power generation, assay labs, administration and so on. The bit of water through the trees that way, that's what's left of Henry Nathan's lake."

After they had landed, she gave him a walking tour.

In the mill, she said, "Before the ore reaches here, it has already been broken up by the rock breaker—a big pneumatic drill—and gone through the primary crusher. By the time it hits these crushers"—she indicated a series of enormous turning drums with spikes protruding from them—"the chunks are about six inches across. By the time they come out of here, they would fit, as you can see, nicely in your palm. Then they go through the rod mill to be ground to about the consistency of sand, then the ball mill to what we call 'flour.' The flour enters a series of floatation tanks and, after it is filtered, goes to the refinery. Here, let me show you."

"Just a minute."

Gould was staring at the conveyer belt that carried the palm sized fragments on to the next crusher. His hand darted out once, twice.

"Can I have these?" he asked, showing Stahr the pieces he had retrieved.

"Souvenirs, Inspector?"

"In a manner of speaking."

"Of course. Suit yourself."

They walked on. Stahr made a commanding and insistently sensuous figure in her fur coat. There was the smell of oil and dust, the growl of crushers, the bass rumble of heavy engines. Here and there, a worker stood at the controls of one of the big machines. The ones who saw Gould and Stahr nodded and then looked quickly away, either shy or embarrassed or defensive, or maybe just concentrating on the job at hand.

They passed through some metal doors into a big square room with a dirt floor. It was quieter here and very warm. They watched, from a safe distance, as a worker dressed in a fire-resistant suit and visor poured liquid silver from a caldron into a mold. "Over two thousand degrees Fahrenheit," Stahr explained. As the mold filled, slag ("lead and zinc mostly") poured off the sides. A couple of minutes later, the worker tipped the mold with a pair of tongs, and a silver bar, still glowing from within, landed in the dirt at his feet. All the while, a nearby security guard, in blue uniform and a white hard hat, held a shotgun and watched.

Stahr offered to take Gould down into the mine itself next, but Gould, in the interests of time, declined. He was a little amused—and somewhat moved—by Stahr's obvious enjoyment of the tour. Pride of ownership seemed to mingle in her with a genuine enthusiasm for the technology. While she had explained the refining process to him, she had seemed to Gould a lot like Sergeant Bacon detailing the wonders of his latest gadget.

As they walked back to the helicopter, Gould said, "I'm surprised by how few workers I've seen. Is that usual?"

Stahr smiled. "You've got to remember, Inspector, that a mine is like an ice-berg—most of it is underground. Down below, off the main shaft, there are equipment depots, repair stations, lunch rooms, washrooms, first-aid and fire-fighting stations, not to mention the primary crusher and related machinery. And, of course, mining these days is highly mechanized, so the tasks that are actually performed above ground don't require that much manpower. Our mill uses the latest technology. At certain times, you'd be hard pressed to find more than a handful of workers there."

"And the strike. There's no evidence from here that a strike is even on."

Stahr's smile faded. Her face took on a look of grim determination. "I've paid a heavy price," she said, "but it's been worth it." She gestured down the main road in the direction of the front gate, a kilometer away through the trees. "The strike stays out there. Out there they can march back and forth all they want—'til hell freezes over, for all I care. In here, we get on with the job."

Back at the house, she showed him the way.

From the entrance way—which was tall enough to drive a dump truck through—they passed through a set of French doors to a bright sitting room with a grand piano in it (polished oak floors, a Persian rug, some gigantic potted ferns) and on into the library. Against one wall of the library there was a marble fireplace with a brass and glass screen in four hinged panels, behind which flames now silently danced. The desk, which had the well-ordered look of a senior executive's, was large and antique, and stood before a tall latticed window, the curtains of which were half-drawn or half-open. The surrounding shelves contained an impressive collection of rare-looking books, narratives of travel and discovery, except for one glass-doored area, which was devoted to a display of antique plate. "Bottger, Ridgeway, Tungstall, that sort of thing," Stahr explained. "I only collect the early types, the blue and white glazes, some earthenware. I don't know why, but it speaks to me. I can still remember the first pieces I ever saw. They were in a cluttered little antique shop near Stoke-on-Trent, a plate, a tea-pot, a couple of cups and saucers, that's all, set up on blue felt on a table. When I picked the plate up—it was that one there—I could feel the roughness of the edges, the raw, beaded feel, and when I held it on edge I could see the rings, like the rings of a tree, where it had been turned by hand, and here and there were imperfections, bits of sand embedded like insects in amber into the glaze. That combination of roughness, of something marked by its making, and fragility (for that plate is almost two hundred years old and it amazes me to think of it still uncracked)—that was it for me. Collecting them has become a pet project of mine. Sit, sit. Feliciana will be here in a minute with the coffee."

They took their coats off and sat in facing leather chairs before the fire. Stahr, Gould could now see, wore a black blazer to go with the black dress. On the lapel of the blazer was a silver pin, a hunting eagle.

Feliciana brought in a tray and set it on a low table between them. Stahr leaned forward to pour coffee from a silver pot. Neither she nor Gould bothered with the accompanying plate of cookies.

After they had sipped from their cups, Stahr smiled again and said, "The famous Inspector Gould," and Gould, not missing a beat, replied, "The famous Lena Stahr."

"Where shall we begin?"

"At the beginning, of course, with the Soledads."

"You mean, did I kill them?"

"Did you?"

Stahr laughed, a low-voiced chuckle, and set her cup and saucer on the table. "No, Inspector, I did not kill Enrique and Camilla Soledad. I was not involved in any way in their killing and I have no idea who was. This is not to say I could never have killed them. Under the right circumstances, I'm sure I could kill someone. Of course, under the right circumstances, I could also lie through my teeth."

"What circumstances are those?"

Stahr swept the room with her hand. "To protect this and"—tapping herself above the heart—"this."

There was a pause. Gould pretended to admire the carved wooden arm of the chair he sat in. Stahr gazed into the fire.

"You have to remember, Inspector, that mining is a tough, sometimes a vicious business. Lots of con artists and predators. Even if you operate honestly there are usually battles over claims and rights and lots of pushing and shoving to attract investors, not to mention dancing on a pin to keep the investors happy until the ore starts to flow—if it ever flows. To survive, much less to prosper, you have to have certain instincts. And if you are a woman, well, you have to have those instincts in spades."

She gestured vaguely at the house again. "Most people, when they first meet me, they go, how? In such a man's world, such a man's man's world. I tell them by the usual combination of hard work and luck. They usually nod their heads, but the expression on their faces says 'yeah, yeah, now tell us the real story.' I rarely tell it, the real story. One of the first lessons you learn as a woman in this business is to avoid unnecessary intimacy. Let me just say this. I've taken my share of kicks in life and I'll be damned before I ever let anyone take away what I've got."

"And the Soledads? They didn't threaten what you've got?"

"On the contrary. They were an important part of my plan to survive this latest challenge."

"How and when did you first meet them?"

"In the summer, August, mid-August. I was introduced to them by Wallace Lies. Wallace and I—well, you're bound to find out, Wallace and I have been romantically involved for the past while. They came to me with an offer. That's why they asked Wallace to introduce us. As you probably know, things weren't going very well for them by that time. You've heard about Enrique and the high school?"

Gould nodded.

"Rather irresponsible on his part, I'd say. But, anyway, they were quite desperate for money, and things were difficult for me too, so I listened to what they had to say."

"And then you took them on."

"Yes."

"To do what?"

"To prospect."

"Prospect?"

"To look for further deposits—you know, the key to all mining. They'd never done any before, but Enrique claimed to have a strong knowledge of geology and to have worked around drills enough to know how to take core samples, and he claimed, absolutely insisted, that he had a sixth sense. He said he'd use Camilla as an assistant. In other circumstances, I wouldn't have given them the time of day. But it's no secret that Cyclops has been financially squeezed the last while, and, as I said, the Soledads seemed desperate. So I thought what the hell, what's there to lose? They agreed to work on spec. I gave them enough money to keep them afloat and in exchange they were to get a percentage of anything valuable they found."

"Did they find anything?"

"Nothing worth finding, unfortunately."

"And this went on right until they disappeared?"

"I have their work plans on file if you're interested."

Stahr contemplated the fire again for a few seconds. Then she looked Gould in the eye and smiled—her welcoming, practiced, convincing smile. "The thing to remember, Inspector, is this: why would I kill two people who might have been my salvation?"

As Stahr talked, Gould reflected on the other evidence about Stahr's relationship with the Soledads that he had heard: the confession of Sergeant Wright, the letter from his father. Both of these hinted at things much darker. Unfortunately, without a copy of the original documents—Stahr's alleged letter identifying the Soledads "as workers who posed special security and financial problems" and the Board's heavy-handed reply to her—his father's letter was little more than hearsay. Robert Gould's word against that of Lena Stahr. And Sergeant Wright's story, without the video-tape, was not much better.

This put Gould in a difficult position. If he pressed the point now, he would tip his hand and lose the psychological advantage of springing the accusation on her at just the right moment. A well-timed accusation could sometimes lead to a confession (especially if it hinted that the investigator was already in possession of the truth); a poorly-timed accusation only served to put a perpetrator on his—or her—guard. And Stahr's response to an accusation would no doubt include trying to find out where Gould had got his information. What would he do if she were successful?

He decided on some delicate probing.

"Tell me," he said. "During the time that the Soledads worked for you, did you get to know them very well?"

"Not very well."

"Your relationship was strictly professional."

"Yes, that's right."

"Did they ever indicate to you that they were worried about anything?"

"Nothing."

"That they felt threatened?"

"Only in the obvious way."

"By the union?"

"It has been a very violent strike, as you know, Inspector."

"I saw the news-story about the truck-driver, what was his name—Luke Carson?—the one who suffered the concussion."

"Just one of many incidents."

"I also noticed the other morning that Carson's rig, smashed windows and all, is still just inside the main gate."

Stahr gave Gould a knowing look. "My official explanation is that the insurance company won't send a tow-truck driver because it's too dangerous. Between you and me, though, let's just say the rig has a certain propaganda value."

Gould tilted his head slightly, an ironic salute. Then he undid the expression and said, "I'm curious. You obviously have an antagonistic attitude towards unions. You see the B.M.U. as a threat to this"—a wave of the hand—"and this."

"Let me tell you something." Stahr now leaned forward to make her point. "My father was a union man. I've got nothing against unions—in theory. But I created Cyclops Silver, I'm the one who took the chances, I'm the one who did the hustling, in every sense of the word. And from the very beginning I decided on one thing: I would treat my workers fairly and, in return, they would deal directly with me. A simple thing. A matter of mutual respect. Heaven knows I've been screwed around by companies myself before. But the deal was, if I treated them fairly, and I did treat them fairly, no unions."

"The union might challenge your definition of 'fairly.'"

Stahr was now angled very far forward, her body tense as a sprinter in the blocks. She tapped her right finger into her left palm for emphasis. "A miner working for my company earns not much less than a university professor. The work is dirty and dangerous, but there are lots of dirty and dangerous jobs out there that don't pay half or even a third as much. On top of that—" The finger stopped in mid-tap. Tension uncoiled from her shoulders, her jaw. She wagged the finger in Gould's direction. "You're baiting me, Inspector."

Gould sipped from his cup.

"Did the Soledads ever say they had been threatened by someone in the union?"

"No."

"But their house was vandalized at Thanksgiving."

"Apparently."

"The union?"

"Everybody seems to think so."

Stahr leaned forward to pick up her cup and gestured to the coffee pot, but Gould shook his head. She resettled herself. "You know," she said, "maybe it was someone from the union who killed the Soledads. You can't rule it out. They certainly had a motive, and they certainly have enough hotheads. And yet, if you want my honest opinion, I don't think so, somehow. The last few times I saw them, the Soledads seemed to have a lot on their minds. Maybe they were worried about something back in their home country."

"But you told me earlier that they didn't seem worried about anything."

"They didn't indicate they were worried. That's true. But they seemed, I don't know, preoccupied. And somebody from in town—who was it?—said they saw a mysterious car on the morning they disappeared."

"Alexander MacKenzie."

"A black car of some kind, wasn't it?"

"I've talked to MacKenzie."

"And?"

"He talked mostly about you."

Stahr laughed. She sipped her coffee and looked Gould in the eye. She seemed totally at ease. "Alex and I do go back a while."

Gould changed the topic. "A few things still puzzle me," he said. "For instance, in your statement on October 28th, you declined to specify the work the Soledads had been doing for you. But you tell me now. Why?"

"You surprise me, Inspector. I thought that would be obvious to someone with your powers of deduction."

"I'd like to hear it in your own words."

Stahr shrugged. "When I was interviewed on the 28th, the Soledads were only missing. The bodies had not yet been found. From the beginning I had tried to keep what they were doing a secret, because I knew that, even more than if they were just crossing the picket lines to work with the other replacements, it would make them targets for retaliation. Think of it, Inspector. If they had found a new vein, it would have changed everything."

"So you were protecting them."

"As far as I could. Yes."

"Something else, then. I wonder about the Soledads staying in their house after it was vandalized. Did you ever talk to them about moving in with the other replacement workers?"

"They would never have gone."

"Why not?"

"The Soledads weren't like the others. For one thing, they were from here, or at least they aspired to be from here. The other workers we'd flown in from all over the country, a lot of them from Northern Ontario where times are grim for hard rock miners. But the Soledads, they had a commitment to community. Don't ask me why, after being here only a few months and after not exactly being welcomed with open arms."

"For another thing?"

"This is trickier. One of the ways we thought to protect the Soledads was to have them cultivate a certain ambiguity. To suggest that though they were working for me they weren't entirely working for me. And living outside of the compound, where they were more vulnerable, helped to encourage that ambiguity."

Stahr, either because of her last answer or for another reason, now grew thoughtful. She gazed at the flames framed by the brass and glass panels over the fireplace. She raised her right hand, still holding her coffee cup, and slowly ran her outstretched thumb the length of the brooch on her lapel.

The silence grew, a few more drops falling into the bottomless well of time.

Gould said, "Now, tell me about Wallace Lies."

"Is Wallace a suspect?"

"I never rule anyone out. Including, of course, yourself."

"Of course."

Another silence. Gould was ramrod, his hands flat on his thighs.

"I don't see how it could possibly have a bearing," said Stahr, finally, "but I did say I would co-operate. Well. As you may or may not know, Inspector, Wallace has had something of a crush on me for a number of years now. For a long time he tried to get my attention by proposing we do business together. But I am a one venture woman, and Wallace, for all his other virtues, doesn't know a thing about mining. Anyway, last summer, the last time he phoned me up with some proposal, I said, 'This has got to stop. I simply am not interested in doing business with you.' But I also knew that the business proposals were only half of his interest. So I said, 'Look. If you'll promise not to come to me with any more schemes, I'll agree to have dinner with you, once, here at my house.' Of course he agreed. Then a funny thing happened. He came over one night. We had dinner. And we had a wonderful time. We've been seeing each other ever since."

"And business?"

"No business. That's our one rule. Our relationship is strictly personal. I know that for a while Wallace pretended we had business dealings in order to hide our relationship. But that's over now. Everything, as you know, is out in the open."

"I find this rather hard to believe."

"What? Never been in love, Inspector?"

"I've been in love. I know the so-called 'craziness' of love. But part of my job is to be a judge of character. And, if you will excuse the presumption, what you have just told me seems very much out of your character."

"That is presumptuous."

"So be it. But I look at you and I see a woman who has made it in a man's world, a woman with business instincts in spades. And right in the middle of a strike that threatens to destroy everything she has ever built, and with no ulterior motive, and after years of holding herself aloof from affairs in the town, she falls in love? The man she falls in love with is the town mayor, a notorious wheeler dealer. But it has nothing to do with dealing."

"I admit, it does sound improbable."

There was a catch in the mine owner's voice. Either Stahr was an accomplished actor or Gould had struck a genuine note of sadness in her, of vulnerability.

"Yes, there is more to my relationship with Wallace," Stahr said, finally. "Maybe I should have admitted it from the start, but, you know, unnecessary intimacy." She drank some more coffee, slowly, as if to steel herself. Then she gazed—rather bleakly, it seemed—into the fire. "The thing, Inspector, is this. I have found this strike hurtful. Deeply, personally hurtful. Suddenly, after years of having my place in this community—I am somewhat aloof, I admit, but I always thought I was respected, even admired—after years of living here, I find myself suddenly vilified. The Yankee Carpetbagger. The Bitch Exploiter. Oh yes, I've heard and read them all."

"You don't seem like the kind of person to worry about the world's opinion of you."

"Only to a point. I've even had run-ins with my neighbours before. Take this house, for instance. To build it I had to tear down the old Nathan mansion. The thing was falling apart, but some people considered it a sacrilege. Anyway, I did what I had to do, took the criticism in stride, then did penance by donating heavily to the foundation that runs the Miner's Museum, and things turned out okay. But this, this strike. To be quite frank with you, Inspector, I don't know how I will ever make things okay again."

"And Wallace?"

"I'm not sure how he fits exactly. It's all muddled up in my mind. Can you imagine? Me, Lena Stahr, muddled! Maybe I just needed someone then, anyone, and he happened to come along. Maybe unconsciously I was trying to show something to the people of Silver. But what that something was, is, to be honest with you, I really don't know."

Chapter Fifteen

I told him about the first time I saw her.

It was at a reception for the English Department, her department. One advantage of being in Interdisciplinary Studies is that you can invite yourself almost anywhere, though, of course, you never really belong anywhere either. So there I was, standing alone by the cheese table, prospecting the room, when I noticed her. She was a smallish young woman with bobbed brown hair and round spectacles. She wore blue jeans and a black leather jacket. She was holding a glass of red wine in one hand and her elbow in the other, her weight shifted a little onto one hip, looking up to a half-circle of grey beards, watching, just watching. Conversation was in the air like windchimes. From somewhere came the truck-sound of a laugh. She seemed . . . self-contained. Contemptuous? A little. At ease? Hardly. More like, *I take no shit and I want it all*. Dissecting the grey beards through her round spectacles.

Eventually, I introduced myself. As it turned out, we had a number of friends in common.

"What can I say about her?" I said. "A group of us headed off together after the reception. Jayne. Me. Some other grad students, some of whom we both knew. We went to a campus pub called The Anti-Thesis Lounge and drank beer and talked until closing. Then we went to somebody's place, shared a couple of joints, and talked some more. As the night went on, there were, I don't know, signs. At one point she got into an argument with another student, a rather self-important guy named Patrick. The issue was some nuance in the work of Michel Foucault, whom they both adored, and the two of them were hardly letting each other speak, their faces were this close, they kept shouting phrases like 'technologies of power' or 'discursive formation,' they quoted authorities I had never heard of in languages I didn't speak. Right in the midst of this she glanced over at me. She was more than a little drunk, probably quite stoned too. To this day I do not know what she was handing me with that look. There was contempt in it, like the look at the reception. But there was something else. As if, all the time she had been arguing with this guy, she had been studying me. And now she had figured something out."

Like the other businesses off the Trans-Canada, The Red Grizzly had a wide slab of asphalt out front. As you might expect, given the general condition of the place, this slab was buckled and cracked, with pools of gravel here and there like spilled guts. A couple of potholes still had water in them from the recent rains, and in the morning, when Gould had first set out, they were knitted with ice. Something else Gould noticed. Along one edge of the lot, there was a neat, and growing, row of dog shit. Large piles. Piles that, except for their distinctive light-brown colour and tubular shape, might have come from a bear. Gould had just avoided one the first time he walked to the Igloo. That first time, the night he told me off, there had been two piles side by side. Now there were six, in a neat row. It was as if someone walked their dog along the highway in the morning before anyone else was awake, and the dog, either by preference or because of its internal rhythms or because its master had trained it to, always stopped to squat at just this spot. Odd thing was, there were no houses out this way, no place where one would reasonably expect anyone to keep a pet.

Gould locked his car. He cast a glance at the Igloo sign, visible just down the strip. Then he turned, briefcase in hand, and headed towards the shot-gunned sign of the grizzly.

Margot, as always seemed to be the case, was behind the front desk. Gould said hello and she did not respond. He hesitated. She was smoking a cigarette and staring bleakly into space, her eyes swollen and red.

"Are you—"

"I feel like crud, Inspector."

"I'm sorry to hear that."

"Yeah, well, I'm pretty sorry about it myself."

She went back to staring. Gould, taking it as a dismissal, started to go.

"Wait." Margot stabbed out her cigarette and now pushed away her chair. "Wait, Inspector, if you've got a minute. I wouldn't mind telling someone about it."

They faced each other across the counter. Standing straight up, Margot's mouth was at the level of Gould's chest. She gave a despairing, self-deprecating laugh. "Jesus," she said, "maybe I'm the one you should be investigating. What you see, Inspector, right here before your eyes, is a violent woman."

"How so?"

"Let me tell you." She looked down at her work station, apparently for her cigarettes, but could not find them. Then, with a wave at the air, she said, "It's like this. Last night, Rennie and me—that's my boyfriend—we had a few beers, quite a few, to be honest, and we went back to my place. Well, one thing led to another and we had a fight. We've had fights before, we both have tempers, but we always work them out. Even last night, we were smart enough to realize it was the beer talking, and after a while we calmed down and made some coffee. So we're sitting at the kitchen table drinking coffee, nothing doing, and Rennie's got one of his hands flat on the table like this. He's looking at me kind of content, kind of smug even, like he knows what I'm thinking and it suits him just fine. Well, all of a sudden, I don't know why, but I'm furious again, and I reach out and grab the pointer finger on his hand, like this. I yell at him that he's a bastard and I bend the finger up and up, and the next thing he's shouting 'you broke my fucking finger!' and it's true, I even heard the crack."

Margot paused, her eyes reddening again at the memory.

"What happened then?"

"What do you think? He screamed that I was out of my fucking mind and ran out to his truck. Drove himself to the hospital. Jesus, Inspector, I think I could've ripped that finger right off." Margot held one of her pudgy hands out like a starfish, as if still dazzled at the power in it. "What I don't understand is, not only doesn't he want to press charges, but later he came back to my place. I thought he was going to beat me up. But when I opened the door he just says, 'I forgive you, Margot.' Then, once I let him inside, he takes me by the shoulders and says, 'Christ, I'm so fucking horny now I could burst. If my finger wasn't in splints and I wasn't in so much goddamn pain I'd pull your clothes off and do you right here on the floor.'"

Margot threw herself back into her chair with a groan. She started feeling around for her cigarettes and found them under some papers. She tapped one out, then scowled, bulldog-like, and jabbed it at Gould instead. "You're a man, Inspector," she said, "you tell me. What's the turn on about people who can hurt you?"

Sergeant Wright was also looking bleak. When Gould came into the murder room, he was leaned against the front row of tables, arms crossed, staring into space. Nearby, Corporal Elderkin entered information into a laptop computer.

Wright, when he noticed the Inspector, blinked and rubbed his eyes. "Sorry," he said. "Late nights, you know. That and the fact we can't find the damn thing."

Before the morning meeting of the investigative team, Wright had reported to Gould about his third night searching the Soledad house. Again, no video-tape. And with the basement now almost completely gone over, it looked like the tape was not to be found.

"It may be somewhere else," said Gould.

"I've been thinking about that. But where? The Soledads didn't have a safety deposit box, at least we've found no evidence of one. What about the children? Have you talked to them yet?"

"In a day or two."

"I guess I'll know, one way or the other, by then."

"Anything else?"

Wright seemed to shake himself into action. He turned for a file that was on the table behind him and handed it to Gould. "Allison and Dagg just reported back," he said. "They tracked down the last people on their list this morning. They confirmed what the others said yesterday, that there were in fact Statewide agents on the road that morning. Consensus is that they were right about here." He pointed to the map.

"We better check with the Statewide people. If they had agents on the road that morning, they might have seen something."

"Right away."

"No, actually, I'll take care of it myself. You, Sergeant, if I may say so, need some sleep. You won't be any use to me if you burn yourself out."

"I'm not sure I could sleep now, even if I tried."

"Well, I'm giving you the rest of the day off anyway. Elderkin can hold the fort. Now, go home."

The lounge at the Selkirk Inn was housed in the old government claims office, a thick-walled log cabin built in 1898. Hitching posts with iron rings stood out front, and on the porch there were seats L-cut out of solid logs of Douglas fir. Behind the lounge and off to one side rose a two-story addition that was the inn proper.

The B.M.U. had rooms on the first floor, at the back, with views of the Columbia River at the bottom of a downslope of rock and trees.

Al Goodwin answered the door himself. He answered like a man with better things to do than answer doors. Gould flashed his badge.

"Oh," said Goodwin. "Hey, clear out you guys, will you? Come on in, Inspector."

Two men with picket signs pushed past Gould as he made his way into the room. One looked down at the floor sheepishly, the other glared as if only the merest whim kept him from driving the stake of his sign through the policeman's heart.

"The coffee tastes like tar, but you're welcome to some if you're interested."

"No thank you."

"Suit yourself."

The two men soon faced each other from identical plain wooden chairs. Gould noted that the bed or beds had been removed from the room, but the other furniture—a bureau, an end table, a chair—had been enlisted into service. Goodwin rested one elbow on a folding table, pushed against a wall, that served as a desk. Thumb-tacked above the table was the same map of the mine Gould had seen in the police station. A second table, this one piled high with placards, empty fast food containers and other items, was against the opposite wall.

"I don't mind telling you right off, Inspector, that I've never had much use for cops."

Gould swallowed a smart reply about what he had no use for, and asked, instead, "Why?"

"Because, one way or another, when it comes to situations like this one, the cops always end up breaking the heads of the working men."

"We don't make the laws."

"You're just following orders, I know. God, how many times in human history are we going to hear that?"

"Look, Mr. Goodwin. You said you were eager to tell your side of the story."

"I did."

Goodwin crossed his arms over his chest. He was a compact man with a heavily freckled face. A high forehead, ginger-coloured hair (thinning on top and rather wild on the sides), and small hazel eyes. He wore a somewhat ratty, green sweater, blue jeans, and sneakers. During the interview he smoked two cigarettes, thoughtfully, with obvious relish. At regular intervals he tapped the ashes into a soft drink can on the desk.

"All right. Where should I start?"

"Start with the Soledads. What was your relationship with them?"

"Hardly knew them. When they first came here they were caught up in that crowd over at the church, with Bentley and Lies and so on. And I was too busy getting my teeth kicked in—sorry, I was too busy with the strike to bother with them."

"I've been told that they had a way of antagonizing people."

"I wasn't around them enough to know."

"And yet you were antagonized by Enrique Soledad, the day before he disappeared, enough to chase him into the street and call him a 'stupid Spic'?"

"Oh that." Goodwin rolled his cigarette around the rim of the soft drink can. "You don't think that was for real do you?"

"You tell me."

"The whole thing was staged. Enrique Soledad came to me that day to say he'd work for us on the inside at the mine. We agreed. We didn't have time to work out any of the details just then, but we figured some kind of intelligence work, maybe some organizing, if it came to that. We also knew that we were being watched. There was a Keystone Cops surveillance team right across the street from us, up there on the second floor above Foshay's Menswear. So we figured to have a little fun and also to work a little decoy to make things easier for Soledad."

Goodwin took a long drag from his cigarette, with an air of satisfaction.

"What made you change your mind?"

"What do you mean?"

"What made you suddenly decide Enrique's offer was a good one?"

"I'm not following you, Inspector."

"Don't be coy, Mr. Goodwin. I know that Enrique Soledad came to you two weeks before as well, and the meeting was a lot less civil."

Goodwin picked a piece of tobacco off his tongue. Then, abruptly, he spat.

"Well, since you already know about it, then you know that the offer was not the same."

"I'd like to hear it in your own words."

Goodwin shrugged. "That earlier meeting, just after Thanksgiving, at that meeting, Soledad tried to appeal to our sense of solidarity. You know, *Workers of the World Unite* and all that. He claimed to be on a secret mission for his comrades in Costaguana. He wouldn't tell me what the mission was, but he claimed that working for Lena Stahr was just part of the plan. He wanted us to be patient. To back off, leave him alone. He was, of course, worried because somebody—I'm not saying who—redecorated his house a little while before."

"And what did you tell him?"

"I told him to go to hell!" Goodwin seemed to catch himself after these words. For a moment he went still, as if he'd just walked into a dark room and heard a sound; then, all at once, he smiled—a mouthful of small, stained teeth.

"It's true," he continued, in a soft voice, "I did tell him to go to hell. But Inspector, you have to understand. What Soledad wanted was for us to stand back and let him do what he wanted, be a scab and work whatever scheme it was he was working, so that he could benefit his comrades back home. In the meantime, he was hurting us. And I'm sorry, when you're in a situation like ours, where you're basically fighting for your life, the only way to survive is to look after Numero Uno. No concessions, not even for comrades in the jungle."

"And the second meeting?"

"It was different."

"How?"

"As soon as he said he'd do some work for us. That was a gesture of good faith. And he said there was more in it for us down the road."

"What?"

Goodwin looked wistful. "I guess we'll never know."

"You struck a deal with him without knowing what your end of it was going to be?"

"I still didn't entirely trust the guy. Who knows what kind of a game he was playing? But, if there was something in it for us, I was willing to give it a try."

"Just like that? I find that hard to believe."

"Frankly, Inspector, I was a bit desperate. This strike, you know."

Gould pondered for a few seconds. Then he said, "What I do know is that you've said—or been quoted as saying—some pretty inflammatory things since this strike began. 'Killing a scab is the same as killing someone breaking into your home.' You still believe that?"

Goodwin took a last drag of his cigarette and inserted it into the can. A faint sizzle as the butt hit liquid in the bottom. "Let me answer you like this, Inspector," he said. "You've interviewed Lena Stahr already, I take it."

"Yes."

"At her home?"

Gould nodded. "Then she probably took you into the library. That's where she always takes people for little heart-to-hearts. She took me there a few times myself when we were on better terms. And she probably showed you around the room too."

"Yes."

"The point is that collection of china, Inspector. 'Bottger, Ridgeway, Tungstall, that sort of thing . . . .' Oh yeah, she's given me the spiel too. I guess she thinks it humanizes her, in some way, to collect things so old and fragile. But it's more appropriate than she thinks."

Goodwin pushed himself to his feet. He went over to the other table, elbowed away some placards (Gould read *Fairness before Profit* and *Canadians fighting Canadians: The American Way*) and reached for the coffee pot. He took up a paper cup and gestured inquiringly at Gould, who shook his head.

"The only way you can condone scab labour—or do scab labour—is to be blind to the history of our country. There is this clichés about Canadians, about how we are so moderate, so wishy-washy. That's bullshit. Anybody who knows anything about Canada knows that our past is filled with violence, that our country was built on violence, particularly violence against workers. Union leaders have been—and still are—persecuted, imprisoned, even murdered. Think of the Winnipeg General Strike or the Dominion Textile Strike or any of dozens of others. Think of Wilfred Gribble, who was tried for sedition in 1915 because he spoke in favour of pacifism, and disappeared into prison never to be heard of again. This is our country, Canada. And exploitation! I won't bore you with all the details. Suffice it to say that more Chinese labourers died building the CPR than there have been policeman killed in the entire history of the country."

"What does this have to do with the china?"

"Do you know how those plates were made? What conditions were like in early English ceramics factories? I bet you don't. Neither does Lena Stahr. She doesn't know that children as young as six worked in those factories. That the average work day was eighteen hours and most of the workers died before the age of forty. That's why she can collect them so happily, the same reason she can use scab labour. If you don't believe me, trying reading the tenth chapter of volume one of *Capital*. Don't be scared because it's Marx. You won't lose your soul from just reading one chapter."

"You still haven't answered my question," said Gould.

"About killing a scab?" Goodwin, finally, poured his coffee. He dropped three cubes of sugar into the cup and shook in whitener from a container. He stirred, then took a sip. "Let me put it this way," he said. He returned to his chair, sat, and set the cup aside. He reached for his cigarettes. "If the Soledads really were scabs"—tapping one onto his palm—"then I'm not sorry they're dead. The situation here has been that serious. But, I'll tell you, since this is obviously what you really want to know, I didn't kill them. I didn't have them killed. Nor did any of my men. I'm quite sure of it. In fact, it doesn't make sense, given what went on between Enrique and I the day before they disappeared."

"If your account of the meeting is true."

Goodwin struck a match. "Too bad the surveillance team was

such a fuck up, eh?"

Suddenly, Gould leaned forward. Goodwin tensed, but the inspector just reached past him to pick up the package of cigarettes off the table. On the package was a large red "X".

"Producto Equis," explained Goodwin.

"These are not legally available in Canada."

The union leader shrugged. "So arrest me."

"Where did you get them?"

"I have a friend who imports them for me. He does it as a personal favour. It's not a big deal. Haven't you heard how easy it is to smuggle stuff through Vancouver?"

Gould tapped the package into the palm of his hand.

"Keep the pack if you want," said Goodwin. "It's not a big deal, like I said. I acquired a taste for them when I spent time in South America. They're only a treat. I can live without them."

"I don't want the pack," said Gould. "What I would like is the butt of that one you're smoking."

"This? Why?"

"I'd like to have it tested. You don't have to give it to me, of course, if you're concerned about it."

"Not me, Inspector. You can have it as soon as I'm done."

"Now," said Gould, "tell me about Terrance Sherwood and Edward Berry."

"What's to tell? Yes, they're members of our local. No, I don't know how they got their hands on those silver bars."

"I find that hard to believe. What about union solidarity? What about the tight ship you're supposed to be running here?"

"What do you expect, Inspector? For six months my men have been getting their heads cracked. For six months they have been living on strike pay, which is less than E.I. if they could qualify for it. Solidarity? Yeah, we have solidarity, for the most part. But there are limits. Push hard enough and far enough and eventually the little guys turn on one another. It's how the ruling class has always kept power."

"You sound bitter. Almost like Berry and Sherwood took those bars from you."

Goodwin considered that for a moment. "I'm speaking in general terms. But, yeah, I'm disappointed in those two. Trying to hawk those bars, that was an act of individual self-interest."

"So the bars did come from one of the union raids on the mine?"

"I'm not saying that. All I'm saying is that however they got them—and, like I said, I don't know how they did—it'd be more in keeping with union solidarity to share with their brothers. Especially at a time like this."

Gould tried what he thought was a good card.

"If Sherwood and Berry were acting on their own—and, frankly, I find that rather hard to believe—but if they were, then tell me: Why did the B.M.U. send its own lawyer to them after their arrest?"

"Brothers are brothers, Inspector. No matter what they've done."

"You know what I think? I think that it would be a public relations disaster for you if it came out that your men had been stealing silver from the mine. I think you have a very strong motive for claiming that Sherwood and Berry acted on their own."

"Think what you want," said the union leader, "I'm not stopping you."

"Okay," said Gould, "let's go back to the Soledads for a moment. I want to ask you something else about your second meeting with Enrique. During that meeting, did Soledad say anything about his relationship with Lena Stahr?"

"No—not really."

"What do you mean, 'Not really?'"

"I mean, no, he didn't say anything."

"Did he imply that there might have been some conflict between them?"

"There probably was."

"Yes?"

"Given what kind of person Stahr is. There's always conflict when you have to work for someone like that."

"I see. Tell me something. How do you think Lena Stahr would have reacted to finding out that the Soledads were working for you?"

"I doubt if she found out."

"Why?"

"I spoke to Soledad alone. No one else was there. And your surveillance team—" Goodwin grinned.

"But if she did?"

"You mean, do I think she would have had them killed?"

"Would she?"

"She's capable of it. No question."

Now Goodwin paused, as if he were trying to remember something. Then, very quietly, he said, "Maybe it was Lena Stahr. I don't know. It's possible. But, you know, somehow I don't think so. I can't tell you why, exactly, except that the second time Enrique came to me, he seemed very desperate. Like he really needed some allies, like someone was seriously on his case. My guess is he was feeling pressure from back home."

"Did he say anything that suggested this to you?"

"No. But there is that black car Alex MacKenzie saw."

"Alexander MacKenzie is a friend of yours, right?"

"Sure."

"Good enough to help you out in a jam?"

"I know what you're saying, Inspector, but I don't believe he made it up. Hey, if you interviewed all my guys again, I bet one or two of them would say they saw a car like that recently too."

"I bet they would."

Goodwin took a last puff and held out what was left of his cigarette. Gould told him to stub it out, then produced some tweezers and a plastic bag from his briefcase.

When the butt was sealed up and labeled and the briefcase snapped shut again, Gould stood as if to go. On the way out, however, he paused at the table stacked with the picket signs. They signs ranged from the basic *B.M.U. Local 73 On Strike for Fair Wages* to direct attacks on *Lena Stahr: Yank the Yank Union Buster.* One read *Enforce Bill 21,* an allusion to the Socialist government's recent labour legislation, which banned the use of replacement workers. Goodwin, who was eyeing Gould from behind, took the opportunity to explain.

"The government claims they can't force Stahr to respect Bill 21 because our strike began before it was passed. In other words, what she's doing is now illegal, but not illegal because she started doing it before it was made illegal, if you follow me. What can I say? To us it's either illegal or not. And the government is selling us down the river because they don't want to be seen as anti-business."

"Maybe they're just trying to be fair. Not take sides."

"You know what I think? I think back in Victoria they are secretly cheering on this strike. They love how violent it has become, all the broken bones and blood, because it proves their argument about why scabs have to be banned. And it does prove it. But to prove it this way, at our expense, that's bullshit."

Chapter Sixteen

In the early days, when we were just getting to know one another, it seemed that all I had to do was make an appearance near one of her favourite haunts, at the university library or Little Sisters Bookstore or the bar in the Sylvia Hotel, and I'd run into her. All I had to do was arrive in the vicinity and there she'd be, her slender form sandwiched between comrades in her black leather jacket, or alone under the ash-grey light floating down from fluorescents in the library, her papers fanned out around her, the hand denied a cigarette flexing on her thigh. I took these meetings as further signs. She said it was a result of my Calvinistic upbringing, always reading for evidence of divine support for what I wanted to do anyway. My brainwashing by Romance. And I did love to tease out connections, to find traces of an underlying inevitability. I wanted to know if she remembered seeing me anywhere before that day at the reception (she said no). I liked to dream aloud about times when we might have been together without knowing it, standing one behind the other in a movie line-up, or at the railing on the ferry to Victoria, or just passing, with an instant of eye contact, on the street. She retorted that she never made eye contact with strange men, that it was a male power trip to get you to acknowledge them.

One day I brought her a dozen red roses. She stopped me at her door and demanded I take them back. "No explanations, just do it." I backed down the stairs, toe-heel toe-heel, each step down my anger rising. I was about to call her impossible when my foot hit concrete, and I spun away, grinding my jaw. I was damned if I was going to take them back. I marched three blocks until I noticed a grandmotherly woman pushing a baby-carriage. I used the baby as an excuse to say hello, made up a story about how wonderful I thought it was, bringing babies into the world. The woman protested that it was her granddaughter but I ignored her. I gave her the roses, leaving her smiling and flustered and speechless. Then I marched back to Jayne's place, pounded on the door, said "they're gone." I expected her to explain later, lecturing me as she was already in the habit of doing, that roses were an implicated gesture, part of the patriarchal romance pattern men have used for so long to put women on a pedestal in order to keep them in their place, like men falling over themselves to open doors in order to emphasize a woman's essential inadequacy ("too fragile to open a goddamn door"). She did bring it up. While the kettle boiled, and she stood by it, and I sat with my hands on the kitchen table. But she only laughed, a sad laugh, and said, "It's not what you think. It's not that. It's just that they always die."

After a while, I became, I admit, obsessed. I thrived on the intensity of our long talks, even arguments like the one I had witnessed with Patrick, and the love-making afterwards. On days when we hadn't planned to meet, I would look for her. Sometimes I spent hours searching systematically, criss-crossing from one favourite haunt to another, scouting her territory. While walking I would imagine where she might be—talking to the man who sold roasted cashews near the Vancouver Public Library, browsing some used bookstore along Robson, holed up with friends in a café somewhere. I was not jealous, not possessive; it wasn't that way. Just that I was dazzled by her, her luminosity, the way I felt in her presence. If I did catch sight of her, I'd take pains to be casual; I knew she'd detest it if she knew I walked the streets looking for her. Prowling, she'd call it. When I approached her she would look up, a little surprised, and smile.

She accused me of domestic urges. She accused me of trying to make her conform to various stereotypical roles, the unattainable ideal, the hysterical woman, the femme fatale. She challenged any assumption I dared to make in her presence. Whether it was an idea I had about literature, history, politics, love, us—whatever—she always goaded me to see other possibilities. Her analyses were brilliant and often exasperating. Sometimes she tore my theories to shreds from two or more mutually contradictory directions. Problematizing them! And she never let up, never let down her critical guard. Apparently, the full professors in her department had learned to hide in their offices when they saw her coming.

After the interview with Goodwin, Gould, for the first time, had the inkling of a pattern behind the events in Silver. Oddly (or appropriately) enough, what brought it to his mind was the unbelievability—the almost certainly false character—of so much that the two main antagonists in the strike had told him. He did not believe that Goodwin's shouting after Enrique Soledad was staged, nor that Goodwin was unaware of where Sherwood and Berry had acquired their silver bars, just as he did not believe key parts of what Lena Stahr had told him: her altruistic attitude towards the Soledads, her all-too-human motivation for becoming involved with Wallace Lies. All lies, Gould thought, all deliberate deceptions. But most telling of all was the strange reluctance the two antagonists had shown towards accusing each other of the murders. By all accounts, Stahr and Goodwin had each stridently accused the other after the disappearances of the Soledads, but then, when it came to the crucial question, there had been a peculiar hesitation. Good manners, Gould decided, could not explain it.

The flipside of this hesitation was how ready each was to point a finger at a killer from Costaguana. And on what evidence? The black car? Even if what Goodwin had said about his first meeting with Enrique Soledad were true (and Gould had doubts about it), the arguments against a killer from Costaguana still seemed overwhelming. It made no sense for the political right in that country—which meant, in effect, the military government—to let the Soledads leave first and then to assassinate them. Much better to kill them at home where they would be just two more political victims noted briefly and then forgotten by the gringo press. In Canada, such a killing would be a serious diplomatic incident, one likely to jeopardize the fragile goodwill that the Canadian government, in defiance of various human rights organizations, was now showing the regime. As for the political left, it made no sense at all. It was especially inexplicable if, as was likely from the evidence so far, the Soledads had maintained some allegiance to their former cause.

With the first inklings of a pattern came the feeling that somewhere, either in the investigation so far or in the investigation just ahead, there was a clue, a missing piece, that would make the pattern come clear. This feeling began to nag at Gould, to nag him and, at the same time, to fill him with anticipation: it meant that he had passed out of the chaotic beginning of the case, where details had proliferated wildly and unexpectedly, to the point where possibilities had finally begun to close.

Back at The Red Grizzly, he recorded the interview with Goodwin, and then, in keeping with his sense of a change in the investigation, wrote out his interpretations. Afterwards, he considered what to do next. The most obvious move was to interview Wallace Lies, to finally pin down the elusive mayor of the town: he had a feeling that the missing piece lay somewhere in that direction.

He reached for the telephone, but, in one of those odd coincidences, it rang just as his fingers closed on the receiver. On the other end was Sergeant Wright.

"I've found it," he said.

"Where are you?"

"At the house."

"I told you to get some rest."

"I tried. But I couldn't. I just kept thinking about where the damn thing could be."

"Are you alone?"

"Yes."

"You better get back here on the double."

Ten minutes later, Wright was standing in the doorway. Gould stepped back to let him enter. The sergeant's face had a flushed, almost feverish look to it, either from fatigue or cold or emotion. He came into the room with a heavy, slow stride, in his regulation black shoes, the stripe on his uniform pants seeming to magnify the length of his legs. The video was in a plastic bag in his hand.

"It was in the darkest corner of the basement," he explained. "A hollowed out space in the wall behind the furnace. Wrapped up in this."

He unwound the plastic bag.

About Sergeant Wright. Something I've been meaning to mention for a while now. I saw him once at the Igloo. He came in for a take-out coffee. He waited just inside the glass door, by the cash register, hatless, in his winter uniform. Even from the other side of the restaurant, I could see how large he was. Six-three or maybe six-four, with enormous hands. The kind of hands that make a coffee cup disappear, or that would make his sidearm—if he ever had to draw it—look like a toy. Hands that hung from his sides like spadeheads.

But that's not what I wanted to say. What I wanted to say is that Wright seemed familiar to me as well, just as he had, though in another way, to Gould. In my case, Wright was the image of the cop who led the raid on the rented house I lived in as an undergraduate. He came in late, after the place was already trashed. He was the only one whose face I saw. All the others were dressed in S.W.A.T.-like outfits, battle fatigues, balaclavas, flak-jackets with POLICE in yellow reflector letters on the back. They smashed in the front door screaming "Police! Get down on the floor! Police! Get down on the floor!" and thundered across the landing. Within ten seconds half the furniture in the place was overturned. Five of us were home at the time. I was at the kitchen table with my roommate Tim, Ron was in the shower, Lou and Jackson were still in bed (it was quarter-to-eight in the morning). I fell to the floor. Tim fell beside me. Next thing there was an M-16 a foot away pointed at my head. "Eyes on the floor!" someone shouted. I felt a knee in the middle of my back and my wrists, one and then the other, were yanked up towards my shoulder blades. The handcuffs felt like they had serrated edges.

Tim and I lay there, chins and noses to the floor, amidst upended chairs and fallen bowls and spoons, stunned, not at all believing what had just happened. Shouting went on for a few more minutes as the cops went through the rest of the house. And then, for what seemed like ages, they just ignored us. Heavy black shoes clumped by this way and that (we could see them out of the corner of our eyes) but nobody spoke to us. Once I tried to turn my head to move the weight onto the flat of my cheek, but a voice shouted "Eyes down!" and I went back to kissing the floor.

They were, no doubt, looking for drugs and guns and whatever else. There wasn't anything to be found. Just the half-dozen or so plants we'd been growing along the back fence. Plants that we'd started almost as a joke but that became a kind of household project after a while, a way of putting our mark on the place, asserting a kind of ownership (illusory as it was). Everything probably would have been okay—the backyard had high fences—except that Ron and Tim both grew up on farms. They knew all about manures and fertilizers. By mid-summer, the plants were seven or eight feet high. We realized we were taking a risk, now that the tasseled tops reached over the fences, but it seemed a shame to cut them down when they had grown so high. A few days before the raid, we got on our rattiest jeans, put blades of grass in our mouths, and took turns posing for pictures before our crop.

The Wright-like officer was the one who informed Tim and I of our rights. He did it while our faces were still pressed into the kitchen floor. He did it with what seemed like barely controlled contempt in his voice. All I could see was part of his black shoes and trousers. He asked us if we understood. We mumbled into the floor, into the wet-spots of drool and condensation that had formed under our chins. "What?" he asked. We mumbled again. "Look at me when I'm talking to you!"

Gould popped the cassette into the VCR he had ordered for the purpose. The television screen showed blue for half a minute, then cut to a shot of the back of Lena Stahr's mansion. Across the bottom of the screen was the time and date: 7:15 PM, October 22. The picture zoomed towards a window on the second floor, until the window, with a small gap in the curtains, filled the screen. The camera then zoomed in on the gap until a grainy view of the room took shape. There was a wait. The time in the bottom right hand corner flipped ahead two hours.

The rest of the cassette captured Inspector Breeze and Lena Stahr in all the classically compromising positions: entering the room together, undressing together, climbing into bed, making love. The picture remained grainy but the protagonists were clearly identifiable. And somehow, by some technical wizardry, the makers of the cassette had provided a crackly version of the sound.

With the cassette literally in his hand, Gould could no longer escape confronting his fellow officer.

This time he waved the duty officer back into his seat. He knocked once on Breeze's door and opened it without waiting for a reply. Breeze was behind his desk, just leaning on his palms, about to rise. He gestured for him to sit. He closed the door gently behind him, marched straight to the desk, and dropped the cassette, like a rock into a pond, onto the papers Breeze had before him. Splash.

"What's this?"

"Enrique Soledad's tape."

Breeze stared at the object before him. He had the expression of someone pondering a suddenly lost position on a chess board. At first he looked for a way out, his face a blend of incredulity and disbelief. As possibilities ran out, and understanding elbowed out hope, his expression became more desperate, grim. Then, all at once, he sagged.

Gould reached for a chair. "You'll have to tell me about it," he said.

Breeze sighed. His eyebrows were pressed into the heels of his hands. He separated his hands just enough to look at the video cassette, the two notched plastic wheels in the plastic shell. "If that contains what Soledad said it contains, then, it's true. I am involved, I am in love with Lena Stahr."

"I want it from the beginning."

Breeze slowly settled back into his chair. When he spoke it was with an air of resignation. "I hardly know where to begin. The roots of it go back a long time before this assignment, before I ever met Lena, with me, with how I am. But you don't want to hear about that, do you?"

"When did you first meet her?"

"In April, of course, when I arrived with the response team. At the beginning she and I had to meet a lot to co-ordinate strategy; the team was called in, after all, mainly to protect her rights. What can I say? I was attracted to her, but didn't think much of it. I'm not in the habit of falling in love on the job. Then one day around the first of May, she sent me flowers, along with a note that read something like 'Thank you for all you've done.' A couple days later she asked if I would come for dinner, a more proper thank you. At first I said no, it was impossible, but she was very insistent—she can be very insistent and, let's face it, I was susceptible—and, well, I gave in. From there things just snowballed."

"Did it ever occur to you that she might have ulterior motives? I mean, she had a very strong interest in influencing the policing of the strike."

"Of course it occurred to me. So I tried to be careful. Right from the start I told her—and I told myself—that I was going to keep my private life and my job separate. That probably seems a pathetic rationalization to you, Gould. A feeble show of professional pride in the midst of a totally compromising situation. But you know what? I really did manage it. I know you won't believe it, but I really am convinced that my decisions here have not been affected by our relationship."

Gould now felt a surge of anger, a strange, exhilarating rush of emotion. "It goes against everything the Force stands for."

"You think I don't know that?"

"I don't know what you know."

Now Breeze was angry too. "Jesus fucking Christ, Gould," he said, almost yelling, "do I have to spell it out for you?" Then, more quietly, "How long have you been a cop?"

"Twenty years."

"I'm closer to thirty. Thirty years of shit like this strike, these murders. Thirty years of the jungle. I'm sick to death of it, Gould, sick of clawing it out with all the other apes. Sick of the way it ruins everything else in your life. You tell me: how many cops do you know who've stayed married after thirty years? How many after five?"

"That's not the point."

"That's the whole point. What I've done here is wrong, I admit it, but for fuck's sake don't rub my nose in it. Sometimes people do desperate things for love."

"Some of us don't."

"Yeah, sure. And end up men-of-action. Principled, rigid, and impotent as hell. That's bullshit, Gould."

Breeze, his hand trembling, shoved the cassette across the desk in Gould's direction. Gould, too dumbfounded to move, watched it tip over the edge and clatter onto the floor. Then, slowly, he reached down and picked it up. He regained his professional manner by reasserting routine: spin the lock on his briefcase, pop the catches, insert the cassette, lift out a notebook and pen, close the lid again.

"There are other questions," he said, finally. He opened the notebook on the briefcase lid. "And I have to warn you. You are now a potential suspect."

"I know my rights."

"Then—"

"Get on with it."

Gould pretended to consult his notebook. After a while, he said, "The obvious place to start is your meeting with Enrique Soledad the day before he disappeared."

"What's to tell? He came in and threatened to expose me if I didn't lean on Lena for him. I tried to bluff him. I said he'd be in even bigger trouble than me if he tried to pull a stunt like that. I told him I could have him shipped back to Costaguana. But he wouldn't buy it. He just got angrier, louder, if that's possible. In fact he never sat still the whole time he was in here. He waved his arms and swore in Spanish and every once in a while he just shouted 'Canadians!' Like he was about to go right over the deep end."

"Why did he want you to lean on Stahr?"

"Wouldn't say exactly. Said I had to make her treat him fairly. Said for me to tell her and she'd know what it meant."

"As if she was cheating him in some way?"

"That's what he thought."

"Did you lean on her?"

"Of course not!"

"Did you tell her of the threat?"

Breeze considered a moment. He lifted the corner of a sheet of paper on his desk and let it fall again. "Frankly, after that little creep was in here, I didn't know what the hell to do. I knew Lena could be hurt by it too. I could imagine the union placards: *Cops and Company in Bed Together!* So, yeah, I told her. Hey, I know what you're thinking, but it didn't happen that way. Lena had nothing to do with the killing."

"What did she say when you told her?"

"She was very calm about it, actually. She's a remarkable woman, Gould, tough as nails, yes, but if you knew the stuff she went through to get where she is."

"What did she say? Exactly."

"She said not to worry. That she understood why Enrique and

Camilla might be mad at her, but that she was going to take care of it."

"Those were her exact words? That she was 'going to take care of it?'"

"Yes."

"She told you that, and a week later, after the Soledads are found with their heads half blown away, you tell me that Stahr didn't have much of a motive?"

"I told you that you shouldn't rule out any possibility."

"Separating your love life from your work."

"That's exactly what I was doing. Everything I told you last week was true. You think I don't know that Lena is a suspect in the case? I know that. But I also know, with as much certainty as I've known anything in my thirty years as a cop, that she didn't do it."

"Then how do you explain her comment?"

"I told you. She was calming. It was in the tone of her voice. It was obvious that she owed the Soledads some money—not surprising, considering what she has was going through with the strike—but that she had found a way to pay them. Maybe she'd just landed some new financing or something."

"What was her reaction to the disappearances?"

"I really don't know. All I know I read in the report of the interview with her."

"Which you did not conduct yourself."

"That's right. As soon as the Soledads disappeared, I knew we had to not see each other for a while. I was sure she had nothing to do with it, but I knew circumstances would look bad for both of us. I phoned her and explained and she agreed. Then I had someone else do the interview."

"And after the bodies were found?"

"She phoned me. She was upset. Upset that I hadn't talked to her in five days, even though she knew why. She said 'You don't think I did it, do you?' and I told her that I loved her and that the only way for things to work out for us was to keep our distances and let the investigation take its course."

"And?"

"She was very upset."

"What did she say?"

"Well, at first she wanted me to handle the investigation myself. I told her that was impossible. And she was furious and called me a useless man."

"And then?"

"We left it at that."

"Now tell me about your meeting, last Thursday night, at the home of Wallace Lies."

Breeze drew a lopsided grin across his square jaw. He slowly shook his head, ran a hand through his salt-and-pepper hair. "Christ," he chuckled, "small towns. I told Lena that that meeting was too risky."

"What happened?"

"It was strange, I'll tell you that." Breeze fiddled with the gold tie-pin at his throat for a minute, staring off into space. Then he said, "Okay, this is the story. Lena called earlier that day, not long after you and I and Viola and Wright had our briefing in the office here. She told me I had to meet her at Lies's place for eight o'clock. I said no way. I repeated what I'd told her before: that the only way for us to make it through this was to lay low and let the investigation take its course. But she insisted. And the fact is I still loved her, still do, and I didn't want us to end another conversation like we ended the last one.

"I didn't know what the hell to make of it. When I got there, Lies and his wife and Lena were waiting for me. We sat around for a while, then suddenly Lena said, 'Wallace and I have something to tell you.' And well, they admitted that they had been seeing one another for months. They said they were in love."

"Did you believe them?"

"I didn't want to. At first I was just in shock. I sat there staring the whole time while they talked. But gradually, yeah, I believed them. It fit some things I remembered."

"Such as?"

"Well. Lena and I had had a very lovely summer. Clandestine meetings, late-night dinners at her house, all very romantic. Then, I don't know when it was exactly, late-August or early-September, things started to change. She became preoccupied, almost evasive at times. I knew she was under pressure from the strike and all, but something about it, about her manner, it did occur to me that there might be another man. Anyway, this went on right until the middle of October. Until she called me one night and we met and it was wonderful. We met three or four times then over a week—posed for Soledad's fucking cameras—and she sent me flowers again."

"The flowers that were still on your desk when I came in for my briefing?"

"That was a little reckless of me, to keep them there like that. But I was ecstatic that things seemed to be back on track with us."

"So the idea of another man faded from your mind."

"Not totally, but yeah."

"Why do you think Lies and Stahr told you about their relationship like that?"

"Who knows? It was weird, like I said. I still can't figure it out. What they said was that with all the awful things that had happened recently, they wanted to make a gesture, to do something up-front, honest. They told all this to Margaret—it seemed to hit her like a ton of bricks."

"When did Philip Bentley come in?"

"Just after the big confession. That was also strange, almost like it had been planned. He stayed downstairs only for a few minutes and then took Margaret Lies upstairs for some counseling. She didn't seem particularly interested in it but Bentley—and Lena and Lies—all insisted."

"A lot of things about that meeting don't sit right," said Gould, after a moment. "For one thing, the next day, you, in this office, you were happy as hell. I remember you cleaning up, redecorating. Hardly the image of a man whose sweet-heart had just confessed to two-timing him for months."

"I know, I know. But listen. The reasons for that came later. After Bentley and Margaret Lies had gone upstairs, there was a long silence. Then Lies went to get something from the kitchen, and Lena, ever so softly, said, 'Can you ever forgive me?' I said, 'I don't know.' And, quickly, she admitted that the whole relationship with Lies was really just physical, based on lust. She said that, in a way, I was responsible. That when we started seeing one another it awakened feelings in her. She said she hadn't been with a man for so long that she went a bit crazy. Maybe the pressure of the strike had something to do with it too. But the thing was, she said, her feelings for me were quite different than her feelings for Lies.

"The long and the short of it is, at the end of the night I felt closer to Lena than I had ever been before. I didn't know if we were going to stay together, if it would all work out for us, but, somehow, all that honesty made me feel okay. And there's something else, too. On the way out to our cars, Lena told me something. She said that she had talked that afternoon with Al Goodwin. She said she couldn't promise anything, but that they had agreed to have their negotiators meet again.

"By the next day, when I met you here, I felt like a huge weight had lifted. I had, still have, this sense that things are going to work out. Hey, I'm about ready to retire from the jungle anyway. Who knows? Maybe after the strike is settled and the killers of the Soledads are found, maybe Lena and I will patch things up. We both, I think, are ready to do some settling down."

"That's a very touching story," Gould said, "but it doesn't change the basic facts. If Stahr ends up implicated in the murders, there is a good chance you'll end up an accessory."

"If Lena is convicted of the murders, I won't much care."

Gould returned his notebook to his briefcase. As he did so he felt a stiffness in his shoulders, an ache that spoke of the effort he'd needed to sit still during the interview. More than once while talking to Breeze he had felt sabotaged by emotion—anger, resentment, frustration—concussions of noisy protest. He was filled with contempt for Breeze, for his unprofessional conduct (it confirmed the negative first impression he had had) and yet, somehow, he felt an oddly contrary emotion as well. It wasn't sympathy, exactly; it was a hybrid, too complex to be named. The effect of it, however, was a subtle ache of loneliness in Gould, an ache similar to something he had felt from time to time during his interview with Lena Stahr. During that interview, and again now, he mentally crossed this ache out. He refused to acknowledge it, refused to allow it a place in his conscious mind. Which, as it turned out, only increased his anger.

He snapped the latches on his briefcase. "I'll be filing my report with O'Brien later today," he said. "No doubt he'll suspend you pending an investigation."

"I'll suspend myself, effective immediately."

"Suit yourself. By the way, what kind of weapon do you carry?"

"Smith and Wesson. A .38. What's it to you?"

"Standard or hollow point ammunition?"

"You know as well as I do, Gould, that hollow points are against regulations."

"Let me see."

Breeze, after a moment's hesitation, reached slowly inside his jacket. His chin lowered. For a moment he almost looked like he was smelling the rose in his lapel. Then he brought out the gun.

"Has it been fired lately?" asked Gould.

"Not long ago. Maybe two weeks. I did some target shooting."

"You had time, with all this?"

"I find that it relaxes me."

Gould took possession of the .38. He balanced it in his palm for a moment, as if admiring it, then suddenly cracked it open and spun the breach. Six bullets dropped into the palm of his right hand. He held one up for Breeze to see. The indented point.

"I'll have to send it to Cramdown for tests."

On the way out, Gould felt a renewed surge of anger. He had an overpowering urge to say something ironic, cutting, vindictive. He looked back from the door and saw Breeze at the desk staring into space.

"*Hasta la vista*, Inspector."

Breeze blinked his eyes. Returned a blank look. "Sorry Gould," he said. "I don't understand a goddamn word of Spanish."

CHAPTER SEVENTEEN

"People do stupid things for love," I said, "and I'm no different than anyone else. But the fact is, being with Jayne was one of the most intense, the most erotic experiences I have ever had. She also pushed me in ways I needed. I wouldn't say that I was lost before I met her or anything as obvious as that, but, in a lot of ways, things had stalled for me. I was sort of going through the motions, taking the path of least resistance. She showed me that I was locked into certain habitual ways of seeing."

"But why did she jump all over you? Why did she accuse you of trying to force her into stereotypical roles? The unattainable ideal, the femme fatale . . . ."

"I just wanted to know her so much, you know what I mean? The more I loved her, the more I wanted to learn everything I could about her, her desires, her fears, where she came from. I could see her every time I closed my eyes. I was convinced that with her I was on the verge of something, something amazing, something I don't know exactly what, that this was a once in a life-time chance and if I didn't make the most of it I would curse away the rest of my life. And, of course, she wouldn't talk about herself. Hardly at all. She said her past was not pertinent. Maybe, in my need, I fell back on certain familiar. . . categories."

"No wonder she told you off. Imagine how she felt."

"My friends thought I was a fool to be with her. That she was the crazy one. They said her main claim to fame was that she was one of the ten most difficult people in the world to get along with. But you know, without her I wouldn't, for instance, have been able to put together my dissertation proposal. I'd known for a while what I wanted to write on but I couldn't figure out a way to do it that wasn't just the same old thing. I wanted to do something distinctive, something a bit different."

"The proposal that was rejected? The reason you quit?"

"Yeah, yeah, I know. Maybe it was too different, for the academics, anyway. For Jayne it wasn't different enough. She said it was a copout, that there were a few bells and whistles in it to get attention but that, basically, it looked like a ploy to get me a job. I guess that's what happens when you try to find middle ground. You get it from both directions."

"Some people call it sitting on the fence."

Around this time, a charter bus had stopped at the Igloo and forty or fifty passengers pushed in through the door for breakfast. For half-an-hour, there was pandemonium. The two waitresses ran this way and that with order pads and pots of coffee, the cook came out from behind the counter with plates balanced on various improbable parts of her body. Tourists in the booth one over started to complain to one another. "You had yours yet? How come they already have theirs?" And, at the end of it all, Nora walked dazed amidst the debris and last stragglers carrying an unclaimed omelet. "Who ordered the omelet special? Did anybody order the omelet special?"

"So," said Gould, "is that why you broke up?"

"It's only part of the story."

"Would either of you like an omelet?" asked Nora. "It's still hot, and the toast is all ready."

On Monday night, Gould returned, a second time, to the Igloo. He came in just as I was finishing my supper, met my eyes from inside the glass door, strode the length and width of the place and slid into the seat across from me. No hesitation, no greeting. When Marlene arrived with a menu, he was all business.

He ordered the same thing I had just had, the hot turkey sandwich, a house specialty. A warmed-up slice of processed turkey on a slab of white (or brown) bread flooded with gravy. Watery mashed potatoes; unfrozen peas and carrots. Cranberry sauce out of one of those rectangular plastic containers, a small brick of red gelatin, tart, with a subtle flavouring of dust and chemicals. Delicious.

There were only a few other customers in the restaurant. Not far from my booth, two truckers in sweatshirts were doing cigarettes-and-coffee at the *Truckers Only* table. In another section, a family of five—four around the table, one in a high-chair—was having a cheap night out. Two lone men and a single woman occupied three other tables, locals or travelers it was hard to tell. Dusk had fallen, making the whole place seem more self-contained, more insular, the overhead lights casting a sheen, like the in-side of a mirror strip, over the windows. In reality, of course, dusk turned the Igloo into a giant fishbowl.

Gould ate in silence. When he was done, he wiped his mouth with a paper napkin. Then he gestured at my journal. "You've obviously thought a lot about the Soledads the last few days. You've listened to all those stories, the competing theories. So what's your best guess? Who did it?"

The question put me on guard. It seemed to nudge against the implied boundary of our acquaintance so far. My opinion on the case? Throughout our conversation of the night before, Gould had seemed to steer away from anything that would treat me as an equal. He had played the professional investigator, sitting in judgement on my journal entries, lecturing me on method. Even his question about Jayne had seemed, at the time, consistent with his method, its systematic pursuit of even the most minor detail. He had studiously (it seemed) avoided any direct discussion of the Soledad case.

My immediate reaction was that the question was a trap, a coyly casual invitation to compromise myself, but the way he spoke, something in it, or rather, some lack it in, seduced my confidence. In the depths of his eyes, I detected no twinkling of irony.

"Lies?" he prompted.

"Maybe."

"Why?"

I grinned self-deprecatingly in the direction of my journal. "From what I know...."

That won me something, an almost imperceptible nod of the head.

I went on. "Lies seems to be at the centre of things around here. I'm not sure why he would have done it, and he's been nice enough to me, but, well, you have to be suspicious of everybody, don't you?"

Gould contemplated his empty plate for a moment, then reached for his coffee cup—which, as it turned out, was empty too. Gazing into its depth, he asked, "What do you think of the rumours about a hit squad from Costaguana?"

"No way."

The way I said it, my sudden confidence, made him look up. "Explain."

Suddenly I was buoyed by his manner towards me. "Let me put it this way. If this was a novel, if this was a detective novel, I'd say yes right away. Because—hey, do you read them?"

"Detective novels? Never."

"Huh. Well, one of the rules of detective fiction is that the least likely suspect is usually the one who did it. And in this case, the hit squad is least likely."

"Why?"

Now I really warmed to the topic. "First of all, there is no real evidence for it. The people who've brought up the idea with me, when I ask them for reasons, they can't give any. Just vague suspicions about why the Soledads moved into that fancy house. Or something about some guy who claims to have seen a black Mercedes. You know about that?"

"Yes."

"Then you know. I mean, gimme a break: a black Mercedes! But more than that." I took a short, quick, excited breath, and plunged on. "Listen. I've really thought about this, and it seems to me that the whole hit squad thing is just too convenient. It, like, gets the town completely off the hook, you know? I mean, this place, not the Igloo itself but Silver, the town—this place is seriously fucked up. The strike has shredded whatever community spirit there was here. Everybody hates everybody else and not just because of the sides they support in the strike. It's like the strike, or something else acting with the strike, has magnified every petty difference between people. I don't know how many times I've had someone get into that seat there and tell me 'the guy you just talked to, he's an asshole.' And for what? This guy thinks his car is so hot, this guy cuts his grass three times a week, this chick thinks she's God's gift to whatever. At first I just ignored stuff like that, but, after a while, I couldn't. I even wrote some of it down in my journal. Anyway, about the only thing people seem to agree on is that they hate—hated—the Soledads. To me, that means someone in this town has to be responsible for the killings. You see what I mean?"

Gould tapped his moustache with a finger. "Your logic is unusual," he said, "but, yes, I do see what you mean."

Believe it or not, it was a decisive moment. I recognized it right away: even with that initial flicker of irony, Gould's response acknowledged me, for the first time, in a new way. Not as a witness, not as a source of information to be twisted and squeezed and discarded, but—as corny as this sounds—as a fellow human being. *Come on in . . . shelter from the storm.*

He confirmed this a few minutes later when he cast his eyes around the restaurant and said, "Ironic, isn't it, that we're discussing the Soledad case here. After all, Wallace Lies could walk in at any second."

"He could. Though I've heard he tends to come and go by the back."

"Ah."

"I did meet him once, though."

"What did you make of him?"

"Well, it was on my first day here, not long after I discovered the bodies. I was, as you can imagine, rather distracted. I also didn't realize who he was at the time, that he had his fingers in so many pies, that he was so close to the Soledads."

Marlene appeared with the coffee pot. She was dressed in the standard Igloo waitress uniform: navy blue slacks and light blue and red pinstriped top, the uniform clashing with the surroundings, which were mostly in browns and greens, as if it had been left over from some previous incarnation of the place. Like the other waitresses, Marlene wore sensible white running shoes.

When our cups were topped up, I continued. "Anyway, the point is, I didn't really make much of him at all. He met me just inside there, introduced himself, and said I could camp in the parking lot if I wanted. He was kind of loud. He pumped my hand in this exaggerated kind of way. You know, one of those I'm-a-virile-go-getter-and-all-round-good-guy handshakes. The funny thing is, though, I can't remember his face. I've tried. It was a natural thing to do once I learned who he was. All I can say is that he struck me as sort of ordinary. Either that or I wasn't paying attention."

"Never met him myself."

"Really? I just assumed, I mean, wasn't he one of the most obvious people to start the investigation with?"

"He was, and I tried to set up an interview with him last week. It didn't work out."

"I've heard he's a rather slippery character."

"That seems to be the general opinion."

"Judith says he's a typical boss. Likes to play the generous rich guy when he's in the mood but look out if you try to stand up for your rights."

"Judith?"

"The night cook. A remarkable person. She and I have talked a lot the last few days. She grew up in Silver and knows a lot about the place, the people."

"What's remarkable about her?"

"Oh, just personal history stuff. I won't bore you with the details. Just say that she comes from a very poor family, her father was abusive, and she's fought every inch of the way to where she is. She got honours in high school. She's a whiz with computers. She's working in the restaurant to save money for university."

Gould gave me an ironic look. I knew what he was thinking. I did not debase myself by claiming the obvious: that Judith and I were only friends.

"About Lies," I said.

"Yes?"

He still had that look on his face. A half-grin. The pompous twit. Who do you think you are? I thought, and out loud said, "Forget it."

He seemed to detect my irritation. The grin dissolved into his usual mask. For a moment, he seemed to waver between assuming his air of superiority, thereby claiming victory in the exchange, and offering me an olive branch. Typically enough, he settled for ambiguity.

"Are you still writing all this down in your notebook?" he asked.

I grunted as if to say More-or-less.

"Good. You never know. Maybe some day I'll show you what a real investigator's notebook looks like."

Gould spent two or three restless hours that night before falling asleep. He should have written a report to O'Brien about Inspector Breeze. He should have prepared for his interview with Wallace Lies, which was finally, definitively, set for ten o'clock the next morning. Instead, he drifted from spot to spot in his room, gazing vacantly at this and that, the framed picture of a knight in a duck-billed helmet holding a lance, a constellation of cigarette burns on the carpet, his unopened briefcase, his hands. Now and then he was aware of rumblings from the Trans-Canada. For a while, he lay fully clothed on his bed, staring up at his reflection in the sixteen mirrors. The smell—part dead salmon, part bile, part disinfectant—was, he noticed, back.

In the end, he forced himself to follow his usual end of day routine. He washed his hands and face, brushed his teeth, put his robe over the back of a chair, took his clothes off and put them in the appropriate places. He felt the coolness of the room on his naked body. He forced down a memory of his father. He thought of Costaguana.

In bed, he remembered the brooch that Lena Stahr had worn that morning on her blazer. A silver eagle. For a while he recreated the image of the brooch for himself, how the eagle rose and fell with her breath, how it caught light from a nearby lamp or the fire behind the glass doors. During the interview, his eyes had been lured to it but had always, out of politeness, moved away. There was something oddly enticing, even familiar, about the brooch. He wondered where it had come from. Stahr, he knew, had begun her career as a teenaged worker in the offices of Silver Eagle Mines. Could it be from there?

He felt an ache of loneliness.

Then, just before he stumbled into sleep, his mind made one of those unusual, half-conscious connections, an explanation for why the brooch seemed familiar to him, one mystery explained by another: the brooch reminded him of the shoe in the tree. Camilla's white shoe. Gleaming, full of significance, inexplicable.

Next morning, after the usual preliminaries, Gould drove back into Silver to interview Wallace Lies. He felt, more or less, himself.

It was a grey morning, a reluctant morning, clouds scraping their underbellies along the mountain peaks. Following Queen Street, its twisting course along the riverbank, gave Gould the impression of travelling up the river itself. On mornings like this, the river the colour of lead, the sky the colour of smoke (as if the union office still burned), Gould felt like Silver was the very end of the world and he travelling towards it in a rusty old metal tub of a boat (this old tub from the carpool) . . . sandbanks, marshes, forests rising on either side into mist. If he'd had a sense of history, which he did not, he might have considered how the place was before the thriving of the town, what it must have been like for those first Europeans huddling at the rest camp there, the log cabins they called Whatcom, how they must have felt walled in by the place, the ramparts of forest spiked with rock and ice, the mysterious beat of un-Westernized places. He might even have considered the eventual conquest of the region, its so-called civilizing and incorporation into the Dominion, which mostly meant taking the land away from people with a different complexion and slightly flatter noses, and rearranging the landscape to suit. The hidden (and not so hidden) savagery of the place.

As it was, the impression of a journey lasted only a moment, chased as it was by Gould's disciplined reviewing of his strategies for the interview ahead. If a trace of the impression remained, it was only in the briefest estrangement as he came into sight of the Silver Municipal Hall. For the space of a heartbeat, the image of the municipal building merged in his mind with an image of the burnt-out union office: the well-kept brick building, and then, superimposed, or as a kind of shadow, a scorched shell half-buried in its own debris. The effect was like the contrast between the Lies and Soledad homes, the one stolidly and brightly present, the other shadowed by the mouth of encroaching forest.

He parked in a space marked *Visitor*.

The building itself was set back from the road, creating a small green space, a walkway up to the main entrance, a couple of benches, gardens. The green space was roughly bordered by a half dozen wrought-iron posts with round white balls on top. At night these lamps were turned on. The idea was to light up the front of the building pleasantly, but Gould, for reasons he couldn't quite put his finger on, found the thought of it slightly chilling.

It was inevitable, after such a build-up, that Gould would find Wallace Lies an anti-climax. He expected a man to inspire awe and fear, someone whom, perhaps, against his own better judgement, he might admire. He expected a man capable of a withering show of sincerity, a man of no restraint, faith, fear—a man who with the kind of physical presence to match his own. Instead, when he had been shown into the Mayor's office, he found a squat, round faced man in a black-and-white checked jacket.

They shook hands. Lies took a step back. "You're looking at my jacket," he said. "No, no, you don't have to admit it, Inspector. Everybody does. It's, well, let's not beat around the bush: it's loud. A loud jacket. Rather like the owner! Sit down, sit down."

They took seats in a nearby arrangement of furniture. The layout and decor of the office reminded Gould of O'Brien's, though the atmosphere, partly because of the appearance of Lies himself, was less muted and affecting. O'Brien's office with the curtains open and balloons hanging from the ceiling.

Gould assumed the jacket was an extension of Lies's strategy for dealing with his name, a way of flaunting his origins as a salesman. Even so, it contributed to the feeling of anticlimax. The jacket only highlighted the extreme ordinariness of the man inside, a man ordinary in complexion, in feature, in manners, and in voice. He was of middle size and average build. His eyes, of the usual blue, were perhaps unusually cunning, and he certainly could focus his glance from time to time, but, all in all, Lies seemed eminently forgettable (which explains, perhaps, my own fuzzy memory of him from that first day in the Igloo). Now and again his lips took on an indefinable, faint expression, something stealthy, a smile or not a smile, something you did remember but couldn't explain. Maybe it was unconscious, this smile; though now and then, just after he had said something, it intensified for an instant. Otherwise he didn't even strike a consistent mood. His face lit up and darkened again like sunshine and shadow on a windy day. Face like an autumn sky, or a spring sky, threatening one minute and inviting the next.

"Let's get right to the Soledads," said Gould.

"Fire away."

"I've been told that you knew them better than almost anyone else in town. Certainly you seem to have had important dealings with them right until the end."

"That's true."

"Tell me how you met."

Lies grinned—or, maybe, not. "Through the church, of course. I'm a deacon, on the board of directors. We had a dinner to officially welcome them to Canada and it went from there."

"Did you become intimate with them early on?"

"Oh no. At first they spent most of their time with the Bentleys."

"When did your friendship develop?"

"I wouldn't call it a 'friendship' exactly. The Soledads were not really 'friendship' kind of people, if you know what I mean. But the beginning, that would have to be the trip to Vancouver."

"In June?"

"I brought them back on the 25th."

"And they had been gone?"

"Ten days or so. They wouldn't tell anyone why. Philip Bentley was quite upset about it."

"How did you come to pick them up?"

"They called from Vancouver and asked if I would."

"Just like that?"

"Just like that."

"It seems like a rather big favour. Why did you agree?"

Lies, who was seated at right angles to Gould, now ran his open hands down the lapels of his checked jacket. "Various reasons," he said, as much to the jacket as to Gould. "They knew I made regular trips back and forth. And I had offered to fly them around before—you know, to see the sights and that. And, well"—he looked up, that stealthy smile again—"I'm just that kind of guy."

"So you went down to pick them up."

"They waited for me at the airport."

"What was their mood when you found them?"

"Very happy to see me, kind of relieved, and also very tired."

Gould now considered a moment. He rubbed his hands slowly on his thighs. Then, slowly, he shook his head. "Too many things about this trip don't sit right. Did they talk at all on the way back?"

"Not much. Except for repeating how grateful they were."

"Nothing that might have indicated the reason for their trip?"

"No. I did find out the reason later, though."

Lies smiled, conscious or unconscious, it was impossible to tell. His eyes gave Gould an appraising look and seemed to decide that he had found a good bargain. Gould grew very still.

"And?"

"They told me when they bought the house. You know the story of that?"

"The basic details."

"Sometimes the deals just seem to find me! Well, fact is, Inspector, I didn't expect to sell the place when I approached them about it. I thought they'd just rent. I knew they were having problems with the Bentleys and my other tenants skipped town because of the strike. But then Enrique flashed that wad of money at me—fifty grand—and said why not sell it to them instead."

"And the trip to Vancouver?"

"That's where the money came from, according to Enrique. When he flashed the wad, of course I was surprised, and he right away started explaining. He said they sold some family heirlooms. Jewelry, probably, though he didn't specify. That was why they didn't tell anybody why they were going and why they called me to bring them back; by that point, they had the cash in their suitcases and were afraid to take the bus."

Gould tapped his moustache. "I'm surprised by this."

"I was pretty surprised too."

"No. I'm surprised you didn't say anything before."

"The Soledads wanted it kept quiet. Last thing they wanted was someone breaking into their house looking for more heirlooms."

"And you didn't tell anyone?"

"Not a soul."

"Didn't you find anything suspicious about it? Think. Ten days alone in Vancouver and later, after apparently hiding it for two months, they produce fifty thousand dollars cash."

"I did find it suspicious. Hey, tongues wagged all over town. But, me, I was mainly just happy for them. It was like one small thing at least had turned out right for them."

"And they weren't any more specific about what they sold than 'heirlooms'?"

"No."

"Maybe they didn't sell anything at all. Did you ever consider that? Maybe they actually borrowed the money."

Lies shrugged, non-committal.

Gould fixed the mayor with his eyes. "They didn't happen to borrow it from you?"

"Certainly not."

"What kind of deal did you give them on the house?"

"Nothing special. Hey, I liked the Soledads, I really did, but I'm a businessman too. I lopped a few thousand off my selling price. And agreed to take back a mortgage, at a reasonable rate, for the balance."

"Now that the Soledads are dead, what happens?"

"The house will have to be sold."

"To pay off the mortgage to you."

"Well—yes. But also to make sure the children receive their inheritance."

"Not considering bidding on it yourself, are you? Estate sales tend to be good bargains."

Lies laughed, then, abruptly, grew serious. "As executor of the estate," he said, "I will make sure everything is fair and above board."

"I'm sure you will."

Gould let a second tick by, two. Then, "Okay. Let's move on to when the Soledads came to you about working for Lena Stahr. When was that?"

"Late July. After the trip to Vancouver but before the house."

"What did they say?"

"Enrique met me here at work. He said that, after much thinking, they'd decided to have a go at the mine. I was surprised, of course, given what I knew about their backgrounds."

"The union work in Costaguana."

"Exactly. But he was insistent."

"Did he say what kind of work he was interested in?"

"No. I just assumed it was the usual. I knew he'd worked at a mine in Costaguana."

"And so you arranged a meeting with Lena Stahr?"

"Uh-huh. Though, you know, Enrique did come to me under a slight misconception."

"How so?"

"He thought I knew Lena because of business dealings. He just assumed, since, let's be frank, I've got my fingers in an awful lot of what goes on economically around here. Of course, he was right that I knew Lena, but you know about Lena and I?"

"I've been told the story."

"Then you know I was both the right and wrong person for him to ask. I did know Lena, but she and I had agreed early on in our relationship never to mix business into it."

"What made you decide to help?"

"I liked the Soledads, like I said. And Enrique seemed truly desperate, unhappy. By that point a number of things had gone very wrong for him and Camilla. You know about Enrique at the high school?"

"Yes."

"Well, Camilla was doing volunteer work in the church office as well, learning to use the computer accounting system and so on, but that didn't go very well either."

"Personality conflicts."

"That's right."

Lies was living up to his name. Gould was sure of it. The problem was, it was hard to know where the lying was or what it was meant to hide or what it might signify. Lies, Gould had to admit, was difficult to read. Not that there seemed to be any great art or intelligence behind the difficulty. In fact, the combination of elements in Lies, the changeable face, the flaunting of name and occupation, the loud jacket, only set out in bas relief the extreme ordinariness of the man: the very tactics designed, apparently, to mask the ordinariness, only drew attention to it. Either Lies really was an ordinary man, with ordinary schemes and tactics, or he possessed a singular talent, one that Gould had never seen before: the ability to present himself as a parody of the ordinary, as an ordinary man locked in a grueling struggle against mediocrity, thereby, by an extraordinary deception, to present himself as ordinary. Somehow, Gould couldn't believe the second possibility. It was just too subtle. Either way, however, the effect was that Lies seemed to have no depth, his character all on the changeable surface, his expressions without anchor.

Gould went on the attack.

"All right. Now tell me about your other trips to Vancouver."

"My other trips?"

"When was the last time you actually flew there?"

Lies's face went through one of its climate changes. A frown, a smile, nervous or knowing, it was hard to tell. After a moment, in his blandest voice, he said, "Probably the Labour Day long weekend. I'd have to check my flight log to be sure."

"And what was the purpose of your trip?"

"I am a man of many interests."

"So I've heard."

Lies displayed his enigmatic smile. He opened his two hands and tapped the spread fingertips against his suit jacket. Like a kid pretending to have wings. "Fact is, Inspector, sometimes I just need to get away. From Silver, from Margaret—love her though I do. I go to Vancouver, check in at a hotel, spend a couple of days taking in the city. Who knows? Maybe someday I'll come across a good business opportunity."

"You wouldn't happen to run errands for Lena Stahr while on these trips?"

"I told you, Inspector, our relationship is strictly personal."

"Except for the Soledads."

"Except for the Soledads."

Gould crossed his arms. Skeptical. Then, assuming his most authoritative tone, he said, "I don't believe you. I don't believe you and Lena Stahr have had a personal relationship only. I believe you are hiding some business arrangement with her. And that arrangement is connected with the Soledads and with Vancouver. Now, you strike me as the kind of man constantly driven to mix business and pleasure and vice versa. I believe your Vancouver trips are connected to this business arrangement. And I also believe that on these trips you always try to mix in a little pleasure."

Lies was silent. Grinning, apparently, to himself. Gould tried to fix him with his most determined look—and failed.

"Let me tell you something," said Gould. "I will find out what you did in Vancouver over the long weekend. I will find out about other trips to Vancouver. I will find out what your business was and what your pleasure was. I suspect the pleasure will turn out to be a lot more embarrassing than the business. So why don't you tell me about the business now and save us both a lot of trouble?"

Lies seemed to consider a moment. A cloud came and passed across his face. Then his lips twitched. "I tell you, Inspector," he said, "this experience has enlarged my mind."

So it went. Gould tried, in various ways, to find out more about Lies' involvement with Lena Stahr. He tried to find out about the intense conversations between Lies and Enrique Soledad that Margaret Lies had reported. But whenever the interview seemed about to break new ground, Lies put on his smile. His ambiguous, bland, but somehow threatening smile. Or the verbal equivalent of that smile: inexplicable fragments of trite philosophy. When pressed about the meeting at his home, Lies only confirmed what Gould already knew. When asked about the Soledads—about whether they seemed anxious or threatened in the days before the disappearance—he gave exactly the answer that Gould might have predicted: that they did seem rather worried, and, somehow, it seemed that they were feeling pressure from back home. He didn't know why the pressure was from Costaguana but he had a gut feeling. And, since he was on the topic, he was also quite sure that neither Lena Stahr nor Al Goodwin were involved in the murders.

As the interview went on, Gould grew more and more still—not the stillness of authority he so often projected, but as if the life were being drained out of him.

At least Lies was not brazen enough to bring up the black Mercedes.

Chapter Eighteen

Once, after a particularly intense argument, I grabbed her by the shoulders. I held her away from me, firmly, at arms length, and gazed down into her eyes.
"What are you doing?" she asked.
"Trying to read the instructions."
She twisted away. "I'm not a cake box, you know."

The interview with Lies left Gould frustrated but also, in an odd way, satisfied. He was frustrated because, let's face it, the interview was not a textbook example of a brilliant detective extracting truth from a witness. Maybe, for all his projection of ability, Gould was a prisoner of his own technique. *Above all, stay firm.* Good advice for most situations, but not much help with the witness who can turn a blank face to your show of strength, or the witness who responds to your irresistible chain of reasoning with the rhetorical equivalent of a blank face. *I tell you, Inspector, this whole experience has enlarged my mind.*

What satisfied Gould about his failure with Wallace Lies was that it added credence to his theory about what he was up against. More and more, with a certain grim pleasure, he was convinced that the main players in the Soledad drama—Goodwin, Stahr, and Lies—had somehow, out of some common interest, coordinated their stories. There was something too neat, too exactly fitting about the evidence each of them had given; there was that strange reluctance by Stahr and Goodwin to point the finger at each other; there was even, he noted when comparing his notebook accounts of the interviews, a repetition of certain key phrases. It was as if, at the beginning of the investigation, traces of the truth lay scattered about, available and disguised only by their ordinariness, but that now, like the debris swept up after a storm, those traces had been gathered, bagged, hauled away somewhere. More and more as the investigation continued it seemed that he was met with small town courtesy, scrubbed and extended hands, and then left to view for himself the blank innocence of the scene.

But if there was some kind of conspiracy, that raised a number of troubling questions. Most obviously, what common interest could have drawn three such different people together? Even if you believed the story of Lies and Stahr innocently in love, which Gould didn't, you had to account for Goodwin. What could Goodwin and Stahr, much less Goodwin and Lies, have in common? If Goodwin's men had been stealing silver bars from the mine, as seemed likely, what possible motivation could Stahr have to keep this theft hushed up? Goodwin, Stahr and Lies may all have disliked the Soledads (discounting their identical disclaimers), they may even have benefited each in some small way from their deaths—but enough to overcome their own differences to actually kill them? It didn't add up. Or maybe the three of them weren't actually involved in the killings, and were just inclined, for some perverse reason, to thwart Gould's attempt to solve the case. That last possibility was even more disturbing than the others.

Even more than before, Gould was convinced that there was something missing, one vital flaw in the stories he had been told, a gleaming trace that had been overlooked and left behind. He had thought, perhaps, to detect this trace in his interview with Wallace Lies, but, in retrospect, he could see that that had been an ill-founded hope: clearly Lies was the best actor of them all, the most accomplished artist, the one least likely to give anything away. What he needed was a starting point, a way in, the proverbial single thread to start the unraveling.

In keeping with everything else about the Soledad investigation, this thread, when it came, came from the absolutely most unexpected source.

Me.

After the interview with Lies, Gould returned to The Red Grizzly. He took his notes, made a few minor interpretations and telephoned Sergeant Bacon in Cramdown. Bacon explained that the tests on the cigarette butts were proceeding well. He was very excited about the technical difficulties. "The hardest part is finding enough of a sample from the first butt to do the DNA test. Saliva doesn't preserve well—usually you need the thicker fluids, semen or blood. But in this case I think we've struck it lucky, because the paper on these cigarettes is unusually thick. With the right extraction process, I think we can get enough material to try for a match. It'll take a couple of days though."

Gould then explained about the Breeze's service revolver. "There will have to be an internal investigation, obviously," he said, "but for now, I'd appreciate it if you'd just take care of the ballistics tests."

After this conversation, Gould opened his portable typewriter to punch out the report about Inspector Breeze. Finally. He had actually tried to start it a couple of times the night before, in the midst of his restlessness, but had been paralyzed by resistance. The resistance isn't hard to explain. Gould had a remarkable capacity for compartmentalizing his thoughts. Once he had decided to carry on with the Soledad case, the possibility of his father's involvement was virtually excised from his mind; it remained only as a dim final outcome of events, the kind of larger significance that, out of habit, he was expert at blanking out. Yet the compartments were not absolutely airtight, and the idea of reporting back to O'Brien, of holding an image of the superintendent in his head and addressing words to it, kept setting off memories from the Friday before. *I know more about you than you realize.*

The resistance, it turned out, was only temporary, a mental hiccup before his habitual reassertion of will. Now, as Gould sat down to write again, his earlier hesitations seemed lamentably self-indulgent. *Thwack, thwack, thwack* went the little typewriter, like a riding crop wielded lightly but firm. Slowly but with assurance the report appeared, first letter to last, Gould's analysis precisely encoded by the single authoritative finger striking keys from each hand.

Then he went to the Igloo for an early dinner.

PROSPECTS UNKNOWN

When Gould came through the glass doors, I was waiting for him. My usual table—dirty cup and spoon, spilled sugar granules, books, condiments (including a four column tray stacked with shots of ten-percent cream), and a stand-up sign advertising a full meal special for two or four—before me. I had been debating since morning whether or not to track him down with my news. Somehow, even though the news was pertinent to the case, I couldn't do it. Or maybe I didn't want to. Of course, I was still dazzled by the beginning of our friendship; only two nights before, he had planted himself across from me and begun his strange overtures. Part of me was bewildered by this attention, disoriented, even suspicious (was he trying to manipulate me?); part of me couldn't believe my good luck. My news was another piece of good fortune, something to savour a few hours, to hold in reserve. I wanted to see if he would actually seek me out a third time. And waiting only sweetened the anticipation. How delicious to see his face when I finally told him!

Gould surveyed the room with a self-contained air, noting my presence but giving away no obvious sign of it, and set out with that steady unhurried pickle-assed walk. His trench coat and suit-jacket were open; his briefcase swung from two fingers. He paused a moment to read the headline of a newspaper left behind at the *Truckers Only* table. Then, with an air of having his mind entirely on something else, he slid into the seat across from me.

I looked at him. He looked at me. "I hope that's not your poker face," he said.

Lillian arrived. Gould placed his order. Then he settled back—the vinyl going *crump*—and folded his arms. I could just make out the flat oval on the end of his revolver butt.

I gave a sheepish smile and reached for my journal.

"Why don't you just tell me in your own words?"

"My—?"

"Own words—unpolished. Without all the attempts at style. It doesn't impress me, you know."

I hesitated. Like so many of Gould's apparently off-hand comments, this one filled me with a subtle dread. I knew—but couldn't prove—I'd been seen into.

"Try it," he said.

So I signaled Lillian to refill my cup. I added a little more sugar than usual. Then sat back too. "It has to do with Judith Mitchell," I said.

"The cook?"

"Yeah. We've struck up a kind of friendship. It started my first day here. She brought my order over personally. Since then we've talked a lot. I told you some of it last night."

"Poor family, abusive father, whiz with computers."

"Right. Well, I came in early this morning to catch her at the end of her shift. She was working grave-yard again. We had breakfast together. She sat right there where you're sitting now. Anyway, she seemed kind of pensive, so I asked her if anything was the matter. She said, 'What isn't?' Turns out her boyfriend has been slapping her around. He's a logger—pickup truck, flannel shirts, the whole bit. I asked her why she didn't leave the guy. I mean, there's no excuse. And she looked at me and said, 'Why don't we go for a walk. I want to show you something.'"

I took a sip of my coffee. Sweet indeed. Gould followed me with his eyes, his usual guarded expression. His forearms were on the table, his fingers intertwined.

"You know what?" I continued. "She was actually married for a while, until last summer. That's what she wanted to talk about. Her husband was her high school sweetheart, a gentle good-natured guy, also interested in computers. They were saving to go to university together. Anyway, not long after their marriage, her husband started feeling sick, and it turned out he had leukemia. The first treatment put him in remission for about six weeks but after that . . . well, he died in July. She showed me his grave, that's where she wanted to go walking. The site is open again, the police barriers gone, but I guess you know that."

"And this—"

"You know it's weird, how you can never tell the significance of things. Not until you know their history. I mean, I actually remembered her husband's grave, I remembered it from when I discovered the bodies. It had this border of stones around the outside. Stones about this big, and round and smooth like eggs. She said she'd tried to make a garden out of it but the flowers wouldn't take."

I paused, deliberately, to let Gould formulate his question. I was pretty sure what the question would be. "And the Soledads?"

(Yes!)

"Of course. The Soledads do fit into it."

Here I sipped my coffee, slowly, theatrically, trying to be as annoying as possible. Gould waited me out.

"It has nothing to do with her seeing anything," I said, "even though she does walk up there a lot. A lot of people do. No. Actually"—I couldn't keep it in any longer—"it has to do with Camilla Soledad, with what really happened between her and Reverend Bentley last summer. Turns out Judith was the one teaching Camilla about the computers in the church office . . . ."

It all rushed out. In the midst of my revelation, Gould's food arrived. The control with which he ate, calmly forking up hot turkey sandwich and chewing thoroughly before sending it down his throat, filled me with admiration. Once he paused to tap his moustache with a finger, a gesture that swelled me with gratification. He gave a nod, almost imperceptible, as if something had fallen into place. Then went back to his meal. He cleaned off his plate just as I finished talking. Our gazes met. Our eyes mirrored one another. He wiped his mouth with a paper napkin, glanced down at his bill, and reached into his pants pocket. His hand came up with two loonies in it, which he slid under the edge of his plate. He eased himself to his feet, palmed the bill up off the table. "I'll need a statement from your friend. Then, I suppose, it will be time to interview the Soledad children." And strutted off in the direction of the cashier.

The Bentleys lived in a small, squat, grayish house, small enough that it made Gould wonder how the Bentleys could have shared it with the Soledads (no wonder they didn't get along). Bentley's land rover was in the driveway. As Gould walked up to the door, he noticed how close the house was to the sidewalk, so close that he could have looked straight through the living room window if the curtains had not been drawn. There was no porch, just a big concrete step with a black rubber doormat on it.

"The children are studying at the kitchen table," Bentley informed him.

Once inside, Gould immediately noticed the smell. It was not an aggressive, vulgar smell like the one at The Red Grizzly, but something more subtle and passive, something suggesting damp coats and rugs often vacuumed—a faint mix of dust, mildew, and the old flesh smell from the church. The living room, which the front door opened onto, continued the pattern of austere simplicity Gould had noted before: a heavy square couch and arm-chairs with clear plastic arm covers on them, a polished and empty coffee table, some simply framed pencil drawings on the walls. The only thing hinting at luxury was an upright piano with ornately carved legs in one corner, and even that had a hymn book conspicuously placed on it as if to counter the effect.

Mrs. Bentley was at the kitchen table with the children. She was a dark-haired, thin woman, with watchful green eyes. She returned the Inspector's formal greeting with an expression that seemed to combine defiance and fear, then said to the children, "Felipe, Gabriela, this is Inspector Gould. The policeman we told you about. He is ready now to ask you some questions about your Mama and Papa. I know this will be hard for you, but it's to help catch whoever did that horrible thing." She gave each of the children a reassuring pat, then, with a comment about not wanting to interfere with "the work of you men," excused herself and left the room.

Gould, with one eye on Reverend Bentley in the doorway, explained his procedure to the children. He spoke as slowly and unthreateningly as he could. He noticed that Felipe nodded in response to his words but that Gabriela kept her eyes on Felipe. He took a chair nearby, opened his briefcase, and asked them a few questions about their earlier statements. He asked them again if they knew of anyone who might want to hurt their parents. Felipe shook his head. Bentley betrayed no response to the question, but continued to stand very still, his large hands clasped in front of him.

Eventually, Gould asked if Felipe had ever noticed a big black car following his parents.

The boy shook his head.

Then Bentley coughed. He put a fist over his mouth and coughed again, loudly. "Can't seem to shake this cold," he explained, with a wan smile.

"Wait, wait," said Felipe. "I remember. I remember a black car. It follow us around sometimes. I remember it parking on our street."

Gould narrowed his eyes. Then, slowly, he asked Felipe, "And when was this?"

"Long time," said Felipe.

"Long time?"

"How you say, many month ago."

"April, May, June? *Abril, Mayo—*"

"*Mayo! Sí.*"

"Just a minute, Inspector"—it was Bentley again—"sorry to interrupt. But Felipe, you should practice saying the right word. Tell the Inspector again properly."

Felipe looked down at his hands, one over the other in his lap. "Yes, yes. I mean 'May.' I see this car in May."

Gould, just then, was struck by a memory of the autopsy lab, of Camilla and Enrique Soledad laid flat on cold slabs. Maybe it was Felipe looking at his hands, those smaller, animated replicas of hands now forever still. Maybe it was the faces, the two unlined, barely-written-upon child faces: earth brown eyes, brown skin, black hair (Gabriela's braided with a black ribbon down her back). The faces had moved him from the start. Now Gould had a vision of death retreating from Enrique and Camilla Soledad, of swollen cheeks deflating back into themselves, bruises fading away, blood stains disappearing fleck by fleck... of skin lambent and lips brightening with breath. The vision ended with Gabriela and Felipe, their serious faces, here and now, in the home of Reverend and Mrs. Bentley.

He brought himself back by a textbook question. "When was the last time you saw the car?"

"I think June."

"I should point out," interrupted Bentley again, "that back in May and June the Soledads were living with us. I have thought about the black car myself a while lately and, I must say, I do vaguely recall something, an unusual, large sedan that parked a few times a few houses down. I remember thinking at the time that one of my neighbours was getting rather ostentatious, but, after a short while, early June I think, as Felipe says, the car wasn't there any more."

Gould took a deep breath, slowly in, slowly out. He shuffled some papers and said, "Let me ask you something else, then."

Just then, there was a sound of piano music from the other room. A very muted, slow, deferential sound—and quite distracting. There was something about the music that seemed to demand Gould's attention, as if he should recognize what was being played, as if there was some important memory attached to it. In a rare failure of his usual mental discipline, he found himself trying to figure out the name of the piece.

"Tell me, Felipe," he said, trying to keep himself focussed, "are you and Gabriela content to be with Reverend and Mrs. Bentley?"

Felipe gazed up from the depths of his brown eyes. Gould thought he saw the shimmer of rising tears. "No, señor. No sir."

Gould's heart rushed a beat. "And why exactly is that?"

"Please sir, we love our mother and father. We want to live with our mother and father."

"But—"

"Yes. I—we know. Our mother and father *estan muertes*. They are dead."

"And the Reverend—"

"Mama Bentley and Papa Bentley, we love them very much too. We are, how you say, so thankful they take care of us. But we miss our mother and father."

Gould could not think of another question. His head was too occupied with the music from the next room. He was sure he had heard the piece before—it was so familiar—and yet still could not place it.

He made a rapid calculation. The fact was, he didn't really expect to gain much from talking to the children at this time. He did need to learn more about the relationship between the Soledads and the Bentleys, and he would have liked to hear the childrens' side of the "inappropriate touching" story, but these topics would have to wait for a more private interview. For the most part, this talk with the children was a pretext: his main purpose was to confront the Bentleys with what he had just learned from me. Time to get to the point.

"That's enough for now, Felipe," he said. "You've been very helpful and brave. And you too Gabriela. I may ask you to come down to the station to talk to me again later. Will you do that when I ask you?"

"Yes, senor."

"Good boy. Now, Reverend Bentley, I need to talk with you and Mrs. Bentley. In the other room."

Before leading Gould out, Bentley addressed the children in a gentle voice: "Back to work now. Another fifteen minutes until study time is up."

Gould was just about to leave the room when there was a shout. He turned to see Felipe Soledad rushing towards him with something in his hand. "Inspector! Inspector! You drop this, Inspector!"

"So I did," said Gould, and, before Bentley could properly react, took the piece of paper offered by Felipe and slipped it into his jacket pocket.

Mrs. Bentley stopped playing as soon as Gould and her husband came into the living room. She said, "I hope I didn't disturb you," but Gould sensed something coy, something disingenuous about the way she said it, her green eyes sizing him up even as her voice seemed to defer to his authority.

"I'd like you both to sit over there," he said.

Soon the Bentleys were side by side on the couch and Gould was in a chair facing them. His briefcase lay unopened on the carpet beside him. He looked first at one and then the other of the couple and, for a full minute, let the silence between them intensify. Once or twice, Bentley glanced with apparent concern at Gould's jacket pocket, the one containing the piece of paper from Felipe.

"Let's drop the false fronts now, shall we?"

The Bentley's looked at each other, surprised or feigning surprise. "Pardon?" said the minister.

"Great shows of virtue can be a disguise, remember?"

"I do remember, but—"

"Don't play coy with me."

Again there was silence. Gould, as always, held himself stiff, authoritative, his suit jacket open to give just a glimpse of the revolver in its holster. The Bentleys matched him stare for stare, their own posture virtuously erect, their faces shaped into masks of innocence (as if they'd been taking lessons from Wallace Lies!). After a few more seconds, Gould crossed his arms and frowned. Disappointed. Like the teacher of a pupil who has squandered a second chance to behave.

"All right," he said. "The trust fund. I know about it. Now—you tell me your side of the story."

At the mention of the words "trust fund," Bentley's shoulders sagged. His mask melted into a grimace. He brought up one of his big awkward hands, ran it through his hair, and, more to his knees than to Gould, said, "It's true."

"Don't say anything, Philip!" It was Mrs. Bentley. Her mask had not melted away at all but had hardened. Now she glared at Gould—self-righteous, defiant, aggressively innocent. "You don't know anything!" she snapped. "You know nothing about me or my husband. Nothing about our lives, the way we have had to live. You come in here and disturb the children and start making accusations."

"Yelling at me will get you nowhere, Mrs. Bentley."

"We have a right to live decently like other people!"

Silence again fell on the room. For some reason, Gould looked up to the ceiling. Directly over where the Bentleys were sitting, there was a brown water mark, rather like the ghost mark sometimes left after cleaning a pool of blood. Someone had tried to cover the area with a patch of white wall-paper, but the stain had leaked through.

"Is that what it's about, then?" asked Gould to Bentley, once he had shifted his attention back again.

Bentley lifted his head to meet Gould's eyes. Slowly, he nodded. Mrs. Bentley made to interrupt before he could speak, but the minister reached over with one large hand and put it on her knee. She acquiesced.

"You see, Inspector, I am not a very good minister."

Bentley took his arm back, now, and brought the fingers of his two hands together in front of him. For a moment, he seemed to be praying, a posture that Gould remembered from the interview in the church office, and which he now found deeply ironic.

"Truly," the minister continued, "without disguise. For one thing, I'm not a very good Christian. I question too much. And when I look down from the pulpit on my congregation, I don't feel kindness or fatherly concern. Sometimes I'm sad, sometimes I get angry. And then I see my flock as a group of self-serving, back-biting hypocrites, all those comfortable people gathered together in the name of simplicity, humility, and the life of the spirit."

Bentley dropped his hands. He stared at a place to the side of Gould's head for a moment, then, in a very soft voice, continued, "I didn't start out in life to be a minister. I've always dreamed of being an artist. The drawings on the wall here, they're mine. But I'm from a poor family. I've made compromises."

"And the trust fund?"

"Wallace Lies set it up for me. He and I worked out the details together. Every month, a certain sum of money gets transferred into an account in my name, but the money does not show up officially in the church records as part of my salary. The idea was for me to be paid what I truly deserved, not the measly amount my hypocritical congregation thinks I should have to live on, and for nobody to get offended. According to Lies and the advice he received, the set up is legal—the payments were authorized by the church deacons, even if they didn't know exactly what they were authorizing—but, of course, if word gets out, my career will be ruined."

"Word will get out," said Gould. "On the basis of the information I received, I have obtained a search warrant for the church premises and this house. As we speak, officers are executing the warrant at the church. Others are waiting for my signal to enter here. The church records and your personal financial records will be turned over to a forensic auditor for examination."

Reverend Bentley reacted to this information by sagging more into himself. His deep set eyes now seemed very tired, his cheekbones gaunt and haggard. Mrs. Bentley's eyes, on the other hand, had a glint of fire in them. She was obviously frightened, but there was something deeply primitive about her response to her fear: she looked like she was barely suppressing an urge to jump to her feet. Whether she wanted to flee from the room or to attack Gould with her bare hands was not clear.

"Well, it's over then," murmured Bentley.

"Not quite."

"Pardon?"

"You still haven't told me about Camilla."

Bentley stared into Gould's eyes. After the count of three, he exhaled sharply—a mirthless laugh. "Is that what you think?"

"You tell me."

"I had absolutely nothing to do with Camilla's death."

"But she did find out about the trust fund."

"Yes."

"And that's why you fought with the Soledads. That's why you filed the complaint with Social Services. Why you expelled them from the church."

"No. That's not true. Camilla found out about the trust fund after we filed our complaint. It is, I am ashamed to admit, the real reason we withdrew the complaint. The Soledads threatened to expose me if we didn't. I'm sorry. I was less than honest about that. For the rest of it, I stand by everything I have said."

"You stand by your belief that there was child abuse?"

"I do."

"And that you expelled the Soledads strictly over your concern for the children?"

"I told you about the way other members of the congregation perceived them. But, yes, that was my primary motivation."

Gould looked Bentley up and down. He tapped his moustache, once, twice. Then, for a moment, his eyes strayed to the sketches on the wall. They were drawings of Silver, the main street, the Church of Christ Redeemer, a stretch of the Trans-Canada as it rose towards the mountains. Cold, hopeless drawings. The one of Henry Street was set at night. There was a single street-lamp on and it seemed pitted feebly against an insinuating darkness. A lone figure shuffled past a half-lit storefront, and both seemed stricken, somehow, by an indrawn look of self-awareness and despair. Everything in the scene seemed to cower from the invisible but somehow powerfully suggested mountains.

"All right," said Gould. "I will now formally serve you with the search warrant."

Gould, as you might expect, was known throughout the RCMP as a shrewd judge of character (it was part of being the professional's professional). He rarely doubted his own powers of judgement, and even on the Soledad investigation, virtually right to the end, he was confident about his ability to read people. Which explains why he was so thoughtful after the interview with the Bentleys. The fact was, he believed Reverend Bentley's new story. He believed that, in spite of the trust fund and the lusting of the Bentleys after the Soledad children, the Bentleys had no direct part in the Soledad murders. There was a ring of truth to the way various parts of their story fit together. Gould could really imagine the Bentleys chafing at the impoverished life they were supposed to lead. He could imagine them convincing themselves that the Soledad children had been abused (though he doubted it himself), then backtracking once confronted by what Camilla had learned. He could not imagine them plotting to murder the Soledads. They were not the type to act so decisively; they were much more likely to weasel their way, to work by indirection (like the trust fund, like the complaint to Social Services).

Certain aspects of the interview did not sit exactly right. Gould wondered about that moment when Bentley had coughed and Felipe—like that—had remembered the black car. Coincidence? And Gould wasn't convinced the Bentleys had been fully honest about their relations with the Soledads or their interest in the children. Still, he was struck by Bentley's transparent guilt regarding the trust fund; it inclined him to believe his later assertions of innocence. And then there was the naming of Wallace Lies. That rang true as well. Clearly, Lies was just the right man to set up something like the trust fund. He had a strong interest in having the Reverend in his debt: there was a lot of business to be done with the church or with members of its congregation, and Lies was the kind of man who lived to get his thumb into as many pies as possible.

If Bentley's story were true, it presented one problem: it did not advance the investigation. If Bentley's story were true (aside from a few, minor, self-interested revisions), then Gould was no closer to solving the murders than he was when he left the Igloo.

For quite a while, he sat with his hands on the steering wheel of his parked car, eyes fixed vacantly ahead. Uncharacteristically, his thoughts wandered. He wondered what was going to become of the Soledad children. From what he had discovered so far, he had his doubts about the suitability of the Bentleys as parents, even if they were named as godparents in the will. But to act on that doubt—assuming the Bentleys had no provable connection to the murders and the trust fund turned out to be legal, which seemed entirely possible—was to go far beyond the boundary of the case. He looked down at the page that Felipe had so bravely slipped to him. It lay unfolded on the seat beside him. A single word, rapidly printed on a piece of scrap paper (on the back of what was obviously part of a draft of one of Reverend Bentley's sermons). *Ayudanos.* Help us. Gould wondered what he could possibly do to help the children. Or if he should.

Then, suddenly, he made two connections.

The first had to do with Mrs. Bentley's music. That maddeningly deferential, distracting piece she had played while Gould interviewed the children. It was, Gould realized, Chopin's *Polonaise in A Flat Major*, the same piece that Glenn had thrashed so many years before in the bank tower lounge. Only while Glenn had finished up in double time, Mrs. Bentley had played slowly, so slowly that the piece itself was hardly recognizable (which is why it took Gould so long to remember). How strange that the same notes, played in the same sequence, could be so different.

Gould was still pondering the significance of this when he made his second connection. He was fingering the note from Felipe again, grimly pondering the childscrawl of that pencilled plea. The single word unleashed a storm of uncertainty in him, a whirlwind of emotions and memories, feelings of loss and anger, images of his father, brother and mother, a memory of walking the beach in Costaguana with Archie. And then, so distinctly that it made him wince as if he'd been struck, a flashback of the dream of the police report in a foreign language. For some reason, the flashback prompted him to turn over the note in his hand. He glanced at the printed words on the other side and recognized them as the opening sentences of the sermon from last Sunday. Our text for today is Luke 8:17, *For nothing is hid*— And he realized what was truly missing from the case.

PROSPECTS UNKNOWN

CHAPTER NINETEEN

She warned me, from the beginning, that she would not be faithful. A month after we began seeing one another, she cancelled a dinner date because she was swamped with work. Around ten I gave her a ring to see how things were going and she told me, straight out, that she had just spent the evening with John, an ex-lover. The next day, after the usual preliminaries, I asked "How was John?" I was trying to signal that I was not jealous, that John was not an emotionally charged or taboo subject for me, but the question set her off. She said it was a manipulative question that showed I was insecure and anxious. I said I was only being polite, but, when prodded, admitted that perhaps a part of me wanted to show that I wasn't insecure and so could talk about an ex-lover of hers in such a casual voice. She said, "Your needing to show that shows you really are insecure."

Another time, she invited a different ex-lover to spend ten days with her in her apartment. She prepared for this by subjecting me to relentless criticism in the week leading up to his arrival. She called me possessive and manipulative. She said that I trivialized her feelings. She said that, during our fight about John, I had tried to adopt the role of the together male while branding her the irrational female making a mountain out of a molehill. By the end of the week, I was exhausted, bitter. I asked her if she wanted to break up. "No," she said, "just that Stephen is coming from Los Angeles tomorrow and I don't want to see you for a while."

After Stephen, I made a show of breaking up with her, but, as a result of what became a regular pattern of coincidence and connivance with us, we were soon back together again. My anger and my love seemed to grow together. Our arguments seemed to grow more erotic as they grew more violent. I wrote long letters defending my side of our latest spat and sometimes sent them to her and sometimes not. I seemed to be seized by an eloquence I had never had before and probably will never have again. I wrote things like: "There is an emptiness in you, Jayne, a darkness that frightens me terribly—something so lost that I can never hope to touch it. You have a capacity, an ability or weakness, to let loose the demon at the heart of anyone, a demon that most of us (me especially) keep boxed in by the sheer weight of our fear, parent of responsibility; it is a monster born out of nothingness, of our knowledge of the meaninglessness that acts as the parentheses, the fore and aft of our lives." I told her constantly that I loved her. She replied just as constantly that the words *I love you* belonged in a Barbara Cartland novel. I arranged more chance meetings.

Once, after we had been to a production of Frank Wedekind's *Spring Awakening* (all those surreal representations of authority and sexuality), we went back to her room and, with a kind of adolescent urgency, peeled off our clothes. We slid into bed and started to make love. I climbed on top, began to move inside of her, but as I moved, she remained still, not moving with me—and I realized that something was wrong. I was seized by such a contradictory blend of anger and desire that I kept on. I moved and moved as she lay perfectly still beneath me. I came—one of the most intense orgasms I have ever had. Then, contrite, realizing what I had done and that she had not had an orgasm herself, I rolled off and tried to caress her with my hand. She lay unresponsive, eyes closed like a statue. Finally, I stretched out on my stomach and rested my head in my arms. After what seemed like an eternity she spoke, in a soft voice. "You are genitally fixated," she said. "I don't trust your desire for me." That night I had a dream of endlessly falling.

Gould returned to The Red Grizzly. On his way in he tipped his head to Margot behind the counter. Then, in his room, he went through all the stacks of paper accumulated since the beginning of the case: the preliminary report, the newspaper clippings from Inspector Breeze, the earlier and later witness statements. He checked one or two things in the report, pulled out a newspaper clipping, and turned his attention to the statements. He went through them carefully, twice, reading only the names at the top. He looked again at the newspaper story he had set aside.

Afterwards, he claimed to have followed an irresistible chain of reasoning. "The catalyst, of course, was the coincidence of name in the epigraph to Bentley's sermon," he explained, "but, really, that coincidence only accelerated a process of deduction I had already begun. I already knew there was something missing. It was only a matter of time before I cross-referenced the available information, the lists of witnesses and the clippings, with the reports we had received."

We were at my booth in the Igloo. It was now Wednesday night, a little over twenty-four hours since I had handed Gould the key to the case. In that time, a number of important details had seemed to fall into place. Soon, it seemed, the entire narrative of the Soledad murders would come together—or at least, as Gould put it, every possible version of the story would be covered and it would only be a matter of time before the correct version singled itself out.

I was, of course, basking in the reflected glory of his apparent triumph. I also made a point of reminding him of my role in making that triumph possible.

"You're welcome," I said, on more than one occasion, "I'm just happy I could help."

What Gould discovered when he went back through the paperwork was that there was no statement from Luke Carson, the driver of the transport truck who had been attacked on his way into the mine. According to the newspaper clipping, Carson had suffered a life-threatening head injury when a brick shattered the windshield of the truck. Gould tracked down Carson's phone number and made a call. The truck driver answered. He agreed to an immediate meeting.

Carson lived a couple of blocks behind the Legion Hall in a small apartment, an eight- or ten-plex, one of those modernist boxes that are all grey concrete and cut-out aluminum windows. Out front there was a yellow lawn with a cedar bush on one side and a crab apple tree on the other. On the lawn were two or three crumpled up plastic bags, a few candy bar wrappers, and various scorched bits of paper and cardboard tubing—the remains of Hallowe'en fireworks.

When Carson pulled open the door, Gould saw a stocky, shortish young man in his early thirties, with a large, balding head (a red surgery scar visible on one side) and stubbles of salt and pepper hair above his ears. He wore blue jeans and a t-shirt, and spoke with one chipped tooth in the front.

"When I got out of the hospital, I wondered why nobody talked to me," Carson said, "but then I figured the big boys must've known what they were doing."

"How is your injury now?"

"This?"—pointing to his head. "Got a steel plate in it, you know. Oh, it's okay. A lot better. It was never quite as bad as they said in the paper. I still get headaches, though, and dizziness sometimes. Which is why I'm at home and not back a work."

During the first part of the interview, Gould asked Carson the usual questions. Carson explained that he had never met the Soledads, that he knew nothing about them but what he had heard from other people (mostly since the murders), that he had no idea who might have killed them or why. He said he knew Stahr, Goodwin, Bentley and Lies by sight but had had few direct dealings with any of them. He did work with Wallace Lies on this last job, which was a little unusual, but not surprising given Lies's reputation around town. He was an independent trucker, had hauled for the Cyclops mine from time to time, and had agreed to bring the supplies from Vancouver strictly for the money. He was not happy about what had happened when he tried to cross the picket line, especially the damage to his cab, but he understood the union's point of view too.

Up to this point, Carson's responses added little to the case. Gould did ask him to clarify the involvement of Wallace Lies and he replied, "He met me in Vancouver, at one of those big storage complexes near the docks. He had the trailer already loaded and waiting for me. He gave me the paperwork and paid me my advance."

Then Gould asked if there was anything else he wanted to add, anything that seemed unusual or suspicious.

"About those supplies I hauled, there was definitely something funny about them."

"In what way?"

"The load was quite heavy, first of all, quite near my limit. I could feel the drag on my engine as I climbed into the foothills. That's not unusual in itself, but just before Roger's Pass I decided I better double-check everything (I was worried about the load shifting). So I pulled over and opened up the back doors. And the funny thing was, that very heavy load only took up about half the space in the trailer. I thought that was kind of weird, so I went in to have a closer look. Everything was covered up by tarps, but I pulled a corner back, and there were these crates."

Gould pricked his moustache.

"They were quite small, about this big"—Carson gestured with his hands—"and they were all seemed to be the same size. Like I was only hauling one thing."

"Maybe it was a special order of some kind."

"Maybe." Carson thought for a moment. He raised a hand to his right ear, which was pierced and contained a gold earring. For a few seconds, he rotated the earring between his finger and thumb, then dropped his hand again.

"The thing is, the crates I could see were all marked with the picture of an orange. Can you believe that? What would a mine be doing with a load of oranges?"

Gould didn't answer.

"Well, it seemed strange to me, but the load was secure and I was in a hurry, so I left it at that. Only the last while, I've started thinking about it again."

"And?"

"I don't think they were really oranges."

"Why?"

"For one thing, the load was too heavy. I didn't cross any scales but I could tell from the drag on my engine. No way a half-a-trailer of oranges would be that heavy. The other thing is, it just doesn't make sense. I mean, really—oranges?"

"Were there any other markings on the crates?"

"Oh yeah. It said 'Product of—' and then one of those Southern American countries. One that started with 'C.' Columbia or Costa Rica. No. It did start with Costa, but it was one word. Costa—"

"Costaguana?"

"That's it. Product of Costaguana. That was on all the crates I saw."

Gould betrayed no emotion. His face was his usual professional mask. Behind his eyes, however, his thoughts were beginning to race from one possibility to another. He stayed with Carson a few minutes longer, clarifying some of the details in the story, then, still without giving away the triumphant feeling that now suffused him, he thanked the truck driver for his assistance and took his leave.

First thing the next morning, Gould telephoned Viola in Vancouver. "Glad you called, Inspector," Viola said, "I've got something to report."

"Go ahead."

"Looks like Sherwood and Berry are headed back to Silver."

"Catch me up, will you?"

"Well, they were released on Monday, as predicted. The Crown says he may lay some charges relating to the illegal possession of found treasure, but anything more serious is on hold until the origins of the silver are clear. They stayed at a hotel in town on Monday night, visited their lawyer in the morning, then went back to their room and didn't come out again until dusk. Then they checked out and started driving east. Last night they stayed in a motel just outside of Merritt. This morning—I just got the call—they got back in their vehicle and continued east."

Gould looked at his watch. "If they drive straight on from there, they should be here about four."

"Uh-huh."

"And the tail?"

"Still with them. Oh, the boys had a good laugh when they saw that car! Nothing like tailing someone in style! And they've done a great job of getting into character too—black hair, sleazy suits, sunglasses. Very convincing."

"Did they let themselves be seen?"

"Like we talked about. As if they didn't intend it. My guess is they managed to spook the suspects. That's why they took off from Vancouver."

Gould then filled in Viola about Carson's story. He asked him to check out the storage facility at which Carson had picked up his load. He asked him to hook up with the Port Police in Vancouver to ask some questions about smuggling and about cargo ships from South America. There were also a couple of things regarding Wallace Lies he asked him to check. He remembered a photograph of Lies in one of the clippings Breeze had given him and said he would fax it to him.

After breakfast, Gould drove to the RCMP station. There he spent an hour briefing Inspector Cullen, who had arrived to take over for Inspector Breeze. Breeze himself had returned to Cramdown.

At the end of the meeting, Gould said he had a request. "I'd like Berry and Sherwood picked up as soon as they get back to town."

"But they've already been through the system. If we pick them up again we're liable for a harassment complaint."

"Regarding the silver bars, yes. But, technically speaking, we haven't interviewed them yet about the murders. Not formally, anyway. And they are striking miners, after all; we have a right to get statements from them like all the others."

"And the real reason?"

"I'd like a go at them myself. A few things have changed in the case and I've an idea that I can make them talk."

Cullen laughed. "I'd like to see that. I'll let you know when they're brought in."

Later that morning, Gould spoke to Sergeant Bacon in Cramdown.

"Silver is a soft metal, right?" he said.

"One of the softest."

"Do you think a large shipment of silver, hauled in a truck, would leave traces behind? Even if the silver had been boarded up in crates?"

"Possibly. Crates are pretty rough containers. If the silver was jostled around at all, particles would have fallen through the planks. There wouldn't have to be many of them for us to find them."

"The thing is this. I need to prove that a certain truck has recently hauled a load of silver. If I can do that, a lot of pieces in this case will fit together."

"I'll send out my best. They should be there in a couple of hours."

By three o'clock, Gould had a forensics team working on Luke Carson's rig. Because the rig was already a known crime scene, it had been easy to obtain a search warrant: all that was required was for Gould to claim he was doing a "follow up" investigation, which—without stretching the definition of the term very far—he was. As he and his officers came into sight of the rig, still in its contorted posture not far from the main gate of the mine, Gould savoured a potential irony. Maybe Stahr's hard-nosed insistence on exploiting the propaganda value of the rig would lead to her own downfall.

The trailer doors were unlocked. Gould looked inside—empty, except for the usual collection of tarps and blankets and straps. He ran his hand slowly over the wooden floor. Then turned things over to the team.

He drove alone down the gravel road until he came to the main cluster of mine buildings. The headframe loomed over the others like a giant grain elevator. He parked, found his way to *Shipping and Receiving* and identified himself to a couple of men in overalls there. Neither of them remembered unloading Luke Carson's truck. And neither of them had any idea what the truck might have contained. Then the department manager came out of his glass-framed office. He asked if he could help. Gould identified himself and said he was following up on a couple of items relating to Luke Carson's truck.

"But I thought you were in charge of the Soledad investigation?"

"I am. And Lena Stahr promised me complete co-operation."

The manager, whose name was Partridge, thought about that for a moment. He raised a couple of fingers to his double chin. Then he shrugged, "All right. What do you want to know?"

Gould asked the same questions. Partridge said he didn't remember how the truck had been unloaded. He went into his office and could find none of the relevant paperwork. He gave Gould a palms-up apology. "It happens," he said, with a rather smug-seeming grin. "The strike—you know. We're short of staff and the staff we do have . . . well."

"Thanks anyway."

Gould then went to the Security office. The Statewide supervisor, a man named Tolomeo, was quite happy to talk. The incident with Carson's truck had as much propaganda value for him as for Lena

Stahr. "Fucking maniacs," he said. "They could've killed somebody."

But Tolomeo couldn't help him either. Gould asked if he could talk to his men.

"Go right ahead."

For the next hour, Gould talked to Statewide agents. Eventually, he made his way back to the main gate. It occurred to him that anyone who had been on guard there would have had to see something. Sure enough, after a half dozen more interviews, he came across two Statewide agents who remembered the trailer being unloaded. "It was at night," they said. "Somebody worked on it all through our shift. A fork-lift, a flat-bed truck, two workers. This was just a couple of days after the thing got smashed." One of the workers, they were sure, had been a woman.

Enrique and Camilla Soledad.

Gould was still interviewing Statewide agents when a call came in for him to say that Sherwood and Berry had been picked up. He did not hurry back. On the contrary, he finished his interviews in his regular way and then conferred briefly with the members of the forensics team. Then he drove to the Selkirk Inn. There he had a long, leisurely dinner, and thought, now and then, of the two miners waiting hungrily in the interrogation room at the station. Over coffee, he flipped through his notebook, reviewing recent developments in the case.

He pulled into the RCMP station a little after seven o'clock. A cold black night with a few flakes of snow in the air.

By the time Gould and Cullen stepped into the interview room, Berry and Sherwood were highly agitated. One of them—it turned out to be Sherwood—jumped up at the sight of the officers. "You guys are in big trouble. You can't do this. We want to call our lawyer."

"Gentleman, gentleman," Gould said, "relax. This has nothing to do with your recent troubles. We just need a statement from you about the Soledads to complete our files. All the other union members have already done it."

"That's not what the stiffs who picked us up implied."

"You can't expect the constables to always understand the finer nuances of things."

Sherwood sat down again. The two men were in chairs on the

other side of a wooden table. They seemed an unlikely pair. Berry was short and fit, with dark hair and blue eyes; he had thick, oddly swept up eyebrows that gave him a look of eccentric intelligence. Sherwood also had an oddly intellectual look about him. He was tall and thin, balding, with an angular nose and roundish spectacles. Gould could picture the two of them as half-dotty professors lecturing on Renaissance literature somewhere but found it hard to imagine them working drills a thousand feet underground in the Cyclops silver mine.

Gould took a seat across from the pair. Cullen stood off to one side with his back against the wall. Gould started by asking some decoy questions about the Soledads. He listened to answers that he had heard a number of times before and then, casually, said, "Oh. We are also looking for a black Mercedes sedan. We have reason to believe the killers used it when they kidnapped the Soledads."

Berry and Sherwood exchanged looks.

"You didn't happen to notice one?"

"No." It was Sherwood who spoke. Berry looked at him but Sherwood warned him off with his eyes. Then he said to Gould, "We've already told you everything we know up to the time of the murders. Now let us go."

"What about after the murders?"

"After the murders, we were busy."

"So I understand. Well, it's not a major point. Just another one of those details we like to track down. But I should tell you both that if you have any information at all that seems connected to the case, you better out with it. Of all the people in this town, you two should be hoping more than anyone that we catch the killers."

Sherwood had half risen to his feet in anticipation of getting out of the room. With Gould's last comment he paused a moment, then gave Gould a skeptical look and stretched to his full height. Berry, on the other hand, remained in his seat. "Why?" he now said.

"Why? Seems like you two clever fellows don't know everything."

"Come on, Ed. Let's go."

"No. I want to hear this."

Sherwood made a move to put his hand on Berry's shoulder, but Berry crossed his arms in front of him—unmovable. Gould let the two men dance their dance until it was over. Then he said to Sherwood, "If you want to hear this, you better sit down too."

Sherwood sat.

After a few seconds, Gould asked, "Aren't you curious why you haven't been charged with theft for having those silver bars? Aren't you the least bit curious why Lena Stahr hasn't reported them missing?"

Sherwood smiled, a knowing smile. "Not in the least."

"Well—I'll tell you. The silver wasn't hers."

Sherwood's smile softened a little. He looked to Berry and back to Gould.

"Aren't you curious whose it was?"

Gould let them wait, ten, fifteen seconds. Then, very softly, with one finger raised, he said, "The same people who killed Enrique and Camilla Soledad. Think about that. Anybody who takes something that belongs to these people . . . ."

"That's who's been following us!" It was Berry.

Sherwood turned. "Shut up, Ed."

"No way. There has been this black car, we thought it was the cops but it sure didn't look like cops."

"What kind of black car?"

"A Mercedes."

Gould laughed. "When was the last time you saw cops driving a Mercedes?"

There was another silence. The two miners seemed to calculate the possibilities. Berry, the more credulous of the two, struggled with his fear. Sherwood still seemed skeptical.

"What about Stahr? If we're in danger, so is she."

Gould put his hands together, then tilted them at the wrist, as if he were praying in the direction of the miners. "I don't know all the ins and outs yet," he said, "but I'm guessing that Lena Stahr knew exactly what she was getting into from the beginning. She's that kind of person. She may have set the whole thing up as part of her response to the strike. Consider. Enrique and Camilla Soledad arrived here, what, two weeks after the strike began. With a horde of stolen silver. Coincidence?"

"What can we do?" It was Berry who spoke.

"The only way I can help you is if you come clean."

For a few seconds there was silence, except for the sound of shallow breathing. Gould contemplated the beads of sweat on the foreheads of the two miners. Then Berry, with reluctant help from Sherwood, began to tell the story of the silver bars.

It turned out that Sherwood and Berry had taken the bars not from the mine property directly but from the union offices, the night after the offices had been torched by the mob. "We went in disguised as volunteer fire fighters. We only took the eight, figuring that in all the confusion they might not notice."

Gould remembered a finger of white smoke pointing up into the darkness. A fire fighter with an empty hose. "How many bars were there altogether?"

"Fifty, maybe sixty."

"And where did the union get them?"

"Where do you think?" Now it was Sherwood talking. "We'd been sending guys over the fence at night to spy or do a bit of mischief, you know, and one night some guys came across these crates in an old shafts. Like a fucking lost treasure, you know? Anyway, the guys that night hauled out as much as they could until a guy in a pickup truck scared them off. The next night there were guards all over that section of the property. And after that, when a couple guys made it to the shaft, they saw the stuff was gone."

"Were either of you directly involved in carrying out the bars?"

"No."

"Can you tell us who was inside?"

"Goodwin. I'm not sure who else."

Gould tapped his moustache with a finger. "Two things still don't make sense to me," he said. "First, why store the silver at the union office? Not a very clever hiding place, really. Didn't they expect an investigation?"

"Hey," said Sherwood, "we're not stupid. Remember what we do for a living. Those bars were well hidden. Nobody who didn't know where they were was going to find them."

"There was talk of hiding the bars out in the hills somewhere," added Berry, softly, "but, to tell the truth, we didn't trust each other."

"Why doesn't that surprise me?"

"You don't know how it is."

"Yes, well. The second thing is this. If what you've told me is true, why did the union send a lawyer to protect you in Vancouver? I mean, if you'd stolen their silver. Why weren't they just ticked off?"

"I—we don't know. We couldn't figure it out ourselves. What they said was that everything would be all right, everything forgiven, if we said nothing about where we got the bars. And if we said anything, there would be hell to pay."

Gould crossed his arms. "I guess that puts you in a tight spot, doesn't it?"

Jamie Dopp

Chapter Twenty

The day I made my exit from Vancouver, Jayne phoned me around noon. "How are you?" I asked. "Not so good," she said. "Something has happened."

Seems that the day before she had taken some Atom, a drug that is a chemical equivalent to mushrooms, and had gone for a walk to a nearby park. There she had picked up a Native Indian man. She had noticed him rummaging in the garbage and had bought a couple of hot dogs and Sprites and offered to share them with him. "Thanks," he said, "I'm hungry." "Yeah, I know. I saw you rummaging." "Don't ever look at me when I do that! That's my world. I don't ever want you to look at me when I do that." He tried to talk her into going out with him to his sister's place in Surrey, but she said, "Why don't you come to my place instead?" As they walked together, many heads turned. They went up to her room. They made love. Afterwards, he gave her a rough ring "a Satan's Choice member had given him." She gave him an old guitar, then walked back with him to a used clothing store she had bought all sorts of things at before. The owner, who was usually very friendly, glowered as the man tried on a leather jacket. "How much?" asked Jayne. "Eighty-five," said the owner. "Isn't that a lot?" (she'd remembered a similar jacket for sixty two months before). "Would you take sixty for it?" "Either pay the eighty-five or get the fuck out of here!"

After she told me what had happened, she asked if I would come over. She said she wanted to spend time with a "good" person.

She met me at the door.

"I told you I would hurt you," she said.

"There's a stack of mail in the box here," I said. "You want me to bring it inside?"

On Wednesday night, when Gould told me about the load of silver, I was incredulous. "What makes you think that's what was in the truck?"

"So many things point to it. How heavy the load was. The fact that the crates were marked Product of Costaguana. The unlikelihood that the mine would actually order a truck load of oranges. Other things."

"How much silver are we talking about?"

"Hard to say. The truck was not officially weighed. But from Carson's description, it would have to have been a number of tonnes. Twenty or thirty maybe."

"How much would that be worth?"

"Six or seven, maybe eight million dollars."

"Wow! And you think Stahr melted this silver back down to pass it off as her own?"

"What better place to fence stolen silver but through a silver mine?"

"From what I know of her, I can imagine Lena Stahr agreeing to something like that."

"At the best of times. But especially during a strike, when there were so many financial pressures on her. She might even have used the silver to keep up the illusion that production was just fine. Imagine the effect on negotiations."

"But how could you remelt all that silver without a whole lot of people knowing?"

"Lena Stahr took me on a tour of the Cyclops operation when I first interviewed her. It's all state of the art, which means that in fact very few workers are involved, especially in the processing and refining end. With the help of a couple of accomplices, it wouldn't have been particularly hard. It would have to be done over time to avoid suspicion, of course. Oh, one other thing. When I was interviewing people at the mine today, I learned the Soledads actually worked the night shift for their first six weeks. I don't know how I missed that before. They only shifted to day work two weeks before they were killed. By that point, the silver was probably all melted down."

"But twenty to thirty tonnes! Imagine hiding that."

"Not so hard. Remember that the silver wouldn't have taken up all that much room. But also, have you ever seen a map of the Cyclops property?"

"No."

"There are dozens of derelict shafts on it. It would have been easy to find some out of the way hiding spot."

"And then, at night, bit by bit, the Soledads brought bars of it into the smelter to be remelted and stamped."

"Exactly."

I sipped my coffee. It was almost eleven o'clock. Gould and I were alone in the Igloo except for one driver at the *Truckers Only* table and two tables of people near the entrance. A Hank Williams Sr. tune filled the air with plaintive sound.

"But I still don't understand something," I said, after a moment. "How could they have gotten that much silver into the country in the first place?"

"It seems unbelievable, even if it was rather feebly disguised as a cargo of oranges. But the Port of Vancouver handles millions of tonnes of cargo a year, and it's one of the easiest ports in the world to smuggle things through. They may also have had some kind of professional help. The most likely scenario is that the Soledads picked up the silver in June when they spent those ten days in Vancouver. That means someone else would have had to bring the silver up from Costaguana, arrange for the cargo ship and so on."

"I guess this explains why Lena Stahr hired the Soledads in the first place, and why nobody could quite figure out what they were doing for her."

"The theory I'm working on is that the Soledads approached her, maybe through Wallace Lies, to cut some kind of deal. The money they used to buy the house was a down payment. But once Stahr had control of the silver, she reneged on her part of the bargain. That would explain Enrique Soledad's anger towards her, his enlisting of Sergeant Wright to blackmail her into treating him 'fairly,' as he put it."

"It would also explain why Lena Stahr didn't claim the silver bars stolen by those miners."

Gould raised an eyebrow at me in a half-ironic tribute.

The next day, Thursday November 9th, a member of the Richmond city police discovered the Soledad car. It had been left on a residential street not far from the city centre. For over ten days it had sat unnoticed: the residents of the neighbourhood did not know each other very well and each assumed it belonged to someone else. Then one night, some vandals, with that sixth sense vandals have about abandoned things, punctured the tires. Two days later, with the car now an obvious eyesore and no one taking charge of it, someone finally complained to the city.

The police arrived with a tow truck. They ran the license through their computer and a Canada wide alert came up. A forensics team was called in. They dusted for prints and took hair and particle samples from the inside. In the trunk they found Camilla's purse, two Statewide Security uniforms, a magnetized facsimile of the Statewide name and logo that would fit on a vehicle door, and a bloodied billy club.

"So," Gould told me later, "now we know how the killers lured the Soledads out of their car. They posed as Statewide agents. Maybe they pretended there was a security check on the road to the replacement workers' camp. Maybe they asked Enrique to open the trunk of his car for inspection. Whatever. One way or another, they got him out, and when his back was turned one of them clubbed him."

"That explains the Statewide agents some of the replacement workers saw on the road that morning."

"Right. I've also made some further inquiries. According to the local Statewide supervisor, there was no security check on the road that morning. And according to the American head office, some uniforms and other equipment were stolen from one of their depots about a month ago. They think it was an inside job. Oh—one other thing. I checked back with some of the replacement workers. Turns out the agents they saw on the morning of the disappearance were in a black van."

"Alex MacKenzie's black Mercedes?"

"Once the fake logo was stripped back off of it."

That same day, Viola phoned in from Vancouver. "Got that information from Conlon's Storage for you, Inspector. Piece of cake. The manager keeps good records and Enrique Soledad signed for the unit in his own name."

"What were the dates?"

"Rented June 16th until August 31st."

"That fits."

"How so?"

"The Soledads made a ten day trip to Vancouver ending June 25th. Carson picked up his load on August 31st. How large was the unit?"

"Eighteen by twenty-five by eight feet high. Like an extra long two car garage."

"Big enough. Did you learn anything else?"

"The manager remembered them. Said they identified themselves as recent immigrants and that they would be storing their belongings in the unit. He remembered joking with them—he was an immigrant too and had arrived with only a suitcase—and they laughed and said yes they were lucky to have brought so much with them. A couple of days later the Soledads unloaded a tractor trailer, but he took no notice of what they were unloading."

"What about when the unit was emptied?"

"He was on duty that day but didn't see much. However, he did say that it was Enrique Soledad who turned in their keys, that the wife was not there. Also: he was not alone. There was another man with him."

"Did you show him the photograph of Wallace Lies?"

"He said maybe it was him, maybe not. Though he did say this man seemed very self-important and loud. He remembered that distinctly. He was all chummy and making stupid small talk."

"Did he inspect the unit after Enrique turned in the keys?"

"Had to before he could turn over the deposit. He said it was spotless."

"I see."

"And something else. According to the manager, the other man who was with Enrique, whoever he was, showed up again about three weeks ago, about the middle of October, and asked some strange questions. He wanted to know if the storage facility was in a 'rough' neighbourhood and didn't the 'underworld' operate near the harbour, stuff like that. Then he asked if there were any bars around where he could go to check out some of the local 'characters.' He said he was from a small town and had never really seen the 'underside' of things."

"What did he tell him?"

"He was pretty put off, really. He said this guy just walked in like he was a long lost friend or something and put on the chummy act that he remembered from before. So, basically, he told him to get lost."

"Nice work, George."

"Thanks. I'm off now to pass Lies's photo around the local bars."

"Don't be over-indulging in the local brew."

"Only in the line of duty, Inspector. Only in the line of duty."

Also on November 9th Gould had a team search the ruins of the union office. They found no trace of the silver Sherwood and Berry had described. Gould hadn't expected them to. The union had had a number of days by that point to clean out the remaining bars.

Around dinner time, Viola reported in from Vancouver again. "Got something for you, Inspector. Turns out that the manager of a pub called The Barnacle, five blocks from Conlon's, is an old acquaintance of mine. I helped him out long ago in my idealistic youth. Anyway, turns out one of his bartenders complained to him three weeks back about this odd character who came in, all chummy and talkative, looking for some 'tough guys to do a dirty job.' When the bartender told him he didn't know anyone, the guy got more pushy, insisting that in a 'rough area' like this there had to be someone. Then he slipped him some money. Two hundred bucks. The bartender took the money—he was broke and easily tempted—and told him to come back the same time next day. He really didn't know anybody. At first he figured the customer for a sucker and assumed he could make something up. But over night he started getting cold feet. What if this guy really was some kind of hood? According to the bartender, he dressed like one. So, he went to my old acquaintance the manager for advice. He was furious, both at the bartender and the customer. He chewed the bartender's ear off, told him to give him the money, and said he'd handle the situation himself. Next day he waited in his office for the bartender to call him, but, apparently, the customer never came back."

"Did you show the bartender the photo?"

"It was his off day, but I went straight over."

"And?"

"It was Wallace Lies."

"He was sure?"

"Definitely. He recognized the checked jacket."

"Bingo."

Thursday night in the Igloo, Gould was completely full of himself. It was marvelous to see. He came in through the door with that walk of his, nose so high it was surprising he could tell where he was going, and I almost expected him to give the Royal Family wave to the tables he passed (show the back of your hand, a little flick of the wrist). When he sat down he gave me a look of utter condescension that made me shiver with delight.

"Simple," he said, as much to himself as to me. He ordered a coffee from Marlene.

"You solved the case?"

He fixed me with his tropical blue eyes, a look that seemed to blend pity and scorn. As so often happened when he looked at me like that, I felt naked. Blood rushed to my face, gathered in a warm halo around my eyes.

"Ah Tucker," he said, "I suppose I shall have to fill you in again."

So he told me of the day's developments. The car found in Richmond, Viola's discoveries in Vancouver. As he spoke—or, rather, lectured—he gave me the full array of Gould gestures: the unmoved face, the finger tapping at the moustache, the subtly narrowed eyes. Now and then I asked a question, especially about the treasure of silver, which I was still having trouble believing in (it seemed incredible and even romantic to me), but not too many and only for clarification. He was not in the mood to be interrupted. At the end of his discourse, he leaned back in his seat like he had just finished a marvelous

Christmas dinner and said, "So there you have it."

"Have what?" I asked. "Seems to me you haven't really proven anything yet. You've got a hint that maybe Lies hired the killers, but you don't have any real proof."

Gould shook his head sadly. He gestured for Marlene to come back with the coffee pot. After she had poured, he took a cultured sip and held the coffee in his mouth a couple of seconds before swallowing. I slopped cream into my own cup, which I had gotten her to top up as well.

"What I have, Tucker, is all the angles covered. I have something on each of the possible suspects in the case, each of the possible members of the conspiracy. All it will take is for one of these leads to come through. Here. Let me show you."

He reached over to the cream dispenser and lifted down a number of the plastic containers. He piled them up in one of his hands and held them out for me to see—like a jumble of oversized dice.

"Let's start with the long shots," he said. "Philip Bentley." And he placed a container on the table. "For the last two days a forensic auditor has been going through the church records. If the trust fund turns out to be illegal, that solidifies the Bentleys' motives to kill the Soledads and further implicates Wallace Lies (who was responsible for the arrangement). Inspector Breeze." Another container. "His involvement with Lena Stahr is compromising enough, but it is also possible that his service revolver was the murder weapon. Lent to the killers, perhaps, to make sure the murder weapon was not traced (who would think to suspect a cop?). Al Goodwin. The cigarette butt may put him at the scene of the crime. Lena Stahr. Once the tests come back positive from Luke Carson's truck, we will have enough evidence to raid her offices and property and seize her financial records. Somewhere there will be a record of the $50,000 payout to the Soledads and the payout to the professional killers who pulled the trigger. Wallace Lies. He may in fact give us the smoking gun, if Viola's work in Vancouver bears fruit. It is a lot harder than most people think to arrange a murder and keep it quiet. Too much money and too many egos involved. In any case, Lies is involved in various ways. With the Bentleys, with Breeze and Stahr. No doubt in other ways I haven't discovered yet."

Gould paused for a moment, as if to catch his breath. There were now five containers on the table between us. He opened one hand wide and made a roof over them. "The point is, if any of these leads comes through, the whole conspiracy will soon be revealed. And at that point, other evidence from the scene of the crime will come into play. Using the ore samples I took from the processing plant, I may be able to prove that the nuggets at the crime scene were from the Cyclops mine. I wouldn't be surprised if Al Goodwin drank Banner Premium Ale and wore plaid shirts. The shoe in the tree . . . the shoe in the tree . . . ."

"The shoe in the tree?" I repeated.

Gould laughed. "Even that will be explained in time. Just you wait and see."

By this point, Gould's know-it-all act was starting to wear thin on me. I was still basking in that aura of assurance, still taking vicarious pleasure from his obvious command of the situation, but, at the same time, I was getting a little peeved. For one thing, Gould remained intent on refusing to acknowledge my contribution to the case. The night before I had inserted a number of variations on "only glad I could help" into his monologue, pointedly challenging him to actually thank me, and each time he had gone on just as pointedly to ignore me. Tonight it was like I didn't even exist for him, not in any significant way, or like I was just a convenient device for him to exercise his ego, a passive audience, vacuous and adoring, to be shown a few tricks and dismissed at the end of the show.

And something else about Gould's manner bothered me, something about the extremity, the absoluteness, of it. All his gestures, his tone of voice, his body language (sitting across from me like he was in the saddle)—they were so refined that they seemed like caricatures, almost as if he was parodying himself. And if he was parodying himself, then he was doing it to make fun of me.

I decided to play devil's advocate.

"So," I said, "you really do think there was a conspiracy. That Stahr and Goodwin and Lies and maybe Bentley and even Breeze were all in on the murders together, each for his or her own reasons."

Gould gave me a condescending grin. "And you are going to tell me differently?"

"I wouldn't presume. Besides, it's consistent with my analysis of the town, about it being fucked up and everything. Still—"

Now I took a sip of coffee. Gould watched me, unmoved. I held my words as long as I could, then continued, "Still, the horde of silver changes things."

"How so?"

"Like, whose silver was it in the first place?"

"It could have been stolen from the San Tomé mine, in which case it came from the government of Costaguana. It could have been stolen from the Front for the Liberation of Costaguana, which is known to finance its operations in part with its own stolen or manufactured silver. Or maybe it was just found."

"Found?"

"Costaguana, my dear Tucker, has many legends about fabulous treasures stashed away in its rugged country side. But really, it doesn't matter. The point is, it came to Canada. The rest is immaterial."

"Is it? I hate to bring this up. But doesn't this raise the spectre of the black car again? Doesn't this create a motive for the government of Costaguana to kill the Soledads?"

"How?"

"Maybe the government let the Soledads out of the country and then followed them in hopes of finding the silver. And once the treasure had been melted down again and lost for good . . . well, maybe they settled for revenge. Or if the silver had been to finance the rebels and the Soledads somehow had double-crossed them . . . ."

"Possible. But I still don't think it was someone from Costaguana."

"Why?"

"First of all, if the government of Costaguana knew the Soledads had the silver in Canada, they could quite easily have gotten Canadian authorities to investigate for them. They have full diplomatic relations with us, after all, and it would have saved them effort and the potential embarrassment of violating Canadian territorial integrity by acting on their own. More importantly, the silver creates a much stronger motive for our local suspects."

"But a conspiracy raises questions too. Things that need to be accounted for."

"Like?"

"Like the role of Al Goodwin. I can see Lies and Stahr working together, but I don't see the logic of the union leader getting involved too."

Gould raised an eyebrow, just a fraction, and said, as if offering a clue, "The silver."

"Goodwin was bought off?"

"Maybe he wasn't part of the original plan. But he did learn about the silver, through the actions of his raiding strikers, and he was just as uncooperative as the others when I arrived. Maybe the three of them realized that there was enough silver for everybody."

"But Goodwin and Stahr are such enemies. If they could come together over the silver, who's to say there weren't others? That's the problem with a conspiracy. How do you know where it ends?"

"Maybe it doesn't end."

Gould said this slowly, his eyes focused on a point beside my head. It was as if he were suddenly lost in possibilities or had just discovered something to himself. I found it rather spooky.

"Maybe," he said, without looking at me, "it just goes on and on. Maybe it will finally expose, expose—"

"Expose who?"

He blinked and was his assured self again. "Everyone, of course," he said, with an ironic grin, "everyone who is involved."

We sat in silence for a while. The Hank Williams tape by this time had been replaced by the greatest hits of Patsy Cline. The current song was *I Fall To Pieces*. I wondered how many times someone had listened to her sing those words over the years. Millions, no doubt. The song wrapped up, with its final repetition of the title and for a few seconds there was complete silence. Then I heard the opening bars of *So Wrong*.

On the table before me was the usual collection of things. Two cups, saucers and spoons resting on Myths of Canada placemats, my books, my journal, now almost half full. Outside the darkness was cut by the orange glow of halogen lights. Two transport trucks idled nearby, their running lights glowing like crowns on the hood of their cabs. There were only men in the restaurant now, as was usual at this time of the night. Except for the workers: the cook and the remaining waitress (Marlene, who was finishing a double shift). Marlene was at this moment cleaning in a section of tables that had been closed off until morning.

I decided to change tack. Enough of the skeptical side-kick act. "Well, it does seem like it's only a matter of time before the case is solved," I said. "You seem to have all the angles covered."

"That's what a professional investigation does."

"Uh-huh. So, um, tell me, Inspector. How'd you get into police work, anyway?"

He just looked at me. Blank.

"I mean, it seems kind of thankless, you know what I mean?"

"A man must work to some end."

"Yeah, yeah. But your family. I've heard you come from a rich family."

"Who told you that?"

"Oh—I don't know. Someone. Everyone wants to talk to me, remember?"

"Why do you want to know?"

"Just curious, that's all."

Gould stared me down for a minute or two. Then he did something very strange. He asked me if I had a photograph of Jayne.

"One," I said.

"Got it with you?"

"Well, yes I do. In my wallet."

"May I see it?"

Slowly, with my eyes hardly leaving Gould's unreadable face, I got out my wallet. The photograph was taken by a mutual friend and showed Jayne sitting in a café. The black leather jacket, the cigarette, a cup of cappuccino in front of her. I handed it over.

Gould held the photograph in front of him for a full half-minute. Then he bent his wrist and looked me in the eye.

"You know," he said, "I considered doing a background check on you at the beginning of this investigation."

"Why?"

"Common procedure. You'd be surprised how many criminals report their own crimes. Either to make themselves look innocent or just for the thrill of it. Like the arsonists who call the fire department and want to help with the hoses. Or the murderers who join the crowd at the funeral."

With his free hand, he cleared aside his cup and saucer and the collection of cream containers. Then he reached below the table and brought up his briefcase.

"I'm going to take this photograph with me," he said. "To make a copy for my files." He snapped the catches, lifted the lid, and tossed the photograph inside. He grinned at me—"Just in case"—and the lid came down again.

Then he was on his feet, brushing the wrinkles out of his blazer. "It's getting late," he said. "I've got a long day ahead of me."

"But—" I said.

"Yes?"

"When do I get—"

"—to see me again?"

He laughed. Beneficent. Self-important. "Tomorrow, late. And if things go as planned, you'll be able to hear about everything."

Neither of us knew, at that moment, how surprisingly true his prediction would be. I just sat there, eyes blurred by the hour and too much coffee, and watched his upright departing back. My only photograph of Jayne in his briefcase.

"Pompous twit," I grumbled.

CHAPTER TWENTY-ONE

Gould was in a triumphant frame of mind when he arrived back at The Red Grizzly. He walked under the sign of the boxing bear (as he thought of it now) and pulled open the door. When he stepped into the lobby, he saw that Margot was not alone. Leaning on the counter was a stocky, puffy faced man with stringy dark hair and a moustache. He was wearing a lumberjack's jacket, green and red plaid, and drinking a can of beer. The pointer finger on his right hand was in a metal splint.

"Oh hi, Inspector," said Margot, rising. "This is Rennie. We've made up."

"Congratulations."

He said it with just a trace of irony. Margot and Rennie did not seem to notice. He considered lecturing Rennie about the can of beer (the lobby was not a licensed area), but then noticed the kind of beer it was. For a few seconds, he considered the possibilities . . . and then, all at once, realized that Rennie's jacket was also torn.

"Where did you rip your jacket, Rennie?" he asked.

"What?"

"Your jacket. It's ripped. Where did it happen?"

"I did it, Inspector." It was Margot.

"Do you remember where?"

"Distinctly."

Awareness now registered in Rennie's dark, not-to-intelligent eyes. He smiled a gap-toothed smile.

"In the woods," continued Margot, "up behind the cemetery. Rennie and I went for a walk."

"We got it on," chuckled Rennie. "She likes it rough and grabbed my jacket."

Margot threw him a warning glance.

"It's alright," said Gould. "Don't be embarrassed. This is helpful to me. You'd like to be helpful, wouldn't you?"

"Sure," said Margot.

"Then tell me, when did you go for your walk?"

Margot sighed. "Two days before the Soledads disappeared. As soon as I heard where the bodies were found I figured it out in my mind. Gives me the creeps to think about it. We were there, exactly the same spot, exactly two days before."

"Good. And Rennie, did you have a beer while you were there?"

"Helps me get in the mood."

"Same brand—Banner Premium Ale?"

"Always."

Gould put his hand out and set it flat on top of the beer can. "I'd like to take this can as evidence in the Soledad murders," he said. "And your jacket too."

"Are we in trouble?" asked Margot.

"No. Quite the contrary. It seems you've just helped account for a couple of the items found near the murder site."

"The bit from Rennie's jacket?"

"And a can. Though you know, Rennie, it's illegal to drink in public like that."

"Not exactly in public."

"You know what I mean."

Rennie gave his broken-toothed smile and handed Gould the jacket.

After a brief visit to the murder room, where he turned over the beer can and jacket to the night duty officer, Gould returned to his room. The encounter with Margot and Rennie had left him strangely shaken—strangely, because on the surface of it, there was nothing at all about it that should have bothered him. An integral part of any investigation is to eliminate details from the crime scene that are irrelevant to the case, and from that point of view the story of the beer can and jacket had helped Gould in his work. And yet he was bothered, even disappointed, by it. He didn't like the fact that it added no support to his theory about a conspiracy. Even more, he was unsettled by the fact that the beer can and strip of fabric had turned out to be dead ends. If he were a superstitious man (which he emphatically was not) he might have considered this feeling a premonition about other dead ends to come. As it was, he chastised himself for being unprofessional.

That night, while he slept under the mosaic of mirrors over his motel room bed, he was plagued by restless and confused dreams. He had a dream in which the indecipherable police report was oddly mixed up with the file of blank paper he had stolen from O'Brien. He had another about a storm and the wooden finger falling from the steeple of the Church of Christ Redeemer, except that the finger ended up falling through the plate glass window of the B.M.U. office, causing a long thin line of smoke to rise into the air. He had a dream about opening his briefcase and finding the white shoe. This one made him bolt awake. It was the dead of night. He lay frigidly still, under the covers, on his back. The room was faintly lit by orange light creeping in around the edges of the curtains. There was no sound, not even of vehicles passing on the highway. Eventually he raised a shaky hand to press his moustache.

Movement. Overhead.

He looked up, and there, staring down at him, was the face of his father.

In retrospect, I should have known Gould would have some kind of breakdown. I should have recognized the signs. It's a cliché of modern fiction, after all, the character obsessed with order who is trying to repress some terrible truth. It's a part of this cliché that the truth—that dark secret hidden in the character's past—always reveals itself, usually with devastating consequences. That Gould befriended me at all, after his first fiery dismissal, was a clue that something was wrong with him. I have to admit that, by the second or third day after his return from Cramdown, I pretty well blanked out the implications of his confiding in me. I had too much need of our friendship to worry about its origins. This perhaps explains why I didn't see the mania behind Gould's fixation on the idea of a conspiracy. I figured it was just another example of his self-assurance, his egotistical belief in his own powers of deduction, and, in a way, I suppose it was, only exaggerated to a pathological degree. Until the night he confessed so much, I knew nothing about his father's potential implication in the case, otherwise I might have recognized the doubleness in those lines about the conspiracy "not ending." Maybe he was hoping to expose his father through the investigation. Maybe he knew that that was the only way he could free himself. I don't know. Then again, he might have been obsessed with solving the case simply as a way of re-establishing his professional credentials to himself, a way of keeping his family secrets locked away in some forgotten cupboard of his mind.

Early the next morning, Gould got a call from the forensic auditor assigned to examine the Church of Christ Redeemer records.

"Edwards here," said the voice on the line. "Thought you might want to know. My preliminary take on the church records is that the trust fund for Reverend Bentley was legal. And there are no other irregularities, as far as I can see, in the church finances. I've got some detail work to do yet to be absolutely sure, but that's the way it's looking."

After taking this call, Gould stared into space for a full minute with the receiver in his hand. When he finally lowered it into its holder, the phone rang again immediately.

"Bacon here, Inspector."

"Sergeant."

"Got a few things to report."

Gould raised a finger to his moustache. "Go ahead."

"First, the tests on Inspector Breeze's gun came up negative. It definitely was not the murder weapon."

"Yes."

"Also, I managed to get enough material to test the cigarette butts. I'm rather proud of that, though I know you're not interested in the technical details. Unfortunately, the results were negative. The butt at the scene and the butt you gave me were not smoked by the same person."

"I see."

"And the dust samples from the truck. They tested for statistically insignificant amounts of silver. If there'd been silver in that truck recently the cargo must have been very carefully crated, either that or the truck was professionally cleaned before we got there. Or maybe it was just luck. Who knows? That's possible too."

"Bad luck on our part or good luck on someone else's?"

"You're the interpreter, Inspector."

"Well—thanks for your work."

"One other thing. The tests on the nuggets from the Cyclops mine are done too. There's another whole technical explanation I could give you here—the ratios of magnesium and lead and minute fractions of gold—but the bottom line is that the comparison with the nuggets from the crime scene is inconclusive."

"Inconclusive?"

"Yeah. They could be from the same geological site but it's not very certain. These kinds of comparisons are generally imprecise anyway."

Bacon's report agitated Gould, so much so that Sergeant Wright, who was in the murder room with him when he took the call, asked him if he was feeling ill. Gould looked back blankly. A shiver seemed to make him insubstantial for a moment—as if his body were somehow blurred in space—then his jaw muscles locked to form his usual, rigid expression.

"It doesn't matter," he said, though whether he meant about the information from Bacon or the question of his own health was not clear.

For much of the morning, Gould drifted back and forth between his own room and the murder room. He poured over his notes—those precisely encoded, remarkably complete records of his work so far—and seemed to take heart from them. To his mind, the conspiracy theory explained so much about what he had uncovered. It made the earlier interviews with Lies, Goodwin and Stahr make sense in a way that they had not before. He took notes towards some future interviews and by noon seemed quite over his disappointment about Bacon's call.

Then word came that Lena Stahr and Al Goodwin were to hold a joint news conference at one o'clock. Gould and Wright grabbed a bite at the Igloo (I was out stretching my legs) and drove to the municipal hall.

The news conference was held in a makeshift media centre set up in a meeting room. On one side there was a long table with microphones on it. Four rows of chairs were lined up facing the table. When Gould and Wright arrived there was a CBC television crew present as well as eight or ten print reporters.

Stahr and Goodwin came in together, accompanied by a half-dozen men in suits and ties—advisors or body-guards, it was hard to tell. After this group came Wallace Lies. The mine owner and union leader sat side-by-side at the table, opening their briefcases and arranging papers before them. Two of the suits and ties waited at the entrance to the room and the others dispersed into the audience. Lies remained standing. When everyone was settled, he called out, "Ladies and Gentlemen. We would like to begin now. Ms. Stahr and Mr. Goodwin will make a joint statement—it should take five minutes or so—and then they will answer questions." Then he sat in the front row.

Lena Stahr was dressed in a long-sleeved black turtleneck and skirt and a bright red, tasseled poncho. When she sat down, instead of taking her poncho off (as Goodwin had his coat), she pulled it open and threw the two halves back over her shoulders like a cape. She wore silver shell earrings and a bracelet around one wrist made out of a series of geometrically shaped loops linked together. Her lips were red like her poncho. When she spoke, it was with her usual low, sensuous and commanding voice.

Al Goodwin, on the other hand, looked like an usher at a wedding, stiff and formal, in a solid dark grey suit. His orange hair was raked down and, Gould thought, probably sprayed into place. He spoke with the slightly disoriented euphoria of a man who has just won a lottery.

Together they announced that a tentative agreement had been reached to end the strike. Reading alternately from a single, prepared text, they explained that the full terms of the agreement would not be announced until after the union membership had ratified it (a foregone conclusion, they seemed to imply). They could, however, say this much: Lena Stahr had agreed to live with a union at the Cyclops mine, and in exchange, the workers would return to the job for about the same compensation package as before. "After all," Stahr explained (with Goodwin nodding beside her), "the strike was much more about principles than money."

During the question period, a Vancouver *Planet* reporter asked about the effect of the Soledad murders on negotiations. Goodwin and Stahr agreed that the murders had helped them to put some things in perspective. "We are really fortunate in this country," they said. "We argue over who gets what and sometimes things get a little rough, but it's important to keep things in perspective. If we stay reasonable, we can work things out. Nobody gets killed. Back where the Soledads came from . . . ."

"Are you implying that a hit squad from Costaguana killed the Soledads?" asked the reporter.

"We're not implying anything. Figuring out who killed the Soledads is the business of the police. All we can say is that we're proud of our Canadian ability to compromise."

"The word around town is that the police are trying to track down a black Mercedes thought to be involved in the killings. Do you know anything about that?"

"Only that there have been various sightings of this car by different people—some mine workers, some others. The meaning of it we'll have to leave to the police."

By the end of the questions, Gould, that model of discipline and self-control, could barely keep himself in his chair. He had a powerful, almost overwhelming urge to leap up and denounce Stahr and Goodwin and Lies. *Conspirators!* he wanted to shout. *Murderers!* He also had an urge, as compelling as it was irrational, to shout profanities at the top of his lungs—in Spanish.

Instead he pressed a finger to his moustache, stared for a moment, and came to a snap decision.

His state of mind, perhaps, explains it. Perhaps it was the looks that Goodwin and Stahr flashed him during the conference. Defiant and sheepish and knowing (Goodwin). Practiced and sensuous and knowing (Stahr). Just before his decision, he imagined himself on his feet with his gun out of its holster. Glen Gould (The Other One) with a gun. He imagined raising the weapon above his head and firing. *Enough!* he'd shout, as plaster rained down around him. *Nobody leaves this room until I hear the truth!*

He sent Wright to guard the way out. Then he intercepted Lies,

Stahr and Goodwin at the front of the room and said, in his most authoritative tone, "It's time we talked again. You, you, you and me. Down at the station. All of us. Now."

Ten minutes later, everyone was gathered in the office of Inspector Cullen (once the office of Inspector Breeze, once the office of Sergeant Wright). Lies, Goodwin, Stahr, Wright and Gould. After a look from Gould, Cullen had excused himself. Various suits and ties were left to wait outside in the public area, under the watchful eye of the duty officer. All three suspects had agreed readily to the interview, Goodwin and Stahr delaying only two or three minutes to consult with their advisors. This willingness only deepened Gould's suspicions: it seemed as if the three had anticipated a showdown. Maybe they had even rehearsed for it.

Lies blustered about the room at first, exclaiming to first Wright and then Cullen (on his way out) about how wonderful it was that the strike was over and, with false modesty, beginning the story of his own role in "bringing the parties together." He was dressed in his harlequin jacket and wearing that faint smile of his. His nondescript blue eyes seemed bright and empty at the same time. Gould put an end to his jabber by tapping him on the shoulder. "There," he said, sternly, indicating the least comfortable of the chairs.

He ordered Stahr and Goodwin to sit at opposite ends of the couch, then he positioned himself so that he was their focal point.

For a few seconds there was silence.

Gould let his gaze slowly sweep the arrangement of people. Deliberate, intense, superior. He waited, his briefcase upright on his lap, in the poised, arms-over-the-wheel manner of a cab driver looking for a break in traffic. Wright sat, large and impassive, beside him.

"Coffee?" It was Lies. "Anyone? I know they keep a pot on in the outer office."

"The silver. I want to know about the silver."

Gould spoke softly, almost in a whisper. But the silence that followed seemed to press on the ears—like the silence after a slammed door. Stahr and Goodwin adopted I-don't-know-what-you're-talking-about looks, Goodwin's coloured by his habitual belligerence. Lies opened and closed and opened his mouth again.

"The silver," repeated Gould. "The one piece of evidence I need to go after the killers of the Soledads."

"You know who the killers are?" asked Lies.

"Everyone here knows who the killers are."

Gould slowly met the eyes of each of the suspects. He gave them his most authoritative look, his gunslinger look, his fighter-pilot-closing-in-on-the-target look. Lies, mouth now closed, returned a dead stare. On his face there was not the slightest trace of a grin. Goodwin and Stahr were also poker faced.

"A hit squad," said Gould. "A hit squad from Costaguana. Isn't that what you told me? Isn't that where each one of you ultimately pointed the finger? Well, I'm convinced. You convinced me. Other developments have convinced me. And I am preparing to focus my efforts in that direction. But I can't do it until you tell me about the silver."

"I, for one, have no idea what you're talking about," said Stahr.

"The silver the Soledads brought with them to Canada. The silver that ended up in an abandoned mine shaft on your property. Some of which was carted off by union raiders. The rest of which was melted back down and added to the mine's output."

Lena Stahr shook her right arm and the bracelet jangled, a muted metallic sound against the sleeve of her pullover. She seemed to be absorbed in the bracelet, as if it was the only thing on her mind. She reached over with her other hand to fiddle with a square, a hexagon.

"Let me tell you something," said Gould. "At this point, if you co-operate, the worst that can happen is some relatively minor embarrassment about the silver. Under the circumstances, it's unlikely you will even have to make restitution. Refuse to co-operate, however, and things will go very much harder on you. All of you. I will prove the existence of the silver. And who knows what other secrets I will uncover along the way? I already know that after the Soledads went to you and you"—meaning Lies and Stahr—"for help, Enrique Soledad claimed that you"—meaning Stahr—"had cheated him. I also know that he tried to blackmail you about your relationship with Inspector Breeze."

Stahr looked up from her bracelet. Her eyes met Gould's and gave nothing away. She raised them another half inch and he was gone. Non-existent.

Lies opened and closed and opened his mouth again.

"I have the tape," continued Gould. "But you already know that, don't you?"

Stahr huffed dismissively and refocused her eyes. "I've had men in my bed before, Inspector, and I will have them again. On my own terms, of course. I'm not ashamed of it."

"What relationship?" It was Lies.

Stahr turned on him. Quietly, in a killing voice, she said, "Don't be naive, Wallace."

Gould watched this exchange, this little side-show, with some interest. It was certainly well staged. Lies now gazed at Lena Stahr with what seemed like real anguish in his eyes. The consummate actor. For a moment, Gould tried to imagine the purpose the charade was meant to serve, but then decided not to be distracted by it.

"The point is," he said, commanding Stahr's attention again, "that your failure to reveal your relationship with Inspector Breeze is very close to obstruction of justice. And with the obvious motives you had to murder the Soledads . . . ."

"You said a hit squad did it."

"That's what I believe. But will the crown attorney's office believe it? Would a jury? Remember, I don't make the final call on these things. And who knows what other incriminating evidence I may find as I continue to hunt for the silver? Letters, directives. After your other false statements . . . ."

"None of my statements were false."

"Come now. Amongst other things, you went out of your way to portray yourself as a friend of the Soledads, doing them a favour offering them a job. Prospecting."

Stahr let out a short, scornful laugh. "I did nothing of the sort. I told you they came to me with a business deal, a deal that, under the circumstances, I felt compelled to accept."

"You said they were desperate."

"They were desperate. But the bottom line was that it was a business deal. I told you that before and I still stand by it."

"You stand by the prospecting story too?"

"Have you evidence to the contrary?"

"Well, for one thing, I now know that the Soledads worked their first six weeks at night."

"So?"

"Prospecting—picking over the countryside looking for minerals—in the dark?"

"Thank you for the mining lesson, Inspector. The fact is, the Soledad's began their work underground, so it didn't matter whether they worked at night or during the day."

Gould looked momentary perplexed.

Stahr sighed and flicked her hand. "The first part of their survey was to examine previously abandoned shafts for viable deposits. If you knew anything about mining, you'd know this was the logical place to start. What was uneconomical to mine fifty years ago might be quite economical today. Only the second part of their survey, which they had barely started before they disappeared, was on the surface. And for that they came into work during the day."

"Are you telling me that the Soledads chose to work at night for those first six weeks?"

"Amongst other reasons, there was less danger crossing the picket line."

"Bah!" Gould was angry. A rare emotion for him—almost unheard of during an interview. The anger appeared as a pinkish rash on his neck. "You know and I know, and Mr. Goodwin there knows just as well, what the Soledads were really doing in those old mine shafts. And it wasn't looking for silver."

Stahr looked back at her bracelet. End of discussion. Gould slapped his briefcase down onto his knees and spun the combination lock. He worked too quickly and had to do the combination over again. Then he raised the lid, a little too fast, and reached inside. His notebook.

"You see this?" he asked, holding it up for Al Goodwin to see. "This contains a complete transcript of my interrogation of Sherwood and Berry. So quit playing dumb. Both of you. I know about the silver."

Goodwin now seemed to rise to the occasion. "If you know about the silver, Inspector, then why do you need us to tell you about it?" He gave his "s's" an extra, provocative push of air through his bad teeth.

Gould refused to answer. Instead he glared at Goodwin: *Confess you bastard, confess.*

The union leader, however, took a deep breath and let it slowly back out. Then he said, with an air of smugness, "My guess is that you really don't know about any horde of silver. Your case may depend upon it but you have no proof of its existence. You're at a dead end and you're trying to trick us into helping you get out of it."

Gould was stunned. All at once, he realized he had made a mistake in confronting the suspects like this. Reason told him to retreat, that he needed to be more patient and better armed before a confrontation, but somehow he could just not back down.

"I have sworn statements," he said.

"About what? That some of my men stole silver from the Cyclops mine? Frankly, Inspector, if that were true, it would be up to Ms. Stahr to make a complaint, and, as we both know, she hasn't. In any case, even if the story were true, it wouldn't prove there was a treasure from Costaguana."

"The statements are not the only evidence."

"Yeah, sure. Luke Carson is a friend of mine. I only mention that in passing, because I wouldn't want you to think I was obstructing your investigation."

For a moment, it seemed like the room was full of smoke. Gould couldn't see, couldn't breath. A succession of images raced through his mind: the union office smoldering after the riot, morning on a beach in Costaguana, the raised shoe of Camilla Soledad. Then he forced himself to return his notebook to his briefcase. He closed the top. Snapped the brass catches. Lowered it to the floor.

It was time to up the ante. "Okay," he said. "I didn't want to tell you this, because the fewer people who know the better, but the truth of the matter is that the Soledads were not killed by the government of Costaguana. I said before that they were killed by a hit squad—that's true—and the hit squad was from Costaguana, but, in point of fact, it was not working for the government. Who was it working for? The rebels, the Front for the Liberation of Costaguana. How do we know? Two reasons. First, we have learned definitively that the Soledads were members of a rogue unit within the F.L.C. This unit stole a large cache of silver from the rebels themselves. Apparently, the rebels have, over the years, acquired their own horde. And secondly, we know that agents of the rebels are currently operating in Canada."

Wallace Lies now leaned forward in his chair. Out of the corner of his eye, Gould could see beads of sweat on Lies's forehead. The smile on his face had faded and his mouth was furrowed with anxiety.

Gould continued, "If you don't understand the significance of this, let me spell it out for you. The rebel Front in Costaguana is very brutal in its methods for maintaining loyalty and discipline. Their methods are similar to those of the Mafia. Nobody leaves the family and lives. Nobody steals from the family or profits by that theft and lives."

He let that sink in. Lies grew even more tense and Lena Stahr threw a warning glance in his direction.

"In a certain way," said Gould, "it doesn't matter who killed the Soledads. If, by some obscure chance, the F.L.C. did not kill them, and, as I said before, I intend to focus the investigation almost exclusively in that direction from now on—even if the Soledads were killed by someone else, it wouldn't really matter. The fact is that if you are connected to the silver the Soledads brought to Canada in any way, you are in danger."

"What can we do?" It was Wallace Lies. As soon as he spoke, the words squeaking out as if against his will, he raised his hand to his mouth and looked apologetically at Stahr. She narrowed her eyes at him in turn.

"Tell me everything you know about the silver. The only way I can protect you, the only way I can make sure the rebel operatives cease and desist, is if I have proof of the silver's existence. Only then can I go to C.S.I.S. and tell them, this is what happened, and this is why these operatives are here and we have to stop them."

"You're bluffing—"

"You're bluffing—"

Stahr and Goodwin spoke in unison. For a second or two they exchanged appreciative glances. Then Stahr said, "If you really have proof of F.L.C. operatives working in Canada, you don't need our help to stop them."

"Besides," added Goodwin, "we know about the black Mercedes."

Gould stared blankly at the union leader.

"*That* Mercedes," continued Goodwin, "not the other one—which may or may exist, I don't know."

An awkward silence fell on the room. Sergeant Wright uncrossed his legs and then crossed them again—the only movement or response he had shown during the interview so far. Lies looked from one face to another, confused. He bounced minutely up and down in his chair once, twice, three times, then blurted out, "What are you talking about?"

Al Goodwin laughed. He slouched back on the couch, stretching his legs, and fluffed out his orange hair with his fingers. He wagged his finger at Gould. "The Inspector here has tried to pull this line before. Only when he pulled it before, he used a prop. He figured that Sherwood and Berry would've heard rumours about a black Mercedes around town, about a hit squad following the Soledads and all that, so he got some undercover cops—Mexican looking cops—to follow them in a black Mercedes. Obviously the police have too much money kicking around. Anyway, the idea was to spook Sherwood and Berry into talking, just like he's trying to spook us. It worked on them. But we copped the cops." Goodwin chuckled at his own wit and, with a flagrantly artificial smile, flashed his bad teeth at Gould.

"Is this true, Inspector?"

Gould turned to face Wallace Lies. He had almost run out of cards to play, and knew it. While Goodwin had spoken, it had taken all his strength of will not to jump out of his chair and start shouting. Now he raised his hand to his moustache. His wrist trembled as he pressed his finger into the bristles. The moustache was damp.

Lies, it seemed, was genuinely perplexed. Gould could see it on his face. Or could he? He found it hard to believe that Lies didn't know every detail about what was going on, every nuance of the deceptions being acted out. He had Lies pegged as the mastermind of the whole operation, the chief script-writer, the star actor. And yet....

Gould decided to go for broke.

"Mr. Goodwin is very clever," he said, softly. "Ms. Stahr beside him there is very clever too. In fact, they are both extremely clever, particularly when they are in on something together like they are now. Too bad they didn't fill you in on all the details."

Lies looked Gould in the eye. "What details?"

"You mean you really don't know?"

Lies's face seemed truly blank.

"All right," said Gould, "you asked about the truth. Well, here it is. The truth is, yes, I assigned a black Mercedes to tail Sherwood and Berry and it did spook them into talking. The truth is, yes, the hit squad story was a bluff. It was my attempt to spook you, just as I spooked Berry and Sherwood, into talking. Let's be honest. The truth is, no hit squad from Costaguana killed the Soledads. The hit squad is a complete fantasy, a wish fulfillment, a fabrication. The truth is, the four of us in this office, you and I and him and her, we all know very well who killed the Soledads."

While Gould spoke, light and dark seemed to pass rapidly over the blank canvas of Lies's face. Sun and shadow on a windy day. There was a smile, which was instantaneously uncertain, then anger, then, apparently, sadness on the verge of tears.

"As I was saying"—Gould's voice now returned to its quiet pitch, a voice of intimate command—"your friends here are very clever. Clever enough to get someone else to do the dirty work for them. To get someone else to make the incriminating inquiries, to set the whole thing up. If necessary, to be the fall guy. Ms. Stahr is even clever enough to have a new lover in place just in the case the old one—"

"That's enough—" Lena Stahr had started to her feet.

"Sit!" Gould thundered. "I will tell you when you can leave!"

There was something in Gould's manner now that genuinely seemed to frighten Stahr. As if he threatened her physically. She shrank back onto the couch. Gould turned to Wright. "Any one tries to leave this room, I want them restrained. You understand, Sergeant?"

Wright searched rapidly in Gould's eyes for a clue about his motivation. When he could find none, he maintained his professional mask and deadpanned his response. "Yes sir."

Gould raked the three suspects with his eyes. "I want the truth. And no one leaves this room until I get it! *Entiendez?*"

Nobody spoke. Wright glanced at his superior. He rubbed his big hands on the front of his trousers. Lies's mouth opened and closed, but nothing came out.

"Look, Wallace, this is your chance to come clean. I know how the killings were carried out. The killers used a black van—not a black car—and disguised themselves as Statewide agents. We have the bloodied club used to knock Enrique Soledad out. We have the Soledad car. It's only a matter of time before we find the men who pulled the trigger. And you, I know you were in Vancouver to organize the shipment of the silver. That you were with Enrique Soledad the weekend Luke Carson picked up the trailer. I also know about what you did in Vancouver after that. The inquiries you made.

"The truth is, I believe you were only a go-between. A messenger. It's obvious that you didn't know all the sides Ms. Stahr here was playing at once. Come clean now and things will go easier for you. I will try to get a deal with you from the Crown."

Stahr and Goodwin were now tensed forward on the couch. Gould, out of the corner of his eye, could see they were about to jump into the exchange. He warned them off with a raised finger, never taking his eyes off Wallace Lies.

After a while, Lies smiled apologetically at Stahr and said, "I guess I should tell you, then."

Gould waited. It was one of the longest waits of his life. Lies took a deep breath and summoned up his willpower. Then he said, almost in a whisper, "Yes, I have made a number of trips to Vancouver the last while."

"Yes?"

"Sometimes it was to do things I'm not proud of."

Lies stammered to a halt. He looked at Lena Stahr. He looked at Gould. He looked at Lena Stahr again and said, "Sorry." Then he looked Gould back in the eyes, exhaled sharply and said, "The truth is—I admit it. I have a mistress in Vancouver."

For five seconds there was absolute silence. The room was so still that the people in it could feel the passage of time as a sensation in their bodies, a subtle pulse on their skin.

Then Goodwin and Stahr laughed.

Wallace Lies had his unreadable smile back on his face.

Gould felt like he was trapped in a whirlpool. He grabbed at whatever he could to keep himself afloat. "Don't give me that line!" he shouted. "I know you helped Enrique Soledad load the silver onto Luke Carson's truck."

"It wasn't silver, Inspector. It was mining supplies."

"You expect me to believe that?"

Now Lena Stahr said, "Enrique Soledad was a miner in Costaguana. Remember? One of the side benefits of his working for me was that he arranged to import some supplies."

"Oranges?"

"There were a couple of boxes of oranges, yes. A present to me. But mostly it was just the usual: parts for the processing plant and so on. I'm sure I have a complete list of items somewhere. I can give it to you any time you want. You should have asked me before."

Gould waved her off. He jabbed a finger at Wallace Lies. "I know what you were doing in Vancouver three weeks ago. I have a signed affidavit from a bartender at The Barnacle. He says you gave him two hundred dollars for information about some 'tough guys to do a dirty job.'"

"The two hundred dollars was a tip," said Lies.

"A tip?"

Goodwin and Stahr were now lounged back in their seats.

"Yeah. I was in such a good mood from the time I was having."

"There is a team of detectives going door to door right now with your picture. Every public establishment, every underworld contact in the area is being questioned."

"It was a tip, I tell you."

"You asked for tough guys."

Gould looked from Lies to Stahr to Goodwin and back to Lies. "I want the truth!" he shouted.

Lies flicked imaginary lint from the lapels of his harlequin jacket. Then he raised his eyes back up at Gould, those ordinary blue eyes. If anything, the smile on his face was even more enigmatic than before. "Look, Inspector," he said, "you know me. I was just making conversation."

Gould raised his hand to his mouth. His eyes, against his will, closed tight. Behind his closed eyelids, the world had gone white.

IV

THE SILVER OF THE MINE

There is something in a treasure that fastens upon a man's mind. He will pray and blaspheme and still persevere, and will curse the day he ever heard of it, and will let his last hour come upon him unawares, still believing that he missed it only by a foot. He will see it every time he closes his eyes.

Joseph Conrad, *Nostromo*

Chapter Twenty-Two

A green bottle fly crawled across my table at the Igloo. It wobbled a bit as it went, like a worker, smudged and sapped and sweaty, after a long shift. When it came to the table edge it clawed the air with its front legs, helpless, it seemed, as if it couldn't quite believe that the solid world had ended. Nearby, a bearded man in a John Deere cap hunched over a log book at the Truckers Only table, his eyes crow-lined with concentration, a large hand making a club around a pencil. Now and then he reached for his coffee cup and raised it like a can of beer to his lips. The fly tumbled off the edge of the table. The bearded man did not look up.

Across from me sat Inspector Charles Gould of the RCMP. His blazer hung open to reveal the butt of his gun, like a severed horn, under his right arm. His shoulders were hunched. His face, though apparently unchanged from the last time I had seen it, seemed ten years older. Like the bearded man he also nursed a coffee, but before each sip he gazed into the cup, sometimes for five seconds or more, and seemed to come away disappointed. Each time he tipped his head back to drink, it was as if he wished he were drinking something else. "So—there you have it," he said. "All the facts pertinent to the Soledad investigation."

"All the known facts," I said.

I slid his notebook back across the table to him.

"It certainly is an impressive record. Clearly written. All those details. The virtual transcripts of conversations."

Gould stared past me, his eyes focussed, apparently, on something on the wall. Then, out of the blue, he began to speak, "Once, when we were small, my brother and I managed to escape the bodyguards that were supposed to protect us . . . ." He went on like this for a long time. At some point he reached out his hand, without looking down, and made as if to lower it on his notebook.

And missed.

It was obvious, from the moment he appeared in the Igloo that Friday night, that Gould was in the grips of some kind of mania. Even the way he walked from the door to my booth suggested something was wrong, the way he dragged his feet slightly and curled in his shoulders. He didn't slouch, exactly, but there was a definite softening of his posture. Down the line of the lunch counter, right turn at the high counter . . . . There was something oddly human about him that night, the way he passed the Truckers Only table and, for the briefest of moments, seemed to acknowledge the bearded man as a fellow traveller, the way he was still upright but no longer rigid, as if he had become more frail and more vital at the same time.

He sat down across from me. "It's over," he said.

"You solved the case?"

For a moment there was a flicker of amusement on his face. An ironic tightening of the lips. Then, with hardly a muscle moving, his face collapsed. He looked ten years older and filled with despair.

In the weeks and months that have passed since then, I have, of course, picked over every detail from that night and the events leading up to it. I have wondered long and hard about why Gould tried to confront Stahr, Lies and Goodwin in such a singular, dramatic way. When he admitted the confrontation to me, early in the dark hours that followed, I shook my head in disbelief. "But that's so unprofessional," I said. "What about all the stuff you told me about waiting for the right moment?"

"I felt it was the right moment."

"But you didn't have the evidence. You were just bluffing them."

"That's true."

He looked at me with tragic eyes.

"You know what else it was? Cliché—that's what. I mean, it's like a fucking Third Degree scene in a detective novel. You know—when the brilliant detective gathers everybody together and says: 'Someone in this room is the killer of Madame Moneybags!' You're not Sherlock Holmes, you know."

"I'm aware of that."

"Well, what did you expect? That you could get a confession by the sheer compelling force of your personality?"

"I didn't have a clear plan."

"Obviously."

Gould threw back the remainder of his coffee and signalled Marlene for a refill. I noticed the bottle fly again, crawling slowly across the brown tile floor. When Marlene came with the steaming glass carafe, the fly disappeared for a moment behind—or under—one of her white running shoes. When she walked away it was still there.

"Look," said Gould, with a sigh, "I didn't start out trying to get anyone to confess. I knew none of them would do that, not outright, anyway. All I wanted was to get confirmation about the Soledad silver. I really believed that the treasure was the key. I could see it in my mind—this gleaming horde, the secret behind all the events. Prove its existence and everything else would fall into place. That's what I thought. And I really believed I had a chance to bluff the three of them that far. After all, my absurd story about the hit squad had worked once before."

"Sherwood and Berry aren't exactly rocket scientists."

"That's true."

Gould looked down into his cup. He frowned. He seemed to debate something with himself, then seemed to come out on the losing end of the argument. He raised the cup to his mouth, sipped, and set it back down again.

"Only after I realized they'd seen through my bluff did I try to work on Lies. At a certain point, I remembered something that Breeze had told me. He said that on the night Stahr and Lies confessed to their relationship—you remember, when they all met at Lies's house—Lies was in the kitchen when Stahr and Breeze had their heart-to-heart. And it came to me: maybe this was intentional. Maybe Stahr had deliberately kept Lies in the dark about her other relationship. Maybe she was playing both sides against the middle. And if this was so, then Lies's astonishment at the mention of Breeze and Stahr would have been genuine. So I thought, if Lies is hurt and suspicious .... Well. I was wrong, obviously. Totally wrong."

The way Gould wound down his talk, so sad, so apologetic, gave me pause. I noticed a tone of finality in what he said, as if the case were now absolutely and irredeemably lost. I tried to buoy him up.

"Well, your gamble didn't work out," I said, "but, really, it's not the end of the world. Lies and Stahr and Goodwin probably knew you were on to them anyway."

Gould stared at me with tragic eyes.

"I know the interview was a disaster, but the investigation goes on, right? It might take a little longer than you originally thought."

"The investigation is over."

"But how can that be? The case isn't solved. Surely the world-famous RCMP is not going to give up just because one of their inspectors blew an interview?"

Gould glared at me. I glared back. A quarter minute crawled by, slowly, like a green-bottle fly alive past its season. Then, out of the blue, he said, softly, "It wasn't just Corporal Clearly, you know. It wasn't even that time I tried out for the Canadian national team. There was something else. Something more important."

"What?"

"It's so cliché. It's the kind of thing every second pulp detective has in his background."

"But it is the reason you got into police work?"

"Not on its own. Everything else had a part to play too."

"Yeah, yeah. I don't mean to suggest you're one-dimensional. Still—"

"Still. You're right. She was the most immediate reason."

"So tell me about her."

We talked for hours this way, from ten o'clock on the night after the failed confrontation, past midnight, when the restaurant all but emptied, past the bar rush, with the RCMP cruisers flashing their red and blue lights outside, through the long black hours until dawn bled slowly into the sky, past the breakfast rush and into the full morning, a curtain of sunlight descending from the peaks of the West Columbia

Range, searing off clouds as it went, until in the cool, still November day, we were silenced by the clap of a gun.

What was most astonishing about Gould's talk—besides the sheer fact of his confessing so much to me—was the way it flowed seamlessly back and forth from the Soledad case to his personal life and back again. It was as if he leapt from one to the other in an effort to avoid revealing anything about either, but with each leap he revealed more and more about both. As time went on there seemed to be something at the core of it all, some overriding secret he was circling around, trying to reveal but also trying to hide with all his vacillations. I gradually came to understand that it had to do with his father.

At some point he told me about the letter and his meeting with O'Brien. I don't remember exactly when this was, only that by then he had told me about his brother and mother and much else besides. To end this part of his story he reached inside his briefcase and brought up the file of blank paper. He slapped it on the table between us.

"Exhibit A," he said.

"Hard to believe you stole that right from under his nose. What were you thinking?"

"I was confused. Part of me wanted revenge. I figured that if I had the file I could prove that O'Brien had overstepped his authority. But, deep down, part of me wanted to read the file as well, to read what it had to say about me, where I came from, who I was."

I pulled the tan folder, with its broad white grin, towards me. The label read: *Gould, Charles Robert.* I peeled back the cover.

"Jayne would have a field day with this," I said. "I mean, the fact that the pages are all blank. The symbolism of that."

Gould didn't respond. He just sat there with his forearms on the table watching as I riffled pages. When I closed the file again, I noticed that he had his hands wide open, about a foot apart, as if he were sizing up something or contemplating an invisible cat's cradle. I also noticed, for the first time, that his hands were faintly freckled. This surprised me. Somehow, because his face was so clear (which set up the powerful contrast with his auburn hair), I had expected his hands to be unblemished as well.

"Well," I said, after a while, "it doesn't really matter, does it? For whatever reasons, you decided to stay on the case. So the important thing is to see it through."

His hands collapsed. "The important thing? It's not important that O'Brien put me on the case for political reasons? Not important that my father put him up to it in the first place?"

"How could you know that?"

"My father, as they say, has friends in high places. How do you think he knew so quickly that I was assigned to the case? How do you think he acquired my address here? Think about it. His letter arrived the day after I did."

A thought fell into place for me. "So that's it, then," I said. "That's what's really important for you about this case. Your father. No wonder you've been like you've been. No wonder this case has been so emotional for you. Your odd behaviour, our friendship."

Gould gave me a look that ought to have stuck about five inches out of my back. Evidently, I was getting too close to the truth. He waved his empty cup in Marlene's direction. She came over with the pot. "I'd like another piece of pie as well, please," he said.

"Apple?"

"Heated. Like the other one."

He stuck his nose down into the steam rising from his cup. He frowned in the way he had been doing all night, as if, against all reason, he had expected the cup to be filled with whiskey. Then he looked up at me. Irony returned to his eye.

"What's really important," he said, "is what Jayne would make of that file."

Outside an engine revved. It was an eighteen-wheeler with chrome exhaust pipes rising vertical on either side of the cab. The pipes were perforated with holes near the top, like the muzzle of a machine gun. When the engine revved, black diesel exhaust jetted skyward.

So I told him about Jayne, how she was a small woman, the top of her head just the right height to be kissed. How her hair smelled of apricots. How one time she beat on my chest and said, "I could hurt you. That's why I don't want any commitments. I could hurt you and I don't want to." And I looked down at her standing there, the sleeves of her leather jacket almost covering her fists, and laughed. I told him how the first time we made love, I touched my tongue all over her body, her shoulders, her breasts, her belly, her sex, her thighs, her calves. At some point, I noticed that she was missing part of the two smallest toes on one foot. I hesitated, unsure of the etiquette. She noticed my uncertainty, raised her head slightly and, in a rare moment of personal confession, said, "That happened when I was eleven. I was cutting the lawn barefoot. I was always doing stuff like that when I was a kid."

"So there you have it," I said, "Jayne Whynot in a nutshell. A brilliant, beautiful young woman, but with a bad habit of hurting herself."

"Yeah, yeah," said Gould, "now tell me the real story."

Much later, I told him, "My reactions were always contradictory. When she snubbed me for some other guy, part of me always reacted in the most predictable, most stereotypical way. I knew I was doing it, but I couldn't stop myself. I became The Hurt One, The Ever Faithful, The Ever Suffering. I listened to Country and Western music, the old time stuff, She done me wrong. My taking off from Vancouver was like that. When I think of the drive now, I think of it as a kind of binge. With every mile I sucked up more of my own bleak mood, my hurt, my anger, my confusion. I remember taking special pleasure as the road got more dangerous. By the time I hit Rogers Pass, about two in the morning, there was steady rain and blinding pockets of fog. At times I could hardly see the road in front of me. Trucks coming the other way threw sheets of water onto my windshield. Soon there were mounds of white on either side of the road. I stopped at the Petro Canada station at the summit, pissed a warm stream into the snow (I didn't want to ask for a washroom key, didn't want even that much contact with another human being) and watched the raindrops churning up a puddle beside me. Then, morbidly happy, I drove on, down through the snow shelters and tunnels, the transport trucks looming suddenly in my rear view mirror, flashing their high beams and going by.

"So part of me was like that, The Hurt One, but, strangely enough, part of me was turned on as well. Turned on by her refusal to be with just one man, her refusal of commitment, her recklessness, selfishness, unpredictability. It was like our arguments. After a fight, part of me, the She Done Me Wrong part, would be crushed, defensive, bitter, but another part would be undressing her with my eyes. Even the morning she told me about the Native man I felt a slow burn of desire. That unnerved me a bit: it seemed so weird, to desire her under those circumstances, so contradictory, perverse, even base."

"But what made you break up with her?"

"I don't know. Maybe I didn't believe I was really doing it. Maybe running away was just another melodramatic gesture, an elaborate ploy to get her back again."

"You won't be getting her back."

I stared at him, Inspector Charles Gould, sitting across from me in his I-am-a-plain-clothes-cop blue suit. He was wiping up the last of his omelette with a piece of toast.

"Who says I won't be getting her back?"

"You read her letter. She said not to follow her. She said you would never understand the reasons."

The moment I opened my mouth to talk about Jayne, I realized I'd made a mistake. I had planned to be sketchy, to fob off a few anecdotes on Gould until he was ready to confess what he needed to confess; but as I carried on I found myself getting caught up in the telling. I became ensnared by the different sides of the story, her side, my side, the others. I found myself empathizing with her even as I vented my anger. I was assaulted by my own yearning desire. And I realized I was getting further and further off track, further and further away from Charles Gould and the conduct of the Soledad investigation.

Gould seemed to hang on my every word. He was extremely attentive, asked gently leading questions, and now and then nodded in an appreciative way. While I talked (with an awareness that I was slipping deeper and deeper into emotional quicksand), he seemed to grow calm, to regain his self-assurance, a kind of sanity (or a parody of sanity). I half-expected him to pull out my photograph of Jayne and start admiring it.

I couldn't stand it.

"I've got to take a piss," I said.

My idea was to get away for a few moments, to break the spell of recollections. Splash some water on my face. Get a grip.

The washrooms were on the other side of the restaurant, down a hallway that ran off the end of the lunch counter. I had to walk past the Truckers Only table (empty for the moment), along the high counter, past Marlene and Nora by the warming light, and turn right. I splashed water. I mugged in the mirror. On my way back, I had a long view of the counter, two lone wolves having breakfast with three empty stools between them, the cash register on a short "L" by the far end. Someone pushed in the glass door at the entrance. I saw the aluminum sides of the pastry cabinets, the drink dispensers, a milkshake maker. Also something that gave me pause: behind the lunch counter there was a glass carafe on a burner. The carafe, as usual, had a handle on it for pouring and, logically enough, was boiling (water for tea). Except that inside the carafe there was a goldfish. The goldfish swam around and around behind a wall of rising bubbles.

I stopped at the warming light and said to Marlene, "The fake carafe—that's pretty funny. Is it new?"

She unzipped a big smile. "Oh no, it's been here for ages. You never notice it before?"

"I find it hard to talk about her," I said, "because everything I say seems cliché. This is terribly ironic, of course, since Jayne was unrelenting in her attack on received ideas. Part of the problem is my tendency to fall back on familiar categories, but really, if you think about it, part of it must be love itself, how scripted the roles are. Fall in love and it feels unique, like five billion years of evolution have passed just to lead up to this moment, but really you are just repeating the same old gestures. And the words. Try to talk about love and you realize the words have been spoken a billion times before. How many stories, poems, movies, songs have been written about love? You can't open your mouth without quoting someone."

"But why does that bother you? So what if it's all been said before? If love is so scripted anyway."

"But Jayne—don't you see?—Jayne was different."

Gould leaned back in his seat. On his lips there was a faint but unmistakably smug grin. "Now we're getting somewhere," he said.

"After she told me about the Native man, I took the bus to her apartment. She said, 'I told you I would hurt you,' and I said, 'There's a stack of mail here' and brought it inside with me. The house routine was to sort the mail, take your own, and leave the rest on the landing. I did it for her, quickly, while she looked over my shoulder. Nothing. Nothing for Jayne Whynot. I went to put the stack down, but she reached out her hand. 'That one's for me,' she said. A letter, in the usual white envelope, Canadian postage, a return address in Ontario. I could see it didn't have her name on it. 'From my family,' she said. 'I never open them.' She led me up stairs and into her bedroom. She hid nothing but also explained nothing. She opened the drawer of her bedside table (the one with the Peter Rabbit ashtray on it) and dropped the letter inside. Before she closed up again, I saw the stack of letters I had seen before. After that, we made tea, sat down at the kitchen table, and had a spit-in-your-face argument. She charged me with the usual things, I made the usual denials. She said I was always trying to police her behaviour, that that was why I had really come over that day. I shouted, 'You asked me over!' She accused me of hiding my real feelings. I swooned in disbelief. As the argument became more violent, I had the usual contradictory clash of reactions. Eventually I yelled, 'I may not know you but you don't know me either!' And left."

Gould stared at me. Something shone in his eyes that had nothing—or everything—to do with irony.

I didn't care. Something had just dawned on me. I went on working it out for myself.

"But that's it," I said, "that's what running away was really about for me. That's why I broke up with her. Why didn't I see it before?"

Nearby, a goldfish swam behind a wall of bubbles.

I smiled. I made little quotation marks with my fingers. "*I never knew her*," I said, to myself, to Gould, to my journal, to the goldfish, to the green bottle fly. "Never could, not in the way I craved. You can't know anyone like that, of course, but Jayne, Jayne lived and breathed the impossibility."

By this point, I had accepted that Gould's confessions were over, that I had disrupted them for good. I accepted that I would never know about his father, that, whether he carried on with the investigation or not, I would never know who killed the Soledads. I wasn't really disappointed. My confessions about Jayne had given me a sense of relief, of release. Not that I had "solved" our relationship in any final way (my explanations did not—could not—tell the whole story), but, somehow, I felt less haunted, less obsessed by that single question—*What about Jayne?*—and so less inclined to run away from the contradictory tangle of my life.

It was broad daylight now. The glass door of the restaurant opened and closed. People took off coats or put them on again. Others sat at tables eating pancakes or two eggs over easy. Voices. Country music. The dull clink of cutlery on dishes. The sound of water filling a glass.

"Think he'll get out?" asked Gould.

"What?"

It was the fly. It had made its way, somehow, improbably, to the window beside us. It was standing on its back legs on the sill with its other legs spread on the glass. A blue pickup truck went by. The dog in the back panted and drooled and was gone. Now the fly turned a complete circle, first upside down and then upright again, trying, apparently, to get out.

"No," he said, after a while, "that wasn't the whole story."

Somewhere, a bugle sounded.

"I did vow to be the most a-political, professional cop ever—that much is true. I also did vow that no rich kids like Michael Roberts would ever get off scot-free again. But there was more to the trial than that."

Gould made to raise his coffee cup to his lips. Then stopped. He looked inside, frowned, and lowered his arm again.

"You see," he said, "the car Roberts was driving was a Hatfield."

The music in the restaurant abruptly stopped. Talking went on around us as usual for a few seconds, then grew quieter.

"The Hatfield was a futuristic-type sports car with wing doors. An amazing design for a car in the mid-fifties. It was so aerodynamic. You can see its shape in the new cars of today, the rounded bodies.

Anyway, the Hatfield was the pride of New Brunswick in the age of Jimmy Dean and Marilyn Monroe. A space aged car, locally designed and manufactured. A lot of people saw it as the ticket to New Brunswick prosperity, a chance to recapture some of the manufacturing base that had gradually bled to Ontario since Confederation.

"Problem was, the car didn't sell. It was very expensive. The design, though aerodynamic and in fact quite common-looking today, was back then an anomaly: remember this was the time of huge tail fins and monster chrome. And, worst of all, though the exterior of the car was very impressive, what was inside, the internal mechanics of the thing, were terrible. Shortly after they came into production the Hatfields gained a reputation for unreliability, for mechanical failure.

"As a result, the main buyers were the local elite. They bought the things to promote the project, but also because they all knew Bennie Hatfield—he was one of them—and many of them had bought shares in the company. A lot of them probably got special deals on the cars too.

"So, as visionary seeming as it was, the Hatfield was an economic disaster from Day One. The project would never have lasted the four years it did if it wasn't for the project's Number One Fan."

The fly was getting desperate. It was turning round and round on the window sill. I couldn't look at Gould. I could hear the anguish in his voice.

He took a deep breath.

"Shortly after taking office in 1952, my father entered into various funding agreements with Bennie Hatfield. All those idealistic capitalistic reasons. He pumped tens of millions of dollars into the plant over the next few years, until incredible losses were exposed shortly after his re-election in 1956. The closing of the Hatfield plant and the public inquiry that followed were major factors in my father's defeat in 1961—maybe as important as the scandal with my mother. At the inquiry, my father admitted that he and Bennie Hatfield had conspired together to cover up the extent of the mechanical problems with the car. When challenged about it—*But what about the safety of the people in the cars?*—he said, 'Well, we took that into consideration. We calculated how much it would cost to settle lawsuits versus how much it would cost to change the design and we made the best business decision that we could.' The newspapers had a field day with it.

Premier claims a human life just another cost of production."

Gould raised a hand to make a visor over his eyes. He sat that way for a quarter minute, like a man thinking, or praying, or hiding, or on the verge of tears.

Then, more to himself than to me, he said, "What it comes down to is that Michael Roberts was driving a Hatfield. At the trial, his defense argued that the major cause of the accident was not his drinking, or the speed at which he drove, but the car itself. A 1957 Hatfield. Using evidence from the scene, they proved, quite conclusively, that the steering column on the car had seized before the accident. My father, in other words, was partly responsible for Archie's death."

Outside, from the direction of the War Memorial, there was the clap of the gun.

I looked for the green bottle fly.

It was gone.

Gould stayed in Silver for two days after that. We were in the Igloo at the same time once or twice but hardly spoke. Early on Monday, he did tell me that Viola had scaled back his efforts in Vancouver. After days of door to door inquiries using a team of detectives called in from the Vancouver City Police, he had come up with nothing new on Lies, except to confirm the existence of the girl-friend, a woman named Lorna Jackson, who seemed to collaborate everything Lies had said.

Later that day, I turned into the parking lot at the Igloo to see Gould's car already there. Gould, I saw, was sitting at the wheel. I pulled into the space beside him. He got out.

He was wearing his blue blazer and trench coat and the tie with the red schooners on it. He came slowly around the back of his car to meet me, his new, tentative, half-shuffling stride. His hands were in his pockets.

I could tell from the expression on his face that this was, truly, the end. That he had pulled himself from the case and I would have to go back to Vancouver.

"A failure of the imagination," he said.

"What?"

"That's why I stayed on the case. I just couldn't imagine an alternative."

We stood there looking at each other, blue eyes to blue eyes. From behind my back came the explosive hiss of air breaks.

"You mean O'Brien was right?" I asked.

"It just took me a couple of extra weeks," he said.

"To imagine yourself—"

"— differently. Right."

"How so?"

He told me about his decision to quit the Force. His proposed holiday in Costaguana. I was stunned for a moment—and then I saw the logic in it.

"Something I should tell you," I said.

"Yes?"

"About Jayne."

A gust of wind stirred Gould's auburn hair.

"You may feel the most alive you have ever felt. You may feel that the possibilities are endless, that you've discovered an inexhaustible treasure. But it will hurt like hell."

"This is not about Jayne," he said.

I let him keep the photograph.

CHAPTER TWENTY-THREE

I can only imagine what Gould was thinking as the airliner's shadow flitted across the coastal plain of Costaguana. The Cordillera, dominated by the massive white shoulder of Higuerota towering above the other peaks, would have given way suddenly to hills, then to flat green lands, then to the tangled mosaic that was the city of Sulaco. Perhaps the jet would follow the same landing pattern as years before, cruising out over the Placid Gulf and banking back sharply again, in which case Gould would again have a view of blue-green water, of three small islands, and—in an order depending on which side of the plane he was on—of Punta Mala to the north and Azuera to the south. If he did, he would probably remember the legend of the gringos on Azuera, the American adventurers who had disappeared seeking a treasure of silver. With an inward irony and, perhaps, a note of sadness for the Soledads, he would wonder if their souls still haunted the gleaming horde they had died for.

Once he had cleared customs at Sulaco International Airport, he carried his one bag out through the sliding doors to where a row of taxis waited. Immediately, like the backdraft of his own breath from a pillow, he was met by hot, humid air. He was still blinded by the glare of sunlight when three tawny-skinned men converged on him. "Taxi, señor!" they shouted, each gesturing back towards his car. All of the cars seemed to be Volkswagen Beetles. Gould picked a man with one tooth showing in the top row and said, in Spanish, that he wanted to be taken to the Hotel Avellanos. When the words formed in his mouth he was affected by a strange yearning, a wave of desire he often experienced when he spoke in a foreign language. The yearning was of the kind he had refused to indulge himself in almost his entire adult life. Now, however, even as he haggled with the driver over the fare, he gave himself over to it, and was rewarded with a brief, pleasantly disorienting glimpse of what those other words seemed to harbour: vast unexplored regions of geography and self.

The driver took his bag, put it in the boot of the car and gestured for him to get inside. The passenger side door and seat had both been removed. Gould stepped through empty space and into the back.

Just before the car roared off, leaving behind a cloud of dust and exhaust, Gould noticed a flag lying limp on a brass standard atop the terminal building. He knew from his guidebook—the same one that he had brought with him twenty years before—that if the flag had been flat out, he would have seen red and yellow diagonals, with two green palm trees in the middle.

Costaguana. The very name had an aura of magic, of strange possibility to him. As the car veered and hooted its way from the airport towards the centre of Sulaco, Gould was entranced by the white walls flashing by, punctuated here and there by doors or windows with iron grill-work over them. At one point, through the black bars of a large gate, he had a glimpse of orange trees, rows upon rows of deep green boughs laden with fruit. Then there were some beggars crouched in the portal of a church. Then, for the length of a city block, a market with the look of a tent city, heaps of food or woven goods or pots and pans raised up on odd pieces of plank and sheltered by canvas, Indian women squatting on mats cooking food in earthen pots.... Just before the market disappeared, Gould heard, amongst the roar of traffic and people, a few notes from some kind of stringed musical instrument accompanied by a drum.

And yet, for all the aura of dream about it, Costaguana seemed immediately familiar to Gould. Every new image he encountered seemed, at the same time, surprising and completely expected. He was thousands of miles away from his birthplace in Fredericton, New Brunswick, Canada, in a country where he spoke the language imperfectly and a city where he recognized not a single street name, and yet he felt that he had arrived somehow—that he was, at last, in the place he truly belonged.

The Hotel Avellanos bordered Revolution Square, Plaza de la Revolución. Gould's window faced east onto the plaza, a great white stone square with a statue of a man on horseback in one corner, a fountain in another, a pavilion in the middle and various trees growing up through their own rings of protected earth. Vendors were scattered here and there, children selling pencils or Chiclets, lottery ticket sellers, men in ponchos and hats each with a handcart, hawking some combination of cana, dulces, fruit or cigarettes. People walked by or rested on benches—Indian servants with children, groups of teenagers, some older couples—and now and then a man in a suit strode past on his way from one place to another.

Gould went into the bathroom, ran some water into his hands and splashed his face. He arranged his toiletries neatly, in the way that he always did. For a moment, he considered his own face in the mirror, and, as he had been doing very often lately, imagined his reflected image as a photograph in a museum with a cryptic caption: *Gould (The Other One)*. As always, at times like these, he was reminded of his father, the trace elements of the old man in his face, and though he felt relieved of his father's presence to a certain extent, he knew there was no way to entirely free himself. Nor was that what he wanted. He could also see, in the turn of his nose and a certain lighter quality in the blue of his eyes, elements of his mother. *Contra-Diction*. He smiled at that, and the smile reminded him of his mother too.

He spent the afternoon and the early evening resting or walking about the plaza, a tall, auburn-haired man who drew many interested glances. At times, he felt like he should be wearing a big sign: *Gringo*. He bought a large straw hat from a nearby shop, partly to protect himself from the sun, partly as a disguise. He ate at the Café Lambroso, where the waitress, who didn't look much like a local herself (she was pale-skinned and blue-eyed), gave him a suspicious look. He ordered his food in Spanish and defied her to reply in any other way. Afterwards, he watched from his window as the evening shadows spread across the square, and the haze that had overtopped the buildings seemed to dissipate. All at once a clear view of Higuerota presented itself to him, an unmoving white pinnacle looming over the city. For a brilliant half-hour, then, the square was all in darkness while the sun lit up the glacier on the mountain. As Gould watched, a line of shadow crept upwards, above which the snow blazed blinding white, and then, like a match blown out, the last spark of light went out, leaving behind a lavender after-image of the whole that soon faded into the blackness of the night.

    He dozed fitfully in the tropical heat and in the morning caught a bus to Puerta des Mujeres.

What did Gould expect to find? My guess is he really did not know. You know how it is when you make those melodramatic gestures (I certainly do): you flee the scene, you jump in your car or minibus or on a plane, with only a few hastily gathered things, but even if you have an actual destination, you don't know what you'll find when you get there. The best you can do is keep your eye out for signs. The one that says: *Information Ahead*. The one that says: *Far Enough*. The one that says: *Dig Here*.

    One thing is certain: Puerta des Mujeres was not at all like Gould remembered it. Rather than the undeveloped hippie hangout that it was in the summer of 1975, the town was now a fully developed tourist resort. Mid-sized hotels and time share condos overshadowed the beach. The ciderblock hostel where he had stayed was gone, and none of the night-clubs or cafés that he remembered were there any longer. Even the town market, which had seemed a timeless feature of the place, had been moved some blocks further from the beach in order to make room for development. The only thing that seemed the same was the beach itself—a long arc of white sand and the rhythmic submissions of the sea.

    There was also an aura of uneasiness and decay about the place. Few tourists were visible, even taking into account the season, and the buildings themselves had a water-stained, chipped concrete look, as if they had been thrown up hastily and never taken care of. Soldiers in full dress uniform stood on most street corners. Gleaming buttons, aviator sunglasses, helmets, rifles. White gloves—as still as mimes. No doubt the soldiers were meant to inspire confidence, but like most flagrant shows of authority they had a way of calling to mind what they were guarding against. The people, in private, called the soldiers *pin-*

tureros, peacocks, in honour of their fancy uniforms, and with the implication that, like peacocks, all they would do if an enemy appeared was to spread their colourful and gaudy tails. According to official reports, the rebels were contained on the other side of the mountains, in the plains to the south of the capital of Santa Marta. Nobody believed these reports.

For three days, Gould walked the asphalt and sand of Puerta des Mujeres. At times, he seemed to move from place to place in a methodical way, as if he were conducting an investigation, but, as I suggested before, he didn't really know what he was looking for. Maybe he hoped to find a trace of his earlier self. Maybe he was hoping to trigger a memory of Archie that would make her real to him again.

On the third day, after walking back and forth along the length of the beach much of the afternoon, he set himself down on a sand dune to watch the sunset. He took off his straw hat. A gentle Pacific breeze cooled the sweat on his forehead. There was no one else in sight. As so often happens in the tropics, the sun seemed to drop rapidly out of the sky, leaving only the briefest traces of itself, and then the black night took over. Stars came out, so large and close they seemed like opening and closing hands. Gould did not move. He kept staring out to sea, out to the place where the sun had disappeared. What he was thinking I do not know. He stayed this way most of the night, only getting up now and then to stretch his legs or to piss against the trunk of a palm tree. Around four o'clock in the morning, the stars began to fade: it was the beginning of the sun's long climb over the mountains to the east. For what seemed like hours, the sky grew brighter by degrees, changing from charcoal grey to the colour of tin to a chalky blue. Gould kept looking out to sea. Then, all at once, a sliver of orange light came from somewhere behind him. The colour of the sky became richer, took on hints of turquoise and tangerine. Gould stood up. He walked, a few shaky steps, towards the water, where the waves now drifted in with gleaming crests of silver. At the place where dry and wet sand met, he squatted, dug down with his hands, and made a loose ball of sand. He stood upright again. For a minute or two he balanced the ball in the palm of his left hand. It was streaked with dark and light veins of sand. Once, twice, he seemed to feel the ball's weight, and then, with all his might, he threw it at the empty horizon.

He took an early bus back to Sulaco. All through the ride he was aware of the grit around his eyes, the salt on his lips. By noon he had checked back into the Hotel Avellanos. He slept until early evening, had a shower, put on clean clothes, and went to the Café Lambroso for dinner.

I should point out that although Gould was on leave, he was still technically a member of the RCMP. O'Brien, in fact, had refused to consider Gould's resignation. I can just imagine his reaction upon receiving Gould's formal notice. He would have called the inspector into his office, played the fatherly authority figure, genial and dangerous, maybe insisted on pouring Gould a drink. No mention of the missing file would be made. O'Brien's heavy, lined face would look as inscrutable, as intelligent and formidable as ever. He would tell Gould of the confidence he had in him, of Gould's potential, of the satisfaction he felt at Gould's handling of the Soledad case. He would simply not hear of Gould throwing away such a promising career. And Gould, being Charles Gould, would, in spite of everything, remain civil. He would think longingly of his brother. He would imagine himself on a horse somewhere. Then he would accept O'Brien's proposal of leave in lieu of resignation. At some point, perhaps as Gould was preparing to depart, O'Brien would remark on the loose ends in the Soledad case that seemed to emanate from Costaguana. Gould, with one hand on the brass door knob, would insist that he had purely personal reasons to visit Costaguana, that he was not going to involve himself in police work while he was there. O'Brien would say, "Of course, of course" and then go on to remark, in a casual seeming way, that Gould's latest report noted that the ex-girlfriend of Phil Tucker is said to have gone to Costaguana. And he would ask, "Are you entirely confident about this Tucker character?" Gould, as was his habit, would remain silent. "Well," continued O'Brien, "if you're not, if you're at all suspicious about his role in the affair, it might be useful to at least look up the girlfriend. The ex-girlfriend, I mean. Maybe she could help put your mind at ease about him."

Gould, for whatever reason, ended up staking out a table at the Café Lambroso. More often than not, he was served by the pale-skinned, blue-eyed waitress. At some point, he admitted to her that he was Canadian, and feigned an interest in the military memorabilia that decorated the place: a framed map of the country with various arrows and lines penciled over it, crossed bolt action rifles from about the time of World War One, a silver tasseled flag of Costaguana (with what looked like bullet holes in it), black and white photographs of soldiers, news clippings, and a display case containing a large silver medallion on a ribbon of red, yellow and green.

The waitress, lapsing into English, explained that the Café Lambroso had been central to the Revolution of 1911 that reunited the country. "Back about the turn of the century," she said, "this part of Costaguana declared itself an independent country—the Occidental Republic—controlled, really, by the European investors who controlled the San Tomé silver mine. Have you heard of the mine?"

Gould nodded.

"Well, it wasn't until 1911 that the country was reunited and the mine nationalized. And a lot of the planning for the revolution took place right here, when the place was run by Don Pepe's great-grandfather. That medallion in the case, that was given to his great-grandfather by President Montero, the first president of the reunited country."

Don Pepe, on hearing his name linked to the word "revolution," one of the few words of English he could confidently recognize, set down his newspaper. He eased himself to his feet and made his way to Gould's table, a slightly round, florid man of about fifty, wiping his hands on his apron. He conferred briefly with the waitress in Spanish and then said to Gould, also in Spanish, "It's true, señor, my great-grandfather played a small part in the glorious revolution that reunited my country. These days, however, I am just a poor café owner. I have nothing to do with politics. I am not a political man."

It was, apparently, a standard disclaimer.

Would Jayne have been attracted to Gould? Hard to say. My own failures suggest that I shouldn't pretend to know anything of Jayne's desires. And, of course, I have no clear idea about what she was doing in Costaguana. Still, Gould was an attractive man, with his clear blue eyes and fresh face. Even with the changes that had happened to him in Silver, he would have retained a fascinating presence. He may have seemed even more attractive without his ramrod bearing; certainly he would have seemed more approachable, even a little vulnerable (though I can't be sure Jayne would have necessarily liked that). Also, let's face it, the same background that made Gould an Upper Class Twit gave him an unusual, even glamorous past, a past filled with drama and tragedy. Told in the right way, Gould's life history could be very seductive.

Gould spent the rest of his two weeks hanging out at the Café Lambroso. Gradually, day by day, he insinuated himself in with Jayne. Maybe he asked her to join him for a cup of coffee. Maybe there were signs. At some point, she would have suspected his interest in her and probably decided (for her own protection, if nothing else) to find out who he was.

"So, Charles," she said one day (either standing there before he ordered or nursing a cup of coffee across from him at the end of her shift), "what do you do for a living?"

"I'm a capitalistic lackey," he said. A line he had prepared in advance.

She met his fighter-pilot blue eyes with her own intense pale gaze. For once his ability to control his expression was useful for more than projecting authority.

"A fascist," he explained. "A cop."

Jayne continued to stare into his dead-pan eyes. Her lips showed the trace of a smile. "I believe it," she said.

Some time later, Gould's body curled into its most vulnerable posture, a posture I encountered the night he told me so much. "I know you've probably heard this kind of thing before," he said, "but I'm actually in the process of quitting police work. For a whole series of reasons, though mainly because of the last case I was on. That's why I'm here in Costaguana, to think things over."

Jayne's eyes flashed. "You're right," she said, "I have heard that kind of thing before."

At some point, either to impress her or to give some weight to his claims about being disillusioned, he told her the story of the Soledad investigation. He told how he had received the call while at his mother's home on Galiano Island, about his return to Cramdown and O'Brien's warnings about the political sensitivity of the case (warnings that became deeply ironic, as things turned out). He told about arriving in the town, how it was deeply divided but oddly united in its dislike of the victims. He exposed the main players in the conspiracy—Lies, Goodwin and Stahr—and explained how he uncovered the story of the treasure (the testimony of Luke Carson, the reluctant confirmations of Sherwood and Berry.) He told about the distractions of Inspector Breeze and the Bentleys, gave a few sympathetic words to Margaret Lies and a deep felt sigh for the Soledad children. He confessed, as frankly as he could, his father's possible complicity. He did not mention Alex MacKenzie, whose testimony he considered irrelevant. For obvious reasons, he also made no mention of me.

Another time he told her the story of his family, putting special emphasis on his mother's disappearance and name change, his ultimate reconciliation with her. Jayne was visibly moved (as he knew she would be). Then, in a halting voice, she told him that "Jayne Whynot" was not her original name either.

They went for walks.

One day, Jayne asked, "What would you do if you weren't a cop?"

It was a Sunday afternoon. People in their church clothes strolled along the four edges of the plaza, or sat on benches, or stopped to buy something from a vendor. Ribboned girls and boys with slicked back hair ran this way and that. A brass band belted out tunes from the pavilion. Here and there, soldiers stood on guard, some of them in the fancy dress uniforms Gould had seen in Puerta des Mujeres.

"Something with horses."

"Horses?"

"Yes. I told you about how I used to ride when I was a boy. I have this idea that I'd like to have a stable somewhere, maybe give lessons or take people on outback excursions. Something like that."

"You know that Costaguana is famous for its horses and riders?"

"Really?"

"Absolutely. There is a great tradition of gauchos because of all the cattle ranches. In fact, Don Pepe knows a number of ranch owners on this side of the mountains. I bet, if you asked him, he'd give you an introduction. You could do some riding."

"When's your next day off?"

"Tomorrow."

"Why don't you come with me?"

So it went. Eventually, it was the day before he was to return to Canada. On that day, he told Jayne that he loved her. She shook her head. "You are leaving for Canada tomorrow."

He raised one finger. "Wait."

Back at the Hotel Avellanos, he telephoned O'Brien.

"I've cashed in my plane ticket," he said. "I am not coming back."

There was a long pause. Then, softly, O'Brien said, "What are your plans?"

"I told you before. I'm resigning from the Force."

The line was extremely clear. Gould could hear the superintendent breath once, twice. Then O'Brien said, with authority, "I'm putting you on indefinite leave."

"I don't want to be on leave."

"You've been under a lot of pressure, Charles. I refuse to let you throw away your career. No matter what you say right now, I'm going to make sure that the door stays open."

"I don't want it open!"

"Sorry. No choice. It's my prerogative. You're a throwback, Charles, but you're too good of a cop to call it quits. Take as long as you like. Rest up, get a load off your mind. Eventually you'll see it for yourself. Mark my word, Charles, eventually you will see it. And when you do, I'll be here to welcome you back."

Time passed. And one day, the inevitable came to pass.

Charles and Jayne and Don Pepe were sharing a table at the café. It was after hours; only a few lights were on. Don Pepe was smoking his pipe and, as usual, leafing through the local newspaper, the Sulaco

Independente. Jayne and Charles were talking. They may have been holding hands across the table.

Under the table, Charles ran his toe along Jayne's calf. He glanced down to admire her bare leg and saw the shoes, the low-heeled white pumps she'd found in a used clothing store back in Vancouver. For some reason the sight of the shoes filled him with desire. He decided to steal a kiss. He looked over to Don Pepe to make sure he was absorbed in the news. And saw the photograph.

Next thing he had asked for the newspaper. The photograph was of a murdered Costaguanero, a villager. He was lying face down with his hands tied behind his back. Clearly visible, in the dust at his feet, were two grey stones. "Impossible," Gould whispered.

"What is it?" asked Jayne.

"The solution to the Soledad case."

"But I thought you had nothing to do with police work any more."

"I don't. But look. This could almost be a photograph of the Soledad crime scene. The bullet to the head, the nuggets of silver—and the hands. Why didn't I make this connection before? Look. The rope used to tie the hands of the victim. It's a lanyard from the dress uniform of a Costaguanian soldier, the silver-threaded lanyard of a *pinturero.*"

"So?"

"So it means the Soledads were killed by someone from Costaguana. A hit squad. Not a government one, but a hit squad from the rebels. That means they must have been involved in some kind of double-cross with the treasure. Maybe they were supposed to sell it and send the money back to the F.L.C. and instead kept it for themselves. They bought a new house, you know, just weeks before they were killed."

Jayne shook her head. "You are so like Phil," she said.

"What? Who?"

"Someone you don't know. A guy I went out with for a while. He always wanted to tie things up into neat little packages too. You said before that you don't believe in simple solutions anymore but you really do."

"But, the facts . . . ."

"What are facts? Maybe they don't mean anything. Or maybe they could mean so many different things at once that you can never decide what they mean."

Gould smiled benignly. He had, after all, been warned about Jayne's tendency to argue.

Jayne got up from the table. She walked to the far side of the room, stopping in front of the battered flag of Costaguana. "Don Pepe, you tell him," she said. "*Dise el gringo. Diselo.*"

Slowly, Don Pepe pushed back his chair. He came over to where Gould sat, the newspaper spread out before him. "*El asesinato?*" he asked.

"*El asesinato,*" said Jayne.

Don Pepe ran a hand slowly across his damp forehead. Then, in Spanish, he said, "I am not a political man, señor, I am just the owner of this café, but I listen enough to know about things. Now, this photograph, this story, you are not to take it at face value. There was a time, oh, five or six years ago, at the beginning of this last guerrilla war, when the rebels, the Front as they are called, used the sign of the silver nuggets to mark their work. It was a way of showing that they had infiltrated the most important industry in the country, the San Tomé mine. But, you see, after a while the army and police began to use the same sign. Perhaps to show who really controlled the mine but also as a devious way to confuse people, to turn them away from the rebels. The army, say, would commit a murder and leave the rebel sign, then they would have it reported on the television and radio and newspapers, all of which, of course, are controlled by the government. This newspaper here, for instance, the *Independente*, is owned by a cousin of the President. So you see, the picture and story probably mean the opposite of what they seem. They probably mean that the government killed a supporter of the rebels and then set it up to look like the rebels were responsible. To shock ordinary people, as I said, but also as a coded warning to the rebels: *beware!* Although, of course, it is possible that the story is for real. There is no way to say for sure. I do not know your country, señor, I have never been there, but in Costaguana things like this happen all the time."

Charles lifted his eyes to Jayne, who stood with her arms crossed, furious, against the silver-tasseled flag of Costaguana.

"I am a fool," he said. "Forgive me. I love you. Forgive me."

Chapter Twenty-Four

When the strike was settled in Silver, and the atmosphere in the town changed so much for the better, I toyed with the idea of staying on. Wallace Lies offered me a job waiting on tables in the Igloo until I found something better. He said that since I was obviously a writer of some kind I might also be interested in volunteering at the Silver *Claim*, and hinted that, in time, a real job might turn up for me there. Judith confessed that she would be sad to see me go and implied that she might leave her boyfriend soon. She said I could crash on her couch until I found a place of my own. It was a tempting offer, but I couldn't take her up on it—no more than I could take up the offers from Wallace Lies. By then I knew I had to return to Vancouver.

After Gould left, I lingered for three days. On Monday, just after I watched him pull out of the Igloo parking lot for the last time, it began to snow. Dark bellied clouds sagged over the mountains, dropping flakes like shredded paper. It snowed off and on for two days. By then the place seemed transformed, whiteness was everywhere, gleaming at the least suggestion of sun. Even the air smelt different, smelt white somehow—a suggestion of Christmas trees, peppermint candy, fresh sheets on a bed. Out of nowhere, sport vehicles began appearing with ski racks on the roof.

On Thursday morning, I awoke to a blinding glare of sunlight. My body ached all over. By this point I had spent over two weeks in the microbus, in the middle of the mountains, with frost heavy on the windshield each morning and a thin foam mattress barely cushioning me from the ridged metal floor. I was looking forward to stretching out on a real bed again.

For my last breakfast at the Igloo, I had eggs over easy, sausages, hashbrowns and toast. The coffee was as musty, as scorched-tasting as always. I picked up a copy of the new Silver *Claim* from the free-box near the cashier. It was the third number to come out since my arrival. The first had been a special Friday edition devoted to the Soledad investigation. Gould was in it, Breeze was in it (his then two-day-old gaffe about the union repeated one more time). Oddly enough, there was no mention of my role in discovering the bodies. The second edition, the next Thursday (the usual day of publication), led off with a story about Philip Bentley, the police raids on his home and the Church of Christ Redeemer offices. Bentley denied any wrongdoing, but also announced that he and his family would be leaving Silver. "Mrs. Bentley and I thought it best for the children to have a fresh start."

In this third edition, the Soledad investigation had been relegated to a short report on an inside page. *The investigation continues....* The front page was taken up with good news stories, the settlement of the strike, the imminent departure of the E.R.T., the approval of a new highway sign for the town. On the second page there was an illustration of this sign: a gleaming arch, like a rainbow or a band of precious metal, over a vista of mountains and trees. Down below were the words: *Silver, Town of Many Prospects.* Also in a prominent position was an item about Wallace Lies and Lena Stahr. Apparently they had put together a proposal to buy the town-owned ski hill and turn it into a resort. A chalet-type hotel, bigger runs, state of the art lifts. Lies would run the place, Stahr would be the financial backer. "Council members have already told me informally that the proposal is a good one," Lies announced. "When the formal sale vote occurs, I will, of course, excuse myself to prevent any appearance of conflict of interest."

As I warmed up the engine on the microbus, I took one last look around me, the Igloo sign towering over the parking lot, the other service stations, a corner of The Red Grizzly down the way. It surprised me, as it had a number of times since my arrival from Vancouver, how close the mountains felt. I'd lived on the coast for many years, always in the vicinity of the Rockies, but I'd never been in the interior before, never had those dark shapes hulking in every direction. In Vancouver, the mountains seem in the hazy blue distance and there is always the escape of the sea, but in Silver, it's like being at the bottom of a well. I also noticed, on the first rise straight across the highway, the ski hill—a series of vertical white runs on a dark-green slope. The runs looked like the claw marks of some giant animal. Funny that I had never noticed them before.

I shifted into gear.

I've been back three months now. The early spring flowers—snow drops, grape hyacinths, primroses—are making their usual February appearance. I will always remember leaving the snow behind in the mountains and driving into the grey mist that covers Vancouver most of the winter. It was a strange feeling, navigating my microbus through the traffic, pulling into the parking lot of my building. When I turned the key in my apartment door, I felt like I had slipped back into a role I had played many times before, as if, by the very fact of occupying the space my body had occupied before, I was pouring myself into a mold. And yet I also knew that although I could slip back into my former identity, that, in fact, I had decided to pick up the pieces and get on with my life, I would never be entirely the same. Oh I could play the part, could use the same name and occupy the same space and speak the same lines as before, but there would always be a difference. Like a landscape made strange by a shoe in a tree. Like the image of Charles Gould fractured by sixteen mirrors over a bed.

On the kitchen table was a stack of mail, including the opened note from Jayne. *I don't believe in beginnings or endings.* I still don't know exactly what that phrase means. It has the kind of flagrant intellectualism that used to drive me nuts about her sometimes. And yet I do have a sense of what she was getting at: there are no neatly defined moments when you can say "now this begins" or "now it's over." Where we think something begins is only a point in time we've chosen for our convenience (how far back do you need to go to understand the murder of the Soledads?) and events resonate long after we've shifted our attention elsewhere. Gould is getting over his father but there will be no simple point when he has put his father behind him. I am getting over Jayne....

Sometimes it is strange for me to sit in café where Jayne and I used to drink coffee together and argue half the night. The thrill of those arguments, the anger that could turn so urgently into love. I regularly walk the beach at English Bay—a favourite pastime of ours—and sometimes take the ferry to Granville Island. I've come to love the market over there, the seaweed-incense-leather smell of the place, the carnival atmosphere, buskers, children eating candies out of bags, the concrete shadow of the bridge overhead. I get a kick out of the fact that the ferry has to cross False Creek to arrive, though the nature of the kick depends on the nature of my mood. Sometimes I still indulge my self-pitying Frankie and Johnnie mood (oh false woman). Sometimes I laugh at my own failures to understand (oh false reasoning, oh false perception). But more often than not, I feel buoyed by the fact that something "false" can be a true passage of another kind. False Creek. A true inlet. Passage to the island market—a place Jayne and I often talked about but never actually went to.

I still imagine Jayne's critical voice sometimes. I try to accept it as a part of me, a true voice, but not the only one I listen to. I can imagine what she'd say, for instance, about my decision to return to school. She'd accuse me, like she did many times before, of angling for an academic job. Well, she'd be right, but not necessarily for the right reasons. Why go back? There is no simple answer. While in Silver, I escaped for a while from the tangled mess of motivations and desires that is my life, into a world where there was the prospect of a clear answer to a clear problem (a prospect guaranteed by the unshaken assurance of Charles Gould), but now I know there is no escape, not for me or Charles Gould or anyone else. The stew of mixed motives that led me to grad school in the first place—fear of poverty, desire for recognition, fear of risk, desire for purpose, fear of meaninglessness, desire for love, inertia—is still there. The only way forward for me is to work through these motives.

For the new title of my dissertation, I have inserted an academic colon: *Prospects Unknown: An Analysis of Four Key Socio-Political Trends in Canada of the 1990s*. A longer subtitle on the first page lists the four areas of study as "religion," "labour relations," "multinational corporations," and "foreign affairs." My supervisor thinks my argument is still too vague and I am probably biting off more than I can chew, but he is pleased that I seem to have finally "grasped the bull by the horns." Sometimes I get real pleasure out of being polemical, presenting evidence, making a case. Sometimes, as I work on it, I feel like I am dying inside. Mainly I write in the academic mode demanded of me, no conclusions not supported by the facts, no extended personal anecdotes (only controlled allusions to myself in the introduction and conclusion), no pretentious literary echoes. But now and then I catch a fragment of myself in the multiple mirrors of my words, or realize I'm repeating phrases from a novel I once read, and experience a delicious, subversive moment of pleasure. I keep all the subversive bits, as long as they don't disturb the surface conformity of the text. They are my little joke. My little difference. What I sometimes need to bring me back to life again.

Sometimes, I have to admit, I get out my notebook and go back over what I recorded about events in Silver. Sometimes I add new details as I remember them. Now and then I get the idea that I should make another text out of my notes—a novel or a true account—but, for the most part, I am content to leave them as they are. If I tried to write something more formal, it would probably come out as a thinly veiled allegory, something about the nature of truth mixed up in the condition of the country, and would probably get panned for trying to do "too much" (whatever that means when it comes to a book). Or maybe it would get panned for being too obvious, for being cliché—that's just as likely. In any case, trying to polish up my notes right now would be like trying to follow Gould to Costaguana. The idea is tempting, but, for the time being at least, it is not for me.

And Gould himself? Will he ever return to Canada? To his career at the RCMP? I honestly don't know. If he did return, it would be like my returning to work on my dissertation—a mixed gesture, an acknowledgement of the tangle of living. Of course, no matter what he did, Gould could never be the professional's professional he once was. Oh he could adopt the role again, in the same way that I have slipped back into my role as a PhD student, but there would always be a difference. Sometimes he would be haunted by O'Brien or by his father and would know that there are no truly impartial agents. Other times he would perform small acts of subversion, of humanity, and would experience a delicious moment of pleasure.

Sometimes, when I think of him, I feel a deep sense of loss. I know he is doing well in Costaguana—I know it is the place for him right now, that he feels at home there—but, especially at night, when I have an accumulation of things to get off my chest, I ache for his company. A part of me will always yearn to be humming and hawing with him again at the Igloo, to be drinking too much coffee, hearing Country music in the background mixed in with the rude release of air breaks, watching some poor fly doing cart-wheels against the window glass. A part of me will always yearn to talk all night with him until dawn slowly revives the world. Hokey, I know. Low-brow, romantic, clichéd. But *real*.

When I think of the town of Silver itself, I tend to get angry. There are, after all, too many loose ends back there. Gould's lucky find perhaps explains who pulled the trigger on the Soledads (or at least narrows it down to two equally foreign—and hence, safely other—possibilities) but, for my money, it doesn't absolve any of the townspeople for their actions. Goodwin, Stahr, Lies, Bentley, Breeze—they all wanted the Soledads dead, and some combination of them was probably conspiring to have the deed done (does anybody believe Lies's explanation about his time in Vancouver?), but then along came the assassins from Costaguana and *eureka!* I can just imagine the reaction, the mad scramble to cover up their own incriminating activities, Stahr and Lies with their feeble attempt to portray themselves as innocent lovers, Goodwin covering up traces of the stolen (or twice stolen) silver, the Bentleys hiding the trust account and their interest in the children, Breeze . . . well, you get the point. Maybe they weren't all in it from the start. Maybe Breeze and Bentley remained unwitting dupes on the periphery (Gould seemed to think so). But the fact remains, they all closed ranks, in one way or another, when that chance opportunity presented itself.

Occasionally I indulge myself in a fantasy about Sergeant Wright. I imagine that he is still on the case, that he will not rest until all the bad guys are brought to justice, that it is still a question of redemption for him, a point of honour. Maybe this is true, but somehow, I don't think so. As that other Philip, Philip Marlowe once said, "This is not a game for knights. Knights have no meaning in this game."

Probably the most shadowy person, in the end, is Gould's father. In a way, the senior Gould was the one furthest away from events, the one with the most tangential involvement. He never made a personal appearance; his only direct communication came in the form of a letter. And yet, in so many ways, he seems behind everything that happened in Silver. Even if you discount his direct involvement in pressuring Lena Stahr to take any steps necessary to safeguard the profitability of the mine, or if you ignore his part in a government that has maintained business as usual relations with the regime in Costaguana, you have to consider his lifetime promotion of what he called "material interests." If so much good follows on the nurturing of those interests (as the Senator often argued), then the fact that things might get a little messy in the short term is just a price we have to pay. Strictly from a business point of view, the deaths of the Soledads were not such a bad thing. The killings did make possible the settlement of the strike. They did ultimately profit both the owners and the workers . . . .

I rant? I suppose I do. Maybe it is out of loyalty to Charles, whom I do consider, after all, my friend. Nobody should have to carry the burden of family history that Charles Gould had to carry. People tend to look at someone like Gould—born with a silver spoon etcetera—pretty much as they look at a country like Canada. They think, hey, only the most boring of histories could have produced that. No drama, no heroism, no emotion, no blood, no violence, no sacrifice, no betrayal. But think of what the weight of history drove Charles Gould to, all those years playing at the professional's professional; then his assignment to the Soledad case and his dramatic and unprofessional confiding in me; then, clinging to one last hope, off to Costaguana. And consider the most cynical but probable outcome of the senator's influence: that without Charles Gould's personal attention, the Soledad file will languish and the loose ends in Silver will never be tied up.

These days, when I try to tell my friends about what happened to me in Silver, they give me twisted looks. When I try to tell them about Gould they say, "You must be joking. He sounds like a character from a novel." Frankly, I don't blame them. Sometimes the whole experience seems unreal to me as well. Sometimes I almost believe I made the whole thing up (as more than one friend has accused me of doing). And Gould, well, on the surface of it, his entire character is composed of clichés from detective fiction. The ramrod bearing, the clear-eyed reading of the scene of the crime . . . I mean, really. The truth is, I needed him too much to view him objectively. I needed his unshaken assurance, his fantastic presence. Who knows how much that need warped my understanding?

One thing I do know: my attraction to Gould was contradictory from the start. Part of me wanted to use him to escape my life, to indulge in a fantasy of being a side-kick in order to avoid the implications of my own failures, but another part of me, maybe unconscious and maybe not, knew all along that he would make me confront myself. Even now, I remember that first time he appeared at the Igloo, his implacable calm, the walk, the way he made it clear he would get at the truth no matter what. It was as if his manner—the same professional manner that seemed to preclude my getting to know him—contained the promise that my own problems would be investigated, uncovered, resolved. I can't explain where this promise came from. I can't be sure if Gould sensed something reciprocal when he first met me. All I know is that, whether it began as a figment of my imagination or not, this promise did, in the end, come true.

Then again, I shouldn't be too bold about what is true or not. What is truth anyway? One thing Silver taught me is to beware my own thirst for answers, to beware my own craving to know. I didn't know Jayne—even the memories of her that I conjured up are tainted by my own hurt and desire—and when I remember Gould or the events in Silver, there is at least as much falsehood as fact. What do I really know about police work? About life in a B.C. interior town? About mining? I tap the rock of events but it is just a rock to me, and so naturally I fall back on the books I've read, their words substituting for the geology itself, as if you could take "silver" to the bank. No—I don't blame my friends for being suspicious. I don't blame them for being suspicious at all.

Oddly enough, the falseness in it all comforts me, comforts me like that ride across to Granville Island. A true passage of another kind. Maybe, in spite of myself, of all my posturing and phoniness, I have managed to create a little something that shines, a glint of the truth that is a mystery at the core. Like the shoe in the tree. Like those letters to someone who is not and is Jayne Whynot. Jayne, in the end, has kept her secrets—as she must, as she always will. She remains more than my memory or account of her (in the falseness of my recollections, there is this truth). This is why I can take hope from the image of Jayne and Charles at that café table in Costaguana. The two of them are drinking coffee. On the wall nearby is a silver-tasseled flag, red and yellow, with two green palm trees in the middle. Jayne lights up a cigarette. The match flares for a moment, lights her face like sun on the glacier of Higuerota. Charles is, as always, inscrutable. Now and then his finger comes up to tap at his moustache. His eyes are slightly narrowed—as if, from force of habit or out of some desperate desire, he is trying to read the situation.

PROSPECTS UNKNOWN

Acknowledgements

Every text, according to Roland Barthes, is a tissue of quotations, but this one is more explicitly so than most. The astute reader will notice many echoes of other texts within its pages. There are also a number of echoes and a few characters from Canadian history.

I am most obviously indebted to Joseph Conrad's *Nostromo*, which forms a kind of ironic backdrop for this story. *Nostromo* is the "guidebook" to Costaguana in Chapters 6 and 23, the source of the quote from the "great author" mentioned by O'Brien in Chapter 10, and the source of the political speech in Chapter 9 of which Tucker asks "Is that a quote?" – amongst a number of other fragments and echoes. Conrad's *Heart of Darkness* supplies some of the flavour of Gould's drive up the river in Chapter 9 and some of the inspiration for the character of Wallace Lies. The character of O'Brien first appeared in George Orwell's *1984* and my police superintendent is indebted to him. Part of the description of O'Brien in Chapter 1 is a near quote from *1984*, and some of the atmosphere of O'Brien's office in Chapter 10 is inspired by O'Brien's apartment in *1984*. The lines "It is called wine. You may have heard about it in books" were first in *1984* (though in a radically different context!). My Reverend and Mrs. Bentley echo the Bentleys from Sinclair Ross's *As For Me and My House*. Some details of character and place related to my Bentleys are citations or near citations of Ross. For instance, the drawings on the wall in the living room of my Bentleys are uncannily like drawings made by Reverend Bentley in Ross. Ross's Mrs. Bentley does play Chopin's *Polonaise in A Flat Minor*. The name Munro Stahr first appeared in *The Last Tycoon* by F. Scott Fitzgerald. The name Annie Torrent appeared in *Ana Historic* by Daphne Marlatt.

Much of my meagre knowledge about mining came from Mike MacBeth's *Silver Threads Among the Gold: The Rags to Riches Story of a Man and His Mines* and E.L. Faulkner's *Introduction to Prospecting* (Geological Survey Branch, Mineral Resources Division, Paper 1986-4, Government of British Columbia). I also consulted various general histories of Canada and British Columbia. The most interesting book I read on Glenn Gould was *Glenn Gould: A Life and Variations* by Otto Friedrich.

My very meagre knowledge of police procedures was enhanced by Charles E. O'Hara's excellent *Fundamentals of Criminal Investigation*.

Lastly, I would like to thank my friends and colleagues in the English Department at the University of Victoria, whose names are repeated in the names of various minor characters in the story. Needless to say, characters with these "real" names should always be understood, like the Glen Gould of my story, to be "the other one." Repetition with a difference is not only the general condition of writing (as Derrida argues), but the source of much possibility and joy.